.... OF TORTURED FAUSTIAN SLUMBERS

.... Of Tortured Faustian Slumbers

C. William Giles

authorHOUSE®

AuthorHouse™
1663 Liberty Drive
Bloomington, IN 47403
www.authorhouse.com
Phone: 1-800-839-8640

Published by AuthorHouse   07/28/2012

ISBN: 978-1-4772-2204-1 (sc)
ISBN: 978-1-4772-2203-4 (hc)
ISBN: 978-1-4772-2205-8 (e)

To Tracy

My Muse, My Lily, My Love

&

In Memory Of My Fallen Heroes

Quorthon (1966-2004)
Ronnie James Dio (1942-2010)
My Brother, Chris (1961-2012)
&
My Father, Roland (1935-2010)

cwgimmortal@gmail.com

CHAPTER 1

Unrecognisable words in another's tongue spoken in anger and hate, drifted as smoke through the ethereal air of his mind. A knowing sense of pain, blood and death wrapped itself around him like a suffocating shroud. His left wrist was slammed hard against a surface that was rough and splintered; he felt his bones crack under the force of pressure being applied to hold it in position. He tried to open his swollen tear-filled eyes but through the salient solution he could only see the large black shape of some demonic wretch.

He felt he was indoors, in a windowless room, unable to place the location yet he could somehow sense dark foreboding clouds looming above him. He attempted to struggle but when trying to swing his right arm down to strike his assailant, agonies he could barely comprehend flew through his hand, arm and indeed his whole body yet his limb remained in its' outstretched position. He turned his head to see what restricted his movement, an act of extreme pain in itself. Through the haze of his tears he could see a large dark object in his outstretched palm. Blinking more rapidly to clear his vision, he could now see blood dripping from around the object, more closely he strained to look and what he saw made him gasp with disbelief. The object was a nail.

This was the largest nail he'd ever seen and it was penetrating not only his flesh but also his bones as it held him to something of wooden construction. More words now from his barbarous captor brought his reality into greater focus still, yet he simply couldn't comprehend what was happening to him. The creatures words dripped from an opening in its face, presumably the mouth but it was difficult to tell! He couldn't decipher the obscure language, if it *was* a language yet somehow he could understand its basic meaning. The words seemed sweet to the ears yet at the same time so thick and black, like drowning in aural molasses. Blasphemy—putrid, harsh, dark and horrific, yet sweet. Sweet, sweet blasphemy.

Two amber lights appeared to open in the monstrosity's face, the eyes stared at him, burning into his soul. Again it started to talk, this time in a more mocking tone but the specific words were indecipherable until it said in that sickly drawl of a voice

"Caaaaiiiiinnnnneeeee"

As it spoke his name it brought something into his eyeline, another nail, actually on closer inspection it was more of a railway spike, very long and dark and viciously terrifying in the hands of this maniacal being. The combination of the look in its' eyes and the spike in its' possession caused his bladder and bowel to evacuate all contents, there was nothing he could do except pitifully look down at himself, only then realising that he had been stripped naked. Urine, sweat, faeces and blood ran down his body and dripped off his feet as he dangled helplessly from the position in which he'd been hung.

Looking back at his vicious tormentor, he tried to plead, his chin trembled as he did so and his cheeks streaked with the last tears he had as he begged for his life. The beast bowed its' huge head slightly and made a deep rumbling sound, a laugh. Quickly its' gaze shot back up to him and as its' head rose up so did its' spike-holding claw. In the same darkly and horrendously fluid movement it drew the spike back and with a howl of pleasure and anger it drove the weapon with huge force through the left palm of its victim. Screams of sickening pain and agony leapt from his mouth as he jerked up and out of his bed onto the floor shivering.

Seth Caine lay naked in the foetal position for a few minutes. His eyes alternating between being screwed tight shut and wide, wide open as he surveyed the scene of his bedroom floor. Looking under his bed like the frightened child hoping not to find a monster living there. He felt he was burning up but shivered uncontrollably, not too confident yet sensing he was safe, he uncoiled himself and clambered to his knees. Nervously he looked at his hands, no holes, no scars and no blood. Seth scanned his bedroom again, his heart was still racing but gradually he regained his composure. He got to his feet and moved to the window where the morning light streamed in, tentatively he peered out through the glass not sure what he was expecting to find, discovering nothing out of the ordinary he turned back to his bed. He was greeted by the pungent stench of sweat, urine and fear.

"Oh for fucks sake, not again"

Seth grabbed the corner of his sheets and dragged them off the bed, walked back over to the window and opened it to let the scent drift out on the morning breeze. Letting go of the bedding it dropped to the floor where it could remain for all he cared.

He went to his bathroom, desperate to shower. Once there he looked into the mirror, the man staring back at him didn't appeal to Seth at all. His long once blond hair looked lank, dirty and greasy. His blue eyes suddenly seemed as grey and soulless as his life had become. Seth only shaved when his face itched too much, now he was noticing tiny grey hairs in the stubble. He was six feet tall, pierced and heavily tattooed but for the first time in his life he was really starting to feel like a man in his early forties. He scowled and the man in the mirror scowled back, the shower and shave could wait, first he needed a cigarette.

Feeling cold, Seth went to his dressing room, basically a spare room with lots of closets but his wife used to refer to it as a dressing room. He grabbed the same jeans and shirt that he'd worn for the past week or so and put them on. He barefoot padded down the stairs into the kitchen, after briskly opening cupboard doors at random he mumbled to himself about there being none of his Colombian blend when he needed it and made himself a cup of instant coffee. Grocery shopping had been on his 'to do' list for the last five days, he would complain about the lack of good coffee in the house again tomorrow too . . . probably.

Coffee made, he sipped at the hot bland liquid and winced "cheap shit" then retrieved his smokes from the living room and lit his first, of many, of the day. Living alone for the last three years, he could smoke anywhere he wanted to in his own house and did so, yet his wife had always hated him smoking indoors and insisted he at least stand in the kitchen doorway. Now alone, Seth still continued with the ritual, at least when he first got out of bed, standing in the doorway blowing plumes of bluey-grey smoke out into the world, each inhalation making him feel better about himself. Along with the cigarette, the coffee didn't seem so bad now, he had no idea what time of day it was and cared even less. It was in fact a clear and sunny late morning; children ran up and down the street as they played, smaller children in pushchairs were being wheeled by mothers in summer dresses, probably off to the shops.

"Must be weekend" Seth thought to himself.

The daylight only temporarily cleared Seth's mind of his horrific dream, as it crept back into his head a shudder slid down his spine. He furrowed his brow as he thought of it then finished his smoke and put it out in the sand bucket as he had been trained to do, good boy Seth. He went back inside, deliberately closing the door on the happy domestic scenes encroaching on his doorstep. Draining his cup he added it to the pile of crockery in the sink that he would get around to, eventually.

The dream now clouding over in his mind as dreams are want to do, he went to his study. Quickly he scribbled down a few choice recollections from the nightmare as memory joggers. The more he wrote the more he remembered, furiously he wrote until his hand and arm ached. Eventually, feverishly he slumped into his leather office chair, he closed his eyes and saw little pinpricks of coloured light in the dark. There was an eerie silence around the place, no matter, Seth switched on his computer and it flickered into life. When ready he typed his password 'lilyseth' and started a new document page, the clean, fresh white screen glared at him and the keyboard awaited his touch.

Seth's hands hovered over the keys as he prepared to write the comeback novel he had been promising himself he could write for as long as he could remember. Come to think of it, he had been promising the same thing for a few years now, to his agent, publisher, friends and most of all Lily. His thoughts trailed off as he thought of his wife, his beautiful wife. Happier times, love, passion, fun.

The phone rang, dragging him back to the here and now, he answered it with his usual simple and abrupt "Yes?"

"Morning Vlad"

It was Karl, Karl Page, Seth's best friend for twenty years or more. They had always had many common bonds such as music and movies but mainly they shared a common sense of humour. Karl often referred to Seth as Vlad due to the writers' long standing love of all things vampiric, be it movies, art, novels or even just a 'mood'!

"Hey Karl, is it morning then?"

"Not for much longer buddy, it's 11:30, you just got out of you're coffin have you?" Karl laughed to himself

"Something like that, what's occurring?"

"Well, it's Saturday and you know what that means don't'cha?" Karl seemed a little too upbeat for this time of day for Seth's liking but he knew where this was heading.

"What've you got in mind Karl? Not the usual fucking places, I'm begging you"

"No no no you grouchy fuck, there's actually a new club opening tonight, Dark Tower or Black Tower or something like that, anyway, rock club, strippers, I know the manager so I've already got the tickets, didn't I tell you about this a few weeks ago?"

"No" Seth replied wearily

"Anyway, that's where we're going" the enthusiasm was obvious in Karls' voice

"Fine, should be a change of faces at least" Seth had become jaded with the local rock scene as a whole and was desperate for something new to shake the whole thing up.

"Cool, I'll get a cab and pick you up about eight so we can have a few in the Dragon first and maybe a couple of other pubs too"

With that Karl hung up, Seth did likewise then turned back to his computer. The clean, blank white page continued to stare back at him, the cursor still awaited instruction and patiently it blinked at him. Seth looked at the pile of paper he'd scrawled his nightmare inspiration on, his motivation subsided, he bent down and switched the computer off.

Chapter 2

Dr Lily Caine sat in her office at her desk and sighed, she hated working on Saturdays, as much as she loved her career, working at the weekends just made her feel that she was missing out on a social life despite her blossoming relationship with a certain co-worker. Her right elbow now rested on the desktop, chin on her knuckles, she gazed out of the window opposite where she sat, at the blue sky and the treetops as they waved their sun dappled leaves at her in the light breeze. Lilys' perfect alabaster skin so smooth and flawless in the morning light, contrasted amazingly with her shoulder length, wild and curly ebony hair. Her hair was like a ravens' wing, so natural and so black that it looked almost blue at a certain angle in a certain light. Lily used to wear it longer, she'd had the romantic look of a gorgeous gypsy girl but motherhood and her career gave her a more 'restrained' look, not-so-deep down though, she was still the untamed beauty.

She was forty three years old but understandably had been mistaken for being much younger on most occasions. She had lips like the perfect rosebud yet delicious and almost edible. Her eyes were hazel and Seth had always said that he could drown a happy man in those beautiful pools. With her tall slender frame and seemingly endless legs she could have been a catwalk model; however her love of psychiatry and a baby had meant there was little room for anything other than her career and family. As usual her thoughts wandered this way and that and her eyes shifted away from the window and to the single silver framed picture sitting on her desk, amidst all the reports and files to be dealt with. It contained a picture of a chubby little tousle-haired six year old, just how Lily liked to remember him, her precious Jack.

Oh how Lily missed her son, taken from her at just sixteen years of age, his whole life spread out before him, awaiting his exploration, then he was snatched so cruelly from this world. Tears welled in those stunningly hazel eyes whenever she thought of him and today was no exception. Time is a great healer it is said but at certain times the pain comes crashing back when you least expect it. Lily's life changed forever that day with Jacks' last breath, as if the whole completed jigsaw of her life had been tossed violently into the air. When it landed, some pieces of that puzzle were missing, including the most important piece of all.

A knock on her office door brought Lily back to the present with a depressing start. It was her secretary asking if she wanted more coffee, Lily simply nodded as she gathered herself and refocused on her reasons for being in the office on a Saturday morning. There could be no greater contrast to thoughts of her cherubic son than to those of her patient, the infamous Severin Frost.

Frost was a man of great intellect and deep thought, or some would say, he had once been so. He was here in the Hoffman Psychiatric Institute thanks to his extreme wealth and therefore extremely devious lawyer who somehow managed to twist Severins' convictions for torture and multiple murders into 'a cry for help' and a medical condition, therefore keeping him out of a lifelong prison sentence or more likely a death sentence.

Severin Frost was a large muscular man in his late forties, shaved head, goatee beard and piercing green eyes that could either charm or chill you, all depending on his mood that day. Severin had a particular penchant for terrorizing then torturing-to-death priests, of any faith. When his exploits were relayed in the court room, the public gallery had to be cleared on account of two people vomiting and one woman fainting. A member of the jury had a nervous breakdown after the trial due to flashbacks of the crime scene photographs and grisly details given, also a police officer had to retire from the force with emotional trauma after witnessing one particularly harrowing scene he viewed through a barricaded church window involving Frost skinning a priest alive as the poor man begged and cried for mercy.

The acts of insanity were argued by his high priced lawyer and miraculously it worked, now in the confines of the Hoffman, Severin Frost loomed large as the subject of academic studies as to how the human mind worked. Many learned men and women from all over the globe came to the Hoffman just to spend time conversing with Frost in order to glean something from behind those eyes, to be the first to discover something new for the intellectuals was a massive ego-trip, invariably they left more shaken than when they first met him. The only person who had managed to interview him for any sustained length of time was Dr Lily Caine, over the last two years she had built up an extensive and exhaustive in-depth file on this beast.

This file she now pondered as she sat drinking the fresh coffee that her secretary had brought for her. Frost had often mentioned his 'dark friends', no names or details, just little verbal grenades thrown into the conversations here and there to peak the interest before moving on. Two days earlier he had started to make comments about Lily's own life, this was a first as he had previously only ever been content to talk about himself, his crimes or hints at his 'dark friends'. To steer the subject to more mundane, everyday things would only serve to incur his wrath. Sensing a breakthrough of sorts, Lily had allowed him to question her, even when a malicious smile crept across his face as he asked about her sex life; she remained the consummate, unflappable professional. Even though she was now in a new relationship with Jason Bolton, a fellow doctor, Frost was curiously only concerned about her previous life with her estranged husband Seth.

"How do you know about my past private life?" she had asked

"Ah" Frost winked "we know all, my pretty Doctor"

"We? I take it by that, you mean your mysterious 'dark friends' again do you?"

"Of course, who else?" A grin spread across his face and he stroked the stubble on his cheeks as he licked his lips, his eyes seeming to penetrate deep into the very heart of Lilys' being.

"That's all in the past Severin" she stammered

"It doesn't have to be that way my dear" then suddenly his voice changed completely to one Lily instantly recognised from her recent past "we can have it all again my darling . . . . Lily Munster"

The sound of Seth's voice seemingly coming out of this monsters' mouth chilled Lily to the bone and jolted her back in her seat.

"H-H-How did you do that?" she gasped

"I have a gift" smiled Frost mockingly

"But how could you know his voice and how could you possibly know that that is what he used to call me?"

"Ha ha ha ha, as I said my dear, we know all . . . ." The smile dropped from his lips and was replaced by a look all the more menacing, yet in Seth's unmistakable voice he spoke again "we really can have it all back again my love, for a time at least"

A pale woman at the best of times, her cheeks had reddened during the conversation, now that crimson faded quickly and she suddenly became nauseous, Lily turned and fled from the room with the sound of Severin Frosts' booming laughter ringing in her ears.

Sitting in her office now, remembering that meeting two days earlier, unsettled Lily but she knew Frost was taunting and mocking her and she scolded herself for allowing herself to be the puppet dancing to his tune. Yet how did he impersonate Seth so perfectly?

"Surely their paths would never have crossed previously and Seth hadn't been to the Hoffman since the separation, even when he had been to see me before then he had never met the patients, besides that, Frost wasn't even a patient here then! Then again Frost was an academic, maybe they met years ago while Seth was researching for a novel, yes, that must be it. That voice was one hell of a party trick though and why wait until now to use it? Mind games, that must be it, I must be close to something in him and he's trying to unsettle me and throw me off. But how the hell did he know about Lily Munster? Even our closest friends didn't know about that!"

"Are you okay Dr Caine?" Lily's secretary had overheard her talking to herself and come to check on her, Lily hadn't been herself for a couple of days, understandably after the last meeting with Frost.

"Oh . . . er . . . yes . . . . I'm fine Linda, just, er, dictating some notes"

"Okaaaaaaay, but you're Dictaphone is here on my desk, are you sure you're okay?"

"I'm fine" Lily snapped "Just leave me alone!"

An hour later Lily gathered herself, her tape recorder and her notepad and left her office to go and do what she came in to do, speak to Severin Frost. Two days had passed since he scared the hell out of her and she knew she couldn't leave it alone to prey on her mind over the weekend, she kept repeating to herself as she made her way down to the interview rooms,

"Face your fears Lily, you're a pro, you can do this, he's just using your own emotions against you"

On reaching interview room 4 she paused with her hand on the door handle, she took a deep breath, opened the door and entered. There he sat, evil personified, a sadistic killing machine of flesh and blood, strapped to a chair, one very large security guard on either side of him. Frost stared into the middle distance, as Lily closed the door behind her he inhaled deeply and closed his eyes to savour her perfume.

"Ahhhhhh" he exclaimed as he let out an exaggerated sigh "you're wearing my favourite scent"

"I'm not wearing any scent today Severin"

"Exactly!"

Lily tried to rise above this obvious attempt to throw her off her axis early on in the proceedings. Authoritatively she dismissed the guards to stand outside as she usually did, so as to relax her patients. The two men re-checked Frosts' shackles, satisfied he was bound securely, they stepped outside the room. Lily sat on the opposite side of the table at which Severin sat, she got out her tape recorder and opened her notebook. She wanted to ask more about the state of mind he was in when he made a particular attack on two nuns as they slept, this was her 'official' reason for scheduling this interview, as far as the Institutes' Director was concerned anyway, but really she wanted to know more about his knowledge of Seth.

"How do you know Seth" she blurted out without even thinking about it

"You mean your husband?"

"What? Well yes I suppose so" already she felt unusually uncomfortable

"You haven't divorced him yet have you Lily, why not?"

"That's none of your business Severin, I just want to know how you know him"

"Is your marriage a prickly subject for you Lily? My dear sweet Lily" measured almost soothing tones as he spoke.

"Of course not, it's just personal and I like my privacy"

"But I thought you wanted more personal confidences to be shared between us, more intimate little chats so I can open up to you, we can even be friends, isn't that what you want? Don't you feel that the more I confide in you, the more you'll understand my pain and torment?" Frosts' tone turned to that of mocking "In time you can learn, you can put your studies to good use, you can help other tortured souls, you could win a Nobel Prize! You never know you might even fucking save me! Hallelujah praise your fucking Lord!"

"Calm down Severin, just relax and take some deep breaths" Lily tried to pacify Frost and ease the situation, having witnessed first hand and on many occasions how his mood could change from one extreme to another in the blink of an eye, and also a number of the Institutes guards could testify to that with scars to match the specifics.

"I am calm and relaxed and in answer to your question, I don't know your husband at all" his head bowed and his chest rose and fell with his deep breathing, his voice little more than a rumble.

"How can you not know him? You impersonated him perfectly"

Frost simply shrugged

"But the Lily Munster thing? You must have met him at least? That was a private joke between the two of us" Lily's frustration boiled up inside of her as Frost merely shrugged again.

"I'm sorry my darling, I've never even met him, not even once. My dark friends know of him though"

"Really?" a ray of light was beginning to appear to her "Tell me more about them, you've never really spoken in detail about them, how do they know him? Have they met him?"

"You're not listening Doctor, I said they know *of* him, but they will know him soon enough"

"What do you mean Severin? You're talking in riddles"

"Not at all, in time they will give him everything he's ever wanted without him even realising how or why, they are true friends. My darkest friend of all wants to be very good friends with Seth, he feels they could be very beneficial for each other. One way or another Seth will get everything he craves except . . . ." Frost purposely let his words trail off.

"Except what?" Lily was intrigued, her professional exterior began to give way to her natural curiosity as Frost had never spoken like this about his 'dark friends'.

"Even my Darkest Friend cannot bring Jack back!"

Lily's whole world crashed in on her in a second. She recoiled into her chair in horror at Frosts' mention of her sons' name, tears welled in her eyes and rage coursed through her whole body as she dived across the table, screaming like a banshee and grabbing Frost by his shirt front.

"What do you know of my baby?" she howled

The guards on hearing the commotion had already entered the room and were in the process of removing Dr Caine as she screamed at Frost

"What do you know you bastard?" tears streaming down her face

"I told you before, we know all. Goodbye for now my sweet Doctor, I have enjoyed our little chat"

Lily was pulled off the table and towards the door, just before she reached it however, she heard crying, instinctively her stomach turned as she recognised her own sons' distinctive screams for his mother. She span around, trying to slither from the guards grasp, momentarily she managed to free herself and reared up into Severins' face before the security began pulling her away, Frost smiled at her, Lily spat in his face and as she was finally dragged through the door Severins' tongue slipped from his mouth and licked her spit from his lips, savouring each drop.

In her office, Lily sat mumbling to herself in a daze of confusion. She was sat on her couch where the guards had placed her sobbing, questions raced endlessly through her troubled mind.

"How? Why? Who?" The strangeness of Frost knowing of Seth was now completely overshadowed by the knowledge of him knowing about Jack, the idea that this animal could sully Jacks' memory by mentioning his name . . . . Lily sat trembling, trying to compose herself. The memory of Frost impersonating Jacks' cries made her stomach turn again and she cried more tears of pain. Time *was* a great healer but her memories *had* come crashing back when she least expected them and it hurt so very, very much.

She knew she had to know what was going on, that meant that she had to contact the link, Seth.

CHAPTER 3

Seth sat in his favourite black leather reclining armchair, T.V. on relaying various sports information and updates, sound off. An old Van Halen album blasted out of his stereo speakers as he drank coffee with a slug of scotch in it and smoked cigarettes. Excerpts from his nightmare drifted in and out of his mind but not long enough to crystallise a clear image, just hints of pain, agony and desperation. No matter how hard he tried to focus he just could not mould the scenes together to form the idea which he knew existed and would make a great set-piece in one of his storylines.

He gazed around his living room in the vague hope of distracting himself, at least momentarily, from his increasingly frustrating dream. Many paintings and framed photographs decorated his home, mainly portraying various vampiric or demonic women in differing states of undress. That was something that had always been one of Seth's weaknesses, dangerous beauty, innocence mixed with inner fire, women that were almost viciously feminine. Strong and beautiful yet with *something* behind their eyes, Lily to a tee.

The CD finished and the phone, as if waiting for some quiet time, rang.

"Yeah?"

"Seth? It's Lily, can I talk to you for a minute?"

"My God, Lily, I was just thinking about you" he blurted out

"Really? Why?"

"Errr . . . ." he stammered guiltily "oh nothing, it doesn't matter. What can I do for you? It's been a long time since we spoke, is everything alright?"

Since the separation there had been little or no reason for contact between them, Lily had thrown herself into her career and more recently her new relationship with Jason, Seth had immersed himself in as many bottles and girls as he could get his hands on, the latter until recently, he hated dry spells.

"I'm fine, well sort of, I just need to know if you know a man named Severin Frost?"

"Nope sorry, never heard of him" came his brisk response

"Don't be so hasty, think about it Seth, really think about it, please"

Seth did think about it for a few seconds but he knew he didn't know the man in question, despite his mild curiosity as to the relevance of this man he remained unmoved.

"I'm telling you I've never heard of him and I think I'd remember a name like Severin Frost, don't you? I might use a name like that for a character in one of my books though!" Seth chuckled to himself

"About two or three years ago? Maybe just a Mr Frost?" Lily was getting frustrated and mumbled under her breath "A false name! that must be it, he used a false name"

Seth heard her and tutted and sighed to himself in exasperation.

"Lily, listen to me, I've never heard of Severin Frost, never met a Mr Frost, Jack Frost or even Frosty the fuckin Snowman for that matter and if this guy was using a false name how the hell would I know if it's the same joker you're asking about?"

"Jack!!" Lily half shouted and half sobbed down the phone.

"Jack Frost? Lily I told you I don't . . . ." Seth, still not comprehending the situation sighed to himself wearily.

"Severin Frost is a patient of mine, he knows you . . . . I think . . . or his friends do . . . or they know of you, oh, I don't know Seth. I'm just trying to find out what the hell's going on. I interviewed him on Thursday, then again this morning and both times he started talking about you and us."

Lily sighed and paused, Seth was silent, he could tell from her tone of voice that she was holding back a flood of tears and this was genuinely upsetting for her.

"Go on" he gently and softly encouraged her

"Today was different, he's mentioned you a few times recently but . . . ." She paused again and cleared her throat, pre-empting her voice about to break and gathered together her composure.

"Lily? . . . . But what?"

"He talked about Jack, my Jack, our Jack"

She needed say no more, it was Seth's turn to hold back the tears, he slumped down in his seat and lit a cigarette, memories of his son came hurtling to the forefront of his mind. Not pleasant sun-filled memories either, just blood, glass, twisted metal and screaming followed by a seemingly never ending silence. The room suddenly seemed much colder now as the hairs on his arms and neck stood to attention.

"He mentioned Jack? Why?" Seth whispered hoarsely

"Frost's a psychopath, he's a really dangerous man Seth, he even impersonated you're voice perfectly, I'm frightened, he called me Lily Munster too! Then he started to go on about his sinister dark friends."

"Dark friends? Who the hell are they and what about Jack?" now Seth was getting flustered and frustrated.

"Severin said that even his darkest friends couldn't bring Jack back to me."

"Lily listen to me" Seth tried to make reason of all this information in his head but none of it seemed to fall into place "This nutjob could've read about Jack in the papers and recognised our names, he's trying to get under your skin darling, don't some of your patients do this sort of thing?"

"Not like this" Lily interrupted "I've thought all about that but this was different, so different, your voice? Lily fucking Munster?" she rarely swore, a sure sign of her anger and frustration but that faded back to grief as she said softly "he even cried Seth, he cried in exactly the same way Jack used to cry, it *was* Jack for a few seconds, it *was* my baby"

Seth heard what she said but immediately barriers came up in his head to block it out, he'd had many nightmares and woke up in a cold sweat on countless occasions due to his memories of his son crying in the night or more awfully, screaming on that fateful night. He blocked it all out for such a long time and he had to do so now, for his own sanity and to try to make sense of the current situation.

"You could have, oh I don't know, misheard his accent" Seth was clutching at straws in a vain attempt to rationalise the situation "You're pale with black hair and called Lily, not that big a leap to Lily Munster now is it?"

"You weren't there Seth, he scared the crap out of me, he knows you, he knows us, or at the very least he knows more than he's letting on now, I'm convinced of it" Her voice was becoming more shrill and broken by the second as Seth seemingly wasn't taking her fears seriously at all.

"Lily just calm down and think about it, take deep breaths and relax"

"Don't patronise me Seth, I've done nothing *but* think about all this since it happened!"

"I'm not trying to patronise you, you're a rational and highly intelligent woman and psychiatrist, just think about what you're saying. This isn't like you to get so worked up about a patient, I'll tell you what, I'll have a good think about it all and ask around if anybody knows this guy, I'll go through my old contact books and see if anything stands out too, okay?"

"Thanks Seth, I'm sorry but this just brought everything back to me about Jack, you know?" Lily sniffed down the phone as she tried to control her tears.

"Of course, I understand, it's not a problem, honestly" inadvertently Seth then noticed the clock on the wall "I do have to go now though coz Karl's picking me up in less than an hour."

"Christ Seth, are you still trawling bars for skanks?" a mixture of bitterness, derision and futility tinged her voice, Seth thought he noticed a dash of jealousy in there too but he may have been deluding himself.

"Ah, that's more like the real Lily!" Seth half laughed, more to break the tension as much as anything.

"Oh . . . fuck off Seth, I don't know why I even bothered asking for your help" Lily grunted

"Okay, I'm sorry but I do have to go now and get ready, I will try to find out what I can, I promise and if I come up with anything I'll let you know, okay?"

"Alright, alright" Lily sighed as she finally calmed herself a little "Keep in touch . . . please, bye" Lily hung up before Seth could respond.

"Bye then!" Seth sarcastically answered to the dead line and tossed the phone onto the couch. "Right" he said to himself as he rubbed his hands together "Alcohol and women" he sniffed under his arm "shower first though!"

Seth turned to the stereo and thumbed through his CD collection; he looked at all the extreme and aggressive music that he usually listened to, he pondered everything from Bathory to Kreator, Overkill to Satyricon before deciding that he was still in a more nostalgic mood as he had been for most of the afternoon, hence the Van Halen session, he went through the entire A-Z before returning back to the beginning and AC/DC.

"Perfect" he said as he selected the "Dirty Deeds" album and replaced the Van Halen disc with it. He looked at his watch, realising that he was running a little late he pressed 'play' turned up the volume and sprinted upstairs to the bathroom. He stopped off in his bedroom to pour himself a large vodka from the bottle on his bedside table, taking it with him, drinking and singing along to the music as he prepared for the night of, hopefully, debauchery ahead.

After shaving and showering he selected a clean pair of black jeans, put on his most comfortable boots and his favourite black silk shirt before slipping downstairs draining the last of his vodka from the glass. Seth retrieved enough cash from his wallet then put on his rings and watch, all silver. Always and only silver, he'd always hated gold jewellery even when he could afford it, gold just looked tacky, fake and cheap to Seth, much like the majority of people who wore it in volume. He had forever been attracted to the cold and clinical elegance of silver or chrome or even just plain polished steel, to Seth Caine, silver was a wonderful and almost erotic substance.

Seths' tastes in women were much the same, in that society is led to believe that all men preferred blondes especially with huge breasts. However he had always had an over whelming desire for brunettes or red-heads and if smaller tits were added to the equation, he almost became a salivating idiot. Being an obsessive fan of rock music all his life meant that he almost exclusively dated (or just simply slept with) girls of the rock or gothic persuasion. Naturally this suited Seth perfectly, lots of such girls had that 'dangerous beauty' he always craved and chased. He'd tried dating 'outside the faith' before but it was always a disaster. No common ground existed and that led to long periods of silence and discomfort, sadly, even when it came to sex there was generally very little to retain his attention for very long, they mainly seemed to be blond for some reason too!

Seth had had a few blond partners over the years, busty ones at that but they seemed to be the exception that proved the rule, as he liked to think. No, he wanted a slim or athletic brunette (black haired if possible) or red-headed rock chick who had a strong will and an independent mind, a love of all things medieval and/or horror movies and various sexual positions, that's all he wanted, what was so difficult about that? Why couldn't he find one that he wanted to stay with? Well, another one after Lily.

He stood at the front door now, waiting for Karl, the last strains of 'Squealer' in the background, one of his favourite songs and a great last song to hear before he went out. The sun was making a hasty retreat in the distance as the darkness ebbed in and Seth wondered where the day had gone. He patted his jeans pockets to confirm he'd picked up his cash, then he grabbed his leather jacket to check for his phone, lighter and smokes, all present and correct, he was good to go. As he waited he lit a cigarette, the CD finished and he found himself mulling over the phone conversation with Lily.

Thinking about Jack, thinking about Lily and just who the hell was Severin Frost? As his mind wandered backwards and forwards, he didn't hear the car horn as the taxi pulled up on the road in front of his house.

"Vlad!" Karl hung half out of the car window "Come on, time's a-wasting!"

Seth looked up and broke out into a huge grin, he closed the front door and locked it behind himself then jogged down to the waiting car, taking a last drag from his cigarette and flicking it into the road.

"Alright?" Seth beamed

"I'm great, you looked miles away though, what's up?" replied his shaven-headed friend

"Oh nothing, just had a phone call earlier from Lily that's all, forget it"

"Already have mate" Karl shrugged

"Right, what's the plan of action for tonight then?"

"Well" Karl mimicked consternation "I thought we'd get smashed and see about getting laid, unless you've got any better ideas?"

"No, you read my mind, that's just what I need" Seth smiled to himself

Idle conversation passed between the two until they reached The Dragon, a rock bar. Bikers, rockers, goths and punks milled around inside and out. Security was never an issue at the door, it was the kind of place that policed itself, even more so now that Big Mick ran the place! As they pulled up outside Seth opened his door,

"Your turn to pay innit?" he said before getting out and slamming the door before Karl could argue the point.

"Shit!" tutted Karl who did indeed pay, again.

He caught up to Seth just as he lit a cigarette standing outside the bar

"You just put one out you anti-social bastard!"

"If I could smoke inside like I could in the good old days, I would"

"So, it's my round first is it?" Karl asked sarcastically, not expecting an answer.

"Or you can wait here til I'm finished" but before Karl could reply "look, by the time I'm done you'll have been served and then we can get started and you know I always pay my way so what's the problem?"

"Ok" Karl sighed "no problem, I'll get them in"

"Good boy" Seth smiled, Karl scowled.

As Karl went to the bar Seth leaned back against the wall of the building and looked up as he blew his smoke into the now darkened night sky. It always felt great to be out with his old buddy on a Saturday night. Seth looked back down again to survey the scene of his fellow patrons, hair, leather, shaved heads, boots, Mohawks, jeans, bodices, piercings, tattoos, studs. Rough looking bikers in leathers and beautiful girls in impossibly tight jeans or skirts that were little more than belts! Seth felt at home, as he looked around he noticed a woman from behind looking off into the distance, long perfectly straight red hair spilling down a narrow-fitted black leather jacket. Faded blue jeans, so tight that he could see she was wearing either no underwear at all or a very fine g-string (another thing Seth loved, attractive and very feminine underwear or nothing). All this complemented by black knee-length stiletto-heeled suede boots, perfection! He stared at her and she turned as if knowing she was being watched and from where, she stared directly back into his eyes, she was even more breath-taking from the front, thin lips, green eyes, only a hint of make-up, absolutely gorgeous.

"No tables" mumbled Karl on his return as he handed Seth his beer, Seth glanced momentarily from the beauty to his friend then immediately back to the vision he had just witnessed. Where the hell did she go? He spun on his heels, looking in every direction but could find no trace.

"What's up?"

"Red-head! You see her?"

"No, I was getting the fuckin drinks in, remember?"

"Shit, how far could she have gone?"

"Relax, she's probably in the ladies, she'll be back. If not, there's a couple of very tasty ones in there" Karl smiled and winked as he nodded in the direction of two girls sat at a table through the window inside the bar.

Seth had only seen the red haired angel for a remarkably short expanse of time yet he knew he wanted her, he knew he had to have her. There was something in those eyes that he must know, it all seemed so ridiculous in his head and there was no way he would say that to Karl but he knew that no-one else would suffice tonight, he would rather go home alone, he had to find her, whoever she was.

CHAPTER 4

Seth and Karl stood and drank for a couple of hours as they talked and put the world to rights while always keeping an eye out for women as they wandered in and out of the bar. An occasional raise of the eyebrows and a nod in a specific direction was all it took to keep each other in the loop regarding particularly attractive females. Seth was especially looking to sight the stunning red-head but as yet he'd had no luck.

"So what did Lily want?" asked Karl, not especially interested but conversation had started to run low.

"Oh just some patient of hers' mentioned me by name, he's making out that he knows me or his friends do or something like that." Seth didn't particularly want to talk about this on a night out.

"So what? You used to be a bit famous you know, I'm pretty sure a lot of people have told someone that they know you, what's the big deal with that?"

"Well, it freaked her out a bit, she thinks there's more to it than just knowing me and he's apparently some sort of psycho."

"Face it buddy, you've known a lot of people over the years, especially weirdos present company included!!" Karl said with a smile causing Seth to grin "and how many of those weirdos were women that you ended up screwing? I'd be surprised if you haven't even got a few stalkers out there" Karl laughed

"Thanks for that! I know what you mean but he also mentioned Jack, that's what's upset her the most, I think that's always going to be a very raw nerve for both of us . . . ." Seth sighed ". . . for as long as we both shall live" he finished with a frown, lamenting his lost son and lost marriage equally.

"It's your round" Karl said, deliberately trying to change the subject and lighten the mood which had quickly become very heavy.

"What?" Seth was still adrift and alone in his own mind.

"I said it's your round, large vodka and lime I think, let's kick things up a notch or two"

"Good idea" Seth replied, trying to shake off his malaise "I'll join you".

Seth went inside to the bar and after a few minutes wait he ordered, as the drinks were being poured he gazed into the large mirror behind the bar reflecting all the customers, the place was full as usual and chatter filled the room along with the constant, high-volume barrage of rock music which helped keep the 'normal' patrons out, thankfully.

The drinks arrived and he paid, as he waited for his change he looked at himself in the mirror, at that moment he saw the reflection of *his* red-head walk past him, he spun around as before looking to see where she had gone but no matter how quickly he shot his glance around the room she was nowhere to be seen.

"Fuck!!"

A tap on his shoulder had Seth spinning around in hope with a stupid expectant grin on his face, only to be confronted by the scowling pierced face and long grizzly beard of Big Mick behind the bar holding out his hand with Seths' change.

"Oh, right" Seth's grin faded very quickly "Thanks Mick" he mumbled sheepishly as he accepted his money and went back outside to Karl who was in the process of being turned down by a buxom blond in a low-cut black dress that she was practically spilling out of. Karl accepted his drink from his friend and suggested they go inside the bar for a change of scenery as they'd checked out all the girls outside.

They entered the building and found the only vacant area to stand, at the bottom of the stairs leading to the customers' restrooms; there they resumed an earlier debate around upcoming gigs and albums when Seth casually dropped into the conversation

"I had another fuckin dream last night"

"Another one, Christ man, what's that, the fifth or sixth this month?"

"Seventh I think, it's really starting to mess with my mind" Seth shook his head and took a deep drink from his glass.

"I'm not surprised, it's amazing that it's taken this long, what was it this time?"

"Crucified!" answered Seth wearily

"Crucified? Fuck me!"

"I know, I've been skinned alive, dismembered, had my eyes gouged out, disembowelled, beheaded . . . twice and now crucified, yep, that' seven and always by this big black fucking shadow thing that I can hardly make out"

"Jesus, shooting and drowning for the full house and you win a set of steak knives my friend" Karls' dry wit made Seth roll his eyes. "Sorry pal, I've told you before though, you need to see somebody about this, a shrink or someone."

"See a shrink? I've been married to a shrink for twenty years!"

"No, you idiot, a different one. It's probably just stress related, you ain't had much success writing for a while, you're marriage is long dead and come to think of it you ain't been getting laid as much recently either have you, probably coz you're getting older"

"Thanks a fuckin bunch for your honesty *mate*! No need to spare my feelings, how long have you been waiting to point all that out?" Seth snapped back but he knew Karl was right.

"Calm down, that's the point, I'm trying to be honest with you. All those things together, and that's just off the top of my head" Seth scowled and snorted as Karl spoke "Seth, your mind's gonna be a bit fucked up. Ask Lily if she can refer you to someone, it's all done confidentially so she wouldn't need to know too much"

Once Karl had finished his mini lecture, Seth simply looked at him with a withering stare.

"No thanks, I don't want her thinking I'm cracking up, besides she seems in a state over her patient as it is, my impending insanity is probably the last thing she needs right now."

"Fair enough buddy, she can find out when you're admitted to the Hoffman as her next lab rat" Karl laughed to himself

"Anyway" Seth snapped again "if I take you're advice, and that's a big if, I'll get one myself, they advertise, they're in phone books." As soon as he said it he knew it didn't seem like a great way to find a good therapist but then realistically what could go wrong? They finished their drinks and Karl made his way back to the bar for yet more refills.

As Seth stood there waiting for his friend and drink, looking down at the ground at nothing in particular, he suddenly felt he had to look up, as if someone had grabbed a fistful of his hair and raised his head. He found himself immediately staring directly into the eyes, the beautiful green eyes of his red-headed angel.

She was no more than ten feet away and walking right up to him, she didn't smile or even acknowledge him, she just looked into his eyes, deeply, as she walked up to, then past him, all the while with perfectly unbroken eye contact. As she passed, his head swivelled and his mouth gaped open like some pimply-faced adolescent. She walked up the stairs to the bathrooms while Seth stood frozen to the spot, unable to move or speak and unwilling to even blink for fear of losing sight of this amazing vision.

He watched her ascend the staircase, there seemed to be something about her, something otherworldly, something in her movement, something beautiful yet sinfully wicked, a wicked angel. Then she was gone from his sight again, a voice in his head implored him to go after her but his body stubbornly refused to obey the command.

"Here" Karl had returned and was offering Seth his drink "What's up with you? You look like you've just seen a ghost, all the colour's drained out of your face."

"I . . . erm . . . red . . . girl" muttered Seth

"Red girl? Oh, you've seen the red-head again? She's only a girl mate, there's loads of them in here tonight, look at that one!" Karl nodded over at a brunette standing with her friends next to the open entrance door.

"You don't understand Karl" Seth said as he regained his power of speech "She's amazing"

"They're all amazing, until the next morning Seth . . . ." Karl's cynical words hung in the air as he stopped mid speech because he'd turned his gaze at the precise moment that the red-head started back down the stairs and he beheld her image for the first time, Seth hadn't taken his eyes off the staircase since she ascended.

They both stood and stared as she now made her return journey, her hips swaying naturally almost to the hard beat of the loud pulsing music which now seemed so distant in the background. Under her open black leather jacket she was wearing a blood-red boned corset which pushed her small breasts up to the maximum. She had almost deathly pale skin which contrasted in a wonderfully harsh way against the red of her corset, hair and lips and the black of her jacket, a vision indeed.

She reached the bottom of the staircase and in one completely fluid movement of calm and grace she put her hand on Seths' face, without words, she bid his head to lower to hers' as she kissed him deeply on the lips. She pulled back, Seth remained slightly bent forwards, his eyes closed and lips ever so slightly still pouted, Karl looked on open-mouthed and amazed.

"I'm Alex" she said in a soft yet mildly husky voice.

"I . . . I . . . I'm Seth" came an almost robotic response as he opened his eyes almost in hope of confirmation that this was the same beauty he had seen earlier.

"I know" she replied but before Seth could even think about questioning how she knew him, she spoke again "there is a car outside waiting for us" without even looking at the disbelieving Karl she continued "the two of us . . . now follow me" with that she walked past them both and out of the front door of the bar.

Seth, without even realising it, immediately dropped his glass on the stone floor, as it shattered into dozens of tiny pieces the people in the near vicinity all stopped and stared at him, silently Seth left Karl standing at the foot of the stairs and walked out into the street. Outside into the now cold crisp night air he stepped, somehow no-one even seemed to notice the huge gleaming black Jaguar with black tinted windows parked in front of the bar, engine revving impatiently.

Almost magnetically Seth moved to the car, as he approached, the engine growled like an actual big cat warning off a potential enemy. The rear passenger door silently swung open to allow him access, without thinking he got in, he didn't even have time to reach out and close the door behind him as it slammed shut. There she was beside him, Alex, as he now knew her. She looked at him and yet still there was no smile, just an intensity and power, reminiscent of a wild animal contemplating its' prey.

The car roared into life and pulled away into the night. Seth looked at Alex, he could hardly take his eyes off her, he had no idea who she was or how she knew him. He didn't know where he was being taken or even who the hell was driving! He just knew that he wanted her, badly, he assumed she just wanted him and evidently she simply wanted to get straight to the point, he wasn't going to argue with that! He glanced at her long slender legs encased in denim and suede, her left hand, where it rested on her thigh, bore multiple silver rings but no obvious wedding or engagement ring, perfect. As she breathed lightly, her breasts rose and fell exquisitely, the tips of her hair fell over her leather covered shoulders and brushed her smooth pale neck, savouring all this brought his mind into focus with the situation. A wry smile spread across his face as he got comfortable in his seat, he looked out of the window as the city sped by, he didn't recognise anything but then he wasn't interested in sight seeing, he whispered to himself under his breath

"Seth, you lucky, lucky bastard."

CHAPTER 5

Following a silent and seemingly short but very comfortable journey, the Jag slammed to a halt, the rear passenger door opened as if soundlessly asking, or ordering him to get out, which he did and the door automatically slammed shut behind him. The cars wheels screeched into life and the machine bulleted off into the darkness. Seth was left standing outside a huge building which looked like a disused factory, he hadn't heard Alex get out of the car but clearly she had as she now walked on five or six paces in front of him, naturally he followed like a bemused puppy eager to play.

They walked into the foreboding building through a foyer that seemed long-since abandoned, dust and cobwebs covered most of the interior and floor though curiously it seemed that only Alex's footprints were visible in the quite thick dust on what sounded like very old floorboards, judging by the echo. Was she the only one who lived here? Did she in fact actually live here or were they here because she had some kinky fetish about being fucked in old factories? Not that Seth was overly concerned at his point.

All of this was a minor insignificance to Seth as they entered an elevator whose doors had already been open and waiting for them as they approached, the doors closed and they rode to the top floor. When they disembarked at their destination, they were greeted by a huge steel door which seemed more in keeping with a bank vault. On the wall next to the door was a very high tech looking keypad where Alex typed in a code, upon which much clicking and bleeping issued forth from the door and it opened to allow entry.

"Security, can't be too careful these days" Seth joked, for the first time now feeling a little nervous and uneasy.

She looked at him and for the first time he saw her smile, though very slightly. Her lips parted and the tip of her tongue slid gently between and across her teeth. There was a strange feeling inside of Seth, an odd combination of fear, foreboding, intense excitement and extreme lust. He'd never wanted any woman as much as he wanted Alex yet he was becoming unusually anxious about what was on the other side of that door.

Alex pushed it open and Seth peered in. His fears, though he didn't quite know what they were, seemed to ease almost at once. This was just a loft apartment, big and dark but a loft apartment all the same. She walked in and with his confidence swelling back, Seth followed. Alex took off her jacket revealing her bare shoulders and threw it on a nearby chair to one side of the rooms' entrance; Seth removed his leather and threw it on the same chair. He surveyed the room, it was indeed very large, plasma screen television mounted on one wall with two sumptuous over stuffed purple velvet-covered armchairs in front of it. Facing the TV and chairs, against the opposite wall stood two enormous, heavy-looking and impressively ornate bookcases. Seth wandered over to them and saw that they were filled with volume upon dusty volume about philosophy, law, religion, medicine, archaeology, architecture and other such subjects, the amount of which he wasn't used to seeing in his usual dates apartments.

The entire room was dark yet eerily candlelit through out, surely she wouldn't have left all these candles burning while she was out, he thought to himself, she couldn't be that reckless, the whole place could've burned down. Such mundane thoughts immediately seemed trivial, she must have a maid or housekeeper, the interior looked old yet expensive so she probably did have staff, it seemed she had a chauffeur he reasoned to himself, so why not a maid?

At the far end of the room under a huge picture window was an even bigger bed, arguably the biggest bed Seth had ever encountered and he'd experienced quite a few in his time. He turned back to see Alex in a small kitchen area, the only small thing in the whole place it seemed, she was pouring drinks and getting ice from the freezer.

"Amazing place" he almost had to shout his compliment over to her "you must be doing well for yourself"

"I get by" she replied without looking up

"What did you say you did again?"

"I didn't" she said as she finished in the kitchen and brought over the drinks "vodka and lime, right?"

"Er yes, thanks, how did you know?" his mild curiosity rose

"Lucky guess"

"Lucky guess about my name too I suppose?" Seth was starting to become a little concerned as he had never even seen this woman before and she wasn't the sort of woman he would forget. How did she know him though? Was he really that much of a fixture in the Dragon that everyone knew who he was and what he drank?

"Relax Seth, friends of mine told me about you"

"Friends? What Friends?" Seth was beginning to panic, something felt awfully wrong here.

"They suggested that I should introduce myself, they thought we might 'hit it off' . . . and here we are" intensity in her eyes but no smile to ease his concerns.

"Ex-girlfriends of mine? Is this some sort of set-up or twisted game, revenge maybe for my not calling them?" his panic was starting to set in and beginning to merge into paranoia.

"Believe me Seth, life is just a game, whether twisted or otherwise. Though I have nothing against doing things that are a little twisted, in fact, the more twisted the better!" she smiled in an incredibly seductive manner making his heart beat faster by the second. "They aren't mutual acquaintances, they are my friends, my dark friends and you don't know them . . . yet" her now sinister tone quickly put him back on alert, a more sober Seth might have got the hell out of there but the phrase she used peaked his curiosity.

"Dark friends?" he questioned, his brow furrowed, the second time he'd heard that phrase today and the whole atmosphere made him more uneasy than ever. She didn't reply, she just put her hand on his upper arm and stroked it, he felt soothed at once and calmed from her touch, he took a drink from his glass of vodka and breathed a little easier.

"Is there a bathroom?" he asked "I think I need to freshen up"

"Yes, just through that door" that little smile returned as she pointed to a door next to the kitchen, he gave her his glass and went to hopefully clear his head.

In the cold, clinical, chrome and glass bathroom with its' harsh fluorescent lighting, Seth gazed into the mirror and tried to snap back into himself. He couldn't remember being so spooked by any woman like this before. He'd been out with a few strange even creepy girls in the past, he kind of liked it but he always knew it was just an image that most of them liked to portray, he'd also been involved with a couple of self-styled witches and they had been great, then there were the younger ones in their late teens who were either just trying to piss their parents off or seeking attention. This, this was different, he'd never met anyone who he felt so scared of but drawn to in equal measures.

"Pull yourself together you idiot, you've done this dozens of times before" he said to the man in the mirror by way of a pep talk. "She knows my drink? She's heard me order at the bar. She knows my name? So do lots of people in the Dragon and I'm an author, she might have read one of my books, she might even be a fan! Ha ha, fat fuckin chance, knowing my luck she'll be a stalker." He smiled to himself "if I'm gonna have a stalker I might as well have one that looks like that!"

He chose to conveniently forget about the 'dark friends' portion of the conversation and instead ran some cold water in the sink, he splashed his face a couple of times with the refreshing liquid before drying himself on a nearby towel, he looked again at the man in the mirror, smiled and said "Let's do this!"

Seth walked out of the bathroom and turned off the light, immediately the dark yet candlelit gloom of her living area appeared far more inviting and seductive. It also seemed much, much warmer than he had noticed before, maybe it was the contrast to the coldness of the bathroom but it was definitely a pleasurable feeling. He walked past the kitchen where his vodka waited patiently on the counter for his return, he picked it up and drained the glass before returning it to the work surface.

Where was she? On the approach to the bed, on either side of the room, there were ceiling to floor lengths of beads and silks in varying shades of red and purple, partly drawn across the room giving a tantalising view of the bed while still partitioning it away from the rest of the living area.

"Alex?" Seth called as he moved slowly through the cavernous room towards the bed. As he approached, a plume of smoke was blown out from the left-sided curtains, he stopped dead in his tracks about twelve feet away.

Alex stepped out from behind the curtain and Seths' chin nearly hit the floor. She stood there wearing the same black knee-length suede boots as before but this time she had put on a black lace bra and removed everything else! Standing in front of him, naked save for the boots and bra with one hand on her hip and the other delicately holding a cigarette, this was everything he'd ever fantasised about.

Her long red hair seemed even redder still now as it hung over her shoulders against that milky white flesh. Seth drank in the sight, looking at her breasts cupped beautifully in the fine black lace, her smooth, slightly taught abdomen down to her hips where her hand rested and her pubic hair neatly shaved into a fine stripe, half an inch or so wide. Her thighs were perfection, in fact her whole body seemed in perfect proportion and it stood there now practically screaming out for his attention. As if reading his mind she turned around to put her back to him, Seth gasped as she did so. She had such a smooth and elegant back, so pale and flawless, easing down to her exquisitely firm ass, a small and faint strawberry shaped birthmark on her left cheek, the equivalent of a signature on a masterpiece work of art, she would be the perfect sculpture had it not been that she was oh so real and for tonight at least, she was his. He stared at her ass as she waited, temptingly like the first succulent peach of summer awaiting his bite.

He could control himself no longer and moved up behind her, putting his arms around her waist he kissed her shoulders then brushed her hair aside so as to gain access to her neck. She took a long draw on her cigarette, dropped it to the wooden floor and extinguished it under her boot. She tilted her head back and blew the smoke into the air as Seth licked and kissed her neck from behind. As he did this she glanced sideways at him, stepped forward and turned to face him. Without a word she unbuttoned his shirt and slipped it off his shoulders, letting it fall to the floor. Next she turned Seth and sat him on the bed, once there she removed his boots and socks.

Taking him by the hands she stood him back up and proceeded to undo his jeans. She pulled them and his underwear down to his knees as Seth looked down, unbelieving of this glorious sight playing out in front of him. At that point she stopped again and kneeling down she looked into his eyes with the most lascivious smile on her face that he'd ever seen in his life. Alex reached behind her back and unhooked her bra, letting it fall to join his garments on the floor, her naked breasts looked even better than he'd anticipated, small and ever so slightly uptilted, deliciously perfect.

Seth bent to touch her breasts but she pushed his hands away, instead she took hold of his know straining cock. Alex squeezed it before leaning forward and gently kissing the tip then lightly she traced around the head with her tongue. Parting her lips she took it into her mouth, Seth could barely control himself at the wonderfully soft, warm, wet feeling. The movement of her tongue as she moved his phallus in and out of her mouth while continuing to stare at him with those beautiful green eyes made him feel like he was going to explode at any second. As if knowing his exact thought she suddenly stopped, she didn't speak, she simply stared at him. No words were necessary, this scene was to be played out in near silence, animal instinct and primitive passion held sway in this place at this moment.

Seth was utterly amazed that he hadn't climaxed already at her first touch, still holding him in her hand she slowly stood so as to graze his member along her skin as she rose, sliding it down her chin and throat, between her breasts and down her stomach until she stood in front of him again. He wanted to say something but nothing would come out of his mouth, all words failed him, no words could describe what he felt. She gently pushed him back onto the bed and as he lay there she slid off his jeans and underwear completely.

Seth suddenly had a feeling that they weren't alone, he looked around from where he lay, scanning the room but could see no-one, he put it down to the candle-light dancing images across the walls and he wasn't really in the mood to go exploring around the apartment! Alex climbed onto the bed and sat astride him, on his stomach, stroking his chest and pierced nipples, gently at first then harder she tugged the rings in his flesh. He winced but enjoyed the intensity of what she was doing, that's what they were there for after all, then she spoke;
"Pierced tongue too I see" she rolled off him and lay by his side "now's the time to use it Seth"

He sat up and moved over her, kissing and sucking on her breasts, teasing the nipples with his tongue. Alex put her hand on the top of his head and began to almost forcefully ease him down to her now parted thighs. Seth had wanted to work his way down slowly but it was clear who was in control of this situation so he dutifully did as he was bid. Softly he kissed his way down her abdomen, her delicate feminine scent intoxicating him as he reached her most intimate and moist lips. Repositioning himself between her legs so he could watch her and see every fluctuation in her body, he settled into motion. This was always a particularly favourite pastime of Seths'. A chore to some men, he relished having a woman squirming on the end of each stroke of his tongue and squirm in delight she did.

Her juices flowed and dripped, mingling with his own saliva as he placed his hands under her ass and lifted her as a starving man would lift a bowl to his hungry mouth. Seth plunged his tongue ever deeper into the scalding inner depths of her cunt and her body convulsed in his eye line. He could see her breasts move as he traced her labia and flicked her clitoris with the stud in his tongue, he couldn't help but smile a little to himself anytime he did this but this woman more than any before seemed to double his pleasure by her reactions, spurring Seth on in his endeavours to please her. Alex almost howled as she came, her body shuddering to a climax the like of which he hadn't witnessed before.

Seth eased her back down onto the bed and wiped her delicious juices from his chin and lips. Alex lay there panting and breathless but quickly regained her composure as she saw him stand up, his erection still straining in front of him. She rose from the bed and he stepped back, allowing her to stand, as she got to her still-booted feet she took hold of it firmly in her palm and massaged it for a few seconds, she tilted her head up and kissed him deeply on the mouth so as to savour her own taste on his lips. Still holding his cock she led him to the side of the room where she released his member from her grasp. She was the image of wantonness wearing just her suede boots with her perspiration soaked hair now sticking to her face and damp naked flesh, even more so when she turned her back to him, bent forward and placed her hands on the wall.

"Now fuck me . . . hard and slow" was all she said over her shoulder to him.

Seth didn't need to be told twice, the sight of her sumptuous ass in the air was more than he could bear, he had to be inside her. He knelt behind her and stroked her soft smooth rump before kissing each cheek lightly, tasting the salty sweat on her skin while her gentle moans increased his ardour. He parted her buttocks in order to catch a glimpse of her rosebud like asshole. Slowly he licked all the way down between the cheeks, stopping only to tease the small warm hole with the tip of his tongue. She tensed, writhed a little then relaxed at his touch. Next he moved to lick her pussy, again to more moans from his subject, continuing where he had left off on the bed but he knew what she wanted, she had been brutally forthright about that. He rose to stand behind her now, while she reached back and took hold of his cock with one hand as he parted her moist lips himself to gain access, as he penetrated, the heat from her inner flesh was as shocking and stimulating as his first sight of her naked.

Seth eased his length into her and she gasped sharply, gradually more and more until he was inside her fully. He caught his own breath and composed himself then took hold of her hips. As she had instructed, she wanted to be fucked hard but slowly, Seth was more than happy to oblige! Withdrawing almost fully then gliding forward slowly but hard and to his hilt, at first she yelped, then again and again but a little less each time. Seth continued with long deep hard strokes until naturally his rhythm began to intensify with the excitement, fluid began to stream down her inner thighs as he fucked her with increasing ferocity and vigour. He smacked her right ass cheek hard, leaving a faint red palm print, Alex didn't protest so he did it again and again as he ploughed into her. Their timing became intertwined and she pushed herself back onto him as he thrust forward to gain maximum penetration while Seth alternated between smacking her ass and reaching forward to stroke her breasts.

He could hold back no longer however and shot his seed deep into the maelstrom of her body, his cock pulsed and jerked inside her until he was sated. They stood joined as if one being, sweat dripping from every pore until Seths' knees buckled from exertion and they both collapsed to the floor. As they lay in each others moist and dripping embrace Seth thought he could hear a deep throaty laugh from somewhere in the room, he couldn't be sure and at that moment he cared even less.

At that precise moment, across the city in the Hoffman Psychiatric Institute, Severin Frost lay on his bunk, wide awake and mumbling to himself, or so it seemed. Suddenly he stopped and sniffed at the air like a great beast in the wild sensing its' prey, a smile spread across his malevolent face.

"Ah, first contact, we are so looking forward to working with you Mr Caine"

Severin turned over on his bunk and closed his eyes, knowing that he would sleep deeply for the first time in a long, long while, the sleep of the not-so-just.

Chapter 6

Seth woke on his living room floor with a splitting headache. Fully clothed, he could smell and taste tobacco and alcohol. He gingerly got to his feet and stumbled to the kitchen where he ran cold water into his hands to rinse his face while also filling a glass from the pile of used crockery still in the sink in order to slake his raging thirst. This was definitely not the first time Seth had woken up in this condition but it did seem a long time since he had been in such a particularly bad state. Realising he was still wearing his jacket; he hunted down his cigarettes and lit one before removing the leather and dropping it on the floor. He unlocked and opened the kitchen door for some much needed fresh air; the sun was immediately blinding and took him by surprise, rocking him back on his heels. He sat down on the step, one eye closed, the other squinting to keep the light from penetrating too deeply into his skull.

Seth tried to recall the events of the previous evening. He remembered being in the Dragon with Karl, drinking a lot, nothing unusual so far, then being in some sort or expensive taxi or possibly a limo! He also remembered an amazing dream about a red-head, he wished he could have dreams like that as often as he had nightmares. A muffled repetitive sound then had Seth turning to his jacket lying beside him on the floor, he fumbled through the pockets until he found his phone, as much to turn off the irritating noise as to answer the damned thing, the display showed that it was Karl.

"Yeah?" he said in an even more unpleasant voice than usual

"Fucking hell Seth, how'd you get on?" he sounded remarkably excited

"What're you talking about?"

"What am I talking about? Are you serious? That girl, she was amazing you lucky dog, are you still at her place or did you take her back to yours?"

Puzzled, Seth looked around from where he sat for evidence of a female somewhere in the vicinity, he didn't look for long though as it hurt too much when he craned his neck.

"Sorry mate, the last thing I remember is being with you in the Dragon, the vodka was flowing like water and I ended up in some designer taxi back home, that must've cost me a fortune." He said as he pulled the loose cash from his pocket "I just woke up on the living room floor with the mother of all headaches, man I feel like shit!"

"Maybe she drugged you? You know like in all those urban legends, drugged you then took your kidney to sell on the black market, you still got all the body parts you left the house with?" chuckled Karl

"Of course I have" replied Seth, though he also lifted his shirt to inspect his torso for any new scars "I did have an awesome dream about some girl but . . . ." Seth trailed off.

"Dream? Are you fuckin kidding me? Don't tell me, slim, perky, hotter-than-hell red-head in leather and a corset?"

"What! Are you saying all that was real? Fuck!!!" Seth found it hard to believe it hadn't all just been a gorgeous dream.

"Well give the man a prize! You spent all night waiting for her then without even a word to me from either of you, she takes you home and, I assume, fucks your brains out. She did fuck your brains out didn't she? I mean with a body like that and the way she introduced herself and . . . ."

Karl was talking but Seth had stopped listening since it dawned on him that last nights exploits hadn't been a dream after all, even more now, the actual facts and details of his lost hours filtered back to him, her body, the apartment, the sex, the sweat, the taste of her, everything. The whole sensation and imagery of their time together was suddenly filling his mind. Then he was frantically rummaging through the pockets of his jeans and jacket, checking his arms, though there was little space between his tattoos, and the backs of his hands for a phone number that he was hoping she'd given him, no number.

"Shit, shit, shit, fucking shit!" he yelled

"Now what's wrong?"

"I ain't got her phone number, never seen her before and probably never will again now" Seth sighed in immediate defeat and frustration

"Wow stud, you must've put on quite a show if you're that confident" mocked Karl as he laughed "don't worry about it, I'll tell you what, we'll go back next weekend and see if she's there"

"Karl, we go to the Dragon most weekends, this is the first time we've seen her, what's to say she'll go back?"

"How about because she wants to see you again and she forgot to give you her number, maybe she's sat at home now wishing you had given her your number, have you thought of that?"

"Good point" Seth suddenly felt more confident "yeah, she might be planning to come looking for me, you never know"

"True, she's probably at home now writing 'Mrs Alex Caine' over and over in the margins of her algebra book" Karl laughed heartily to himself then said "seriously though, we should go back next Saturday"

"What's in it for you?" Seth sounded sceptical

"Because I'm your friend" Karl almost sounded hurt until he laughed again "no, really, she might have a hot little friend or two, she knows that you were out with me and she might just want to bring someone to occupy me, which I'm totally cool with by the way!" Karls' leering was almost visible through the phone which made Seth half-laugh despite his disappointment at not having Alexs' number.

"Okay, next week it is. Usual time if you don't hear from me?"

"Abso-fuckin-lutely mate! See you then" Karl sounded positively giddy.

They both hung up, Seth threw the phone onto his discarded jacket and lit another cigarette, then he sat for a few minutes with his head in his hands, mumbling abuse at himself as he thought about the possibility of maybe *not* seeing Alex again.

Later that day, following his Sunday service, Father Seymour Duncan was making his rounds at the Hoffman Institute. He was a vibrant priest, late thirties, thin of build with a hairline that had been receding since his mid twenties and deep dark brown eyes that seemed to help his flock trust in his friendship and guidance. His voice was velvet soft and he avoided wearing any of the traditional priestly attire of his calling except during services. He had always felt that people treated him differently in his religious regalia and therefore no-one ever really opened up to him. He wanted the patients in the Hoffman, in particular, to be comfortable in his presence. Therefore in the three weeks or so since he started in his new post, he only ever went about his business in a non-threatening sweater and cotton trousers.

Father Duncan had seen almost all of the patients in the Institute on a one to one basis, most if not all had been very open and receptive to his charm and message. Those who hadn't had usually been very heavily sedated or too disturbed to understand or converse with him, he felt he would get back to them all at some point, the sedated ones when they were a little more 'lively'. He felt that he could always, given time, steer anyone onto the right path, as he saw it to be.

There was only one patient that Seymour hadn't been able to see so far, Severin Frost. Father Duncan had specifically asked not to be told of the patients past or their misdemeanours so as not to allow himself to become biased or judgemental of his newly found sheep. The Institutes Director however had explained, even warned the priest, that Frost, in particular, was not to be taken lightly. To which the good Father had replied, rather predictably that "we are all Gods' creatures."

Father Duncan walked down the long white-washed corridor to Frosts' room with a wry smile of self-satisfaction on his face that he was finally, after stalling from the directors, getting his way. Two guards accompanied him to which he had vehemently protested, but it had been made crystal clear to him that without an escort present he wasn't going to see Frost at all, this was a concession that he had no choice but to accept. He knew Frost was supposedly a very dangerous man, and he had also been told that the 'patient' would try to scare him with stories of his past deeds but then again how horrific could it possibly be? In his teenage years, the young Seymour had been quite the horror movie buff, werewolves, vampires, even the odd zombie flick on occasion, this would be fine, wouldn't it?

Arriving at Frosts' room, Seymour waited as one of the guards swiped a key card through the doors access system to allow entry, access was granted but as the priest made to step foot in the room a guards' heavy hand gripped his shoulder tightly while the other man checked the room first. Seymour could hear chains being rattled as they were checked behind the partially closed door before the first guard re-appeared and gestured for him to enter. Seymour was dwarfed by the size of the guards and as he peered around the bulk of the one in front of him, he saw the back of a man sitting in a chair in the centre of the room, light from a small high window sent a shaft bouncing of his smoothly shaven skull.

"Mr Severin Frost?" enquired Seymour politely

"I think you have the wrong room priest" came the curt reply

As if not hearing the cold response Father Duncan pulled a nearby chair over to sit close to Frost, the guards moved in, standing either side of the two, facing Frost. Severin swivelled around in his office style chair to face the priest. His wrists had been shackled in preparation of Seymours' visit with heavy-looking chains but with enough length to allow him some movement, he lent on the armrest as he stroked his goatee beard, pondering his visitor.

"I didn't think priest was on the lunch menu today so why are you here?" not a hint of humour was in Frosts' voice despite his sickly smile.

"Good day my friend, I am Father Seymour Duncan."

"I know *who* you are, I asked *why* you are here" his sickly smile was replaced with a glare of utter contempt.

"Oh come now Mr Frost, there is no need for that tone, I am the new, what shall we say, spiritual advisor for this facility" as usual, Seymour tried to remain upbeat no matter what the circumstances.

"What makes you think I need advice in such matters, priest?" Frost leaned forward slightly in his seat, the contempt ever more obvious in his eyes as he studied the young cleric. This automatically caused the two guards to tense themselves and both moved their hands to the sticks and pepper spray canisters on their belts. Frost simply tilted his head up fractionally and raised an eyebrow as he glanced at each of the men in turn, who moved their hands away from their weapons and tried to relax, though it was never easy to relax in Severin Frosts' company.

"I believe that everyone at times needs guidance or advice in such matters, my friend. That's my role here, I've spoken to the other patients in this fine Institution and I must say that I've had quite the positive response so far." Seymours' jocular nature seemed to grate with Frost.

"Until now priest, and don't ever refer to me as your friend" icily Frost spoke and icily he stared "Why do you do this so-called work? For your God? You should get a real job."

"I do this because I feel it is my calling to help those people not fortunate to have a clear sight about their past, present or indeed future and sometimes they seem confused about life in general, from a spiritual point of view. I try to guide them in the right directions and give them some hope and encouragement too." Seymour was feeling more comfortable and confident as he settled into his role.

"Point them in the right directions? You mean towards your God?" sneered Severin

"Mr Frost, you seem to have adopted a rather hostile tone in your voce, believe me, it isn't warranted on my account my friend"

"I told you not to call me friend, whatever you may think we are, whatever your calling, we are not and never will be friends" Frost spoke through gritted teeth

"That's alright, if you're uncomfortable with that term for now, I'd like to think I can be a mentor too, a guide maybe or a confidant, I could even just act as a sounding board if you like, is there anything you would like to get off your chest?"

"I have nothing to get off my chest and my soul is not in need of saving, especially by *your* God so unless there's something else, you can fuck off back to your blind sheep, I'm sure you have a choirboy or two to molest." Spat Severin, his words filled with hate and vitriol.

"Sir, I find that last remark to be highly offensive and . . . ." Seymour sat upright in his seat as he almost shouted back at Frost but he also misread the others' twisted smile at the indignant priest "Oh, I see, you are trying to get a reaction out of me, not to worry, I have heard that sort of thing before, I do apologise if I sounded aggressive, it's rather out of character for me to react like that. I am intrigued as to why you refer to Him as *your* God though? There seems to be a deep seated resentment in you voice. Also, don't you think the term *save your soul* that you used before is a little archaic? We live in modern times Severin."

"I prefer archaic, vengeance, torture, an eye for an eye, everything that your *modern* God and your faith would be offended by I'm sure. Your weak, impotent, compassionate, pathetic God, turn the other cheek? Ha, I shall slay my enemies" Genuine bile and loathing were in his words as Frost practically spat them at Father Duncan.

"You're trying to provoke me again Severin" Seymours' fists clenched in anger at the slur but he tried to keep his composure "and what about the Old Testament? A vengeful God indeed, surely?"

"You people make me sick, nothing is ever your Gods' fault but you want to commend him with everything that is good in your eyes. War is mans' sickness yet how many wars have been fought and are still being fought in his name? He's merciful or vengeful depending on how it suits your view and which side of the fence you're sitting on, are the deaths of innocent children *His* will? If you can't explain something then you put it down to Him moving in a mysterious fucking way! And by the way, isn't the Old Testament *a bit archaic?*"

Seymour reached out and rested his hand on Frosts' knee, patting it as if soothing an agitated victim of mental health in a very condescending manner. Frosts' eyes seemed to bore into the priest and he slightly swivelled his chair to move his knee from the priests' reach, both guards immediately braced themselves for any physical outburst, hoping desperately that it wouldn't come to that. The movement of the guards caused Severin to look up at them again, as he glanced back and forth between the two burly men he remembered that on separate occasions he had hospitalised both of them, Frost gave a withering smile and said

"Relax boys, I'm actually in a good mood today, can't you tell?"

The men slipped back to Defcon 3 and gave uneasy smiles in return.

"Really Severin, why are you in a good mood today, are you expecting visitors?" asked Seymour, hoping to lighten the very tense feeling filling the room.

"I don't have visitors, well not in the conventional sense at least, let's just say that things are developing well after last night and leave it at that" replied Frost with a wry smile, the guards looked at each other and furrowed their brows, that sounded like trouble to them.

"Hmm very cryptic Severin, almost like you're trying to scare me" Seymour laughed, nervously, but a laugh all the same. Big mistake.

"You're laughing at me?" the smile completely slipped from Frosts' face as his eyes narrowed as if trying to read the priests mind or look deep into his heart "I'm curious, what did they tell you about me and why I'm here?"

"Well actually they were trying to tell me but I refused the information, I prefer not to know too much about my charges before I meet them, I find that approach stops me forming preconceived ideas about them."

A smile crept back to Severin Frosts' face and he licked his lips as if preparing to tuck into his favourite meal. He always loved this part of an interview, it happened so rarely these days as most of his *subjects* knew of his crimes. Frost was like a cat tossing an injured mouse into the air for sport before death, torment was second only to torture in his eyes.

"Okay, so do you want to know of my *so-called* crimes?"

"Only if you want to tell me as a confidant, unfortunately with the guards here it won't actually be a formal confession but it may help you to talk about them."

"Priest, formal confession is for someone seeking forgiveness, that is something that I neither want or need." Was Frosts' abrupt reply and before Seymour could react "I'm here because I have a penchant, no sorry, more of a *calling* if you will, for torturing certain 'people' . . . to death" theatrically he let those last few words dangle maliciously in the air.

Seymour nervously looked up to his right at the guard standing there who in turn looked down and very slightly nodded his head. The room suddenly seemed much darker and colder than it had previously, the timbre of Frosts' voice, his eyes, those dark green pools, seemed to dance with black light as he spoke. This was no mind game, this was the truth about to open up before Father Duncan.

"Err . . . certain people? You said certain people, what sort of . . . people exactly?" Stammered Seymour, a sickly feeling suddenly at the back of his throat made him swallow hard.

Frost bent forward with that twisted smile on his face as if to whisper a delicious secret to a favourite child, he lifted his hand making his chains rattle and beckoned with his finger for the priest to join him in a confidential moment. Against his better judgement and almost against his will, Seymour bent forward too. The guards inched forward also, again reluctantly, they knew exactly what Frosts' acts of horror were and didn't particularly want to hear about them again but they were here to protect Father Duncan or get him out of there if things did turn ugly.

"Prriiiieeessssttttssss" hissed Frost like a huge serpent taunting its' prey, then he simply sat back in his chair to allow the word to take the desired effect. Immediately images of pain, death, destruction, brutality, decay, horror and torture rushed like a macabre avalanche through Seymours' mind. He couldn't tell if Frost was still talking, his lips were moving and presumably he was telling his horrific tales but it felt like all Father Duncans' nightmares had been fused together with a few choice cuts from other monstrous scenarios and were now playing like a movie in his head and Seymour couldn't switch it off.

As the images eventually faded, Seymour hunched over for no more than a minute or two before gingerly moving back in his seat, beads of sweat rolling down his temples and brow, all colour drained from his now ashen face. The priest almost painfully craned his neck to look to his left at the other guard for some reassurance that this wasn't really happening, reassurance there was none as the guard almost apologetically looked down at his boots, unable to make eye contact with the internally squirming young priest.

Had the guards heard Frost tell him those things? Or had Frost somehow put the images in Seymours' head? Frost must have spoken of such things because the guards knew what was going on in Seymours' mind by their reaction, surely? Tormenting questions all seemed to confuse the issues more and made matters worse in the priests' head, he could continue no more and fumbled to his feet with the aid of a guard. He looked like a man with sea-sickness on the bow of a ship trying to withstand a tidal wave. He stumbled to the door as the other guard unlocked it, as he did so Seymour looked over his shoulder

"Clever party trick Mr Frost" he mumbled

"That was no trick priest, just the truth and there is plenty more when you have the time, or the stomach for it. Leaving so soon? Pity, I was just getting comfortable with you"

"I . . . I . . . I have to go, other people to see, busy day you know"

"You were right Father, it does feel better to get things off my chest, we must do this again sometime . . . my friend"

On the other side of the door Father Duncan collapsed to his knees and vomited on the floor, coinciding with a deep and sustained laugh from Severin Frost.

CHAPTER 7

Seth drove through the early hours, he knew he should be asleep, he had a big day tomorrow, or should that be today? It was 2:30 in the morning and this was the last place he wanted to be, the fucking motorway.

His son Jack was sat in the back with his moronic sidekick Spud. Why the kid had been given such a ridiculous nickname Seth neither knew nor cared. This was unfair, he should be resting in his bed. It was crucial that the meeting with his publisher went well in the morning, his future and in part therefore Jacks' could depend on it. He looked again in the rear view mirror at the boys, everyone had said how much like his father Jack had looked, 'maybe a few years ago' Seth frowned 'not now'.

Those years ago, Jack had been a likeable kid, in his early teens he had been polite, friendly and well-mannered but he'd done the classic thing and *fallen in with a bad crowd* (or so the saying went). Now he was a moody, arrogant and self-centred 16 year old. Everyone changes of course thought Seth to himself, he used to be carefree and relaxed himself, spontaneous and fun-loving too, up until a few years ago that was, that was when his book sales had slowed down as his writing dried up. The poorer the writing, the worse the sales, the sales made him more desperate and stressed and therefore his writing suffered further and so the spiral went ever downwards. Added to that, Lily had had a brief, and immediately regretted affair with some bastard called Scott at work, what kind of fucking name was Scott anyway? He felt he was entitled to feel hard done by. As far as he could understand, Jack had never found out that his mother had been unfaithful and was still very close to her. In moments of weakness, drunkenness or self-pity, Seth had almost let it slip to the boy but his love for his son and his wife always reined him back from the edge of that precipice. He did understand why Lily had strayed, albeit briefly, Seth must've been hell to live with when things were professionally on the slide for him, Jack was going through difficult times at school and then a new doctor arrives at her Institute, young, successful, rich and most important of all, no wife or kids to complicate matters, what was a girl to do?

Now here Seth was, half asleep and getting more stressed with every mile covered, all due to his upcoming meeting and what was he doing? He was driving his ungrateful son and his chain-smoking loser of a friend home from their latest concert.

"Missed the last train home and we can't find Eddie to get a lift, can you come and pick us up Dad? It's freezing"

That had been the extent of the phone call that got Seth out of his bed, no "sorry Dad but . . . ." or even a "please", Seth had grown used to this by now though, conversation hadn't even got started in the car, not that Seth was looking for a happy chat. Just a combination of private jokes sniggered at between the teenagers or moody silences as they stared out of the window as Seth chauffeured them home.

The more Seth thought, the more his mood darkened, the more irritable he became, the faster his heart beat and the tighter his chest became. He needed to sleep, oh God he needed to sleep. Everything would be fine if he could just get a good nights uninterrupted sleep, fat chance! If he could just get through tonight and tomorrow went well, everything would be fine, he told himself. As he thought of all this, the anxiety distracted him from the increasing pressure he was applying to the accelerator.

Seths' teeth ground together as his migraine decided to kicked in, *if* he could have been allowed to concentrate more on his writing, *if* Lily hadn't cheated on him, *if* his son had worked harder and applied himself more at school, it was all other peoples' fault. His knuckles turned whiter as they gripped the steering wheel harder and harder, the vein in his forehead that Lily once thought was so cute began to pulse. His son in the back was wrapped up in his own little world, oblivious to what speed they were travelling at.

Seths' heart beat faster and faster still, his head hurt, too much thinking, too much stress, too little sleep. He looked down and realised his speed and eased up but the blood was pumping through his cholesterol-filled veins and arteries at seemingly greater speeds. His heart still galloped, cold sweat trickled down his spine and the all too familiar shooting pains raced down his left arm. Seth crumpled like a rag doll over the steering wheel.

Jack and Spud at last realising there was a problem jerked forward, as did the car.

"Dad, Dad!!" screamed Jack, the car sped on out of control, lurching this way and that. No other vehicles were on the road at that time of the morning but an immobilised driver at ninety-five miles per hour is only going to result in one thing sooner or later.

Sooner rather than later the inevitable did happen, the car skidded from side to side, weaving like a punch-drunk boxer. Jack tried to steer the car over his stricken fathers shoulder from the backseat all the while screaming for his daddy. Spud by his friends side, screamed in near hysterics as he bounced of the front passenger seat and side door, tears streaming down both their faces. Then Jack lost what minimal control he had and the vehicle hit the central reservation, mounted it and flew up and over the crash barrier. Spinning in mid-air like a childs' toy it landed on its' roof and slid another hundred yards, leaving a stream of sparks until it eventually came to rest on the opposite side of the motorway against a grass bank.

A torn and crumpled wreck of mangled, twisted metal and broken bones, shattered glass lay all over the road and twinkled under the moon and road lights like Christmas tree decorations. Oil, blood, fuel and tears swam together, glistening in iridescent pools. No more private jokes, no more sniggering, no more pent up anxiety and rage, no more moody teenage silences, just silence. In the far distance the sirens wailed, the approaching emergency services were speeding to the scene, they would do what they could, they would do their best but it would be too late.

Seth lay barely conscious, a jumble of thoughts spinning through his lacerated head. He thought of his beloved Lily and their courtship, their simple wedding in a forest, the birth of their beautiful baby boy and how everyone said that he looked just like his proud dad. He thought of their home together and how his life was just perfect with them in it.

There was no white light, no-one beckoning him through an open doorway to a better place, nothing. Seth lay in agony, with his memories of happier times to comfort him, those times were all with his family, he had been a lucky man, he thought to himself.

A single tear rolled down his blood-stained cheek as he caught sight of Jack in the broken rear view mirror, his lifeless eyes stared back at his father. Trapped and unable to hold him and unable to bear the sight of his dead son, Seth closed his own eyes and silently prayed for merciful death to take him by the hand.

Seth jerked upright in his bed; a dark shape loomed over him inquisitorially. In the half light coming in from the moon Seth was unsure who or even what he was looking at, was it a man? It didn't appear to be the same beast from his nightmares. He was still in a cold sweat from his horrendous dream of Jack but what the fuck was this new nightmare vision?

It seemed to be a large man in a black cowl and cloak, Seth inched forward, the 'thing' seemed to be covered from head to foot in leather, old, cracked, black leather. The more his eyes grew accustomed to the lighting the more he realised 'it' wasn't wearing leather at all, the leather was 'it's' skin! The creature was actually perched on the foot of Seths' bed like some huge bird of prey, an analogy made all the more chillingly clear upon Seths' realisation that there was no cloak and cowl, as a right limb unfurled, revealing a monstrous ragged leathery wing stretching almost halfway across the large room. As Seth glared motionlessly at his watcher, its' features came into view, a sight Seth would rather not have seen, the thing had only a half-fleshed face. Bone, gristle, tendon and savagely sharp teeth gleamed in the moonlight as it smiled a taunting rictus grin, a crackling sound issued forth from its' jaws as bone ground against bone and muscle twisted to form the unearthly sight.

Seth stayed frozen to the spot, slowly the creature began to unfurl its' left wing. It was holding something, something quite large but Seth couldn't quite make out what it was. Curiously the beast seemed to be showing whatever it was to Seth but as he could hardly move through fear, the monster held out its' huge wing further as if to show Seth an offering it was making.

Sensing that the beast wasn't there to hurt him, just to show him *something*, Seth moved a little closer, but soon wished he hadn't, on closer inspection it was clear that the 'offering' was human! Seth jumped back again with a yell of horror. A throaty laugh belched forth from his visitor as its' head tilted back in its' enjoyment, Seth could see the glisten of saliva in its' partly exposed gullet. The body was held out to Seth again and he looked at it not realising what was expected of him. As he looked, the head of the lifeless corpse lolled to one side exposing a face, a face that Seth had longed desperately to see again but not like this. It was Jack, his eyes open, his face streaked with blood, exactly the same as five years ago, the last time he'd seen his son in the mangled carnage of his wrecked car.

Seth wept in despair and rage as he lunged forward to rescue his dead sons' body from the clutches of this monster. As he did so, the beast swept the boy back up beneath its' wing and swung its' other limb round, slicing across Seths' face with the three talons that lined its' tip. Seth recoiled back onto the bed, the creature looked down at the boy as a mother would cradle and gaze upon her new born child, then it looked back at Seth with what appeared to be a cross between a snarl and a sickly smile and hissed at him

"Miiiiinnnnneeee!"

Seth woke up screaming Jacks' name and crying like a baby, sweat dripped off his body as if he had spent the night sleeping in a sauna. He felt drained and weak, his phone at his bedside beeped at him to remind him he had missed calls or messages. Realising he had been dreaming about Jack and the crash again but also nightmarish winged beasts he calmed himself by checking the phone.

"12 missed calls and 20 missed texts!! What the fuck" he checked the time and then inadvertently noticed the date, he had been asleep for around 42 hours!

Seth went to the bathroom to wash the clammy sweat from his face. He had been having awful nightmares for a while now and wished he could make them stop. However the one he hated the most was of the night he lost his son. If he could, he would trade having nightmares of being tortured every night for the rest of his life if it meant not having to re-live the car crash again. Just as unnerving was the creature holding Jack, he'd never had that one before and he hoped it wouldn't become a regular feature in his night time terrors.

He filled the sink and rinsed his face, he straightened to look in the glass and stood rigid with shock and horror, the man in the mirror now had three deep lacerations in his cheek.

CHAPTER 8

Seth stared in disbelief at the man in the mirror. No matter how much he had been drinking recently, he knew those scars hadn't been there when he went to sleep. A chill caressed his soul at the thought of his nightmare being a reality, this was quickly replaced by fear, was that thing still in the house? Jack?

He ran out of the bathroom yelling his sons' name, oblivious to what might be lurking in the shadows. Seth ran downstairs still shouting in near hysterics, through the kitchen and living room, nothing. He flung open his front door and stood on the porch looking up and down the street, again he shouted Jacks' name but heard no response.

A woman was in her garden, attending to her rose bushes, hearing Seths' cries she peered over the fence and gasped. He didn't know her name as he had never bothered to meet his neighbours, she scowled at him and he sneered back, he was in no mood for pleasantries. He turned back into the house, slamming the door and bolting it behind him, just in case. After a final look around the house for his own satisfaction that he was alone, Seth sat on the floor in the middle of his living room and wept, he wept tears of grief for his son and he wept for his own sanity that he felt he was losing.

His sobbing was interrupted after a few minutes by a knock on the door; he wiped his eyes, stood and walked over to it. Suddenly he stopped and the ludicrous thought that the demon would be standing there crossed his mind, he dismissed the idea immediately but that didn't stop him from picking up his baseball bat from behind the door, again, just in case. Another knock at the door, this time harder made his heart beat a little faster, he unbolted the door and lifted the bat over his head, bracing himself ready to strike.

"It's open" he shouted through the door, then to himself "steady, steady"

The door was pushed open and he took a deep breath as he raised the bat further and his whole body tensed and strained to deliver the kind of blow that may be necessary.

"Lily? What the fuck?"

"It's great to see you too Seth" she looked him up and down "nice greeting by the way"

A smile of relief crept along his stunned looking face; this was a very unexpected yet very pleasant surprise. He realised he was still holding the bat, waiting to pounce, and lowered it.

"Come in" he muttered

As she entered the house she looked him up and down again and gave him a weary and withering smile, simply saying

"For Christs' sake Seth, it's 2 in the afternoon, put some pants on!"

Seth looked down at himself, realising for the first time since he woke up that he was still completely naked! Suddenly it dawned on him why his neighbour had given him such a glare, 'fuck her' he thought with a wry smile.

"Sorry, I'll just er . . . get dressed"

"Got a wild one this time have you?" asked Lily

"What do you mean?"

"Those look fresh" Lily replied as she gestured to the scars on his cheek.

Seth had completely forgotten about the marks and didn't quite know how to explain them, what rational explanation could he use?

"Erm . . . well" was all he could come up with on the spot and he inadvertently looked upstairs to the scene of his earlier horror.

"Oh Seth, for crying out loud, she isn't still up there is she?"

"No, no you've got it all wrong, it isn't like that at all, I promise." Seth exclaimed, he still cared what she thought of him despite his usual behaviour to the contrary.

"Whatever you say Seth, just get dressed and I'll make some coffee" Lily made her way to the kitchen shaking her head and mumbling under her breath, her mumbling became louder once she reached the kitchen and saw the state of it and the pile of dirty dishes in the sink. Seth did as he was told and went upstairs to dress.

On his return in his usual jeans and t-shirt, he stopped at the bottom of the stairs as they led into the kitchen. Lily stood at the sink, gazing out of the window above it as she drank her coffee. Seth couldn't help but look her up and down, long flowing cotton skirt and matching sleeveless top, all in a creamy off-white colour. A thick brown leather belt loosely tied at the waist and Egyptian style sandals of a similar coloured leather complimenting her perfectly pedicured feet. With the afternoon sun flowing through the window she looked almost otherworldly in the haze and Seth could barely take his eyes off her. She turned and smiled a little smile as she caught him watching her.

"Coffee?" she gestured over to the table in the middle of the room. "It's cheap because it's all you have and it's black because your milks expired, big surprise."

"Thanks" her comment would have got a reaction out of him usually but he just didn't want to get into a fight over something so trivial, not after what he had or hadn't experienced, besides that, he was just so pleased to see her.

"So, what did you do with her? By that, I mean where have you hidden her or has she already made her escape?"

"I told you Lily, there isn't a girl, this was . . . ." he stopped as he grazed the scars on his cheek, they stung to his touch.

"What, a man? Let me guess, you've worked you're way through the cities entire female population and now you're having a go at the men?" Her sarcasm was biting as she laughed to herself.

"Don't be so ridiculous Lily" sighed Seth

"Ridiculous? What, that you've run out of women or that you've turned to men?"

"Both, this is nothing to do with sex" but Seth wasn't rising to her taunts and she seemed puzzled, he continued "What can I do for you?"

"What can you do for me? I asked you to find out about Severin Frost, remember? You haven't got back to me even though I've been ringing you and left you countless texts."

Seth had no reply, he just stood there looking sheepish, like a guilty schoolboy who'd not done his homework despite saying he had.

"I don't believe it, then again I do, it's just sheer ignorance on your part Seth, you are so unreliable. You know I've been going out of my mind over this and you're just going out getting drunk with your mate and screwing anything with a pulse and . . . ." Lily was on a roll now, for such a normally calm and rational person she was becoming almost hysterical, Seth stepped up close to her and lifted his hand up to her face gently putting his finger on her lips.

"Shhhh" he said simply

Her eyes widened with anger and her nostrils flared as if she was going to explode, that she didn't fly into a rage at his perceived belittlement of her was due to the look that she saw in his eyes. It was a look of upset, loss, confusion and weariness, he looked a beaten man, he looked a broken man, he now seemed grey and empty, as if someone had reached inside him and taken out his spirit. His hand fell from her lips and he pulled out a chair from the table and sat down heavily with his head in his hands.

"Seth, are you okay?" she hadn't seen him like this for a number of years, five years to be precise, her temper cooled quicker than it had risen "What is it?"

"It's Jack, Lily. Please, sit down"

She did as he asked though in slow motion, Seths' hands released his face and moved down to the tabletop where they grasped Lilys' now shaking hands, she didn't flinch away, instead she instinctively held his hands tighter in reassurance, whether she was giving reassurance or hoping to receive it she wasn't completely sure.

Seth took a deep breath and told her everything about the dreams he'd been having over the last few months and how he hadn't been sleeping properly, then he stopped and looked at her with his ever more grey and gaunt expression. She looked concerned for him what he'd said hadn't warranted a mention of their son.

"And Jack? What's all this got to do with my baby?" she questioned

"All that was up until the last couple of days, while you've obviously been trying to get hold of me, I finally slept deeply, too deeply"

"For two days?" her brow furrowed

Seth then very reluctantly told Lily about the nightmare of Jack and the beast that followed and the scars on his face and how he felt he was losing his mind. She sat there in stunned silence, a single tear rolled down her cheek, followed closely by more. Seth squeezed her hands to let her know he was there for her as she stared into space.

"It's ok, I'm fine" she said in a tiny broken voice, giving him a little smile as before "or I will be anyway."

Seth stood and opened the kitchen door, he took a packet of cigarettes from a drawer and lit one as he stood on the back porch. Lily came over to him, he was about to apologise for smoking when she took the cigarette as it protruded from his lips and started to smoke it herself. She had quit smoking many years before, in fact when she fell pregnant with Jack. No words were needed now as Seth lit another cigarette for himself and they stood there in quiet contemplation in the suns warm rays of the late afternoon.

After they had finished their smoke they both walked back into the kitchen, an atmosphere hung heavy in the air, neither of them knowing what to say until Lily broke the silence.

"You need to get some help Seth, a good psychiatrist might be able to get to the bottom of these dreams, it may be psychological or emotional problems or it may be just be work related, either way, you need to get the problem resolved."

"Hmm, that's what Karl thought it might be too" interrupted Seth

"Karl? Well if that's what you're drinking buddy has come up with from his analysis I'd have to concur with his findings" sarcasm dripped from every word.

Seth sighed without reply, his head bowed, the anguish on his face was enough evidence that he didn't want another argument.

"I'm sorry" she whispered as her hand came up to stroke his injured cheek tenderly "Please Seth, if you do nothing else, please get some help."

"Thanks, I will I promise, what about this Frost guy?"

"For now, forget him, just get yourself together. I have to go now but I'll be in touch." Lily moved forward and kissed him gently on the lips, then without another word she made her exit.

With Lily gone, Seth sat at his desk and stared at nothing in particular. His thoughts meandered about Jack, he could still smell his wifes' scent in the room and the way she had looked in the kitchens sunlight, his warm happy memories were fractured however with his nightmare creature show. He rubbed his eyes as he took a deep breath to clear his mind before picking up the telephone directory.

Seth flicked through the book until he found a section for 'Psychoanalysts/Psychiatrists', he glared at the pages in frustration, how the hell was he supposed to pick one out from the others? They all looked the same, a name followed by letters of qualification, which meant nothing to him, an address and phone number. Page after page he thumbed through not quite knowing what he was looking for when suddenly on one page all the listings seemed to merge and blur into one almighty mess albeit for one tiny name and number right in the centre of the page, Dr Roth.

Seth rubbed his eyes again, trying to correct his vision, then flicked on a few pages and then back again, this time nothing at all stood out. He threw the book down on his desk and found himself picking up his phone and dialling a number he didn't know, a receptionist answered.

"I'd like to make an appointment with Dr Roth please, sometime next week."

"Dr Roth will see you tomorrow at 11am sir"

"Er . . . ok, that'll be fine, thank you." Seth said robotically

"Thank you Mr Caine" she hung up

Seth put the receiver down and sat in his chair in a daze, trying to work out just what had happened. He couldn't remember the number he had called, there was no address but somehow he knew exactly where he had to go and just how did she know his name? One thing he did know though was that he felt so much better than he had in a long, long time. A huge weight seemed to have vanished from his shoulders, calm and tranquillity seemed to wash over him, Seth sat and basked in his new-found inner peace for a couple of hours before deciding he wanted an early night in order to be fresh for his appointment. He went to bed sober and for the first time in months, he went without fear or trepidation. What will be will be, seemed to be the mantra tripping through his thoughts as he slipped between his sheets to await whatever would be waiting.

CHAPTER 9

Seth slept deeply until his slumber was interrupted by nothing more trivial than a need to visit the bathroom, something that he'd noticed happening more and more as he got older, very depressing. He threw back the sheets and clambered out of bed still half asleep, self consciously he switched on the bedside lamp and squinted into the partially lit room expecting *something* to be there, lurking in the dark, there was nothing. He smiled to himself; it must've simply been the call of nature responsible for his waking.

He went to his en suite bathroom, not bothering to switch on the light, the glow of his lamp would suffice and he hoped not to dazzle the sleep out of his eyes with too much brightness, therefore getting back to his restful sleep as soon as possible. Seth urinated while trying to keep his eyes closed as much as he could in his attempt not to fully wake up. Once finished he sighed and rinsed his hands in the sink before returning to the comfort of his still warm bed, closing the bathroom door behind him and switching off his lamp. Settling down under the covers he sighed again and closed his eyes as he curled up to resume his slumbers.

As the calm washed over him again, Seth heard something faintly in the background as he lay with his back to the bathroom. He opened his eyes but couldn't be sure, he held his breath so as to hear more clearly, all he could hear was silence, not even a passing car interrupted the stillness. Putting it out of his mind he nestled back into his bedding and pillows as if about to hibernate. His mind wandered without prompting to thoughts of Lily, pleasurable thoughts, his lips formed a slight smile and his member stirred into life of its' own accord. His hand moved to massage the swelling as the intimate times with his wife flicked through the mental rolladex of their past sexual exploits.

A noise, this time he knew he'd heard something, he switched the lamp back on and sat upright in his bed looking around the room, he was beginning to always suspect the worst but again there was nothing and no-one there. Seth was just about to lie back down when heard what sounded like water, he could've sworn that he'd turned the tap off in the bathroom and it didn't sound like a dripping tap. It sounded more like pouring water rather than dripping as it came again, then it stopped. A few seconds later and more pouring, then it stopped. He could tell it was coming from the bathroom and he threw back the sheets to explore, after recent events, he was hoping that it was nothing more than a mere broken water pipe threatening to ruin his home.

Just as he reached the bathroom he lifted his hand to push open the door and heard the pouring again but also a distinctly female voice, laughing softly. Seth stopped dead in his tracks, the way things had been going recently a broken pipe was the least of his troubles, whoever was in his bathroom, they weren't there five minutes ago! He looked around in the dark for a weapon but couldn't think of anything to use before dashing downstairs as quickly as he could to retrieve his baseball bat. Whether it was a woman or not he wanted protection, once back upstairs he waited quietly outside the bathroom door, secretly hoping that whoever it was had gone as quickly as they had arrived.

No such luck as the pouring and gentle laughter continued as before. Seth stood with one hand on the door and the other holding the bat above his head in what now felt like his traditional naked stance. A feeling of déjà vu came over him as he thought of Lilys' visit earlier, somehow he knew this wasn't Lily and therefore, an enemy. He braced himself and took a deep breath, his knuckles white as they gripped tightly to the bat, whispering to himself

"Come on, one, two . . . ." He hesitated ". . . three!!"

Seth pushed the door open as fast as he could to give himself the element of surprise but it was he who was surprised, deeply surprised.

Sat in his bathtub was indeed a woman and what a woman she was, more than she greeted his eyes however. The beautiful woman was bathing in blood. The bathtub, his bathtub, was three quarters full of pure thick blood, in all his novels Seth had never dreamed up a scenario such as this. Moreover, kneeling at the side of the bath was another woman with a large pitcher which she continually filled from the bath before pouring it over her companion, to giggles and squeals of seeming delight from the bathing beauty.

As he had burst in through the door, neither of them had even flinched let alone acknowledged his presence, as if they were expecting him, they just continued as if he wasn't even there. The kneeling girls' face he couldn't see as her long black hair and bowed head hid her features from view. She was naked save for thick shining silver chains which loosely manacled her ankles and the same at her wrists, skin the colour of cappuccino, she was slim, toned and athletic, almost muscular in a very feminine way.

Seth turned his gaze back to her 'mistress' being bathed. The first thing that he noticed was the redness, so much blood everywhere. The woman was sat upright with her hands resting on either side of the tub, blood dripping from her fingertips back into the bath. As he looked at her he could see some patches of blood drying and coagulating on her exquisite body, that is until her 'slave girl' poured more fresh liquid over her to yet more howls of joy and pleasure. Firm round breasts, nipples gleaming and hard in the crimson flow, hair long and dark hung down over her shoulders and stuck to her flesh, the exact colour of her hair was difficult to ascertain due to it being blood soaked as it was.

With each pitcher of blood poured over her she smiled a delirious smile, this exposed the gleaming white of her teeth which stood out even greater against the over-whelming scarlet of the scene. That was until she opened her eyes to look directly into Seths' eyes. They were the most stunning shade of purple that he'd ever seen, like two amethyst crystals held up to the light, he'd never known of anything like it. As she stared at him, another flood of crimson poured down over her shoulders and breasts. Her eyes seemed to flare as they widened and emphasised the beautiful colour, her stare held his and he felt he could almost feel her body pulse and swell as if in orgasm at what she was feeling.

"Do you like what you see Seth?" she said in an almost musically carefree voice.

Seth was taken aback as she spoke initially as his vision was now being stolen by the slave girl taking a large sponge and soaking it in the bath before squeezing it out over the bathers' breasts and massaging them with it.

"I'll take that as a yes shall I?" she whispered huskily as she looked down at his straining erection. Seth was transfixed by the sight and still didn't react. "I am Angelique and this is my handmaiden Richelle" she closed her eyes as she spoke and reclined back in the bath.

"W-what are you doing here, how did you get in?" he spoke meekly, and as he did, Richelles' hand slipped down her mistress' torso and disappeared between her thighs into the blood, Angeliques' smile grew wider as her handmaiden pleasured her.

"You ask too many questions Seth, there are pleasures to be had in life if only you would open your eyes and let someone show them to you."

"What the hell are you talking about?" aroused intensely yet frustrated Seth questioned, part of him was horrified by this literal bloodbath, part of him just wanted to know who they were and what they wanted, yet mostly part of him just wanted to jump in the bath with them!

Angelique shivered and groaned as Richelle brought her quickly and expertly to orgasm. No answers were forthcoming from either of them, Richelle stood with her back to Seth and held up a huge thick white towel for her mistress. Angelique stood up in the bath and stepped out, she was covered from head to toe in gleaming blood, Seth ached for her and reached out to touch her, he got close enough to feel heat radiate from her flesh before Richelle wrapped the towel around her and he was briefly distracted as he heard a noise from over his shoulder back in his bedroom. He quickly drew his hand back and spun around then turned back to the women to ask what it was but they were gone.

Not only that but the bathroom showed no sign of either of them, no beautiful women, not even a single drop of blood in or around a bath that a few seconds ago was full of it. The white of the bath gleamed back at him as if taunting him and Seth stood and rubbed his eyes. He looked in the mirror, the scars on his face from his previous 'nightmare' stared angrily back, he was losing his grasp on reality, he could no longer decide what was a dream and what was not, the scars looked and surely felt real but the lines between fact and fiction were more than simply blurred now.

As he continued to stare and study the man in the mirror, hoping to find answers to questions that he wasn't sure about, he heard the growling again. He must have dropped his bat, though he wasn't aware of doing so and he retrieved it from the bathroom floor to confront his next probable visitor.

Seth walked back into his bedroom very warily but could see no-one, he crossed to the other side of the room and found nothing out of the ordinary but for a smell of decay or something that had been dead for a very long time. He switched the main light on and as the room was illuminated there was a yelp of distress from the corner, a figure stood hunched over, dressed in rags. Seth moved closer with his trusty bat in hand, this was no stunning naked girl to throw him off guard, nor was it a monstrous winged beast.

"Who the fuck are you?" Seth shouted at the intruder

"Turn off the light!" croaked the stranger

"Tell me who you are and what you want or I swear I'll take your fucking head clean off" retorted Seth

"I'm not here to harm you, please just turn off the light and I shall explain all, it hurts my eyes" anguished and breathless, the man didn't appear a threat at all, Seth turned the main light off but quickly moved back over to stand by his lamp which he felt may still give him some sort of 'protection'.

"Thank you" growled the ragged man

"Right, so who the fuck are you and what are you doing in my house?"

"How very eloquent, you are indeed a literary man" a half laugh came from the man but Seth was in no mood for joking. He raised the bat over his head again, ready for a fight "fear not Seth, as I said, I am not here to harm you"

"So, what are you here for? I mean, this is some kind of dream isn't it?"

"Of sorts, you could say" the hunched man moved forward with arms outstretched to show he was unarmed, in doing so he also stood up to his full height, almost dwarfing Seth in the process. "I say again, no harm will come to you from my hand, this night"

The man now stood almost seven feet tall, with grey tangled hair hanging to the floor and a waist length beard. Parts of his hair and beard were in long braids, tied with silver clasps. His smile was more of a sneer, his crooked mouth and cracked lips parting to display long yellow and very sharp teeth. His hands were held out in front of him still, elongated bony fingers with jagged broken nails constantly moving as if grasping or clawing for something out of his reach. His flesh looked old and cracked like museum-quality parchment, brown and dusty. His clothes were little more than rags, it was difficult to see what they once were, or even if they were ever meant to be used as clothing, possibly a cloak or overcoat of some kind. They were filthy though and as he drew closer the smell of lingering death became almost overpowering.

"That's close enough" Seth said, holding out the bat at arms length, the man duly stopped and tipped his head courteously, despite the offensive bat resting in his stomach.

"I am Mammon" said the man "a scholarly man such as yourself may have heard of me?"

Seth looked curiously at him and furrowed his brow, he had indeed heard of Mammon, he had studied demonology in his spare time and used a lot of his findings in his own works of fiction. But could this 'being' really be stood in Seths' bedroom chatting to him now? He had to check himself, it was surely just a dream, but why couldn't Seth ever be just playing poker with the Pope and Clint Eastwood in his strangest dreams. He waited for a few seconds to collect his thoughts before replying.

"You mean the demon Mammon? Lord of avarice and greed?"

"You are indeed well read, that is exactly who I am."

"No you're not, Mammon isn't a real demon, it was just a name given to the sin of greed in ancient times not an actual demon, you'll have to do better than that, whoever you are" Seth pushed with the bat, rocking the man back, slightly.

The mans' nostrils flared at Seths' insolence, this was an insult and a growl emanated from somewhere deep inside his body. His eyes, as grey as his hair, narrowed and bored into Seth as his hand shot up and grabbed the bat where it rested against his midriff before Seth could even think of defending himself with it. A cracking noise came from the bat as the man squeezed with one hand, more and more he squeezed until the bat splintered into two under the incredible force. Seth stood rigid with fear at the power of this seemingly broken old man.

"He is who he says he is" Seths' head jerked to the side to see the beautiful Angelique emerge from the bathroom in Louis XIV period couture looking every inch the stunning aristocratic goddess of the 'Sun Kings' court, Richelle, head bowed as before dutifully walking behind her mistress in a maids outfit of the same period but with her hands and feet chained in silver as before.

Angelique walked over to them and offered her hand; Mammon released what was left of the bat and took it, lifting it gently to his lips and kissing it, ever the gentleman it seemed. Seth stood in disbelief for a second; she was *not* in the bathroom! He'd been sure of it, but then could he be sure of anything in his life at the moment? He tried to convince himself he was dreaming, then she stroked his cheek and he could smell her perfume.

"Listen to what he has to say Seth, all will be well and you will come to no harm"

Seth looked down at the pile of matchwood that had been his baseball bat and he found that difficult to believe, she smiled her radiant smile "I promise, just listen to him."

With those words she turned and walked out of the room with Richelle, leaving Seth alone with his 'visitor'.

"I am Mammon" he said again "Mortals have always tried to explain away what they don't understand or what they fear as myth or legend or claim myself and my kind are nothing more than stories to frighten wrong-doers. I have been Lord of Avarice since long before it was even considered a sin by man. Humans do not fully understand what lies beyond their earthly realm and therefore so-called learned men will claim to know secrets and thus elevate themselves above the common man. Please, sit down Seth." Mammons' tone was gentle now, his anger having subsided, Seth sat on his bed and pulled the covers' over his lap, feeling vulnerable in his still naked state.

"So, what do you want with me? Are you responsible for all my strange nightmares recently and why am I having them? Is this really a dream or not because it feels all too real to me." Seth felt calm as he spoke, though he felt he should be more freaked out by the thought of demonic visitations.

"First of all I will reassure you, you are still sleeping at the moment and you will remember me as a very vivid dream and yes we are responsible for your recent spate of nightmares. I apologise for the graphic nature of some of those scenes, mortal tolerance of such things can be somewhat limited, though I do assure you that there is much, much worse that we could have inflicted upon your mind. However, we needed to get your attention as opposed to mentally incapacitating you, we have achieved that, I believe."

"You keep referring to *we*, do you mean yourself and Angelique? Where does she fit into all this and why exactly are you trying to get my attention anyway?"

"Angelique is my companion or consort you might say, she becomes restless or bored from time to time and likes to play, therefore she requested to accompany me while I pay you a visit, Richelle is Angeliques' personal plaything. Trivial I know but she enjoyed turning your head and getting your attention and I think you enjoyed it too, didn't you?"

"Of course I did but why are you doing all this? And you still haven't told me who 'we' are yet?" Seth was becoming exasperated.

"If you think about it, you know exactly who we are but all your questions will be answered in the fullness of time. I have been sent to explain to you about the possibilities open to you should you co-operate with us."

"Co-operate? What do you mean?" a puzzled Seth furrowed his brow again and shrugged.

"No more questions" Mammon raised his wizened hand "You used to have everything you could ever have wanted Seth, beautiful wife, son, happiness, money, fame, infamy, influence."

Seth looked down at the floor and sighed, he knew that part of his life all too well and didn't care to have it read back to him.

"What's your fucking point?" he scowled

"My *fucking point* as you put it, is that you can have it back."

"Really? How?" sarcasm crept back into Seths' voice "time travel?"

"No, with us. I can't bring your son back to you but think to yourself, how did it all fall apart for you in the first place? Where did the fabric of your life start to unravel?" before Seth could answer, Mammon continued "your writing died, the talent you had suddenly started to desert you. You lost the fame and notoriety and the money, your wife was unfaithful . . . ."

"I killed my son and my wife left me" Seth wept quietly as he finished Mammons' sentence for him.

"You didn't kill your son, that was an accident and your wife left because of the pressure of the situation you both found yourself in and it tore you apart." Mammon sounded almost tender and sympathetic in his speech.

"This isn't what I expected from a demonic presence" sniffed Seth

"I am tasked with opening you mind to our possibilities. You may ignore us though that will be very difficult to do as we can be amazingly persuasive but should you co-operate with us as I've said, willingly, you could have your fame and fortune back as before, you may even resume a semblance of your old life with which to rekindle your life with Lily, I know that deep down that's all you really want." Mammon paused as Seth looked at him and nodded in agreement.

"At the end of the day Seth" Mammon continued "all men want money and power, clichés about health and happiness are all well and good but it is undeniable that money brings a more stress-free existence." As he spoke of wealth Mammons' eyes seemed to dance and his fingers grasped ever more frantically.

"Or" the demon tried to ram the point home "you could carry on chasing empty vessels until you can no longer catch them? Another faceless woman and another bottle, drinking yourself into ever declining squalor, drowning in self-pity, unwanted and unloved. Do you really want to continue on this constantly decreasing spiral of despair and self-loathing? Or do you want to regain your life of financial security and the freedom that it brings with it? You are still a relatively young man Seth, many years are stretched out before you, it's your choice as to how you want to live out those years, we can help bring almost everything you want back to you." Mammons' words struck home immediately with Seth.

"What do I have to do?" he said

"You will know everything, all in good time, for now however, my task is done. You will do well to ponder on my words Seth. No, we can't bring your son back but the rest of your life could be transformed back to the way it used to be, when you were genuinely happy. All you have to do is reach out and grasp it, think on."

Seth woke with a jolt and sat upright in his bed, daylight flooded in, he was alone.

"Just another fucking dream" He sighed to himself

But he thought again when he peered over the edge of his bed and saw lying there the two halves of his crushed and splintered baseball bat.

CHAPTER 10

Severin Frost sat chained to a chair in front of a large table in interview room 7, guards either side and facing him, he waited for his latest visitors. Dr Lily Caine and Father Seymour Duncan arrived promptly at 10am as arranged. Neither said a word as they entered the room, they were both distracted in their thoughts but for partly different reasons. Lilys' pain was caused partly by Frost from their last interview, she simply couldn't get the killers' reference to her son out of her mind but also having left Seth in such a state the day before, she was concerned for him too, therefore she'd had a very restless night and very little sleep herself.

Father Duncan however had been having a number of restless nights since his encounter with Frost. Images of torture and death filled his waking hours and dominated his sleep, the images put there by Severin. Seymour had requested this second interview, he'd said, in order to get some 'closure and understanding' of Frost, Dr Caine had been scheduled to see Severin so she had agreed to his request.

Lily opened her briefcase, retrieving a pocket cassette recorder and her notepad and pen as she always did to start a session. Earlier she had listened back to tapes of recent interviews with Severin and couldn't get the impersonation of Seth out of her mind, she tried to block out those thoughts as she started the recording by reciting the date and time of the interview as well as those people present, then she began the session.

"Severin, I'd like you to tell me about your attacks on the priests in your own words, do any specific motivations, thoughts or prejudices spring to mind?"

"We've been through all this many, many times before doctor, do you really want to hear about all that again?" replied Severin in a very courteous and civilised manner.

"Yes I know we have and I'm sorry but as you can see we have a guest today who has his own reasons for wanting to hear your story from your own lips, if you wouldn't mind that is."

"As you wish my dear doctor" a serpents' smile slithered across Severin Frosts' lips as he glanced at the priest who sat all too quietly by Lilys' side, stroking the crucifix on his rosary.

"My attacks were enjoyable in the extreme, delicious and oh so sweet. First there was a middle aged priest, the names are forgettable and irrelevant to me, I hung him by the wrists from a beam above his font. He was stripped naked so that I could more easily access his flesh, I took my favourite set of hunting knives to him, slicing strip after strip from his thighs as he wailed his prayers for help and his blood dripped to fill the font. Gradually I worked my way around his whole body, well almost, his pitiful screams alerted passers-by it seems who in turn contacted the police. I had barricaded the church doors but they managed to see my work through one of the stained glass windows. It was a nuisance which sadly forced me to bring a halt to proceedings early so as to make my escape. As you know doctor, I have never explained how I make my escapes and nor will I as I like to keep a little mystery for myself. I seem to recall that my victim died from his injuries at some point, although it did take some time." Frost smiled at Father Duncan, trying to make the priest squirm in his seat.

"I dismembered the next on his altar, a swift knock-out blow to the back of the head rendered him powerless. When he came round he was lying on his altar, I waited until he opened his eyes then I swooped down with an axe, taking his left arm clean off, as he screamed I deftly moved around and took his right arm. A leg, I think the right one, followed but sadly he passed out just before I took the other. It was almost orgasmic to hear his screams, a sound unmatched in life. Oh well, at least he knew sheer pain and torment before I left him to bleed to death.

I decided to follow that up with a more intimate approach. I waited in line with the sheep for Holy Communion, one by one they drifted to the priest for their symbolic bullshit. I allowed them each to go ahead of me like the good soul they thought I was until finally it was my turn. I knelt in front of him and received the bread but then as he bent to offer me the wine I raised my hands and grasped his head tightly, I forced my thumbs into his eyes and pressed firmly but slowly, naturally he dropped his goblet which caused a stir, his colleagues stood in disbelief, not knowing what to do, people screamed but I continued to press, his blood poured down his face and onto the steps below. He dropped to his knees and I rose from mine in a glorious role reversal, a member of his flock ran over to drag me off but was in no way strong enough to break my grip. Finally as I managed to push the priests' eyes into the back of his brain he crumpled to the floor, dead. I turned and smiled at his supposed rescuer who just stood there white as a sheet with shock and fear, I then turned back to the priest and spat out the 'bread' into his lifeless face before calmly making my exit."

Dr Caine sat quietly, she had heard nothing new from Severin although it chilled her soul knowing what this monster was capable of, she turned to Father Duncan to check if he was alright to carry on. Not surprisingly he was looking a little pale and Lily thought she saw the merest glimpse of a tear in his eye for his fallen brothers, however, he steeled himself and silently gestured for the interview to continue.

"My next victim didn't come along for another year or so, I realised that my last kill had been a little public and if at all possible, I wanted to continue with my reign. I went back to the scene of my first strike, it had taken a while for a replacement to be found after what had befallen the previous incumbent of that post, so once he had settled in, I took him too. He was younger than his predecessor by a number of years and in quite good physical shape, very reminiscent of you actually Father" Severin paused for a reaction but nothing came from the priest.

"Please Severin, I know you like to incite but try to keep your provocation to the minimum" interjected Dr Caine.

"I do apologise" a nod of his head and a sly wink to the unmoving cleric before the killer continued with his tale.

"As I was saying, he was a young priest and I decided on disembowelment, it was a lot easier than I had imagined actually, too easy in fact. I simply crept up behind him and grabbed his chin with my left hand, twisting it to the side before reaching over him with my blade in the other hand. I stabbed it into the left side of his abdomen then drew it deeply across his stomach before pulling it out. I stood him up straight for a few seconds so as to watch his reaction as his entrails spilled out onto the floor of the church, then he fell backwards with a wide and gaping bloody smile where his stomach used to be. I must admit I didn't get too much satisfaction from that, well not as much as I'd hoped for anyway. I decided that I wanted to take them with style and panache, anyone can stab someone, there is no art to it, it happens every day, in every city all over the world.

Therefore I decided on beheading, my plan was to take two priests from adjoining parishes on consecutive nights. The authorities would not be expecting that you see and by that time, there was quite a task force set up to track me down. I was proving elusive to the police because there were gaps in my time frame, there didn't appear to be any motive or link between the victims aside from them being priests of course and I was moving around to different areas so as not to make it too easy for them, they had no idea where I would strike next or when or indeed *if* I would kill again!

The first was an elderly priest who I had knocked out and draped over his pulpit, I waited for him to come around as I had done previously, he looked to the side in his dazed and confused state, to where I stood, I simply smiled and raised my trusty axe before bringing it down squarely on the back of his neck. His head separated very easily from his body, I had expected to take two or three swings at it but was really pleased with myself for getting it done in one fell swoop, as they say. I wonder if that's where the saying comes from? One fell swoop, hmm"

Severin mused on this to himself for a few seconds but neither Dr Caine nor Father Duncan wanted to debate the origins of the phrase, Frost broke the awkward silence by continuing with his tales.

"The local communities were indeed shocked that I had struck again and because of that they weren't expecting me to take another victim so soon, as I had planned. In the next district, prayers were said the following day for the fallen holy man and I sat outside listening to the horrified flock as they left in their grief. Once they had gone, I sneaked inside and pounced without warning on my next subject.

This was another relatively young priest who managed to put up quite a fight before succumbing to my will. I had to tie this one down on his lectern in order to complete my mission, I decided to lie him on his back due to all the trouble he had caused me in daring to fight back and I also felt that he should see my blade coming, for maximum effect. The look in his eyes was priceless, I even allowed him time to say a prayer to his impotent God, while he prayed it struck me that throughout all these executions there had been no saviour for any of them, no lightning to strike me down, nothing.

I raised my axe again as he stared at the ceiling with tears in his eyes, then I swung down with all the force that I could muster. With his neck stretched as his head hung backward, arterial spray plumed out many feet into the air before coming to rest and bathing the steps and floor in crimson, it was a beautiful sight."

Father Duncan stood and walked over to a water cooler in the corner of the room, he poured himself a cup of water and gulped it down, then a second. He lent on the wall, his shoulders tense, Severin watched him intently, the guards were coiled and taut, waiting to see what would happen next, Lily watched Seymour with great sympathy. She was about to call a halt to proceedings when the priest broke the silence by screwing up the little plastic cup and throwing it in a waste bin next to the cooler, he then moved back over to his chair and sat down. Ashen faced he gestured again to Lily for them to continue, he wanted to hear it all, he didn't speak for fear of his voice breaking with emotion. Severin produced a sly and cruel grin as he continued.

"Finally, there was the crucifixion of the nun, an attractive young thing, wasted on the church I felt. She was simply unlucky to be in the wrong place at the wrong time, I had been tracking a specific priest for some time but for one reason or another I was unable to locate him and my desire to kill had grown considerably, sadly for her. She was unfortunately the closest thing to a priest that I could find. She sat at prayer and I watched from a distance, when she had finished I approached and, quite brazenly, I told her flat out who I was. Amazingly she smiled, no doubt thinking me quite mad but the look in my eyes then convinced her otherwise. I think she would have tried to run but fear paralysed her legs, I picked her up and threw her over my shoulder, taking her up to the altar where I first of all stripped her and then lay her. I tied her hands and feet and gagged her before climbing up to dismount the eight foot high crucifix hanging on the wall above us. I took her off the altar and lay her on the back of the cross, back to back with the effigy of *your saviour.*" Bile in Severins' voice as he spat out those last few words directly at Father Duncan, a sneer on Frosts' face, filled with loathing and hatred as his eyes narrowed.

"As I said, I had been tracking the priest for a while and knew how I was going to do this and therefore I had brought along a set of suitable nails and a solid hammer with which to carry out my duty."

Severin was revelling in his story now, there was positively glee in his voice as he openly taunted Father Duncan, he was begging for a reaction of some kind as he'd had on their first meeting. Seymour sat stock still, rigid but not through fear, not anymore.

"She cried as I brought out my tools, lying there naked and helpless, my sympathies were only that she was not my originally intended victim. I raised the hammer and sent the first nail crashing through her hand and another through her wrist, muffled screams through the gag echoed through the church and again as I nailed her other arm in the same fashion. I decided to tie her legs to the cross and for extra support I bound a rope around her shoulders to hold her upright. I stood the crucified nun against the wall for maximum effect, as I did this, I took her gag off, I really don't know why.

Surprisingly she didn't scream, perhaps through shock, she did beg for her life though, yet the manner of her begging surprised me. She begged *me* for her life, I could have been her saviour had I wanted to be, she had no doubt dedicated her whole life to her God yet here I was holding what was left of it in my hands. I knew there was nothing her God or the pathetic limp creature on the other side of the cross could do for her, yet it now seemed that her faith had deserted her and she now pleaded with me to save her, ironic I thought, don't you?"

Father Duncan sat glaring at Frost as he paused, Lily looked at him with concern as he continued stroking the rosary in front of him, more forcefully though now.

"Anyway, my musings on her plight as I watched her were alas to be my downfall. It seems the priest, my intended victim, had returned and seen what was going on. Sadly for me, he had alerted the police and they rushed me from all sides as I watched her dying from her wounds and blood loss. Needless to say, they were too late to save her."

As Severin finished his horrendous tale he looked directly at the young priest, tauntingly, goading him into some kind of response. Father Duncan stared back, unflinching, his shock and horror of their previous encounter now replaced by anger, hatred and loathing. Dr Caine tried to break the tension that was so obvious in the room by suggesting a break in the proceedings but as she started to speak Severin turned his attention and gaze towards her, this was the moment that Seymour had been waiting for and he seized it.

The priest immediately jumped to his feet and dived across the table, as he moved he unsheathed a small hidden yet extremely sharp dagger from inside the crucifix on his rosary. He caught everyone unawares with his attack and he plunged the small blade into Severin Frosts' throat then again and then twice more with speed into Frosts' face, aiming for but narrowly missing his eyes'. As quickly as they could, the guards grabbed Seymour, dragged him off the table and threw him into the corner of the room. Lily ran over to the wall and slammed her hand against the panic alarm button and screamed into the intercom for immediate medical assistance, then she ran around the table to help the guards to put pressure on the veins and arteries spurting Severins' blood all over the table and floor.

Within seconds, medics and extra guards rushed in, quickly two of the guards bundled Father Duncan out of the room while the medical team attended to Severin. As he was being dragged into the corridor Seymour looked over his shoulder at Frost with a crazed look in his eye and a maniacal grin on his face, in return Severin Frost glared at his assailant with pure hatred and an inner fuming lust for revenge.

Across the city, at the same time Seth Caine had arrived for his own meeting. He didn't really know where he was or how he had gotten here, he had just been drawn to this place, he couldn't even remember being in this part of the city before. He had set off walking out of his house and seemed to instinctively find himself being pulled towards the office building he now found himself standing in front of.

It was a huge and very stylish modern building, as Seth entered he noticed that wherever he looked it was glass, black marble and chrome. He walked to the elevators, a long list of steel plaques' bearing company names and office numbers gleamed at him from the wall, right at the very top of the list was 'Dr Roth', no office or floor number, just the name. He pushed the button for the elevator and the doors immediately opened as if they had been waiting for him.

Seth got in and before he could select the correct button (he assumed that he wanted the top floor) the elevators' doors silently closed and he was whisked away at seemingly great speed. Once it had stopped at its' destination, the doors opened and he was confronted by a large wooden door, very heavy looking and seemingly more in keeping with an ancient country house than a modern office complex. Seth stepped out of the elevator which promptly closed and left him there, there were no other doors, no receptionist that he had thought that he'd spoken to, just a very foreboding door. He made to knock but before his knuckles could connect with the surface, the door quietly opened, warily Seth entered.

Floor to ceiling windows greeted Seth as he entered, giving spectacular panoramic views of the city. Deep plush red carpet gave his arrival virtual silence, in front of the windows stood a very heavy antique desk made of oak. On top of the desk stood a sleek computer screen and keyboard and various files piled to one side. A black leather office chair sat behind the desk but swivelled around facing out to the cityscape. Seth approached the desk and coughed gently to announce his presence.

"Er . . . . I have an appointment" he said as he looked at the back of the chair and glanced around the room. There was no answer; standing in front of the desk he noticed a thick, closed file in the centre of it, with his name on it.

His brow furrowed on seeing the file, he was only potentially a new patient, how could they have what looked like a sizeable file on him already? He reached out his hand to take a look and then, just like a naughty child with the cookie jar, snatched it back as the chair spun around to face him.

"Good morning Seth"

"Alex?" Seths' immediate shock soon became delight at seeing his beautiful red-head again. "Well this is an amazing coincidence; I thought I'd never see you again. What are you doing here? I mean, do you work here? I'm here for an appointment with some Dr Roth, is he here?" he babbled just like the awkward, drooling teenager he had become when he'd first met her.

"Dr Alexandra Roth, pleased to meet you Mr Caine, formally that is" she smiled that lascivious smile he remembered "please, take a seat."

Seth retrieved a chair from the back of the room and sat down, his mind was spinning now. She didn't seem shocked or caught off guard in any way. Seth Caine wasn't a common name like John Smith but why wasn't there even a little surprise in her manner or her voice on seeing him stood there? Doubts crept back into his mind, had he indeed been set up the other night? Who would go to such elaborate lengths to take revenge on him? What revenge anyway, what or who had he done to make somebody plot a set up against him? How had he contacted this particular Doctor? His head started to ache with all the questions. She was watching him as if exploring all the dilemmas in his mind, he calmed himself and tried to take control of the situation.

"When I asked you what you did for a living the other night, why were you evasive?"

"I wasn't aware that I was being evasive, I simply didn't want to indulge in any small talk, would it have made a difference if I had told you my profession?"

"No, I suppose not, but all this just seems like too much of a coincidence, I'd been talking to my friend that night about maybe finding a therapist, then you were there and now here you are!"

"Yes Seth, here I am, some things in life happen for a reason" she glanced away as she spoke then looked back at him out of the corner of her eye, half smiling.

"You mean fate?" he was hoping that fate was throwing them together for more than just one night.

"No, not fate exactly Seth, let's just say that when certain stars align, certain events must take place and our meeting was preordained"

Not for the first time Seths' brow furrowed in consternation and as if to throw him off guard even further, Alex stood up and moved away from her desk. She looked stunning with her hair tied back, short black tight skirt and matching jacket with a white silk blouse. She walked over to the long windows and stood with her back to him deliberately in order to show off her long legs and sheer black seamed stockings, black, patent leather stiletto healed shoes completed the ensemble to devastating effect. She looked highly professional, very elegant and incredibly desirable.

"So, why are you looking to see a therapist Seth?" his mind had inevitably drifted back to their night in her apartment, her question made him think for a few seconds before he could come up with the answer.

"I've been having a lot of really bad dreams recently and I was wondering if there's more to them than just being dreams, I mean, is there something going on in my subconscious or maybe deep rooted issues and grief over my son or maybe a mental block with my work?"

Alex partially turned away from the window and looked over her shoulder at Seth, raising her eyebrows questioningly.

"Self-diagnosis already?" she smiled as she moved back to the desk and resumed her seat.

"Well, no not really, you see my wife's a psychiatrist too" her eyebrows raised again and Seth realised what he'd just said "I mean my ex-wife, well not *ex*, I mean, er . . . . We're separated but not divorced, shit!" he wondered to himself if he'd just blown his chances with Alex outside of her office, as she sat in quiet contemplation.

"Tell me about these dreams Seth, give me as much information and detail as you can remember" she said as she opened up his file in front of her and put on a pair of reading glasses which made her look even more alluring.

Seth explained for over an hour about his dreams and nightmares, from the beginning right up to and including the previous nights instalment and his encounter with Mammon and Angelique. As he did so, Alex made notes and ticked boxes in her file while in total silence as he spoke. Everything flowed out of Seth like a river overflowing its' banks, the details which she'd asked for and the clarity with which he remembered everything surprised even Seth. Once he had finished his tale he sat with a calm and assured glow surrounding him, it had felt like a relief to air everything to Lily but this seemed different, as if Alex was the one who he was *supposed* to talk to.

Were his feelings for Alex developing at a rapid pace from sheer lust to something more or was it simply a doctor/patient relationship issue he wondered. He was about to ask her what she thought when she suddenly spoke for the first time since he began his story.

"So, how do you feel now Seth? Relieved? Clear? Unburdened?"

"All of those" he smiled "I feel fantastic"

"Good, you are at peace with your subconscious, sometimes it helps to just be able to speak to a stranger without interruption, not necessarily a therapist. Just getting things off your chest can be a wonderful thing, lightening your load without trying to explain the 'whys and wherefores' of a situation."

"So" asked Seth "What next? I mean is that the nightmares banished? Have I moved past them? I must say that this all seems way too easy."

"I wouldn't say that, what I would say is that you should open yourself up to them more. In fact I would say that you should embrace them" her advice surprised Seth somewhat.

"Embrace them? How do you mean?"

"Well obviously they are trying to tell you something, maybe about yourself, maybe about your past or your future. I would allow the message to come through clearly, as I said, embrace them rather than try to fight them off and shut them out. It could be very freeing and liberating, if you feel this good now just by unloading and accepting them, just think how wonderful you could feel if they have a positive effect on your life, as Mammon has said, you might even enjoy them to an extent!"

Alexs' reference to Mammon as if he were a real life physical person as opposed to a demon in his mind threw Seth for a moment but everything else she had said seemed to make crystal clear sense to him now and he decided that she was absolutely right, 'embrace and open up to them'.

"Thank you Alex, sorry, I mean Dr Roth" he smiled boyishly as he spoke and stood to leave.

"I was just wondering if I can see you again, not as a patient I mean, though that would be wonderful but socially, we could go out for a drink or to dinner?" he could feel himself blushing.

"I'm very busy at the moment Seth but thank you anyway" she said as she walked him out of the room and to the elevator which was already waiting for him without either of them calling for it, doors open expectantly. Disappointed he stepped inside and just as the doors started to close she spoke

"Don't worry Seth, you will see me again soon enough, I promise" she teased with a sin-filled wink and smile as the elevator doors closed completely and Seth was whisked away again, this time with a huge grin on his face.

CHAPTER 11

Dr Lily Caine stood in her office, looking out of the window when Father Seymour Duncan entered. Immediately she turned and despite repeatedly telling herself to keep her composure she yelled at him as he took a seat.

"What the fuck was that?" not a person to swear normally yet Lily could barely keep her anger in check.

Father Duncan sat in silence, staring at the desk in front of him, avoiding eye contact, taking deep breaths, his chest and shoulders rising and falling significantly.

"I'm waiting" Lily glared at the priest as she spoke through gritted teeth, trying to rein herself in.

"He got the very least of what he deserves" Seymours' words were delivered with icy contempt *at* Lily rather than *to* her "you know and have known for a long time what he has done and what he would do all over again without hesitation, should he ever get out of this place."

"Of course I know what he has done, I also know, probably better than anyone of what he is capable of doing. He has done far more than the things you know of, believe me!"

"Such as?" the priests' eyes narrowed as he looked up at her with curiosity

"Well, just as an example, he tried to rape and abuse his way through an entire convent in between his killing spree. You didn't know about that did you?"

"What!" Seymour sat open-mouthed in shock and amazement "why isn't that being investigated, why isn't it on record? Who else knows about this?"

"Just myself and Dr Sterling, the senior consultant here, or rather, she *was*" recalling the events to her mind depressed Lily and calmed her briefly as she sat down behind her desk.

"Dr Sterling?" Father Duncan hadn't heard that name before.

"Yes, she was to all intents and purposes my former boss. She had a few personal problems anyway and then around a year or so ago, she was interviewing Severin during a routine session and he mentioned the events in the convent, yet he went into extreme detail. Needless to say, that had quite an impact on Dr Sterling, she was pregnant at the time and having problems with her husband which all culminated in her having a nervous breakdown and losing her baby, which in turn just added to her torment. She left the Hoffman, officially, soon after. I've been handling the day to day patient-related running of the Institute ever since. The Director handles the over-all running and he is supposedly hiring a new senior consultant soon but I haven't heard anything definite for a while."

Lilys' calmer manner as she spoke seemed to take the heat out of the situation between them. Seymour now felt that he could gain more information.

"So, what did Frost do in the convent?" he inquired

Dr Caine had been briefly lost in her own thoughts of grief for her former colleague and good friend Dr Karen Sterling. Now, on hearing Seymours' question she was brought back to reality and looked cautiously at Father Duncan from the corner of her eye, she sighed and she shook her head before speaking.

"He broke in one night, laying in wait until the sisters' were sleeping and more vulnerable than usual, then he systematically worked his way from dormitory to dormitory, basically raping, abusing or molesting every frightened nun he came across. The terrified women had no idea what was going on in the darkness because it was the very last thing that anyone would've expected to happen, this monster estimated that he defiled at least a dozen of the sisters before someone managed to raise the alarm." She sighed again and shook her head as she told the tale of yet another of Severin Frosts' heinous acts.

"My God, why hasn't he been charged with his vile deeds if he's admitted to all of that horror?" gasped Seymour

"Well, it's complicated, Dr Sterling wasn't recording the interview for some reason that I still don't know, I suspect that that is why he was so blatant, he knew she wasn't recording, she told me the story later and then she gave me her notes for my own files. There was no physical evidence at the scene as the sisters all immediately bathed and scrubbed away all trace of Frost after he escaped. They refused to be examined when the police got there, through a combination of trauma and a misplaced sense of guilt and shame.

There was an investigation yet Severin was never charged because of a lack of evidence. He denied everything when questioned as he does love to torment people and have us running around, added to that is the fact hat he has the slimiest of moral-free lawyers I've ever had the misfortune to meet, all of that combined to keep things dragging on until this day."

They both sat in silence for a few minutes, Lily pondered how Karen Sterling was getting on, Seymour pondered about how or if he could actually kill Severin Frost.

"I wish I'd sliced his jugular" he muttered under his breath, his comment brought Lily straight back to the here and now with clarity.

"Father Duncan, I have to tell you that I have already reported this mornings' incident to the Director, further more, I have recommended to him that your services are dispensed with as soon as possible. He concurs with my view and your position here at the Hoffman Institute has been terminated with immediate effect. Of course you will be notified of our decision in writing but I don't think it is in anyone's best interests for you to return at any point, I do not expect to see you in this facility again."

"You care for that creature!? After all the things he has done or is likely to do if he gets a chance." Seymour spat the words out in contempt.

"I care for my patients, that is my job and I have spent many years doing so. Make no mistake Father Duncan, we could have you arrested and charged on assault or wounding charges, carrying a concealed weapon, anything else?"

"It was attempted murder" coldly and clinically the priest replied.

"Father, I will pretend I didn't hear that and purely because I can understand your feelings towards Frost, his crimes are horrendous for anyone to hear and provocation is an art form that he loves to engage in. So, to that end you will leave here with a clean slate to go back to your life outside these walls and hopefully, for your own sake, you will forget you ever even heard the name Severin Frost. Please don't make this more difficult for us with legalities and you also have to be aware that Severin may insist on pressing charges against you himself, although I will try to persuade him otherwise."

Seymour was aghast at the thought of Frost suing him or bringing a court case of any kind against him, the thought seemed ludicrous against all he knew of the monster and his crimes, let alone his innocent victims.

"I will leave without fuss, don't worry Doctor" Seymour stood, walked over and opened the office door before turning back and adding "but I will never forget or forgive Severin Frost, neither will God."

Lily sighed and put her head in her hands on her desk, it had been a particularly bad day. It was getting late in the afternoon, she decided that she'd had enough, she really needed a stiff drink. Lily packed her files away, rang through to her secretary Linda to tell her to go home early before grabbing her keys and purse and taking a well earned early finish.

Seth sat at home in a pleasant and relaxed mood, the first time he'd been in such a stress-free mood in months, flicking through coffee-table art books and music magazines, looking at nothing in particular. He decided to put some music on, he hated the whole idea of downloading music and Seth pined for the days of vinyl records and his old collection. His only concession to 'modern day' music was the compact disc and he'd begrudgingly rebuilt his archive in that format and he treasured it but just as he started to thumb through his CD's, the phone rang.

"Yeah?"

"Vlad"

"Hey Karl, how're you doing buddy?"

"Fine, are we still on for Saturday night then?" Karl already sounded very eager.

"Saturday? What's happening Saturday?"

"What's happening? Are you shitting me? Me and you looking for that red-head and hopefully a few of her friends at the Dragon, that's what's happening on Saturday!"

"Oh sorry buddy, I forgot" Seth suddenly felt a little guilty

"What d'ya mean you forgot! How the hell could you forget that? She's your dream girl, remember"

"Well, the thing is . . . ." Seth knew he was going to regret saying this

"The thing? What thing? Tell me what the thing is Seth"

"The thing is, I've already met her" Seth waited for the reaction

"What!! Why didn't you tell me, I thought we were friends?" Karl paused in his minor rage "wait, has she got any friends? Didn't you say you hadn't got her number?"

"It wasn't a date or anything."

"For fucks' sake Seth, stop pissing about and tell me what's going on" Karl's frustration was audible.

"I got a therapist, like we talked about . . . ."

"What the hell's that got to do with it?" Karl interrupted

"Karl, it's her!" Seth was still surprised himself, that was evident in the glee in his voice.

"It's her? What d'ya mean it's her?"

"Well I got a number out of the phone book and showed up for an appointment and lo and behold it's her, Alex, the red-headed sex goddess and she's my therapist!" Seth couldn't help but smile to himself as he said the words out loud.

Karl paused for a moment, taking in the information he'd just received and tried process it before replying.

"Man; that is fucked up!"

"What?" Seth seemed puzzled

"I mean, first of all, good for you for getting a therapist but buddy that is seriously messed up!"

"Hell of a coincidence ain't it?" Seth beamed

"Coincidence? No! Spooky, freaky, weird? Yes. I think you could be heading down a long road of pain my friend, you can't fuck your therapist, she'll be analysing you constantly and you'll be guarding everything you do or say."

"Look Karl, I appreciate what you're saying but I've already asked her out and she said she's too busy at the moment."

"You mean she's blown you off already?" Karl chuckled to himself "so why do you sound so happy about it all then?"

"She hasn't blown me off, she said that I will see her again so I'm assuming that we'll get together when she's free"

"Boy, at times you really are as dumb as wood" mumbled Karl under his breath as he sighed.

"What was that?"

"Nothing, so, are we going out on Saturday anyway then?"

"Er, no, I think I'll give it a miss for once, I'm feeling pretty relaxed so I'm gonna take it easy this weekend, next week if you want?"

"Don't do me any favours!" Karl mumbled again as he hung up in disappointment.

Seth felt bad for not going out with Karl but genuinely he didn't feel like it. For some unfathomable reason his life suddenly felt much more organised, he didn't feel disjointed, surely therapy couldn't be *that* good after such a short spell? She'd hardly said that much and he didn't feel he was there for that long; there must be more to it than that? Not that he cared, as long as he felt like this. As for Karl? He would come round in a few days, they'd fallen out over worse things and more trivial things too but they always got back on track, it would be fine.

Lily stopped off on her way home from the Institute and bought a bottle of vodka, things hadn't been going too well with her partner Jason for a few weeks now, coupling that with her awful day at work made a very large vodka seem very appropriate. Jason and Lily had been together for seven months, he spent most nights at her apartment but recently there had been fewer and fewer.

The two of them had met when he arrived as a newly qualified doctor more than ten years her junior but that hadn't mattered to either of them. It had been a passionate encounter from day one when they passed each other in the corridor at the Hoffman and he smiled as he introduced himself to her, curly brown hair, deep trustful brown eyes and a swimmers lithe build, she was attracted to him immediately and that attraction was more than mutual the minute they shook hands.

Within a week they had been out for a meal and soon after, the affair became physical. Lily had never thought that she was in love with Jason but she did care very deeply for him. Unfortunately, a new nurse, Katie something or other, had arrived at the Institute in the last month and seemed to be circling in on Jason, Lily's longer hours and greater responsibility were suddenly putting pressure on the relationship and she seemed to be seeing less and less of him.

As Lily walked into her apartment something seemed different but she couldn't quite put her finger on what it was or why.

"Jason?" she called out more in hope than expectation.

No answer came and she frowned to herself in disappointment, she kicked off her shoes and put her keys and bag on the coffee table then went to the kitchen. Lily got a large glass from the cupboard and rinsed it before filling it with ice from the freezer. She poured in vodka, over half way up the glass before looking in the refrigerator for something to add, there was no orange juice that she preferred but there was a bottle of lime juice, immediately she thought of Seth with a large vodka and lime in his hand, she smiled as she poured her drink.

Lily went back into the living room and slumped with her drink in an armchair, picking up the TV remote in one not-so-fluid movement. She checked the various news channels to catch up on the days events but nothing held her attention, she switched off the TV and tossed the remote onto the couch. She closed her eyes as she took a mouthful from her glass and sighed as she swallowed, Lily sat in a state of well-earned relaxation for a while before opening her eyes.

Curious to see if Jason had rang her and left a message or maybe a text, she retrieved her bag from the coffee table, it was only then that she noticed an envelope on the table. She hadn't seen it on her arrival home, she'd just put her bag down on top of it. Her name was on the front, handwritten, she felt a knot in her stomach and with trepidation she opened it.

As Lily read the relatively brief two page note, tears welled in her eyes before spilling down her cheeks, taking streaks of mascara with them. Three times she read the letter, it was over he had said, he'd met someone else with whom he had more things in common he'd said. He'd met someone younger she thought.

"Fucking Katie! Bitch!"

Anger, pain, bitterness, jealousy and loneliness all swirled around inside her, mixing a cocktail with the vodka that she'd consumed. The note also told how he had transferred to the night shift until he could get a post at another hospital or clinic because he didn't want to run into Lily and have an awkward situation.

Lily got up and went into the kitchen, she poured herself another drink and looked around her home, only then did she notice the little things that were no longer there, little things of Jasons'. He'd already picked up his stuff, had 'she' been with him Lily wondered in disgust. She'd known all along that she hadn't been in love with him but the feeling of emptiness and betrayal was overwhelming her, which was until the loneliness started to take over again. She drank to blot out and numb the hurt, it didn't work.

Chapter 12

Seth went to bed, no longer fearful of his dreams but almost looking forward to them. Of course he didn't know if he would actually have any and if he did, he didn't know if they would be horrific or if maybe Angelique would make an appearance, he certainly hoped she would. He hadn't even bothered having a drink during the evening, he'd just watched an old movie that seemed to drift by him as he thought of all things Alex Roth. The way she looked, the way she smelled, the way she walked and talked, everything. She was all the more real now he'd met her soberly and everything she'd said seemed to penetrate deep into his mind. It wasn't so much what she'd said, although that had worked, it was more the way she'd said it, as if she knew exactly what his problems were and just reached into his head and fixed them.

He slept deeply until he felt a stroking sensation on his chest, it was extremely pleasurable and he felt himself beginning to rise. He opened his eyes to the darkness and as his sight adjusted, he saw there was a figure on his bed, kneeling at his side and stroking his chest still. It was definitely a woman, a naked woman, he could tell by her silhouette in the moonlight. He lifted his hand to move the long dark hair from her face but she stopped him and turned away. He heard the unmistakable sound of rattling metal. "Richelle?" he'd been hoping to see Angelique again but if her handmaiden was visiting him, that was good enough for Seth.

She didn't answer, instead as she turned away she moved onto her hands and knees, presenting him with her beautiful pert bottom. In the dim light he could still make out that her chains had in fact been removed, still though she wore the clasps around her wrists and ankles like huge and grotesque jewellery. He moved onto his knees behind her, stroking her ass and thighs, she wriggled her butt in encouragement yet still said nothing. Seth knew that he would never turn down an opportunity like this, dream or no dream. Dr Roths' words suddenly came to him as if she was whispering the mantra in his head, "Embrace and accept them, you might even enjoy them."

He spat onto his fingers for basic lubrication and rubbed at her labia, seeking out her clitoris. Quickly he found it and gently he teased it as she made soft muffled moaning sounds as her pussy moistened, once he was satisfied that she was ready, he pressed his cock to her now lubricated entrance. Slight pressure was all that was required for him to slide straight into her, he settled easily into his rhythm and fucked his silent dream partner as hard as he could. Her olive skin gleamed with perspiration in the moons' dull glow as they powered into and onto each other but just as the feeling of orgasm was starting to take hold of him, she pulled away and his cock slipped out of her.

Seth was just about to protest but evidently this was only a temporary halt to the proceedings. Richelle rolled onto her back, legs apart, inviting him back inside her and he duly and eagerly obliged. He penetrated her again and quickly regained his stroke, her long dark hair had fallen across her face when she had moved onto her back, Seth had still not glimpsed what he assumed to be a beauty yet he found himself fucking her hard!

While continuing to pound away at the handmaiden, he moved to grab a handful of her hair to shift it away; he had an overwhelming desire to look deep into her eyes as he came deep inside her. Just as he did manage to uncover her face, the headlights of a passing car shone through his bedroom window, illuminating her and the room and he could finally gaze upon her face unhindered, what he saw stopped his thrusts immediately.

She had most definitely been a great beauty, in fact she obviously still was but she now lay naked in his bed, writhing on his cock with her eyes closed and stitched together and so too her mouth! No wonder she had hidden her face and hadn't even spoken, as he had stopped mid-thrust she started to wriggle her herself back onto him and wrapped her legs around his waist, her leg shackles clinked together as she crossed her ankles behind him, pulling him more into her. Part of Seth wanted to stop in shock and horror but he couldn't as she tightened her grip with her muscular thighs clamping him into her. He realised he was no longer in control of this, but had he ever been in control? She was now using him to fuck herself, harder and faster, harder and faster, he could feel his seed rise as if about to boil over. Instantly she released him from her grip between her thighs and as he fell back his cock slipped out of her just at the very second that he ejaculated. His semen arced into the air and landed on her abdomen, she arched her back as soon as it touched her flesh, splashing on her skin as if it were molten metal scalding her before she settled back into the bed satisfied with her work, savouring his fluids.

"I take it that you enjoyed the gorgeous Richelle? Or would it be more correct to say that she was enjoying you, Mr Caine?"

Startled, Seth looked over to where a huge figure stood in the shadows, then he briefly looked back down to where Richelle was writhing on his bed, massaging his semen into her skin as if it were a luxurious body lotion, she was a sight that would normally would have his cock straining almost immediately, had it not been for the dark shadowy figure.

"Good evening Seth"

"G-good evening" he stammered in reply

"You still sound surprised when we visit you, I had been under the impression that you had become somewhat accustomed to our presence."

"Er, yes, but I'm still getting to grips with how you announce yourselves" Seth looked down at the still writhing Richelle, seemingly lost in her own little world of lust. His heart still raced from his sexual exertions but more now at the ease and immediacy of the way these entities arrived in his home.

"Ha ha ha, we do like to grab the attention" a deep and booming laugh from the *man* still standing in the darkness "and we do know exactly what you like, therefore we give it to you."

Seth climbed down off his bed, as he did so, Richelle had ceased writhing and crawled to the other side of the bed before stepping down and walking over to where his visitor stood, kneeling at his feet just as she had knelt at the side of Angelique in Seths' bath.

"You are doubtlessly wondering who I am, well I gather from my esteemed Lord Mammon that you are well read in our lore, I am Astaroth."

This was indeed another demonic presence that Seth had read about and studied, the newly identified figure stepped forward from the shadows, Seths' jaw dropped in awe at the sight. Again, like Mammon before him, he was very tall by conventional *human* standards but as Seth shifted his weight from side to side to take in the marvel of the demon, without straying from his spot, he could see an unmistakable glow about him. In fact, from different angles Astaroth appeared to be either pure white like freshly fallen snow or as black as polished ebony. As Seth studied the creature, he remembered snippets from research he had done on an occult novel that he'd been writing but never finished.

Lord Astaroth was said to be the foul-breathed commander of forty legions of Hell who rode a dragon and carried a viper at his right hand. As if reading his mind, Astaroth raised his arm and indeed a serpent was wrapped around his wrist, eyeing Seth with malicious intent. It was obvious to him that Astaroth had once been a very handsome 'man', evidently though, countless battles had left him scarred and wounded, his face alone could probably tell endless tales of blood-thirsty mayhem and rage as he led his legions of monstrous soldiers.

Some of the beings' scars looked fresh and open, Seth wondered what kind of man or creature could inflict damage on a demon such as this. His war-weary features were completed by wild, dark eyes and a thin manicured beard, long and braided with an ornate silver clasp at the end, seven or eight inches from the tip of his chin. Astaroth looked every bit the fearsome warrior, yet more than that he looked like the warlord or berserker that he undoubtedly was.

Atop his shaven skull the Demon Lord wore a bejewelled crown befitting of his status as a prince of the underworld. His clothing too seemed to be almost robes of state, more jewels and a medieval style fur-edged cloak, regality dripped from every pore of his dark being. A sword hung from his hip, ornate yet brutal in its' scale, Seth wondered at the bloodshed and death caused by such a weapon in Astaroths' mighty hands.

"No dragon tonight?" Seth smiled nervously

"No, I come only as a messenger, not for war." He smiled as he answered, now at closer quarters Seth caught overwhelming evidence of the demons' legendary halitosis. Not wanting to offend such a powerful entity, Seth resisted the urge to hold his nose or turn away, instead he decided to get this over with as quickly as possible.

"Messenger?" he asked

"I know all secrets Seth, I know your infatuations and cravings, I know your wants and needs, I know your desires and tastes" as he spoke this last part Astaroth looked down and stroked the head of Richelle, who had come forward with him to kneel at his feet obediently.

Seth immediately felt guilty for his lusts but more than that he felt very nervous at the idea that anyone, especially someone like this could know his innermost thoughts and secrets.

"I also know that you crave your past, this is not unusual for mortals, most humans reminisce and pine for their youth. They often make mistakes in life and therefore with age they are living a life with many regrets. Your fame and successes went to your head, you got bloated and lazy, your work suffered and you became sloppy."

"I thought you had a message?" sighed Seth, not wanting to go over all this again, he knew his faults and though he knew they were many he didn't much care to have them repeated to him in a lecture.

"Don't you dare interrupt me Caine" snapped Astaroth as he held up his monstrous right hand, that was also scarred from his many battles, his viper stared directly into Seths' eyes, inches from his face. Seth bowed his head in silence, heeding the warning, Astaroth lowered his mighty hand and continued "I am here at the request of the highest of all powers, you will be of great benefit to my Lord and you in turn will reap great rewards for your services."

"What great rewards?" inquired Seth, excitement now in his voice.

"Ever the money grabbing mercenary eh Caine, you really can be a grubby little man" Astaroth sneered as he looked down at him "you don't even know what we require from you yet already you're only interested in what you will get in return. From what I know of you and how you live your life and of course your *tastes*" he paused and smiled lecherously "you would enjoy our kingdom immensely, don't you agree Richelle?" the handmaiden nodded enthusiastically at his feet.

"Just checking to see if it would be worth my while" replied Seth

"If what would be worth your while?" sneered Astaroth "you don't know anything yet!"

Seth stood silently, realising he wasn't going to get anywhere or in fact get this over with unless he let the demon tell him *their* proposal, he had to shut up and listen, so he did.

"Alright, first of all we would ensure that you regain your former status as a respected novelist, you will achieve great success, wealth beyond even *your* dreams, notoriety and of course the popularity that you mortals seem to crave."

"Is that it?" Seth couldn't help interrupting again, somehow he was expecting more.

"Greed, I like it" smiled Astaroth "Mammon said that he could see the idea of fame and fortune light up in your mind when he spoke to you, I see that too. He is a very good judge of character regarding such things but you are right to be cautious and expect much more when you are going to be putting so much on the line in return."

The last comment didn't fill Seth with too much pleasure but the statement was probably true bearing in mind who he was actually dealing with, there are two sides to any deal, there would undoubtedly be a price to pay.

"Well my dear Caine, your wife could be thrown into the equation too if you so desire and I know that you do still desire, unless you would rather continue to enjoy the delights of our vixens?" he stroked Richelle again as he spoke.

Seth didn't even consider the *vixens* that he was being offered, thoughts of Lily ran through his mind, he had never stopped loving her and no matter the amount of demonic, lust-filled beauties that were put before him he had always only needed or wanted Lily back with him. His life had only ever had sense and purpose when she was in it; since she'd left he was like a rudderless ship crashing onto the rocks, time after time.

"How is that possible? Lily I mean" he asked

"You forget who you are dealing with Caine, we have infinite power and knowledge, we can manipulate circumstances to our favour when it suits our designs. To anticipate your next question, Lily would not be the one being manipulated; she would be acting of her own free will. We would just, as I said before, manipulate various circumstances to our mutual benefit. Should you agree to our terms, we will get what we require and so shall you."

Seth was sorely tempted to agree to just about anything, it would be worth it just to get Lily back, let alone having the finance to live how or wherever they wanted to live. No debt, no starting at the bottom, just Seth and Lily plain sailing through life and happy ever after. His mind was already racing with dream homes and expensive vacations, when he realised that this all seemed too good to be true, he also had to find out what he was going to have to do to get his happy ever after.

"So, what do you want for all that? Who do I have to kill?"

"Ha ha ha, you don't have to kill anybody" his booming laugh echoed around the room "we have many others to do that, although I prefer to do the killing myself" his laughter stopped and the smile dropped from Astaroths' face, in that split second he now seemed more dangerous than ever.

"So?" Seth waited patiently and nervously

"Write a book." Answered Astaroth simply

"Write a book? Is that it?" Seth was surprised, it couldn't be that straight forward could it?

"Not just any book but your greatest work"

"My greatest work? Just like that?" Seth smiled and shook his head "first of all, it's not that easy, I write for a living you know, I know how hard it can be."

"It will be a novel that surpasses all others" Astaroth continued, ignoring Seth's words and doubts "something that will stand alongside the great literary works of the ages; it will make your name rise up above the chaff of your peers. Your career and your success will shine like the brightest of stars and therefore you shall reap the rewards financially, then you can live the lifestyle that Lily and yourself have always dreamt of and more importantly, you will live that dream side by side, hand in hand, together."

It was as if Astaroth had implanted the wonderful image he spoke of directly into Seth's head, like painting a picture on the walls of his mind, he could see it all so clearly, he could almost smell and taste it, however, there was obviously an unavoidable snag in reality.

"I can't write, I've lost my knack for writing, as you probably know, that is why I lost everything in the first place. Massive writers' block that I've never recovered from, how the hell am I gonna come up with this amazing blockbuster of a novel that you're talking about just like that?"

"How the *Hell* indeed! Ah my dear Seth, don't you think we've thought of that? I or rather we are going to give it to you"

"Er, how are you going to do that?" Seth was intrigued

"Questions, questions, questions, do not concern yourself with technicalities Seth, just trust me when I say that if you agree to our terms, then your troubles will be over."

"Er, I do have one more question" mumbled Seth

"Why you?" pre-empted the demonic lord

"Yes"

"You are the perfect candidate, you have opened yourself up to us and accepted us, that is also enough to warrant the rewards we are offering you . . . for now" Astaroth sneered again with a gleam of pride in his eyes at his seemingly successful mission.

"For now?" suddenly doubts crept into Seth's mind again, was this the catch that he'd been expecting?

"Surely you would allow us to visit you again once we have delivered on our promises to you? We might even have another book for you to write, should you be as successful as we anticipate with this one, even more fame and infamy could be on offer, this could be just the start of a beautiful working relationship."

"Er" this request didn't seem to be too unreasonable to Seth "Sure, I don't see why not but are you sure that Lily will go for this and will she still be herself? I don't want her as some glorified sex slave to do my bidding you know?"

"But of course Lily will be herself, we aren't going to visit her or even touch her, she will be entirely as you knew her before, I give you my word" Seth smiled as Astaroth told him what he wanted to believe. "In fact, so sure were we that you would accept our proposal that plans were put into motion some time ago, it shouldn't be too long before Mr and Mrs Caine are reunited."

Seth's joy was almost uncontained and he beamed broadly at what he was hearing, if all this was true he would spend his life trying to make Lily the happiest woman in the world as he felt she should be.

"Your obvious pleasure speaks a thousand words Seth, if you agree then when you awake in a few hours, your book and your future will be ready and waiting for you, all you have to do is let it out and embrace it. So, are we agreed?"

Astaroth held out his powerful and mighty left hand to Seth who enthusiastically and still smiling, took it firmly, it was like a child shaking hands with an adult.

"Agreed?" asked Astaroth in finality

"Agreed" replied Seth.

Astaroth threw back his head and roared with laughter and triumph, as he looked back down at Seth, still laughing, it seemed that all the scars and wounds on his face had opened in their own little gruesome grins and hideous smiles, they all seemed to be laughing in demonic glee at him. Seth wondered nervously just what the fuck he was getting himself into.

CHAPTER 13

Seth woke in the early afternoon with a ringing in his ears and an almighty headache, he crawled out of his bed and went to the bathroom where he took a piss and stretched the sleep out of his system. He brushed his teeth and decided to shower, it was while showering that he began to have very vague recollections about the previous nights dream but nothing cohesive. Once finished, he dried himself off and dressed in his regular jeans and picked out a Death Angel t-shirt then headed down for his usual 'breakfast' of coffee, aspirin and nicotine.

Aspirin taken, mug of coffee in hand, he stood at his back door to watch the world go by as he had done many, many times before. The coffee tasted surprisingly good for instant, the cigarette tasted wonderful, he felt even better inside than he did the day before and much better than he had for a very long time. The only downside was this damn headache and ringing in his ears that he felt unable to shake off. After his smoke he made another cup of coffee and went back inside.

Seth sat in his armchair and switched on the TV, he flicked between various sports shows then a few music channels which only made his headache worse so he switched off the TV and sat in silence. He had a nagging idea that he was supposed to be doing something but for the life of him he couldn't remember what it was.

He went to the kitchen to see if he'd left himself a reminder on the refrigerator as he had done so often in the past, usually a barely legible scrawled note when he was drunk. There was nothing, he opened the fridge to see if he was short on milk or juice or something, no, well no more than normal. He checked his cupboards; they all seemed to have the bare minimum food levels as he usually kept it, nothing stood out as being absent. The headache persisted however so he took a couple more aspirins to hopefully ease the growing discomfort and sat in his chair again, hoping that the lack of movement and sound would dispel the pain.

An hour of stillness and silence later and the pain, instead of easing, instantly seemed to increase ten fold and he fell from his chair and slumped to his knees in agony, clutching his hands over his ears tightly as if his brain was trying to escape and he had to push it back in. It felt like a power drill grinding away at the inside of his skull and he screamed as tears rolled down his face.

Seth crawled across the floor but couldn't move fast enough to leave the agony behind, he had no plan but found himself moving towards his desk. Once there he climbed into his chair and took deep breaths, he had no idea why he was doing it but he switched on his computer and typed in his password. He felt compelled to write, more so than that, he felt he had been told to write, the drilling in his head seemed to have a voice. That voice was telling him to type, it was a cold and nasty voice, strict, harsh and brutal. He felt he had no choice but to do as he was being told and so he did.

The more Seth wrote, the easier it became to tolerate the voice in his mind, the tendons in his hands and arms ached as he typed at a speed he'd never thought himself capable of. Faster he typed, barely catching sight of the words and sentences he was writing as they dashed up the screen to be replaced by another paragraph, then another and another.

Chapter after chapter flooded out of him though he had no idea where it was all coming from, his hands moved over the keys as if possessed of life in their own right, he didn't feel he was controlling any of what was happening. He started to see in his head what he was writing as if he was watching a movie, not thinking about what he was actually typing, not planning characters or developing plots. This seemed pre-planned, a creature that he was giving birth to. The more he wrote, the more excited he became at just what was unfolding before his eyes and in his mind, he knew instinctively that he was creating something amazing all of a sudden, he still didn't know what the hell it was but he knew it was going to be darkly wonderful.

Hours passed, day turned to night and still he typed. Seth could feel the end in sight as he galloped towards the finish line, the voice in his head had stopped screaming at him now as he was obeying its' commands but he wasn't going to take a chance on stopping as he could feel its' malevolent presence as if sat there in his skull, watching and waiting, ready to strike should he slow in his task.

An hour later and Seth was exhausted, he had no choice but to stop and rest for a few minutes, his fingers ached and were swollen and blistered from typing, his back had stiffened badly from being hunched over the keyboard, he hadn't realised just how long he'd been writing.

"I'm just going to take a very short break" he said to 'it' as if requesting a breather at work from his slave-driving boss, there was surprisingly no complaint and no screaming from whatever was inside his head.

He arched his back like a cat stretching out in front of the fire, he had become even more stiffened than he thought and stumbled as he stood, he rubbed his eyes that had grown weary from staring at the computer screen. He gingerly stepped away from his desk, wary of being yelled at and made his way to the kitchen to get coffee, cigarettes and fresh air.

Again he opened the back door and stepped outside to drink his coffee, he was a little taken aback by the darkness that greeted him, it had been after lunch when he'd woken up, but where the hell had the day gone? Seth sat on his step with his coffee mug, sipping and smoking, a wry smile creased his lips as he dared to think of what he was creating, who was creating it? Lily came to his mind then and something about a dream he'd had although he couldn't remember the context of it very well. This was strange in itself as Seth could usually remember his dreams fairly vividly, especially over the last few months.

A warm feeling came over him as he thought of his wife; he wondered where she was and what she was doing. He expected her to be working, he looked at his watch, one a.m., Seth sighed because he knew she wouldn't be working. She'd be at home in her apartment; she'd be with Jason, probably asleep. He hoped she'd be asleep anyway, anything else he just didn't want to contemplate. Melancholy drifted over him now, how easily the happiness of Lily was replaced by the depression that she was no longer his.

Just like a siren going off, the thing in his head screamed at him, his coffee break must be over, he jumped at the noise and dropped his mug which shattered on the concrete beneath his feet. He rubbed his temples in a vain attempt to soothe the howling pain, reluctantly he finished his cigarette and the scream became more insistent.

"Ok, ok, I'm going" he told his supervisor as he put his smoke out in the sand bucket.

Once back at his desk and feeling a little more refreshed at least, he started to read back his last couple of paragraphs to re-acquaint himself with where he was up to but the thing in his head was in charge and 'it' seemed to know exactly where he was up to and screamed at him to write, he wrote. Seth was amazed at just how easily this work was flowing out of him. He hadn't even had to go back and correct a spelling mistake and his punctuation had been exemplary, that was very unlike Seth.

There was no time for coasting and no easing off of the pace, he wished he could write all his novels like this, then again, no. As he typed what was to be the final sentence he looked down at the keyboard for the first time in hours and noticed little smears of dried blood on the keys. He finished the sentence and flopped back in his seat, breathing heavily with relief and exhaustion; he looked at his fingers and realised how much they'd bled. He hadn't noticed this because he hadn't been able to feel his fingertips for many hours, now as he looked at them and blew gently on them they started to tingle as the feeling began to come back.

He sat in his chair and looked out of the living room window, dawn was starting to break over the city, everything was so quiet, not a sound anywhere. He had come home from a night out many times at this hour and enjoyed the quiet but this seemed so much more than that. Added to this he realised the voice in his head had stopped, better still was that he could no longer even sense it sitting there waiting to start again, it had left his mind completely.

It was a great feeling, a feeling of relief and even a job well done, he felt enormous satisfaction because he knew he had something special within his grasp now, even though it had been tantamount to writing at gun point! He stood and stretched again before returning to the kitchen doorway for a cigarette and coffee, this time though, in celebration. A glow of achievement and satisfaction drifted over him, this was something that he hadn't felt in a painfully long time. Not since his heydays of success had he been this confident in his work and ability, he dared to think of better times around the corner and his future, before deciding not to get too carried away. Still he couldn't help himself yelling to whoever was listening
"I'm back motherfuckers!"

He smiled as he looked out at his neighbourhood as it was waking up, lights were being switched on and although he couldn't hear them he knew that alarms were going off all around as people were getting up and going off to work. Seth had done what seemed like a few months work in a little over 12 hours, he deserved his bed.
"Enjoy it mate, it's been a while" he said to himself

He went back inside, to his desk and sat down, he saved his work to a memory stick and to the hard drive before switching the computer off and sitting back. Seth didn't make it to his bed, his tired stinging eyes closed giving instant relief and satisfaction, his body slumped in exhaustion and he fell asleep in his chair, he'd earned the rest.

Dr Lily Caine arrived at work feeling a little worse for wear. She'd drank half a bottle of vodka in her vain attempt to blot out everything that had been going wrong in her life recently. She'd heard more than enough horror stories from Severin Frost, she'd had to dismiss Father Duncan for his attack on Frost which meant that now she would have to be involved in finding a suitable replacement for him. There was the possible fallout from the assault and wounding of a patient by a priest, the notoriety of Frost with the press could cause ripples, reports would need to be filed, authorities to be notified and possibly even court cases. These were all things that the Director and Dr Sterling, as the senior consultant, would normally be dealing with but with Karen Sterling out of the picture and no replacement on the horizon, it just meant more shit for Lily to wade through.

On top of all this, over recent weeks she had found her thoughts drifting more and more to Seth which was troubling. Whether it was Severins *impersonation* of him or thoughts of Jack, again via Severin, was hard to say. Then again she had been having thoughts of Seth before Frost had started his act. Speaking to her estranged husband was difficult on the phone as she had tried to keep it, Lily had always preferred to speak face to face to people but with Seth it was awkward in person because she still loved him and knew she could never stop loving him either. Seth was her first love and her first lover, that was something that could never be erased and he would always hold that special place in her heart, however his place in her heart seemed to be getting bigger and stronger and she didn't know why. He was also the father of her child; he'd been a wonderful father too. It broke her heart when Jack died and it was broken all over again when it came to light how much Seth had blamed himself for the loss of their son, she recalled him telling her recently about his dreams of the crash, at least she didn't have the torture of reliving the experience over and over again as Seth did.

She had felt herself thinking of happier times between the two of them for a while now but always she kept her thoughts well hidden for fear of showing vulnerability. She couldn't rekindle things with Seth, too much alcohol and too many women had flowed under Seth's bridge for that to happen. She was confused and unhappy, throwing herself into her work had kept her from falling apart after Jacks' death, she was sure it would get her through this awkward time too.

The cherry of humiliation on top of this cake of misery and frustration came when Jason had left her, while drinking away her dejection she had felt used and discarded by him. He'd had his fun, screwed his boss and then discovered a younger and firmer plaything. He hadn't even had the decency to talk to Lily about it, just cleared his things from her apartment and left a note, the spineless bastard.

Now here she was, another day another dollar, same shit different day. She checked her minimal make-up in the mirror on her office wall, dismissed how old and unattractive she suddenly felt, took a deep breath and set off on her rounds.

After seeing all but one of her patients she started to feel more like herself, on professional autopilot, it was now mid-afternoon, she'd skipped lunch as she couldn't face it and needed to keep busy for fear of letting her mind drift to her other problems. The one patient that she hadn't seen was inevitably Severin Frost, he was under medical observation in the Institutes private hospital wing. She knew she had to check his medical state first; she also had to determine if he wanted to take the matter of the wounding further legally and part of her just wanted to see him.

It was a strange feeling that most people wouldn't understand but despite what unspeakable crimes he had committed to be in the Hoffman and despite how he had upset her in the past, especially with regard to her son, he was still her patient and she felt a very protective bond and duty to him. Father Duncan had been right in some ways to say she cared for Frost but then she cared for all her patients, past, present and future. Severin however was a special case in every sense of the term, for what he had done coupled with the fact that he hadn't responded to anyone in the Hoffman like he had to her.

When Lily arrived in the hospital wing, she checked with the doctors caring for Severins' wounds and she was reassured that he was going to be fine, there had been no major arteries damaged and despite losing quite a lot of blood, he'd had a transfusion and would make a complete recovery. Instantly she felt a wave of relief, it felt strange, as if she was waiting for news of a friend or relative who had been in an accident, not a psychopathic killer and sadistic torturer.

Lily went to the room that he was staying in, on entry she immediately noticed that he was lay on his back with his hands strapped firmly to the sides of the bed. Bandages swathed around his head and neck like an ancient mummy, she felt for the first time, some sympathy for this creature. His massive chest rose and fell deeply as he slept, she had been warned that he would be heavily sedated to keep him calm until his wounds had healed properly. Having satisfied herself that he was alright and would recover fully, she smiled and stroked his hand and made to leave.

"Dr Caine?" a broken husky voice called after her, she stopped in her tracks and turned back half-smiling.

"Severin?" she whispered "hi, how are you feeling?"

"I will be fine my dear doctor, what are you doing here?" he croaked

"I just came to see you and to make sure you were going to be alright, they've assured me that it all looked worse than it actually was and that you'll be back terrorizing everyone in no time" she half-joked, no matter what he had done, he was still a human being, he needed treatment and she hated to see anyone in pain, violence repulsed her.

"Thank you, that was a very kind gesture and very sweet of you. How is my good friend Seymour?"

"Don't worry Severin, he's gone, we had to get rid of him after this" she thought she would be reassuring him but Frost laughed "why are you laughing?" she asked.

"Because you said don't worry, do you really think I would be worried about him coming to get me?" Severin laughed again to himself

"I suppose not" Lily smiled "Look, Severin, I know this probably isn't the right time or place to ask this but" Lily moved closer to the bed "we're going to have to ask you at some point, do you want press charges against Father Duncan for doing this to you?" she was sombre as she spoke

Severin looked into her eyes, she seemed to have the weight of the world on her shoulders as she sat on the chair at his bedside and he knew it was more than just work troubling her.

"Don't worry about that worm, I have a reputation to think of" he smiled an almost gentle smile beneath his dressings "he was a mere insignificance before and even less of one now. When you hunt for so long as I have, sooner or later your prey will turn and bite back when you least expect it, that's all it was, let's just call it a work related injury shall we? I won't be taking it any further, not legally anyway."

"If you're sure about that, we'll let the matter drop from your point of view at least" She chose to ignore his comment about not taking it further *legally*, after all there was little he could do in the Institute and Father Duncan would be long gone soon. Severins' flippancy was of no real surprise to Lily after the years she had spent with him, what he was to say next however was a surprise.

"Your heart is in pieces my dear, you need to let out the pain before it poisons your mind and soul" Severin looked deep into her with eyes that suddenly seemed so full of compassion and care.

Lily sat open mouthed by his side, he had never spoken or looked at her like that, even when trying to get inside her head. The words were delivered so beautifully, so thoughtful and sincere; his voice gentle and seemingly full of genuine concern. The way he spoke that simple phrase threw her totally off guard and touched her so much that a tear rolled down her pale cheek in her vulnerable state. Maybe there was some semblance of beauty in this beast, she had been searching for it for such a long time, had she finally found it? He strained at his shackles and reached out carefully with his fingers to stroke her hand gently with sympathy, she didn't pull away.

"We are not in session now are we, I take it?" he whispered

"No Severin" she sniffed and wiped the tear with her other hand so as not to break the physical contact with him "we are definitely not in session now" she smiled softly.

"Good, then talk to me. We have known each other for a long time now, I normally tell you about myself and what's in *my* head, take this rare opportunity to let out what's in *your* head. Talk to me once . . . as a friend" the tenderness with which he spoke was overwhelming, he was like a different man, the bandages disguising his features, the words and sentiment of a poet. She had never really opened up to anyone, not like she used to open up to Seth in the early days of their romance, she had forever since bottled up her emotions, as if reading her thoughts he said

"Uncork that bottle Lily"

Lily did just that, first work and the pressure she was under, the priest and the paperwork and then onto Jason and the other girl, how she felt her age and that life was passing her by. Finally she told him of her feelings for Seth and of their previous life together, Jacks' death and the effect of it on the two of them, Seth's fall from grace as a writer, their separation and his subsequent womanising and drinking and finally how her feelings were returning. Her confusion was evident, she bared her soul to Severin, for his part, he listened, stroking her fingers when her voice cracked occasionally, particularly when talking about her son.

After she had finished, she dried her eyes and took a deep breath, for a nightmare split second she realised what she had just done, she'd exposed herself emotionally, totally and completely to a patient and not just any patient but Severin Frost! She looked down at where he still held her hand, suddenly she became very nervous, he could break her fingers like snapping dried twigs, shackled or not. He simply looked at her and as if to alleviate her sudden anxiety he opened his hand wide to let her withdraw hers. She decided it would be best to leave and stood to excuse herself.

"I think it's time I left Severin, I'm glad to see you're going to be alright and I'll see you back in the main unit soon, a couple of days they said."

"Lily" he whispered still "you know what you have to do"

She stood with her hand on the door handle, her back to Frost, wanting to leave but for the first time in her very professional, hard-nosed, calm and calculated and extremely independent adult life, she just wanted someone to tell her what she should do.

"Go to him Lily, go to Seth, you know in your heart and soul that Seth is the only man in this world who can make you feel alive, make you feel loved and make you happy no matter what shit each day throws at you. If I could have found such love in my life maybe things could have been different for me . . . ." he trailed off before continuing "Deep down you know this and Seth feels the same way about you, how could he not? Go to him Lily"

She opened the door and looked back at the stricken man as he lay there, they had both opened up more in one afternoons' conversation than in years of official therapy, she left the room but just before she closed the door she smiled at him over her shoulder and said

"Thank you Severin"

CHAPTER 14

L ily left the Hoffman as the day had drifted into early evening, streetlights came flickering into life as she pulled out of the staff car park and made her way home. She switched on the radio as she drove, thoughts of Severins' words faded in and out of her head until the news came on and she turned up the volume. Reports were relayed of a multiple car crash on the outskirts of the city centre close to her route home, she was glad of the warning as she could now avoid the area and the inevitable detours and delays, she just wanted to get home though she knew that no-one would be waiting for her. The newscaster also mentioned that there had been a number of fatalities including a child, immediately she changed the channel, if she hadn't, then more thoughts of Jack were also inevitable.

She listened to a music station for a while as she continued on her homeward journey, the DJ tried to sound sincere as he dedicated bland pop ballads requested by various bland listeners who had phoned it to get a mention for their no-doubt ever more bland partners. Lily sighed and tutted to herself before switching it off and deciding to enjoy the silence instead as she drove.

On her arrival home, she put her bag and keys on the table as she did every night. Moving into the kitchen, kicking off her shoes as she went, she switched on the coffee machine. Lily then went back into the living room and switched on the TV, the news was on, reporting up to the second information about the crash she'd just heard about, reporters were at the scene and emergency lights flashed in the background as police were sealing off the area, again she switched it off and decided on silence. She went to get a coffee cup from the cupboard and noticed a packet of cigarettes partly hidden.

"The bastard said he'd given up." She said to herself as she realised that they were the brand that Jason 'used' to smoke. Lily took them out of the cupboard and threw them in the trash. Once her coffee was ready she poured herself a cup and went back to the living room, she slouched on the couch and put her aching feet up on the table in front of her. Sipping at the coffee she sighed and tried to let everything wash over and away from her.

After a few minutes she got up again and returned to the kitchen to see what she had to eat, she didn't really want to start cooking. She checked the freezer compartment to see if there was anything worth throwing in the microwave. Nothing tempted her and she stood there looking around the room, not really knowing what she wanted to do. Surprising herself, she opened the bin and picked out the cigarette packet, she opened it, six or seven left, she retrieved a box of matches from a drawer and opened a kitchen window. Smoking a cigarette relieved her boredom but only briefly and she sighed again as she extinguished the tobacco under the kitchen tap before disposing of it in the bin.

She looked around to see if anything needed cleaning, as tired as she was, she felt she needed to keep busy. She didn't want to have the time to dwell on things, any things. Everything was in perfect order and as pristine as ever, just how she liked it, just how she always kept it. She looked around again and noticed her bottles of wine in the small rack on the kitchen counter, Lily pondered them for a few seconds before she picked out two bottles of red and said to herself
"Fuck it!"

Seth had slept for the majority of the daylight hours following his marathon and exhausting writing session. Once he had risen from his deep and remarkably dreamless sleep in his chair, which was far more comfortable than he'd imagined, he'd showered and brushed his teeth then come back downstairs where he excitedly printed of his new novel. Even thinking of it as his new novel, his comeback, maybe even his masterpiece, excited him more than any of his work had excited him before, there was a genuine optimism that this was 'the one'.

Watching his printer spit out page after glorious fresh page as he scanned down it re-reading sections of the story that he had created made him swell with pride.
"Where the hell did this come from? I knew you had it in you Seth my old mate" he told himself as he beamed with self satisfaction.

Once the printer had finished its' job, he piled the sheets neatly on the side of his desk and stood back, glowing at his achievement, this felt even better than the completion of his first book. He went to the kitchen, it was dark outside but he didn't really care where the day had gone this time, for that matter he didn't even care what day it was. He looked in the freezer for some food but nothing took his fancy, he looked in his cupboards, what little there was didn't tempt him either. Seth opened the drawer where he kept all his take-away menus that were constantly being pushed through his letter box and spread them out on the kitchen table, deciding what he wanted to eat. Then there was a knock at the door.

Seth furrowed his brow, he wasn't expecting anyone that he could think of and with curiosity he went to answer it.

"Lily! What are you doing here?" he was incredibly surprised to see her but also absolutely delighted.

"Have you eaten?" she smiled

"No, I was just about to order some take-out, why?"

"Fancy getting pizzas?" she held out the two bottles of red wine in front of her.

"Of course" Seth smiled "Er, please come in"

Lily entered and Seth shut the door behind her, she gave him the bottles and threw her bag and keys on his coffee table as she followed him into the kitchen, kicking her shoes off as she went.

"Make yourself at home" Seth laughed as he watched her

"Oh, sorry, force of habit" Lily went to retrieve her shoes

"Don't be silly, leave them, I'm only joking, relax" Seth thought of how she used to do that in *their* home, it gave him a very warm feeling of love and comfort.

The pizzas were ordered and wine opened, the food arrived and they sat in the living room eating and drinking. Small talk about how they both were gave way, eventually, to a more relaxed feeling, a very comfortable feeling. They talked about the old days and laughed together as they reminisced, Seth seemed in an especially good mood which lightened the weight on Lily's shoulders as it lifted her own mood, as did the wine. They had both always loved to see or make the other laugh. She noticed the pile of papers on his desk; that in itself was a flashback to better times, of Seth being the toast of the literary world, in particular the alternative and darker side of literature. Success and happiness went hand in hand back then.

"What's that?" she nodded over to the pile.

"Ah, it's my new novel" Seth beamed uncontrollably.

"Really? I didn't realise you'd been working on anything, has it taken you long?"

"ha ha, it's funny should you say that, it actually took me just over half a day"

"Oh I see, that's just to type it? That's quick for you. Do you still hand write everything first then type it later?" she asked, remembering how he used to work.

"Actually no, it was the damnedest thing; I woke up with a splitting headache . . ."

"I see" Lily raised her eyebrows and rolled her eyes in mock surprise

""No, not through drinking, I hadn't had a drink that night at all for your information"

They both smiled at her playful teasing, there was a warmth in the room emanating purely from the two of them as they curled up together on the couch, it was all so natural and easy to be in each others company, alone.

"I just woke up with this blinding pain in my head" Seth continued "and I had this strange compulsion to write, the more I wrote, the easier my headache, it was really strange but it worked. By the time I'd finished, my fingers were bleeding and swollen and I'd got a completed novel sat here." He neglected to mention the horrendous yet invisible creature sat there gnawing away at his skull, he felt that that would just cloud his achievement.

"Wow, that's great!" she beamed back at him "but is it any good?"

"Well, you know better than anyone that when it comes to my work I'm my own worst critic but I can honestly say that it's the greatest thing I've ever written . . . by far!" he said with a completely straight face, in fact, a very serious expression, Lily could tell that this wasn't just bravado and she was genuinely delighted for him.

"I'm so pleased for you Seth, really, congratulations."

"Thanks, I think I surprised myself even more than I've surprised you"

"I always knew you had that in you Seth, for what its' worth, I never stopped believing in you, you know?" she smiled

"I know, it's nice to hear though" he returned the smile and almost blushed, with that Seth poured the last drops from the wine bottle and went to the kitchen where he opened the second bottle and brought it back into the living room, he started to pour into Lilys' glass but stopped when he noticed her car keys on the table.

"Er sorry, I forgot that you're driving, do you want a coffee instead? I think I might have some coke or juice or . . . ." he knew that he only had coffee but felt as if he was being a terrible host without an alcohol-free alternative to offer.

"No" she stopped him "I want more wine, I brought two bottles and I intended for us to drink them both. Plus, I know that you always have a few bottles in the house in case we run out" Lily smiled

"Oh" he raised his eyebrows quizzically "taxi home I take it?"

"You also know that I don't like getting taxis home alone at night" as she said this she lent forward, took the bottle from his hand and finished pouring her drink then filled Seths' glass. "and it's Saturday tomorrow, I'm not working this weekend" she smiled a smile that he hadn't seen in years and he responded likewise.

"I really hate to break the mood here Lily, but what about Jason?" he *really* didn't want to break the mood and he *really* couldn't care less about Jason.

"Jason is no longer in the picture, let's just leave it at that, please" her head bowed as she spoke, Seth gently lifted her chin with a single finger and looked into her eyes where the tears started to well. He so wanted to kiss her but she wasn't quite ready for that and she moved her head, wiping her eyes and changing the subject.

"So" she cleared her throat "did you think about getting a therapist as I suggested?"

"Actually I've already been to see one"

"That's' wonderful, anyone I know?" she smiled, pleased with him that he was actually trying to get himself back together, a psychiatrist and a rapidly completed novel, all in quick succession.

"Er, I don't know" he hesitated "Dr Alexandra Roth?" he tried not to wince as he said her name; luckily Lily didn't notice his facial expression. In his head he repeated the thought 'please don't know her, please don't know her'

"Roth? Hmm, no can't say that I do"

Seth just smiled with relief and nodded while thinking 'thank god for that' as he topped up their wine glasses again.

"So, is she any good? How did you find her?"

Too many questions, he didn't really know how to answer them but he knew he couldn't tell her that Alex picked him up in a bar, fucked him and then *appeared* out of the phone book, it was all way too bizarre to explain no matter who he was talking to.

"Phone book" he said, short and simple "just got lucky I suppose and she's really good, made me feel better and clearer about things in our first session" he was grinning as he thought about Alex again "she gave me some mental exercises to help me control my dreams" he lied.

"She does sound good" commented Lily though Seth's stupid grin made her curious at just what he was grinning about, he saw her narrowing her eyes and quickly changed the subject again.

"So, how's work going?" he asked

"Oh, ok I suppose" Lily sighed and visibly slumped at the thought of her own work

"Not that good then really I take it? That's not like you; you always loved your work even on crap days, the highs and the lows."

"Let's just say that the last few days have been a particular low" she took a large gulp from her glass and held it out for a refill "do you have cigarette?"

"Er, yeah sure" a little surprised Seth filled her glass and got his smokes and an ashtray from his desktop "It must've been a really bad week!"

He lit two cigarettes and passed one to Lily who drew heavily on it then took another drink.

"Did you find anymore out about that guy?" Seth queried

"What guy?"

"Frost or something? You asked me about him, he says he knows me?"

Severin Frost back in her mind, something else that she didn't want to think about, especially after that days encounter, now she was starting to have mixed feelings about him, she tried to block the thoughts and feelings out as she finished her cigarette and drained her glass before putting it back on the coffee table then snuggling down on the couch.

"Oh Seth, forget about that" she said wearily lifting her legs up behind her on the sofa, her head now resting on his chest.

He leaned forward and kissed the top of her head, he smelled her hair as he put his arm around her shoulders and squeezed gently. In response she nuzzled deeper into him and he smiled to himself, this really was like the good old days.

Her breathing was steady and peaceful and Seth didn't want to disturb her but after a while his arm began to go numb and he decided it was time for bed.

He slowly and gently eased himself out from under her sleeping body, slipping a cushion under her head to support her. He got her bag and went to the kitchen for a large glass of water then took them upstairs. Lily always seemed to get a phone call or text in the morning from work, even at weekends and he assumed she still did, he didn't want her frantically looking for her phone and breaking the spell that he was under. She also always wanted a glass of water when she woke up, either during the night or first thing in the morning, especially after she had been drinking wine the night before. Lily always seemed genuinely touched and pleased when he used to do things like that for her, trivial to some people but to her, doing the trivial things showed that he cared and Seth had always cared for her, it just came naturally to him and after all this time it did still.

Upstairs he switched the bedside lamp on at the side he knew that she preferred sleeping on and placed her bag on the floor, within easy reach. He put the glass of water on the bedside table, again within her grasp but not too close to the edge so as to be knocked off accidentally. Finally he pulled the duvet back so that he could put her into bed with as little disruption to her slumber as possible.

Seth then went back downstairs and there she was, sleeping beautifully. He knelt in front of the couch, just watching her sleep in peace, his heart ached for her. Ever so gently he moved one arm under her bent knees and the other under shoulders and back, she groaned softly at the movement but didn't wake. He steadied himself and lifted her up into his arms, again she groaned but slept on.

Slowly he made his way to the staircase and step by gentle step he carried her cradled in his arms up to his bedroom, once there he lay her on the bed, now came the dilemma that he hadn't thought of. Should he undress her? A few years ago there would've been no dilemma, he would just naturally undress her and they would laugh about it the next morning, but now? She would be uncomfortable sleeping fully clothed but if he undressed her she might flip out that he had done so. What if she woke up in the middle of him taking her clothes off? Half asleep, she might go ballistic, thinking that he was trying to take advantage of her condition. Didn't she come over for that anyway? That had seemed that implication with the wine and being unable to drive home. For the first time in his life he felt he couldn't read her intentions.

"Fuck it!" he said under his breath, he removed her blouse and skirt. Tempting as it was to remove her underwear, he resisted, he was amazed that she hadn't woken up already but he didn't want to mess things up in the long run between them by getting overly ambitious and pushy now, things had been going so well. He covered her over and went to the bathroom to brush his teeth. He looked at the man in the mirror, the scars on his cheek had nearly gone, just faint red lines remained which was surprising as they were initially quite deep. He smiled ruefully at the man staring back at him and said

"Bigger picture, trust me" before switching off the bathroom light and walking back through the bedroom to go and sleep on the couch. Just as he got through the door he heard a voice

"Seth?" she was looking at him through half closed eyes in the lamplight.

"I'm sorry" he whispered "I didn't mean to wake you"

"Where are you going?" her eyes were open more fully now and she seemed quite awake.

"I just put you to bed, I thought it would be best if I slept on the couch"

"Don't be stupid" Lily slid over to one side of the bed away from where he stood leaving the other side vacant and pulled back the cover invitingly "I didn't just come over here for wine and pizza you know, I could've done that at my place." She smiled coyly as she spoke, Seth smiled back as he undressed and got into bed beside her.

They made love in the truest sense of the words, it was passionate yet tender, aggressive yet beautiful, they rolled around on his bed locked in hot and intensive embraces while Seth was buried deep inside her and Lily clawed at his back and shoulders. They brought each other to realms of pleasure and excitement that only they with their deep knowledge of each others bodies and tastes could have made possible. They came together expertly, each holding off their own orgasm in order to enhance the experience and power for the other. When exhausted, they lay in each others arms and slept through the night in exquisite rapture, it was as if they had never been apart.

CHAPTER 15

The next morning Lily woke alone, she looked around the bedroom and listened to see if Seth was in the bathroom, which he wasn't. She curled up more under the covers, warm and comfortable in her cocoon. Then she heard him coming up the stairs, he carried with him two mugs of coffee, he put one on her side of the bed then walked back to his side, he was wearing a long black bathrobe, normally he wouldn't bother with the robe and he would just walk around as nature intended but was at least trying to make an effort, he took off the robe and got back into bed.

"Good morning" he smiled "coffee?" he nodded over to the mug

"Aww thank you" she smiled sweetly back then sat up a little and picked up the drink.

They both sat in quiet contemplation as they sipped at their hot drinks, occasionally glancing at each other and grinning like teenagers after their first night together. Seth decided to break the mild tension first.

"Er, do you have any regrets, about last night I mean?"

"I know what you mean and no I don't have any regrets, I promise" she reassured him

"That's fantastic" he sighed with relief "I was a bit worried when I was downstairs making the coffee, wondering to myself if you would wake up and run out of here hiding your face in shame" as he explained his fears, she laughed "seriously, I could have come back upstairs to find you hanging outside the window trying to make your escape!"

They both laughed at the thought, it was a great feeling to lie in bed together, laughing and joking, another reminder of how good things used to be.

"No" she smiled "I knew exactly what I was doing when I came over, I brought the wine remember and I had no intention of going home. To be honest and to put it crudely, I just wanted to fuck! Well, actually I just wanted to fuck you" she went a little red with embarrassment as she didn't often speak in such a way.

"It seemed more than that to me" replied Seth, flattered and hurt at the same time.

"Oh it was for me too, don't get me wrong, I'm just saying that that is how it started out, it ended so, so much better though, thank you for that" she beamed

"You're welcome and thank you" he chuckled "but has it ended? Is that it?" he was dreading her response if it was going to be in the negative.

"Honestly Seth" she paused and his stomach knotted "I really hope not but for now, let's just take it easy, is that ok?"

"Oh darling, we can take it as easy as you want to" he said with a relieved smile as he leaned forward and kissed her softly on the lips.

"Thanks for being so understanding Seth" she smiled again "now don't take this the wrong way but I really should be going now"

"Alright but first I have to know what the situation is between you and Jason, I mean, is he going to pop up again somewhere along the line?"

"He's gone Seth, he's left. He found someone younger and prettier" she sighed, not for the loss of Jason but for her supposed loss of her youth.

"Really?" Seth was gob smacked "What a fucking prick! I mean, look at you, you're as stunning as you've ever been"

"Aww Seth, thank you, that's so sweet, believe me when I say that I really needed to hear that" she stroked his cheek as she looked deep into his eyes "But I have to make it clear that this isn't a rebound thing because I'm feeling sorry for myself, I promise you, you've been on my mind a lot recently and I just needed to be with you, do you understand?"

"Lily, I don't care what the reasons are for you being here, I'm just unbelievably happy that you are. All I care about is you, all I've ever cared about is you, you may find that difficult to believe, I don't know, but to be able to hold you in my arms at any point is like an amazing gift. As well as that, I have to say that it's strange because you have been on my mind a hell of a lot too lately, more than usual, I've been aching for you"

She looked deeply at him, his face in anguish as he tried to get his point over to her; right now though, she had no definite answers for him as to what would happen next between them. She loved hearing those words but didn't want to get too carried away, well not yet anyway.

"Maybe it's fate?" she smiled "Now, I really do have to go, I have a lot of paperwork to do at home" she put down her coffee cup and stepped out of bed.

Seth sighed as he looked at her, she still took his breath away now as much as when he first saw her all those years ago. As Lily sorted through her discarded clothes and found her underwear Seth lunged over the bed and grabbed her arm, playfully pulling her back into the bed with him.

"Stay here" he pined as he rained kisses down on her face and neck.

"I can't" she laughed under his barrage "the paperwork!"

"Screw it! Or better yet, go and get it and bring it here to do?" he mumbled as he continued to kiss her, now her shoulders and breasts and down to her abdomen.

He followed his merry journey of kisses down on to her thighs and she could feel her willpower deserting her, she so wanted to stay and continue where they had left off the night before but she knew that she had to go.

"No" she said reluctantly but defiantly, Lily grabbed a fistful of his hair just as he approached her sweet spot "I'm going" she smiled as she lifted his head by his hair and lent forward and kissed him deeply. Lily rolled off the bed and moved out of his reach as he pouted like a schoolboy, she laughed gently at the face he pulled.

Seth watched her dress, which was in itself a pleasure, then as she finished he put his robe back on and followed her downstairs. She put her shoes back on, grabbed her bag and keys and Seth reluctantly walked her to the door, as he opened it for her she kissed him passionately and said

"I really wish I could stay, I'm sorry. I'll see you soon alright, probably during the week, I'll call you" she kissed him again "bye" she jogged down to her car and waved as she left, he blew her a kiss as she set off and all too soon she was gone. Seth closed the door behind himself and stood leaning with his back to it with a huge smile on his face.

Later that morning, after Seth had showered and eaten, he stood at his backdoor with a coffee and cigarette, contemplating the previous nights' events. He was so amazingly happy, he felt that even if it took a while to get Lily back with him properly, it would be worth the wait. Despite the coffee and cigarettes and despite the shower, he felt he could still smell her in his hair, he could still feel her touch on his flesh, skin on skin; he could still taste her on his lips, it was a taste he'd missed desperately and never wanted to go without again.

He needed to keep hold of her this time and he vowed to himself that he would, he needed to prove to her that he had indeed turned his life back around the right way, the book would be the first step along that road. Now he needed to get it published and keep this positive momentum going. To start his journey back he would require a little help to get going, a push start, he knew the very man to push him, his long time friend and agent Gus Knight.

Seth finished his smoke then went to his desk to retrieve Gus' phone number, due to his lack of work over recent years, communication had declined steadily but Seth knew he could always count on Gus' help when he needed it and vice versa. He found the office number then realised it was a Saturday, Gus wouldn't be in the office but Seth really didn't want the fire in his belly to die over the weekend so he called anyway, he could at least leave a message.

The Knight Agencys' phone rang and was surprisingly answered by Gus' secretary, luckily he was in but in a very important meeting. Seth gave the woman his name and pleaded with her just to tell Gus that he wanted to speak to him urgently, eventually and before Seth started swearing at her, she relented and asked him to hold but very quickly came

"Seth? Seth Caine?" exclaimed Gus in shock and surprise

"Hi Gus, how ya doin?"

"Fuck me, Seth Caine, wow, I'm doing great buddy, it's good to hear from you!"

"Glad to hear it"

"I thought you'd died man, it's been such a long time" Gus laughed

"Yeah I know, I'm sorry about that but I had nothing new to give you and . . . ."

"You still could've checked in though" Gus interrupted "I called you a few times and left messages but you didn't return any of them, hold on a minute, you just said you *had* nothing new for me, does that mean you have something new now? Is that why you're calling?" Gus sounded very excited at the prospect.

"It sure is!" Seth sounded very pleased with himself

"That's fantastic news, when can I see it?"

"As soon as possible as far as I'm concerned, Gus I'm sorry I didn't get in touch with you for a while and I know we're friends regardless of work but . . . ."

"Seth we can talk about hurt feelings and crap some other time buddy, I'm over it already" Gus' laugh boomed down the phone "How about Tuesday afternoon? I'm free then" he said while consulting his diary.

"Not soon enough, what about today?" Seths' eagerness was surprising to Gus

"Today? Not possible my friend, I'm only in today for a big deal I'm helping put together for a clients movie, this is gonna take all day I'm afraid, I'm just waiting for the studios' people to get here."

"I don't want to wait with this Gus; it's ready to go and fresh off the press"

"Er, I could juggle things around and I suppose I . . . ." Gus hurriedly flicked through his diary again to see if there was anything he could cancel or at least postpone.

"Tonight" Seth said simply

"Tonight? What d'you mean tonight?"

"On your way home tonight after your meeting, swing by my place and pick it up, it'll be worth it buddy, trust me."

"Erm, ok, this could go on most of the day though so it might get to around six or seven before I can get to you?"

"If that's the best you can do buddy, that's fine, I promise you won't be disappointed, see you later"

Seth hung up, leaving Gus mightily intrigued, just as Seth had hoped for. He knew Gus so well and also knew that his agent would now be sat in his meeting with an itch that he just couldn't scratch over this book. He would be speeding all the way to Seths' with anticipation and Seth knew deep in his heart that it wouldn't be a wasted journey.

Gus was indeed intrigued, his mind was elsewhere throughout his important meeting and as soon as it was over he made his excuses to his celebrating colleagues and client and dashed off to see his old friend Seth.

Seth had once been Gus' star client, his books were continually being sold out prior to release or on some occasions they were banned which just made them more sought after and popular. Everything in his name or even just magazines with him on the cover became collectable and expensive, book signing tours caused pandemonium wherever he went with queues of people snaking around the block just to meet him and Gus likened him to a rock star of the literary world, the bad boy of fiction. When sales of his novels started to decline and Seth was no longer an icon of his time, Gus was the one who tried to prop him back up and orchestrate publicity stunts, unfortunately none of which ever really worked on any consistent extent.

Gus had always said that he would be there to help resurrect his career for him should Seth ever get to a position to do it and now it seemed that that time might have finally arrived. There had of course been a few false dawns but something seemed to be in Seths' voice in their, albeit, brief phone call that had heightened Gus' instinct and he had a natural instinct for business.

He arrived at Seths' in heavy rain and ran from his car to the door, banging on it furiously. Gus was a stocky man, relatively short but built like a bull, thick neck and broad shoulders. He had a receding hairline and wore slim wire-framed spectacles, early fifties, clean shaven and an absolute animal in business. Seth opened the door and Gus barrelled in out of the downpour, soaking wet and panting for breath after his short sprint from the car.

"Gus, great to see you" Seth beamed

"Hey buddy, same here" they embraced like long lost brothers, Seth took Gus' coat, hanging it over the stairs banister to dry a little.

"Have a seat, drink?" Seth offered

"No thanks, I can't stay long, I promised to take Natalie out tonight, we finally managed to get a babysitter so I can't be late home." Natalie was Gus' wife of ten years, nice woman, nearly twenty years his junior. She used to be his personal assistant but their affair ended his previous marriage and he married her soon after his divorce. Most people had assumed that she was only there for his money but she'd proved the doubters wrong by staying the course and giving him the beautiful daughter that he'd always wanted, Alice.

The child had been little more than a year old when Jack had died, understandably Gus and Natalie had been devastated for Seth and Lily, a tragedy that brought the two couples closer together. Natalie and Lily had bonded in particular in the early days and the four of them had had many great times together.

"How are Natalie and Alice?"

"They're fine thanks" replied Gus, eager to get on with the business as always and also to get back to his waiting wife. "So, what's this book you seem so enamoured of?"

Seth smiled, he knew Gus would be like this, rushing around, always looking for the next big deal. He moved over to his desk and picked up the manuscript which was now barely concealed in a large manila envelope.

"Here you are, the future of Seth Caine" Seth oozed confidence and self-assurance as he handed his agent the package, Gus hadn't seen him like this in years, cocky and arrogant in his demeanour but still very likeable.

"Really, you're that sure of yourself?"

"Oh yeah, this is it, you should believe in me" Seth smiled a very broad smile.

"I do believe in you, you know that. I was always the one who believed in you even when things were going down the pan." Gus felt hurt that his faith in Seth was even slightly being questioned.

"I know, I know" Seth raised his hands in surrender at Gus' protests "I know better than anyone how many times I fucked up but you have to trust me now when I tell you that this is it"

"Forgive me for being cynical Seth but you've been out of the loop for a long time now and I say this as a friend but do you still think you've got it in you?" Gus made to open the envelope and Seth stopped him.

"I know what you're saying and there's no reason, apart from our friendship, why you should think any different this time but please, if you never read anything from me again, just read this and believe in me." Seth came across as extremely sincere as he looked at Gus with a knowing look of pride and confidence in his own work. "Just take it home, go and have your night out with Natalie and then tomorrow just clear you're day to sit and digest this, you'll be glad you did"

"My day's free tomorrow as it happens; Natalie's taking Alice to see her grandparents so there won't be any interruptions" he looked at the package again "so for you, I'll give it my undivided attention."

"Call me when you're ready and we can discuss the next steps" Seth said as he retrieved Gus' coat for him.

"You're talking this up pretty big Seth, you do realise that, I hope it delivers the goods"

"Oh trust me Gus, this delivers like no other" Seth held the manuscript while Gus put on his coat.

"You seem different Seth, have you got a new woman in your life or something?"

"Ha ha, you could say that" laughed Seth.

"Really, anyone I know?"

"As a matter of fact yes you could say that, a stunning psychiatrist, goes by the name of Dr Lily Caine" his smile broadened again as he spoke with a glint in his eye.

"Wow, no shit, that's fantastic news. When did this happen? How's it going? We should get together, the four of us, just like old times" Gus took back the book and opened the door to leave.

"Yeah it is fantastic, it's early days yet though so we don't want to rush anything, you understand?"

"Of course, sure I understand" he looked at Seth as he left and smiled "Man, you're glowing, I can't wait to tell Natalie, oh and I promise I'll give this my full attention and get back to you in a few days ok?"

"That's fine Gus, give my love to Natalie and kiss Alice for me will you, have a good night buddy"

"Will do, same goes to Lily ok, speak to you soon, goodnight"

Seth closed the door as Gus ran back down to his car; both men practically had a spring in their step at this new turn of events. All Seth had to do now was wait for the phone to ring, he knew that that wouldn't be too long to wait. Wheels were in motion; he knew that this rollercoaster was going to be the ride of a lifetime.

CHAPTER 16

The following Tuesday morning Seth woke to the sound of his phone ringing. He picked it up from the side of the bed and answered it under his duvet.

"Yeah?" he groaned

"Seth, it's Gus"

"Hi Gus, how you doin? What time is it?" he said as he tried to rub the sleep from his eyes

"Just after 7am and I'm fine, well I'm more than fine, I'm fuckin wired!"

"Oh? I thought you'd given all that up, what've you been on ha ha"

"On? Nothing, it's your book buddy, it's incredible!" Gus trilled

Seth emerged from the darkness and warmth beneath his covers, into the cold light of day and squinted at the suns' unwelcome intrusion into his room.

"Really? You think so?" as proud and confident as Seth undoubtedly was over his book, validation from a straight-talking man like Gus who pulled no punches was always reassuring.

"Absolutely really Seth, it's fantastic, it took me two days to get through but I couldn't put it down, it's wonderful, spell-binding, provocative and poignant, man, I don't know what else to say, it's got it all." Gus gushed like Seth had never heard before

"That's great Gus, I'm so glad you liked it, I did tell you that you would though"

"Liked it? I fucking loved it! You really were right about this, I gotta hand it to you my old friend, you were never more right about anything."

"So, now what?" asked Seth "who'd you think we should approach about publishing?"

"Already working on it buddy, why else would I be in my office at this hour?"

"You're at work already? I thought you were phoning from home, I thought you'd just woken up" Seth had never been an early riser, he was definitely not a morning person.

""I've hardly slept, I couldn't! I've been here for over an hour. I have a lot of work piled up so I do have to do some of that but as far as I'm concerned your 'Suffering Innocence' is going straight to the top of that pile, great title too by the way."

"So, it's going to be all meetings and negotiations from now on I take it?" Seth loathed corporate meetings and loathed people in suits even more.

"Don't you worry about all that, that's why I'm your agent and that's why I'm here at this time of day; I'll deal with everything and you know that I know all the right people in this business" no argument from Seth on that score "so I'm calling in a few favours, this is gonna get fast tracked at light-speed, believe me. Publishing is a foregone conclusion but I'm here looking at the much bigger picture than that Seth, this thing is going to be huge. I've already spoken to some people to get the buzz out there in the right places."

"At this time? They aren't gonna thank you for that Gus" laughed Seth

"Fuck it, sleep when you're dead, that's my motto when it comes to business."

Gus' enthusiasm was heartening for Seth and he knew that if Gus put all his knowledge and commitment into making this happen as quickly as he said he could, then Seth had better buckle himself in very tight.

"Thanks Gus, I really do appreciate your time and effort"

"Thank me? No, thank you Seth, for coming back with this novel, you were spot on when you said that 'Suffering Innocence' delivers the goods, now it's my turn to deliver. I can't wait to get my teeth stuck into it, you know I live for this shit."

"Good to know, glad you ain't losing your touch." Seth joked

"Never! Anyway, you get back to sleep and rest that wonderful grey matter of yours, I've only just gotten started and I've got a lot of calls to make and a lot of people to bully. I'll speak to you soon and update you with the situation as it happens, see you Seth and welcome back."

"Thanks Gus, I knew I could count on you and it's great to be back."

With that they both hung up, Gus went back to strategy planning and flicking through his contact book. Seth curled up into a foetal position of comfort and contentment, with Gus he was definitely in the right hands

Seymour Duncan sat alone in his parents' home. His father had died at the age of just 46, just after Seymour was born, leaving him to be brought up by a cold and puritanical mother who at the time was in her early forties. Initially, the couple had been delighted at finally being blessed with a baby at such a relatively late stage in life but shortly after her husbands' premature death, Seymours' mother became distant and resentful towards him.

He had been a quiet and introverted child, no friends to speak of, well, none that his mother ever approved of. An only and very lonely child, he became a frightened and frail little boy, afraid of the dark, afraid of strangers, afraid of girls, thanks to his mother and generally afraid of his own shadow. He didn't play sports with the other kids after school, he had to run home, do his homework and then go to church with his mother every evening where he would pray for forgiveness for sins that he could barely comprehend let alone commit.

His strict upbringing and very sheltered life led him to the priesthood, just as his mother had always wanted and had told him so from a very young age. It was always his destiny, whether he had chosen it or not was beside the point. Mrs Duncan had wanted a priest for a son and that was that, what little spirit he may have possessed once upon a time was beaten out of Seymour and his will broken very early on in his tender life.

Later, in his early twenties, Seymour had managed to break the apron strings albeit briefly by doing voluntary work in Africa. On his return he was very quickly manipulated by his controlling mother into staying with her through emotional blackmail due to her alleged poor health. Almost ten years passed before her *illness* eventually caught up with her and took her life, Seymour was devastated, no matter how tyrannical she had been, she was the closest thing to love that he had ever known in his entire life.

Now, less than a year later he sat in the family home staring at pictures of his parents. His father had looked a handsome man and Seymour so wished he had known him because in all the old photographs he looked like a genuinely happy guy. His mother also seemed to be full of life in the pictures, pretty and laughing in her summer dress as his dad picked her up in his arms at the side of some lake or other. What had happened to that woman? Seymour often wondered about *that* woman.

He hadn't had the heart to remove her things after her funeral, now the house just seemed cold, dusty and soulless, much like his own life he felt. He put the framed pictures back on the mantel and sat in contemplation of his empty future. He thought about what he had done at the Hoffman Institute, he had enjoyed his brief time, apart from his encounters with

Severin Frost but now that was gone. It was all gone, his entire life would be gone professionally if charges were brought against him.

As he thought about Frost a chill ran down his spine and he could have sworn he heard a womans' voice, he looked around the room. There was nothing, no-one, but it sounded as if he could hear the hysterical giggling of playing children, no, more than that as he listened more intently. It was indeed more like a playful woman and it seemed she was calling him by name, it definitely wasn't his mothers' harsh tone either, it was very joyful in a twisted sort of way. Seymour felt as if a cool breeze was blowing through his mind suddenly and he got up and walked around the room. He looked outside, windows closed to keep the world as far away as possible, no draughts, no children playing in the street, no-one around at all; it was a very quiet day.

"Seeeeeymoooour" the voice whispered

"W-who is it, who's there?" he stammered

"I have come to ease your troubled mind"

"What do you mean? Where are you?" Seymour was beginning to panic and frantically looked around the room "I've got a gun you know!" he lied as he tried to hold himself together.

"You carry a very heavy burden of guilt Seymour, I am here to relieve that burden" her voice, for it was most definitely a womans' voice, was soft and lilting, delicate yet clear in every aspect.

"How do you know all this and who are you?" his own voice now became a little shrill as he spoke while still shooting glances around the room.

"My name is unimportant at this moment Seymour, consider me your inner voice, better yet consider me your guiding angel" as she spoke it was as if she gently kissed his forehead, soothing his panic which instantly drained away and he felt more relaxed than at any other time that he could remember. He fell back into his armchair as if blown down by a beautifully scented but strong breeze.

"Why can't I see you?" he whispered now as she eased his fear with her tone.

"You will see me when the time is right my dear Seymour, you can feel my presence though, I know you can."

As she spoke those words and Seymour was about to reply he felt something brush against his legs softly then move up his body, moving along his bare, short sleeved arms and over his face and the top of his head. It felt like how he imagined a swans' wing would feel, though he couldn't actually see it, he knew it *felt* pure and white. He sighed at this seemingly angelic touch of purity.

"How can I be of service to you" he said with emotion swelling within him, Seymour cried tears of joy and faith and he smiled as he moved from his chair and down onto his knees.

"As I said Seymour, I am here to ease your pain, you feel guilt over this man you have wounded." It was not a question, more a statement of fact.

"I do, it felt right at the time, which I feel ashamed of admitting in your presence."

"Oh Seymour, there is no shame to be had in this."

"But I tried to kill a fellow man, it is sinful to even think of such a thing, for me to try to carry it out is a most heinous act I feel."

"Your remorse is understandable but you must forgive yourself as you will be forgiven due to your repentance. You must look at this man and what he has done, not only is he a killer but he is a killer of men and women of God."

"Are you saying that I did the correct thing?"

"You took what you felt was the correct course of action, man was blessed with free will. You chose the correct path early on in your life and you have followed that path in exemplary fashion ever since. What is more, you chose the right path in this instance too."

"I am honoured that you have come to me, to comfort me, and my mind is rested at the thought, thank you for lightening my burden." Seymours' tears flowed freely as he spoke in hushed tones.

"What you must also understand Seymour and the reason I visit you now, is that there has been a war raging and it has raged for aeons, ever since the rebellious angels were cast down into the pits. They will try to storm our gates again and we need warriors in the mortal realm as well as on the celestial plain if we are to resist and once and for all defeat the fallen angels of darkness." She spoke with a passion that inflamed and reinvigorated his faith.

"You want *me*?" Seymour was amazed at the mere suggestion, he had never thought of himself as a warrior in any way.

"Yes Seymour, will you help us to hold and turn back the dark tide before it engulfs the world of man?"

He hesitated, it wasn't that he didn't want to help, he would help in any way he could but he tried to take in everything she was telling him. Suddenly he felt her hand clasp his shoulder, her grip burned but it was a pleasant heat, like the suns' warmest rays all pulled together just for him, filled with power, filled with love, he had only one answer.

"Yes, yes, a thousand times yes, I will do anything that is required of me."

"Thank you Seymour, you will be rewarded many times over for the love, faith and devotion that you show."

"It is reward enough that you come to me and that I am able to serve you."

"Dear sweet and noble Seymour, I will visit you again, until such time be restful in your thoughts. Be forever guilt-free and also watchful of the darkness."

Seymour felt her gentle kiss on his forehead again and her feather-like touch as if she stroked his cheek with a gossamer palm, then she was gone. He knelt on the floor in his humility and rapture before standing with renewed hope and purpose in his life, a cause to fight for and fight he would.

Severin Frost sat alone in his room staring into the middle distance, he had healed from his wounds sufficiently to return to the Hoffmans' high security wing which had been his home for the last few years. This had been coupled with the fact that he unnerved so many of the staff in the Institutes' hospital that they wanted to get him out of there as soon as possible.

He sat staring into space, talking to himself, or so it seemed to any of the guards who may have looked through the re-enforced glass to check on him.

"My Lord, your plans are coming together well. I sense the doctor, thanks to my influence and of course your expert manipulation of events, is growing closer to her husband. The Lady Angelique visited me in my dreams and assured me that Mr Caine is fulfilling his side of the bargain as I'm sure you are aware and I believe the priest is also receiving a visitor as I speak to you now."

Severin stopped as he listened to his unseen guest, he nodded in agreement, his head bowed at all times in reverence.

"My wounds are healing well thank you, I do not fear the blade nor the shedding of blood as you know. Of course I will continue to do whatever you require of me My Lord, it is my duty and my privilege to serve you and long may I continue in that role."

Chapter 17

A few days later and Seth was lying in his bed, contemplating the beauty that lay beside him. Lily had stayed over again the previous night, she had called him as she promised she would and the two of them had gone out for a meal which was followed by a few drinks afterwards. They had both been having such a good time together that neither wanted it to end so Lily decided to leave her car in the city and they got a taxi back to Seths'

He had vowed to never get another car in his life, he hadn't been able to bring himself to drive since the accident; too many horrendous flashbacks simply destroyed his self-confidence as soon as he got behind the wheel. The sounds of screaming followed by visions of his sons' lifeless eyes resulted in panic attacks and tranquillizers. He never wanted to go through those harrowing scenes again, the dreams of the crash were uncontrollable but his other dreams were seemingly easing off, maybe that one would too, he hoped.

They had dined at Baggios', their favourite Italian restaurant where they had had many of their most memorable evenings, some romantic, some anniversaries or birthdays, some for Lilys' promotions or Seths' book celebrations, whatever the occasion they had always had a great time. This had been Lilys' suggestion and it felt like a first date, they both had butterflies in their stomachs as they dithered over what to wear when getting ready at their respective homes, such was their anxieties and expectations of the evening.

On arrival, they both had seemed shy and nervous which just added to the electricity in the air between them. The wine flowed and gradually they both relaxed and stared into each others' eyes longingly as they enjoyed the evening. Despite having to work the following morning, Lily decided she wanted to go home with Seth, he was so pleased, because it would've been agony to part after such a wonderful time together.

Once they had retired to his home however, the night took an interesting twist as Lily practically dragged Seth to the bedroom. She had been firm and demanding in telling him exactly what she wanted, he was more than delighted to oblige in her requests and orders, even her language became more overtly sexual and explicit, much to Seths' pleasure.

Now she lay on her side in his bed, peaceful and exquisite as she rested, last night had indeed felt just like one of their early dates and they had both loved it. As he watched her sleep, just like he used to, he couldn't help but think that they still had the same magic that they always had. It hadn't deserted them at all, if anything, time had made the magic mature and it was now more potent than ever. With every breath her chest rose and fell, her closed eyes gently flickered and he wondered hopefully that she was having amazing dreams of the two of them together; he felt more in love than at any time in his life.

Just as he thought of such things she rolled onto her back, her eyes opened and she instantly smiled as she saw him looking at her.

"Good morning angel" he whispered softly.

"Mmmm morning" she replied "sleep well?"

"I always do when I'm next to you"

"Uuuuurrggghh! Treacle" she laughed and pulled a face at his overly sugary compliment, Seth laughed too as he heard his words out loud but deep down, he meant what he said.

"What time is it?" Lily asked

"Er" Seth looked behind him at the clock on his table "9:15"

"9:15? Shit!!" She spun around herself to check her watch, which she'd left at the side of the bed, for confirmation. "Shit! I'm really sorry to have to rush off again Seth but I really have to go"

"What? No, stay a while, have some coffee with me at least." He pouted a little.

"Oh Seth, you know I can't, I told you last night that I'd have to run in the morning for work and I've still got to get my car yet" she stroked his cheek as he looked hurt, he simply didn't want her to go "please don't make it harder for me, you know I'd rather stay with you"

He knew she was right, she had said so the night before and in the heat of the moment it was the right thing to do; now however, in the cold light of morning, he resigned himself to her leaving despite his heavy heart.

"Ok, I'll ring you a cab" he sighed as he kissed her.

Lily jumped out of bed and quickly got dressed while Seth went downstairs to get his phone from his jacket to call a taxi for her. There were two missed calls on his phone, both from Gus, hopefully some news on his book. He was very briefly tempted to call Gus straight back but he could hear Lilys' footsteps running frantically around the bedroom above him as she shouted "Where's my other boot?". He smiled to himself and called the taxi first and decided to wait until Lily had gone before returning Gus' calls.

After ordering the cab he went into the kitchen and put on a pot of coffee, Lily came running downstairs with both boots in one hand while trying to straighten her hair with the other.

"So, you found it I see?" he said, nodding towards her boots.

"What? Oh, yeah" she smiled back then looked at her watch.

"Don't worry, it's on its' way, a couple of minutes."

"Thanks Seth, I'm sorry, I hate rushing off like this but . . . ."

"Hey, don't worry about it, I'd rather you stayed of course but I understand totally. I'm just so glad that you stayed in the first place" his smile and words eased her mild guilt at having to leave. "I am going to see you again though, aren't I?"

"Ha ha, aw Seth" She threw her arms around his neck kissed him longingly "you don't have to keep asking that you know, of course you're going to see me again"

She put on her boots and the jacket that had been so quickly discarded on the couch as soon as they had walked through the door the night before, she checked her bag for her keys and phone and quickly checked her face in a small compact she always kept.

"You look gorgeous, you always do" he smiled again as he walked her to the front door just as a taxi pulled up outside.

"Call me, soon" she said as she kissed him again, they both lingered over the kiss goodbye prompting the cab driver to beep his horn. They both tutted and shook their heads as their lips sadly parted at the ignorant interruption.

"I will, soon" his smile continued, though even now it was more one of longing, as she ran down and got into the car, waving as she was driven off into the morning.

Such were Seths' recollections and reminiscences of his night with Lily and the inevitable comparisons with how things used to be between them that it was over an hour after his routine coffee and cigarettes that he remembered to return Gus' calls. Seth was sat at his desk when he rang Gus' office and was greeted by an assistant that he didn't recognise, he told her that he was returning Mr Knights' calls and when he gave her his name she became very flustered. Odd, thought Seth, evidently it seems he was the talk of the office, she told him that she had been tasked with getting hold of him, without success.

"Don't worry about it, tell him you've finally tracked me down"

"Thank you Mr Caine, it's a pleasure to speak to you, I'll put you straight through now."

"Seth?" Gus immediately took the phone call, Seth could hear him telling somebody else in the office to get out "Finally!! I've had Becky trying to get hold of you all morning"

"Yeah, sorry about that, eight times she tried" he lied "very persistent is Becky, she's a keeper"

"As long as I've finally got you, that's all that matters"

"Sounds important"

"It is, I meant what I said before, 'Suffering Innocence' is gonna be fucking huge. I've been working on a deal practically non-stop since you gave it to me. We've got a bidding war going on between three different publishers" Seth could hear the glee in Gus' voice as he spoke "You know I don't like sending important paperwork via e-mail, I prefer the tried and trusted ways, so I had it photocopied and couriered over to them first thing on Tuesday morning, after I'd read it and they're all fighting over it now, ha ha"

"How come we aren't going with George as usual?" George Blackmore was Seths' long-time publisher, another old friend.

"Well, George is in with a pretty good offer and maybe looking to increase it but over the last couple of years I've been working with a couple of other sizeable firms who said if I get anything really hot, and nothing I've ever handled has been this hot, they want first refusal. This way they all get first refusal!" Gus chuckled to himself.

"Very ethical business practices as ever I see"

"Business is business buddy boy, that's why I'm your agent, I'll do the dirty work for you and you don't need to get your hands soiled. We've got Jackson & Crowley and Steinssons' both doing cartwheels over this."

"Sounds promising" Seth said in a very understated manner.

"Promising? Fuckin hell Seth, you haven't even heard the best part yet"

"Really? Go on, I'm listening"

"Well, we've already got two film studios interested and one of those is preparing a substantial financial package as we speak" Gus let his words hang in the air.

Seth had always wanted one of his novels transformed into a movie. However, despite his past successes, initial movie plans had always previously been scrapped due to a lack of funding or executives getting cold feet at the graphic and explicit nature of some of his work or simply Seth himself pulling out as he didn't want his books diluted for the big screen. He desperately wanted to see his vision there as a movie but not as a sanitised piece of crap that bore little if any resemblance to what he had created in the first place.

This had been one of Seths' chief disappointments in his career, he had always been a huge movie fan as a kid and even more so as he grew up. He had spent many an evening in awe at a story that someone had thought up and then developed and then that idea had been captured in film and transported him to another time and place, just like a great book, if it was done well. The imagination could do wonderful things when it was stimulated and wrapped up in a really good storyline. When he'd been writing all day though, he didn't always want his mind to create but he still loved that transportation of thought and escapism that could be achieved through a great movie. Now, finally could it be true that he was going to be able to make that leap onto the silver screen?

"Fuck, Gus are you serious? But"

"Now before you ask" Gus stopped him before he could raise his concerns "I know exactly how you feel about some movies being watered down versions of the original story but as this thing is so hot and in demand already, I have made sure that I have assurances by both companies that you get final say on how it's going to look and dialogue and pretty much everything else, hell, I'm even trying to get you final say on the casting to have it how you want it."

"Wow, thanks Gus, I don't know what else to say"

"Any time buddy, I'm loving all this almost as much as I loved the book! Just imagine Seth, that book in particular as a movie, it'll be awesome!"

Seth did try to imagine it and was quiet for a few seconds, he'd been imagining it in his head as he did with all his work but this one seemed so vivid even though he couldn't really remember how the whole thing came about in the first place. He could see it all so clearly now though, if the studios delivered as they were seemingly promising, then it would be amazing.

"Wow" he said again "I can't believe this is happening, finally. So, all the sex, violence, horror and blasphemy will stay in? I mean, there's quite a lot of it, even for me!" Seth was elated but still surprised and a little sceptical, 'Suffering Innocence' was by far his most controversial book to date, which was a stretch in itself!

"That's right my friend, I mean one or two things you might have to compromise on naturally but there's always gonna be a compromise at some point. Generally speaking though, they'll do it your way or no way. They know that, I spelled it out to them as soon as they started circling."

"Oh Gus, you never cease to amaze me, I can never repay you for all you've done for me" Seth was genuinely overwhelmed.

"You're more than welcome but don't forget I still get my percentage you know? Ha ha" Gus laughed

"You're worth every penny, bud"

"Good to know Seth, now you go and celebrate and I'll get on with negotiations and try to get all these deals tied up. I think we can safely say that you are definitely back this time, bigger, better and badder than ever before. I'll speak to you soon mate."

Gus hung up, as did Seth who sat at his desk and stared around the room as if seeing everything for the first time in his life, he grinned inanely at how his life was turning around so quickly, he couldn't possibly be happier. He was also amazed at just how fast everything was moving, he'd always known that he had a great agent in Gus but this was ridiculous! He even felt like giving himself a mental pinch to see if he was dreaming, then it occurred to him that he hadn't really had a dream since Mammon and Angelique visited him, he remembered something or other on the night before he started writing 'Suffering Innocence' but he couldn't remember clearly for some reason what it was all about.

Maybe Dr Roth had been even better than he thought. His mind felt clear, uncluttered and relaxed and on top of that he'd just produced the best work of his career to date, he had to thank her, if she'd helped to do all that in just one session, just think what she could do over a prolonged period. He picked up his phone to dial but couldn't think of her number, he flicked through his address book but found no listing so he went back to the original phone book. 'Psychiatrists and Therapists' held no listing either, he checked 'R' for Roth then even in desperation under 'A' for Alex! Next he went through every single name and number of therapists, nothing. He got out a map of the city to see if something jogged his memory, if a street name or building stuck in his subconscious, as he tried desperately to remember where her office was, then he tried to think where her apartment was, both times he drew a blank. Frustration crept in and he started to get annoyed with himself but then he thought of Lily and smiled a satisfying smile.

He picked up the phone again but this time he rang Lily, he had to share his good news with somebody and she was the only person that he ever really wanted to share anything with. He thought about ringing Karl but that could wait a few days, he would be in touch the next time he wanted to go out.

"Good morning, Hoffman Institute, how may I help you?"

"Hi, could I speak to Dr Lily Caine please, it's her husband" just saying that gave Seth a tingle of pleasure inside as he waited to be connected.

"Hi Seth, I know you said you'd call soon but this is a bit eager of you" she laughed as she teased and her fun-filled voice pleased Seth instantly.

"Hiya darling, I know you're probably really busy so I'll be quick, I just had to tell somebody my news but you're the only one I want to tell."

"Really? I'm intrigued"

"Well, after you left this morning I called Gus, he'd been leaving messages for me, so anyway, I called and it turns out that he's been really busy putting deals together on my behalf for the book and now there's a bidding war going on with different publishers!"

"Wow Seth, that's fantastic news, congratulations, we'll have to take Gus and Natalie out to celebrate."

Lilys' suggestion of the four of them going out as a group in a celebration sounded wonderful to Seth as it seemed like confirmation to him that they were back together as a couple, this time he hoped it really would be for as long as they both shall live.

"That's a great idea but you haven't heard the best part, apparently there are companies also fighting over the film rights too! Finally, I'm going to get a movie made and I'll be involved in the making of it too!" Seth could feel his enthusiasm rise and threaten to boil over.

"Aw Seth that's amazing, I know that that's what you've always wanted, I'm so happy for you" Lilys' smile at the other end of the phone was just as big as Seths'.

"Be happy for us, not just me Lily, if you're sure you want us to stay together that is, I know we haven't talked about it darling because we were trying to take things slowly but we could have the life we've always wanted."

"I already have the life I've always wanted, I only need to be with you, everything else is just chocolate frosting" Lily cooed

"Oh my love, me too" he wasn't going to spoil things by talking about material wealth after she had just uttered something that was so pleasing to his heart "Sorry to change the subject but are you sure you've never heard of my therapist? I was going to give her a call to arrange another session but I can't find her number anywhere."

"No, I don't think so, what was her name again?"

"Roth, Dr Alexandra Roth" replied Seth.

"Roth, Roth" pondered Lily for a moment "no, sorry, never heard of her. Why don't you just go down to her office and make an appointment?"

"I know this is going to sound really stupid but I can't remember where her office is!" and he wasn't going to admit to having been to her apartment but couldn't remember where that was either.

"You can't remember where her office is even though you where there the other week? Ha ha ha" Lily found that hilarious "Seth, you're one in a million, don't worry, it'll come back to you sooner or later."

"I suppose so; it's just frustrating though because it's on the tip of my tongue."

"Maybe I'll be on the tip of your tongue later" Lily blushed as she didn't usually speak like that in the confines of her office.

"Lily! That's not like you" gasped Seth in mock shock "Although last night . . . ."

"Oh I know, what can I say, I'm just a naughty girl I suppose" she laughed "Who needs a spanking?" Seth finished her thought

"Promises, promises, great minds think alike" she replied and they both laughed together before Seth heard a knock at Lilys' office door through the phone "Oh no, I'm sorry Seth, I have to go, I've got yet another meeting I have to attend."

"It's ok darling, I'll call you later and we'll get together and celebrate alone tonight, we can go out with Gus and Natalie when all the deals are sorted out."

"That sounds great, I'll see you later, bye" Lily blew him a kiss down the line

"I can't wait, bye" they both hung up and Seth sighed with pleasure at the rediscovering of everything that was good in his life in such a short space of time. Was this what they called a whirlwind romance?

Chapter 18

ONE YEAR LATER

The year was incredibly kind to Seth and Lily. The success of 'Suffering Innocence' was phenomenal, greater even than either Seth or Gus had anticipated; the book topped best seller lists on both sides of the Atlantic and was translated into dozens of languages despite its' explicit, horrific, graphic and blasphemic nature or, as Gus would have it, because of such things.

The movie, of the same name, was already being discussed as the hot ticket for all the award nominations later in the year. Box office records were considered to be under threat, the western world in particular had seemed to have been bewitched by the intoxication of the storyline. Even the top actors and actresses of the day, so often dismissive of roles in such dark movies, had been vying for inclusion.

Seth Caines' star wasn't just on the rise, it was at its' zenith. Cynics and critics alike the world over had slammed his book and subsequent movies' content, all of which just whetted the publics insatiable desire for all things Seth Caine-related, his entire back catalogue had to be reprinted twice to keep up with demand and original copies approaching their twentieth anniversary were now changing hands for thousands of dollars over the internet. His face was being plastered across magazine covers and newspapers and much extra rainforest was destroyed in order to maintain the column inches of gossip written about him, slaking the thirst of the public for Seth. Ex brief girlfriends and one night stands had their flirtatious moment in the spotlight to dish their sordid, grubby little stories of sex and salaciousness. Some were just blatant lies, most however were very factual.

None of this distracted from the industry that was Seth Caine, if anything it inflamed it and stoked the flames higher.

Surprisingly, Lily was unaffected by all of the gossip and rumour and restrictions on their freedom, their relationship had in fact grown stronger still. The only truly upsetting times came when a woman in her late twenties claimed that her two year old son was fathered by Seth. He was adamant that he hadn't even met her let alone slept with her. The most sickening part of the claims as far as Lily was concerned was that this bitch had told the papers that she had called her son Jack in honour of Seth and Lilys' son. As it turned out, the woman had indeed created a tissue of lies and as Seth had said all along, they had never even met before.

Seth wanted to sue her; giving any money they received to charity, just in order to set down a precedent to stop future bandwagon jumpers. Lily talked him out of it, as hurt as she was by the whole scandal, she just wanted it over. Seth let it drop but rumours of his initial plans to sue leaked out, that was enough it seemed to deter any future leeches.

There were the occasional fans who camped out near their home which meant they had to buy a new house but they had been thinking of making a fresh start with a new home anyway. They now had the finance to live where they wanted but they had both always loved the city and Lily still loved her career so they just got a larger place on the outskirts instead. A much bigger house; surrounded by their own grounds and edged with high fences and good security.

All of this just meant that whenever Lily wasn't working and Seth wasn't promoting his book and the movie, they endeavoured to spend as much *quality* time together as possible. Following the paternity scandal, Seth promised Lily that once the furore over 'Suffering Innocence' had eventually burnt itself out; he would retire from writing and public appearances completely. Then, when she was ready, they could become reclusive millionaires, relaxing in luxurious but anonymous style, hand in hand, together.

Lily still continued to work even though financially she didn't have to anymore. She liked the normality of day to day life, she looked forward to the day that they could take an early retirement and enjoy each other of course but in the meantime she still enjoyed her work and felt too young to 'retire', she hadn't felt so young and vibrant in years.

Severin Frost had even been the model patient, up until the last couple of weeks that is, where his mood started to become more than a little unpredictable.

Nine months earlier, the Institutes senior consultant role had been taken up by a harsh and cold man in his late fifties, Dr Gunn. However, almost immediately and very mysteriously, he met a bloody and tragic death just a week later when he was found in his bathtub with his throat slit. No-one was ever brought to justice over the murder and so Lily had had to continue in her busy dual role for the time being at least. Otherwise, life was wonderful, if a little hectic at times for the Caines'.

Currently, Lily was attending a large and very important psychiatry conference on the other side of the country and would be there all weekend. Seth was in between promotional engagements and rattling around their new home all alone. He loved the house and though it was indeed huge, he'd never realised just how huge until he was alone in it. It didn't normally affect him day to day while Lily was at work but now she was away for the weekend he felt lost in there without her.

This was the first time that they would sleep apart over night since they got back together and he felt so miserable. She'd called him the minute that she arrived at her hotel and they talked for an hour which seemed like seconds. Less than an hour later and he'd called her back just to hear her voice again, unfortunately she had had to go and meet up with colleagues shortly after so she said she would call again tomorrow, Seth would count the hours until then.

He knew he would go insane waiting for the phone to ring and he knew he couldn't take it much longer so he rang Karl. Their brief feud a year earlier had been just that, very brief. Karl had been delighted for his old friend, along with Gus he had always been there for Seth. Whereas Gus was mainly business, Karl was strictly his social partner. He'd always told Seth he would get back on his feet and reclaim his literary place among the best, though neither of them had expected Seths' meteoric re-emergence in such a dramatic fashion.

"Karl, it's Seth, what're you up to?"

"Hey Vlad, not a lot, why what can I do for you?"

"Well, as you would say, it's Saturday night and you know what that means"
Seth laughed as he said it.

"Oh I see, Lilys' out of town, you're bored coz you haven't got a playmate so you thought you'd ring dependable old Karl, is that it?" Karl was laughing under his breath as he spoke

"Piss off! I was only out with you last month!" Seth knew Karl was only joking but they always enjoyed a bit of banter.

"Yeah I know, so, what do you wanna do?"

"To be honest, nothing fancy, just a few beers in the Dragon if you're up for it? I ain't been in there for ages" it had been at least six months since Seths' last excursion to his favourite watering hole.

"Fancy? Whenever have we ever done anything fucking fancy!! The Dragon is fine by me; meet you there around 9:30 ok?"

"Excellent, see you later mate." They hung up and Seth went to get ready, he had a bit more spring in his step now, at least this would take his mind off how much he was pining for Lily, this would be a good night he felt.

Shortly after 9:30 Seth arrived via a taxi at the Dragon, one or two heads turned as he arrived, he was genuinely someone to recognise now. He stopped outside and lit a cigarette, taking in the night air. As much as he loved his new life and lifestyle he also knew that this is where he belonged, no matter where he lived or however much money he earned, these were the people and surroundings that he felt comfortable with, this was his tribe. What's more, these were not the sort of people to get bowled over with celebrity bullshit, no matter who you were.

Lily was much the same, despite her profession and expensive business suits, deep down she was a true rock chick in jeans and boots, laughing and joking with friends with a drink in her hand in a rock bar or club, just waiting to gyrate and thrash around on a dance floor, always much to Seths' delight as he watched her move and knew he would soon be taking her home. She loved to dance and he loved to watch her, yet another thing he loved about her.

As he smoked and surveyed the scene, he heard a tap at the window from inside and turned around. It was Karl waiting for him, Seth pointed towards the bar and mimed a drink, Karl rolled his eyes, nodded and went to the bar for him while Seth finished his smoke and smiled to himself; it felt so good to be back.

"Alright buddy?" Seth said as he entered and found Karl

"Yeah, great, you?" said Karl as he handed a drink to him

"I am now" replied Seth as he took a long steady gulp from his beer

"So, how's fame treating you these days? Smiled Karl

"I saw you last month remember, nothing different from then"

"I take it you're pissed off now Lily ain't there?"

"Must admit it pal, it's killing me, being without her" Seth sighed

"Aw, shame!" mocked Karl with a laugh

After the initial question and answer session about how the book and movie were doing and how Karl was doing, they settled into their tried and trusted staple conversations about music and other movies, upcoming concerts and women. Many beers later and they moved onto their usual vodka and limes', the natural order of things seemed to be in place.

As they chatted and laughed, the conversation was brought to a halt as a beautiful young red-head walked up to them. Seth and Karl both stopped talking and turned to face her simultaneously. She was stunning, wearing a skin-tight red and black pvc dress with matching boots, tribal tattoos adorned her bare shoulders and a very cute looking nose ring completed the look, then she spoke.

"Excuse me, aren't you Seth Caine?"

"Er, yes I am" he smiled

"Hi, I'm Kelly, I was wondering if I could have your autograph" she said, holding out a pen and piece of paper.

"Of course you can; my pleasure." Seths' smile broadened into a grin, especially when he glanced at Karl and saw him roll his eyes. Seth signed the paper and gave it back to the early twenty-something.

"Thanks" she said as she smiled ever so sweetly "just to let you know, if you want to, later on why don't you come over and have a drink with me and my friend Denise" Kelly pointed over to where her similarly pvc-clad and equally delicious looking friend sat at a table watching them, Denise waved and Seth and Karl responded likewise.

"That's very kind of you Kelly but I don't know how much longer we'll be in here" Seth could sense Karl throwing visual daggers at him.

"Oh ok, but if we don't see you later here's my phone number, maybe we could get together another time?" ever more sweetly she smiled again and walked back over to her friend. Seth and Karl couldn't help but be transfixed by her bottom tightly wrapped in the pvc as she wiggled her way back across the room.

"Oh my God" exclaimed Karl "I don't believe that"

"I know, quite something wasn't she?" replied Seth pocketing her phone number though purely not to offend her.

"No, I mean oh my God, you turned her down!"

"I'm married you prick!"

"You've always been married, it's never stopped you before" Karl said but before Seth could protest "I know, I know, things are different now. It's just difficult to see something like that walk away that's all and before you get all sentimental, I also know how much happier you are now!"

They both stood looking around the bar, occasionally they would glance over at Denise and Kelly, to find them staring back. Seth had no intention of following up on her advances and even less intention of actually calling her. One or two heads turned towards them in curiosity when they noticed Seth being asked for an autograph or when someone else recognised him, whispers and nudges spread around the room but no-one bothered them as they drank.

"Didn't she remind you of anyone?" Karl said a little later

"Who? Kelly?"

"Yeah, beautiful red-head, coming up to you in here?" Karl leered

"Oh yeah, Alex, how could I forget!"

"She was fuckin incredible" Karl shook his head at the thought of Alex "whatever happened to her? You never told me."

"Well, after that night that I told you about, through some bizarre chain of events that I really don't understand to this day, she became my therapist, well sort of. She was brilliant, er, I think!"

"You think?"

"Well yeah, but it's difficult to judge, the session was good even though she didn't say that much. I just sort of unloaded all my shit for ages and she talked for a while about how I'd done the right thing and how I should learn to embrace my dreams."

"Wish I could embrace her in my dreams" interjected Karl

"Just after that, I had 'Suffering Innocence' and there were no more bad dreams so I suppose she unblocked something or other and did a brilliant job."

"Whatever it cost you Seth, it was worth every penny considering how things have gone since then."

"True but that's another thing, I tried to see her again, professionally but I couldn't remember where her office was or her apartment or even her phone number or anything. I don't think she's been in here since that night either. So I didn't even pay for the time I had with her, I had the session and she walked me out, payment was never mentioned at all. She did say that I'd see her again though but that was over a year ago now."

"It's ok, maybe the therapy was free in response to your services rendered at her apartment" laughed Karl

"In that case I owe her a fuckin fortune!" they both laughed and then continued to drink into the early hours of the morning, it was definitely just like the good old days and just what they both needed.

They left the bar and staggered along the street until they managed to hail a taxi, Seth insisted on dropping Karl off at home despite the fact that they now lived on opposite sides of the city, he also insisted on paying as he could afford to do such things now. Secretly, even though he was very drunk, Seth didn't want to go home to his big empty house because he knew he would be alone. Half way to Karls' place he told their driver to turn around and insisted that Karl stayed at his house so they could continue drinking. Karl agreed, he didn't want the night to end either, the taxi turned around and they sped off.

However, once they stumbled into Seths' home, Karl collapsed on the couch and wasn't in any fit state to continue the session. Seth threw a blanket over his friend and, still smiling to himself at his drunken buddy, made his way up to his bed to sleep off the night, at least he wouldn't be alone in his house now.

CHAPTER 19

A few hours later Seth opened his eyes as he felt an aching in his back and shoulders and a stirring in his loins. He looked up and realised immediately that he was hanging from the ceiling! He was chained at the wrists and in turn a further chain suspended him from a large and sturdy wooden beam. It seemed as though, because he had opened his eyes to this scenario, the pain in his wrists, shoulders and back suddenly became excruciating. His head was tilted back and he swung freely, his hands were pale and going numb from the tightness of the chain cutting off the blood supply to them. Very strangely, he felt extreme pain and extreme pleasure at the same time at the same levels, a yin & yang of agony and ecstasy. Seth tilted his head forwards and down, between his outstretched arms in order to see what caused the amazing stirring that he also felt.

On inspection he realised that he hung there completely naked and bizarrely he was being fellated by a nun!! She was kneeling on the floor of a room that he didn't recognise with his member in her hand as she pleasured him with her mouth.

"What the . . . who the fuck are you?" he managed to ask, despite his shock and confusion.

"Don't you know me Seth? That hurts my feelings after all we shared and now you don't even remember my touch." She spoke without lifting her head as she continued to work her magic on his cock.

"I . . . . I don't know you, what's your name?" his vulnerable position was starting to concern him greatly.

"I am Meridiana" still she continued her task

"I have no idea who you are!" he gasped

She ceased her incredible manipulations of him and got to her feet; she lifted her hand and wiped her mouth, all the while with her head bowed.

"I am Meridiana" she said again as she stood in front of Seths' hanging body with her head still down, eyes gazing at the floor "I lived in the Auvergne region of France. In the 10th Century I seduced a young man named Gerbert d'Aurillac. I promised him knowledge, magick, prosperity and success if he stayed loyal to me and that he duly did, that was until he drunkenly fucked a local whore, I forgave him however. In time and with my help he ascended through the ranks to become a Cardinal and then eventually Pope, he became Pope Sylvester II. He liked me dressed as a nun and I thought that you might too." She giggled to herself

"But what the fuck are you telling me all this for? What's that got to do with me?" Seth yelled at her.

"Hush my dear Seth" she gently grazed her long sharp nails down his hanging torso, groin and thighs. "You simply know me by another name" finally she lifted her face to his view.

""Alex!!" he exclaimed in amazement.

"Yes, to you I am Alex or Dr Roth." She smiled "But my real name is Meridiana, I have used many, many names throughout the ages."

Seth was having great difficulty taking all this information in let alone his predicament of hanging naked from a beam in a place that he didn't know! Questions filled his already crowded and jumbled mind.

"10th Century? You said 10th Century, right? But that's a thousand years ago!"

"Oh well done Seth!" she laughed in a mocking tone, she then quickly slipped out of her nuns' habit and let it drop to the floor before she twirled around on the spot for his viewing pleasure, looking as erotically stunning as she had done at her apartment, though now she was naked and gleaming with sweat which dripped off her breasts invitingly. "Don't you think I look wonderful for my age? I see you are filled with curiosity and intrigue my darling"

There was a deep and very ominous growl from the back of the darkened room, Seth felt as if he was hanging in a spotlight, as if on show for everyone to gaze at and mock. He was suddenly even more uncomfortable, if that were possible and his vulnerability was incalculable.

"Ah, someone is here to talk with you and maybe we can answer some of your questions my love, if you're a good boy" she stroked his now distracted and flagging cock and kissed it in her twisted playful manner "allow me to introduce you to his black majesty, Lord Asmodeus"

With her words and the mention of his name, a huge ball of fire and black smoke erupted thirty feet from where Seth hung, almost scorching his naked flesh, such was the extreme heat and intensity. As the fire raged a figure of massive proportions stepped through it. Seth squinted to see amidst the blaze and the monstrous figure approached him.

It was three headed, one of a bull, a second was the head of a ram and in the centre a man, thick black hair with a long braid hanging down from the human head. The creature looked like some bizarre medical experiment or a guardian monster from Greek legend. All three heads looked fierce and moved independently of each other as they surveyed Seth whose already fading erection was completely lost through fear.

Meridianas' beautiful eyes lit up and her nostrils flared as if inflamed by this huge beasts' presence and she bowed her head respectfully. Asmodeus was muscular, very muscular and his powerful legs, like the hind legs of a giant stag, were covered in coarse, thick red hair and culminated in hooves. Those legs brought him over, ever closer to Seth. He stopped a few feet from where Seth hung, his heads looking the author up and down all at the same time before the central human face stared down, deep into Seths' eyes. He was hanging around three feet off the ground, yet still the beast that was Lord Asmodeus looked down at him from it's massive height.

"So" his voice rumbled like thunder "You are Seth Caine"

"Er . . . yes . . . er, sir" he had absolutely no idea how to address someone or something like this but such fear would bring out anybody's' respectful side.

"I will be honest with you Caine, I do not appreciate being asked to perform such menial tasks as this, I have underlings to do my bidding, yet here I am."

"W-what do you want with me?" stammered Seth

"I have your new project, your next task to perform; this one however is for *our* benefit, not yours'"

"What task? I don't know what you're talking about."

"It's quite simple Caine, you performed very well in the first part of our pact and so I am here to give you your next orders."

"But I don't understand what you're talking about, what pact?"

Asmodeus sighed his frustration which sounded more like a storm approaching from the horizon and he looked at Meridiana for clarification and gestured for her to explain, seemingly Asmodeus was already losing patience with his subject and his resentment at having to do an 'underlings' errand was clear to see.

"Have you forgotten your conversations with Mammon and Astaroth?" she asked of Seth.

"I remember Mammon and Angelique" he was trying to help and mentally scanning everything he could for fear of the powerful and temperamental beast now glaring at him.

"And what about Astaroth? Don't you remember him?" grunted Asmodeus

"No, I'm sorry, truly I am" Seth whimpered

"Think Seth, think." Meridiana urged

"After seeing Mammon and Angelique" he began slowly "I went to see Dr Roth, I mean you! That night I did have some sort of dream I think but it's really vague, when I woke up I had a splitting headache but when I wrote it seemed to ease. That was when I wrote my new book and everything changed. I haven't had a dream since then" Seth hesitated and looked at the beauty and beast standing watching him dangling like a marionette, a yard from the stone floor "I take it that this is another dream or visitation?"

"Yes Seth" Meridiana was almost tender as she spoke as if taking pity on him "you must concentrate my love and think of that clouded and vague dream, your life depends on it."

Asmodeus grunted again in agreement at the last and turned his huge back on them as they talked, Seth tried to think deeply and closed his eyes which also helped to block out the monstrous vision that stood impatiently before him.

"Concentrate Seth, Richelle came to you, you enjoyed her . . . do you remember that?" Meridiana led his thoughts and he followed as if following a trail of breadcrumbs, though he wasn't being led out of the enchanted forest, he was being led back to the wicked witches' house.

"I see Richelle!" he yelped in triumph at his recollection

"Yes my dear, now go on, further into the dream" she stroked his thigh in encouragement, this coupled with thoughts of his time with the handmaiden caused his erection to stir back into life, at which she smiled lasciviously and licked her lips.

"I see a man, a very big man, maybe a warrior, with a sword and shaven head, I see a snake and a crown." The mists gradually cleared from his mind as if a light breeze blew the fogs away.

"Keep going darling; that is my Lord Astaroth" Meridiana prompted

"I can see that we talked but . . . . I don't know what he's saying, I don't know what we are talking about" Seth gasped in frustration as he lost the image and hung panting for breath from the chain.

"You did well Seth" she said as she patted his thigh in reassurance

"Enough!!" Asmodeus spun around and stamped his mighty hoof on the ground which cracked under the massive impact.

"You made a pact with us" Meridiana whispered to jog his memory again, she had seen Asmodeus' wrath before, it was always better to ease it rather than inflame.

"I don't know what you're talking about!" yelled Seth in frustration "Please just tell me what I'm supposed to have agreed to" he started to sob.

"We gave you the book which you wrote, in turn this brought you the success that you craved and also it brought your wench back to you" Asmodeus said in a low but surprisingly calm rumble as he tried to hold back his all-consuming rage "in return you agreed to write a special book for us, that was the pact."

"No, I wrote the book, not you" Seth protested "that's what I do! I woke up with a great idea and wrote it down, simple as that" his protests were unwise.

Asmodeus' eyes widened, if Astaroth had been a warrior then this was a whole other kind of war monster, a Warlord indeed. His temper was legendary even in the deepest, darkest pits of hell; one of the most unholy abominations ever issued forth from the fires, even his own peers feared him. His impossibly huge and destructive fists clenched as that temper rose. Meridiana lifted her hand to calm him and he spun around again in rage, trying to hold himself back as he had been asked to do, he moved to one side, allowing her to speak.

"Seth, you made a pact, you *must* fulfil your side of the bargain" she implored.

"What? You're saying that I made some sort of deal with the devil? I don't believe you, I wouldn't be so naïve as to do something so stupid"

"That's exactly what we're saying and that's exactly what you did"

"Why the fuck would I?" he shouted

"Because you craved your success of the past, because you wanted your woman back and because you wanted everything that you'd lost." Meridiana spoke softly but then more sternly "we came to you when you needed us, we gave you back everything that you'd lost as we said we would, there is a price for everything in your world, now you have to pay that price."

"No!" Seth was defiant "this is a dream, at some point I'm going to wake up and you two will be gone. I haven't dreamt in over a year and I've been fine, in fact I've been better than fine, I've been fantastic. My wife came back to me *before* the book came out and I came up with that storyline, not you *people*"

A rumble seemed to come from the bowels of the Earth beneath him; screams of discontent filled the air and built into a strong breeze which swirled around the room causing Seth to swing to and fro from the beam. The screams physical state also caused the hair on the beast that was Asmodeus to move, he stood stock still now in what was becoming a rising gale of howls and pain. Meridiana stood still also but with more difficulty as she was buffeted by the increasing strength of the blackened winds of hate and suffering that gathered. She gazed at Seth and shook her head at his stubbornness to open his eyes to reality.

"Alex" he yelled to her over the building din of despair, using the name that he knew her by "you cured my nightmares, I thank you for that but this is just a lapse, it's all in my imagination, I cannot agree to something that isn't real"

"Seth, listen to us" she implored again

"No, I'm drunk and in bed asleep, that is the reality, you could say I agreed to anything" he swung more wildly from the chains as the screaming winds increased in velocity and anger "Alex, you told me to stay strong and embrace my dreams, I am strong and now I'm taking control, I deny everything you are both saying" Seths' defiance and bravery surprised even he.

"So, you are refusing to honour the pact?" Asmodeus bellowed over his shoulder as he turned back with a seemingly curious and malevolent smile on his human face while the ram and bull heads were contorted by scowls.

"Yes, I'm refusing the pact, no deal" Seths' misplaced bravery swelled again

"Seth, I think you should reconsider" Meridiana shook her head in disappointment as she yelled, imploring him to change his mind.

"No, there's nothing to reconsider"

"In that case" Asmodeus looked to his companion as he sneered his words to Seth "Goodbye Caine, this is not the end however, this is simply the beginning of the end for you, I hope you enjoyed your life, take time to enjoy what little is left. And fear not, you will meet me again one day, and on that day I will not be restrained or restricted."

"Goodbye Seth, for now, I'm sorry" she looked disappointed as they both walked to the back of the room and into the ball of fire where it still raged. As they entered the inferno, the demonic howls and wind quickly faded to nothing, once they had been consumed by the flame it imploded on itself and dispersed. The chain holding Seth snapped instantly, he dropped like a boulder and as he hit the floor he bounced and realised he was at the side of his bed.

Seth looked around his room, he felt weary, his arms, back and wrists hurt and he felt curiously warm. He looked around the room again and saw nothing and no-one. He looked out of the window at his new gardens, in the distance he could see a gardener working on his neighbours' property, it must be mid-morning he thought mundanely to himself. Seth quickly dressed then ran downstairs and saw Karl asleep on the couch; Seth kicked the furniture and shouted "Morning!" loud enough to be heard as he walked past and into the kitchen to make the coffee.

He returned with two mugs of coffee and a lit cigarette dangling from his mouth. He put one on the table in front of Karl and sat in his armchair, smoking.

"She'll kill you"

"What?" replied Seth, furrowing his brow, looking as if he were miles away.

"Lily, she'll kill you when she knows that you've been smoking in here."

"Oh, yeah, probably"

"What's up with you?" Karl asked

"I had a dream last night"

"Really? I was hoping to have a dream about those two girls in the Dragon last night" Karl lecherously smiled and laughed to himself.

"No, like I used to do, you know, with the nightmares, remember?"

"Oh yeah, I'd forgotten about those"

"I hadn't!" Seth grunted

"Cheer up buddy, gives you a good reason to try to look up that shrink again" Karl laughed again to himself as he stretched on the couch.

"She was in it!"

"Really, anything good happen?" suddenly Karl was much more alert.

"Well, yes, but that's not what's on my mind." Seth was clearly troubled

"Ok, what is on your mind then?"

"Alex, who called herself Meridiana, and this demon lord told me that I'd made some sort of pact or deal to get my success back." Seth shook his head and rubbed his eyes as he sighed to himself.

"And did you, make a pact I mean?"

"That's just it, I don't really remember it, after I had therapy with Alex, who's now claiming to be over a thousand years old!" they both raised their eyebrows questioningly as Seth continued "I had this dream, normally I remember the bad dreams but that one was really hazy and they said that's when I made this pact with them."

"So she's one of them now? Seth, she's a girl who picked you up and then coincidentally becomes your therapist, once!" Karl was shaking his head at the absurd fantasy that Seth seemed to be building in his head "I mean, who ever heard of a Therapy Demon?"

They both laughed a little, the more Seth thought about it, the more ridiculous it sounded, his one night stand, his therapist was now in league with dark forces and out to trap him? He hadn't seen her in over a year, it was just a dream, his subconscious, his twisted imagination stimulated into action from his work, it must be, surely?

"I know, it's frustrating though, all this time without the night terrors and now this!" Seth sighed to himself again.

"Seth, you fucked her buddy, did she seem different or anything? I assume you would've mentioned it if she'd had a forked tail ha ha" Karl continued

"Different yes, but only in a fucking great way!" Seth replied and they both laughed

"It might be coz you're on your own?"

"How d'ya mean?" asked Seth

"Think about it, this is the first night you've slept without Lily since you got back together. Now you're slipping back into nightmares that you only had when you were apart, it might just be that you're missing her" Karls' words immediately started to make sense, that must be it!

"Hey, I never thought of it like that, I bet you're right, thanks bud" Seth seemed immediately relieved, it was all so simple now.

"So, in this dream, what did you do, about the pact I mean?"

"I refused, they said I'd agreed to write a special book for them or something and I said no"

"And?"

"And they left, that's when I woke up"

"They just left?" Karl seemed surprised.

"Yeah, they weren't happy and they made some threats but . . . they left and I woke up on the floor at the side of the bed" thinking about it logically now, Seth seemed surprised too.

"Hmm, maybe that's where the phrase 'facing your demons' comes from? I mean, you've done it literally and lived to tell the tale"

"True" Seth smiled, seeming rather pleased with himself for doing just that "what the fuck are you doing here anyway?" he said, changing the subject.

"You invited me!"

"Did I? Oh" Seths' memory of the night before the nightmare was sketchy to say the least.

"I'll get a taxi in a minute, I need my own bed." Karl sipped at his coffee "when does Lily get back?"

"Tomorrow morning, thank God"

"Aww sweet" Karl laughed

"Piss off, I ain't gonna see her til tomorrow night though, I've got another book signing all day but she should be here when I get back" Seth smiled again at the thought of coming home to Lily and wished he could get out of his personal appearance to be there for her to come home to, sadly the signing session had been organised weeks ago.

"Where's it at, this book signing?"

"Simmons & Stanley in the city centre, I'm just thankful that it ain't out of town this time!" Seth was tired of travelling and just wanted to be at home all day with Lily.

"Simmons & Stanley eh?" Karl pondered

"Yeah, you coming down?"

"No chance, I just know to avoid that side of town!" joked Karl.

Chapter 20

Monday morning at Simmons & Stanley books, crowds snaked around the block for a brief audience with their hero, the great and infamous Seth Caine. People of all ages came out to see him, which always surprised Seth, he understood that it was prominently 20-30 year olds who bought his books but then as Gus often reminded him, there were people of that age group twenty years ago when he started and they remained as fans of his work to this day. His catchment group was just that much bigger now; the graphic horror and sexual gratuity in his novels hadn't put off his older readers at all, which delighted him.

Even as he sat in the store signing countless autographs, shaking endless amounts of hands and posing for so many photographs, he thought of Lily. She would be on her way home about now, he pondered as he checked his watch, he so wished that he could be there waiting to greet her as she arrived, he longed for them both to fall into each others arms. He was distracted occasionally and understandably when a girl or woman, again of surprisingly varied age ranges, asked him to sign his name on their breasts or thigh. He'd always thought it was only rock stars that got those sorts of fans but he was always happy to oblige. It was always a pleasant distraction from his pining but never anything more.

Gus accompanied Seth to the event as he usually did and he stood to one side talking to the store manager, no doubt about money or business but Seth could practically see the cash signs lighting up in Gus' eyes, not such a bad trait in an agent he'd always thought.

Late morning and Seth was allowed a short break to stretch his legs and grab a coffee, he decided to take his drink, supplied by the store, and slip out of the back way for some alone time. He stood in the alley behind the bookstore so he could have a cigarette and some peace and quiet. He

143

thought more about Lily but his thoughts were clouded by his nightmare relapse on Saturday night. Sunday night had been featureless and he'd slept very well but the previous nights dream was starting to bother him greatly.

Questions poured through his aching mind again. Did he in fact make some sort of deal or pact? Did 'they' actually give him the story? He still couldn't remember how he'd come up with it in the first place. Could Alex, or Meridiana as she called herself, really have been around since the 10th Century? He'd remembered Astaroth as she guided him but that could have been some sort of suggestive mind trick, then again, maybe she was telling the truth and he had made a pact? One thing was for sure, he never wanted to meet Asmodeus again! He felt like he was trapped in a cross between 'Alice In Wonderland' and a twisted black version of 'A Christmas Carol', with visitations from otherworldly beings giving him messages and threats. It was all way too bizarre.

"You ok Seth?" Gus asked as he appeared at the back door of the bookstore.

"Yeah, fine thanks, just got a few things on my mind that's all"

"When you're ready buddy, the crowd's getting impatient" smiled Gus.

"No problem, I'll just finish these and I'll be right in" Seth held up his coffee and cigarette.

Gus nodded and went back in to reassure the manager that Seth wouldn't be long and Seth finished his cigarette and flicked the butt into a puddle, he drained his coffee cup and returned to duty, putting on his 'show' face as he entered again.

Seth continued to sign, smile and press the flesh of his disciples for a few more hours as he had done many, many times before and nothing seemed out of the ordinary apart from the occasional body part to sign but even that was becoming mundane. He continued right through lunch because, as the manager had said, that would be a busy time as people would come in on their breaks from work. Over and over he asked "What's your name?" or "Where're you from?" or "Who should I make it out to?" until the routine day was shattered when he asked "What's your name?" without looking up properly and got the response

"Angelique"

He stopped immediately, the name was unusual and unforgettable but it was the voice that uttered the word that was unmistakable and caused him to freeze. He slowly raised his head and there she stood. A lot of his younger fans sported the 'Goth' look so she didn't stand out from the crowd too much which was probably just what she wanted. She blended in well with the masses but if only they knew what she really was, then again, Seth wasn't quite sure what she was himself.

She wore a long black hooded cloak, beautifully made from velvet, a similarly exquisitely-styled dress underneath of the same material, flaunting her perfectly smooth and milky-white cleavage and elbow-length evening gloves. Cherry red lips and those stunning purple eyes, which to on-lookers must've seemed like contact lenses but Seth was convinced they were real. To the keen-eyed she did look different but they couldn't quite put their finger on it, she was simply too beautiful to be human! Her flesh seemed so pale and flawless under the fluorescent store lights, especially so to Seth as she wasn't having blood poured over her in his bathtub!

"A-Angelique, h-hello," he replied in a stammered whisper of shock.

"Seth, we meet again my darling. I decided against bringing Richelle with me this time for fear of her face drawing too much attention to my presence, I'm sure you understand."

Seth simply nodded his understanding in his bewildered state

"You do remember Richelle, I take it? And of course, fucking Richelle?"

How could he not remember Richelle, and of course fucking her? It had now turned out to be a pivotal moment in his life, the night that Astaroth came, possibly, though he was still unsure, with the pact that may have changed his life.

"My dear Seth, cat got your tongue?" she said playfully

"Er no, I'm . . . er . . . just wondering, what're you doing here?" he mumbled as he stared at her, trying to figure out if he was imagining all this, had he fallen asleep? Surely not in a bookstore surrounded by fans.

"I see you're doing very well for yourself Seth" Angelique gazed around the store at the throngs of people behind her and queuing out into the street "very well indeed, I'm impressed"

"Thank you" he half smiled

"Yes Seth, thank you, you *should* be thanking us, for it is us who are responsible for all of this."

Seth stayed silent and sheepish as he looked at her, convinced that she was actually living and breathing right in front of him and not just in one of his nightmare visions. He looked around at the other people in line behind her and noticed they were trying to look around her at him; she was definitely physically there as opposed to some bizarre hallucination.

"W-what do you want?" he asked as he scanned the room, dreadfully expecting to see Mammon about to put in another appearance too.

145

"Don't worry Seth, I have come alone" she said as if reading his thoughts "if others had come as they wanted to, they would've laid waste to this place and everyone in it, such is their wrath directed at you."

Her playful manner had gone and her expression grew stern and forceful, her purple eyes darkened and narrowed, Seth immediately felt a chill run down his spine as her gaze bore into him. As beautiful and amazing as she looked, she now seemed terrifying to behold, power and malevolence coursed through her and her nostrils flared as her lips pouted, a gorgeous psychopath from the underworld, literally.

"You must make good on your promise Seth, you must fulfil your side of the pact."

"B-but"

"No buts Seth, you made a bargain, we have delivered on our promise, you live evidence of this every day of your life. However, we can take all of it away and so much more, just as quickly as we gave it all to you. Dire consequences will befall you if you continue in your denial of us and your pact with Astaroth. You do not have a choice in this, one way or another you will do as we ask, it's just a matter of time. It would be far easier for you if you would just comply and accept your fate."

Her expression eased, the light came back to her eyes and the beast left the beauty. From being petrified to enchanted again, Seth was sat writhing in inner turmoil, he seemed in a never ending spiral of emotion at their varying visitations, one moment an elixir the next it was poison. He didn't know what to say or even how to respond.

"This day I am merely a messenger" she continued "and I shall leave you now but be forewarned my darling, honour your debt."

With that, she turned briskly on her heel and left the store, Seth sat bewitched by her beauty yet again but in no small part, frightened at her words and more than ominous tone. There was a coldness to chill even the hottest of blood in the way she spoke and the not-so-subtle threats, Gus came over.

"Who the hell was that?" he exclaimed

Gus' confirmation of Angeliques' presence meant that Seth was immediately relieved that she was no longer just a figment of his imagination, proof that he wasn't going insane but also, on the other side of that twisted coin, was the reality that she was physically real. And if Angelique was physically real, did that mean that all his other visitors were real too? Mammon and Astaroth as physical beings, able to do him harm,

Asmodeus in flesh and blood? The thought chilled Seth further and he tried to avoid the subject.

"Oh, er . . . nobody, just a fan" he said

"How'd you piss her off?"

"I didn't"

"She looked pretty pissed to me bud, she was gorgeous but Christ, I wouldn't want to get on the wrong side of her!" Gus shook his head at the prospect. "You know how it is" Seth tried to laugh it all off, unconvincingly "can't please everyone all the time, er, next?"

The next fan came up and Seth continued to sign, pose and smile but not surprisingly he couldn't get Angelique out of his head, this was all becoming way too real. A year of happiness and totally dream-free, now all this in such a short space of time, what the hell had he done to deserve it all? He composed himself long enough to complete the signing session and then the doors were finally closed. He asked an assistant for another coffee and took it outside to his alleyway retreat. He lit another cigarette and wished the coffee contained something much stronger to calm his nerves.

Seth stood with his back against the wall blowing plumes of smoke into the air as dusk started to take hold of the city. His hands had just about stopped shaking when a mans' voice spoke to him from the shadows.

"Mr Caine?"

"Er, yes" he sighed as he peered into the darkening alley

"I have come to ask you to desist from your work"

"Desist from my work? What the fuck are you talking about?"

"The books you write are anti-christian in doctrine; they are blasphemous, heretical and gratuitous in both violence and sexual promiscuity. You must be stopped from this awful work that you do"

"Just fuck off will you, I'm having a really bad day" Seth was in no mood for lectures and his temper was already bubbling to the surface.

"Mr Caine, I am asking you to stop with your vile works which I feel offend millions of people the world over." The sinister figure stepped out of the shadows and stood face to face with Seth.

"Millions of people? Well, my books sell to other people in the same quantities! Just who the fuck do you people think you are? There is a demand for my *vile works* you know; didn't you see the crowds here today?"

"Many people in this world are misguided Mr Caine and you are helping to misguide them with your filth."

"Who the hell are you anyway?" sighed Seth in frustration

"I am Father Seymour Duncan and I have been chosen and sent by angels to stop you" the priest said with a straight and serious face.

Seth wanted to laugh at him but he was too tired and irritable to get involved with a local religious freak who heard 'angels' talking to him, besides which, his own otherworldly experiences were making such things less ridiculous or outlandish.

"Well Seymour, I think you should leave now, you've made you're point but as I said, I've had a bitch of a day and I've got a lot on my mind, so I think it'd be best for us both if you left." Seth rubbed his eyes as they stung in his exhaustion.

"Mr Caine, please don't try to threaten me, I really feel that . . . ."

"Look!" Seth cut the priest short as his patience snapped "if you don't fuck off out of my life and leave me alone as I so nicely suggested, I'm going to put you're face through that wall, we'll see then if your angels can stop me"

"You do not frighten me Mr Caine, I have encountered far more intimidating creatures than you, just ask your wife, Lily." Seymour stood impassive and unmoved by the threat of violence.

"What did you say?" Seth dropped his cigarette and clenched his fist at the priests' mention of her name.

"I know your wife Mr Caine, a very professional lady, I'm sure you wouldn't want to see her upset would you?"

"Are you trying to threaten *me* now?" Seth sneered through gritted teeth as he squared up to the priest.

"You're wife will come to no harm, I assure you but I must insist that you write no more of your books. In fact I feel you should withhold your services in promoting your evil propaganda immediately"

"Evil propaganda? They're fuckin novels, fiction, you idiot!"

"Nevertheless, you are corrupting the youth, not only of this nation but of the world."

"That's it!" Seth threw his coffee cup to the ground where it smashed and with his clenched right fist he swung and struck the holy man squarely on the jaw, as his victim fell backwards Seth threw another punch, glancing Seymour above the left eye and putting him down on the ground.

"I told you to fuck off but you wouldn't listen would you? You want me to stop do you? Well others, a hell of a lot scarier than you, want me to carry on. I'm damned if I do and damned if I don't. *I* will decide what to do with my life and *I* will decide what do in my career, no-one else" he shouted down as he stood over the stricken priest "And another thing, if you go near or contact my wife in any way, shape or form, I'll kill you, that's not an idle threat by the way, I *will* kill you, believe it."

Seth opened the backdoor and went back inside the bookstore, breathing heavily, adrenalin racing through his veins. He picked up his jacket from where he'd left it on the back of his chair, he was in an even more foul mood and desperate to get out of there.

"Hello grumpy"

"Lily! What're you doing here?" his mood immediately brightened

"I was going to go into work when I got back from the conference but the traffic was awful and it was late so I decided to surprise you and give you a lift home" her delightful smile lifted his heart and he practically ran over to where she sat on the stores' counter.

"God I've missed you" he said as he wrapped his arms around her and kissed her deeply while he lifted her down to the floor.

"Aww darling, I've missed you too. Why did you look so angry when you came in?" she asked when their lips parted.

"Nothing important, forget it. Where's Gus?" he said as he put his jacket on and as he raised his hand Lily noticed the swelling and an open cut on it.

"Forget Gus! What the hell have you done to your hand?"

"I told you, forget it, it's nothing" Seth said as he took her hand and started to walk to the door but Lily stayed put.

"Seth, tell me"

"Ok, ok, I was having a smoke outside and this religious nut starts banging on at me about how I'm evil and corrupting the youth of today blah blah, I've heard it all before."

"And you hit him? Why did you hit him if you've heard it all before?" Lily was staying stock still and stern faced until she got some real answers.

"Because he mentioned you" Seth sighed "Ok? He mentioned you and it sounded like some sort of veiled threat and I lost it, I know you hate violence and I'm sorry but"

"He mentioned me, why?" Lily cut his apology off with her curiosity

"I don't know, he said he knew you and how I wouldn't want to see you upset, I assumed that he did know you and was trying to threaten me or you, it wasn't so much what he said as the way he said it, look I'm sorry but can we go now?" Seth pouted like a school child.

"Did he give you his name?" Lily was calm and her brow furrowed.

"Seymour I think, Seymour Denton?"

"Duncan, Father Seymour Duncan" she gasped breathlessly and the colour drained from Lilys' face as she mentioned his name, she hadn't heard from him since she recommended his dismissal from the Hoffman Institute after he went crazy and stabbed Severin Frost, just over a year ago.

"Yeah that's him, Seymour Duncan, little shit. I'll beat the crap out of him if I see him again, now, can we go? Please" Seth whined

Lily looked distant as Seth confirmed Seymours' identity, there was something sinister in that man which had been well hidden, probably for a very long time. She had mused after the Frost stabbing that she'd have liked to interview and analyse the priest, there had to have been something more to him in order to make him explode the way he had done.

"Lily?" she heard her name then her hand being squeezed

"Lily, are you okay?" Seth said again

"Er. Yeah" she replied "What?"

"I said, can we go now? Are you sure you're ok?"

"Sure" Lily said as she came out of her daze and returned his loving squeeze of her hand "let's go home"

CHAPTER 21

The following day Seth and Lily sat quietly having breakfast together, both in their own little worlds. Seth was pondering the recent events surrounding the return of his nightmares and the new turn that they had taken in him getting visitors from his dreams in public places. He felt himself questioning his writing ability and even his own mind, was his novel all his own work of inspiration and his creative mind or was it in actual fact given to him by these mysterious and menacing third parties as they had insisted? He even went as far as to question his whole career. Had he been having subliminal dreams all his adult life or possibly even as a child? Maybe he was and they were only manifesting themselves as works of imaginative and disturbingly dark fiction. It that was indeed the case, did it also follow that in recent times their influence was getting stronger and the dreams more powerful? If so, where would it all end? With Seth in the Hoffman Institute being monitored by his own wife?

Lily was considering the sudden and much unexpected reappearance of Father Duncan. Why had he shown up now after all this time and why go to see Seth? What did he want? It surely couldn't be a coincidence that it was her husband that Seymour had tangled with, could it? Why was Seth so quiet? He hadn't discussed his day at the signing session at all, apart from his reluctant explanation of his encounter with the priest, that wasn't like him at all. He'd seemed very withdrawn throughout the previous night and again that morning, it had been a long time since she'd seen him like that.

"Are you ok?" Lily broke the silence to no response from her husband before again she tried to coax him "Seth?"

"Sorry, what?" he belatedly looked to her

"I said, are you alright?"

"Eh? Oh, er yeah, fine"

"You seem very quiet" Lily frowned "you were the same last night"

Seth didn't reply, he just stared into his coffee cup as if an answer to a great mystery lay there, deep in the dark liquid. Lily put her own thoughts to one side such was her concern for him. She got up from her seat and went around to the other side of the table, squeezing herself between Seth and the table and she sat on his lap. With Seths' concentration broken, he looked up at her and smiled.

"Come on darling, tell me" she smiled back

"It's nothing for you to worry about"

"Tell me anyway, please?" she pouted jokingly

"It's just my nightmares, they've started again" there was no way he was going to tell her about Angelique, just in case he actually *was* going insane.

"Really? I wouldn't worry about that too much, you've beaten them once and moved on with your life and look how much happier you are" Lily was ever the optimist and just for good measure she used her fingers to turn the edges of his mouth into a smile, at which they both laughed.

"I know" he sighed as his fake smile slipped "It's just really frustrating"

"Think of it like an addiction, you were doing so well, controlling them and keeping it all together then through no fault of your own, you fell off the wagon. That doesn't mean you've failed my love, it just means you're human and you need to get back up and carry on with even more resolve to beat them"

"Controlling them?" he asked

"Yes, you said that your therapist gave you exercises to control them, I assumed you were keeping all that up and that's why you hadn't had any problems for so long."

"Oh yeah, the exercises" Seth tried to dodge the issue and the fact that no such exercises existed; luckily Lily did the dodging for him.

"Look, you've done so well, if you've got nothing else planned for today then maybe you should try to see her again. If she's the miracle worker that you say she is then maybe she might be able to help you overcome this little lapse." Lily had always been sceptical about this *Dr Roth* but she seemed to have worked wonders for Seth, maybe it was at least worth a shot for his own peace of mind.

"I suppose I could try and track her down again" since his last dream he had kept telling himself that Meridiana was just a dream and he was over that but maybe, if he could actually track her down, Alex Roth could provide some answers to the riddles that were threatening to rip his mind to shreds.

"I've got to go to work now sweetie" she said looking at her watch "have a good day and try to get your head back in the game" she kissed his forehead and then kissed him properly on the lips as she climbed off his lap and retrieved her bag and keys before leaving.

"Love you" she shouted over to him with a smile as she stepped out of the front door.

"Love you too" he replied semi-cheerfully as he watched her go.

Seth got dressed and steeled himself; after Lily had gone he'd sat for a while and come to the conclusion that he wasn't going to let figments of his imagination push him around anymore. He denied to himself that Angelique was real or that Alex had got anything to do with the whole twisted kaleidoscope of a tale that was his life. He convinced himself that everything was just psychosomatic and there simply had to be a root cause. Lots of people have hallucinations, he reasoned, and a course of medications might be all that he needed, maybe.

Seth came up with a plan, such as it was, that he would spend the whole day wandering around the city until he eventually found something or other that he vaguely recognised in connection with Dr Roths' office building or even her apartment, anything that would jolt his memory. He felt that once he'd seen her he could get some perspective on the matters at hand and hopefully at least part of the puzzle could be put into place.

Seth got a taxi into the city and asked to be dropped at the Dragon, the place and surrounding area that he was always most comfortable and familiar with. He resisted the almost over-whelming urge to get a drink first and instead started to walk. He set off in no particular direction, he just walked, his eyes scanning ahead and up at the skyscrapers and imposing office complexes of the huge City. Once he realised he was moving away from any kind of developed area and there was nothing on the horizon, he stopped and turned back to the Dragon to start again. Over and over he repeated this pattern until without really knowing how he'd managed it, he found himself standing at the foot of Dr Roths' building. He looked back the way he thought he had just come but had no idea how he had found it or even where he was, he'd lived in this city for most of his life yet this seemed a very busy section of town that he didn't recognise at all. This was the second time he had been here but couldn't understand how. As he walked into the lobby he expected to find a table with a bottle of potion and a piece of cake labelled "Drink me" and "Eat me" respectively, though this was Seth in a very scary wonderland.

He went to the elevator which waited for him again as on his last visit and on his entrance it closed and shot him up the glass tower without him selecting a floor. The doors opened and deposited him at Dr Roths' office door then the elevator fired off again. He approached the medieval-looking, dark wooden door and just as he expected, it opened, bidding him to enter before closing behind him.

"Seth, good morning" she sat behind her desk looking stunning, her hair tied up and glasses' on the tip of her nose. Black business suit and stockings as before, he noticed as she deliberately crossed her legs beneath the desk top. She looked as though she had been expecting him.

"You don't seem surprised to see me" he said

"I'm not, I think we've got a lot to talk about and I'm pretty sure you've got a lot on your mind."

"Well, it *has* been over a year since I saw you . . . *hasn't it*?" he questioned himself as much as her.

Alex just smiled her delicious smile and gestured for him to take a seat on the chair in front of her desk.

"Please begin Seth, what can I do for you?"

"My dreams, they're back"

"Oh?" she said innocently with raised eyebrows as if mocking him

"Yes and my head is all over the place with them"

"I believe you're a big star these days, success, money, notoriety and fame, shouldn't your head be in the clouds with a big smile rather than all over the place?" she teased

"Yes it should be that way but the nightmares are back and I think they're getting worse than ever."

"Hmm, tell me about them Seth, is it the same 'people' as before?"

"Well, yes and a few others, including you!"

"Really?" she feigned shock and concealed a small grin.

"Really!"

"Well we can get to that later; tell me, what did your visitors want of you?"

"They say that I've made some sort of pact, a demonic pact, with them and that they gave me the book that resurrected my career. They're now also saying that in return I have to write a book for them, some special sort of book, my fucking head is spinning with all of it and just when my life had fallen back into place. I've started to question my own sanity; I *know* that I wrote that book"

"Maybe physically you wrote it but . . . ." she left the thought in the air,

"What do you mean?" he snapped back defensively

"Nothing, it doesn't matter. So, why don't you just do what they want and write this other book?"

"Why? Because I refuse to be threatened by a fucking dream that's why, I don't like being threatened by anyone let alone some mythical monsters"

She looked calm as she studied Seth, he on the other hand seemed to be becoming more and more agitated as the conversation continued. Alex had initially looked to be playful and seductive but now she seemed to be looking down at him as if with derision and scorn with a definite air of contempt. Her head tilted to the right as her eyes bored coldly into him as she spoke

"Mythical? Interesting that you, of all people, should think so? Especially bearing in mind the subjects you deal with in your books. Surely Seth, you must have studied these subjects to a certain level in your previous research? I'm sure you realise that very little of what you studied is 'mythical'?" an icy tone in her voice yet alternately a raging furnace seemed to blaze in her eyes.

"Er, well, yes" he mumbled as he was caught off guard by the strangeness of the contradiction between her voice and her eyes "but a lot of what I've read and studied is open to conjecture and peoples individual belief systems."

"So, where do I come in, in your nightmares, I mean?" her tone and appearance seemed to change again, she seemed to purr and the room seemed to glow and pulse with her quickening heartbeat as her eyes now seemed like deep and seductive pools.

"Well" Seth surprisingly found himself reddening as he spoke "I . . . . I was naked and hanging from a chain and you?..,,,,, . . . you were dressed as a . . . nun"

"Oooooooh Seth, a fetish lover, I knew you would be" she laughed which made him squirm in his seat "please, continue"

"And you were . . . ." his embarrassment grew even though he had had an amazingly wild and intimate night with this woman, he was totally in her control and she knew how to twist him around her little finger.

"Yeeessssssss?" she hissed like the serpent of dark delights that she undoubtedly was and Seth couldn't take being toyed with any longer.

"Alright! You were sucking my cock!" he shouted back at her and jumped to his feet

"Mmm, yummy, that takes me back to my apartment" she laughed again "you do realise that lots of people fantasise about their doctors, don't be embarrassed"

"It wasn't that sort of dream" he sighed to himself and slumped back down into his chair, he wanted answers not more fucking games. "you were calling yourself Meridiana and you said you were from the 10th Century and you'd seduced a pope or you'd made a guy a pope or something like that"

Alex nodded but Seth wasn't sure if it was as an acknowledgement of what he told her as a tale or whether she was nodding to confirm the *facts* of his story, which simply served to unnerve him further!

"So, who are the other characters Seth? Who do you remember?" she asked, all of a sudden back to the therapist-side of her multiple and changeable moods.

"Well, there was Angelique and Richelle who came with Mammon who I told you about, oh and that's another thing; I had a hallucination about Angelique. Well I think it was a hallucination, anyway, she came to see me at a bookstore and threatened me."

"Hallucination?" Alex questioned with a raised eyebrow "are you sure about that?"

"I don't know!" he yelled "I don't know anything about anything these days, how can she have been a hallucination, other people saw her too! But if she wasn't a hallucination then that means she was real and if she was real then how many of the others are real too?" he started to panic and sweat, his chest started to ache and his pulse raced.

"Seth calm down, look at me and take some deep breaths, look at me Seth"

He looked up at her, she stared back at him, their eyes met and it felt as if she flowed across the desk like a river bursting its' banks and surging towards him, reaching out to him. Her waters cooled his pulsed and soothed his heart, washing away his anxiety as if he were standing under a waterfall. He opened his eyes that he hadn't realised he'd closed and looked across at where she still sat.

"Feeling better?" she said calmly, Seth nodded and she told him to continue when he was ready, he took a deep breath and tried to finish his story.

"Well, then I came to see you and that night I had a dream that I've since learned was Richelle again and the Demonic Warlord Astaroth" as Seth uttered his name Alex smiled to herself "that's when I'm supposed to have made this fucking pact. I wrote my book 'Suffering Innocence' the next day, which they are now saying that they gave me, all that was just over a year ago. Now, right out of the blue I've got this fucking huge demon, Asmodeus, stomping around my nightmares threatening God only knows' what, and you chaining me up and . . . ." Seth stopped and thought for a few seconds and stared at her. His mind was suddenly trying to put the pieces of the puzzle together and some pieces were starting to fit.

"Yes?" she smiled teasingly at him "do you want to say anything else?" she probed his head, knowingly, as if with a sweet and alluring but very sharp stick.

"Astaroth, Alex Roth? You've gotta be fucking kidding me!" he pointed an accusing finger at her though he wasn't quite sure of what he was accusing her of at that precise moment "or are you gonna tell me that that is just a coincidence?" he stood up and his chair fell back behind him, Seth stumbled as he backed away from the desk.

"Busted!" she laughed to herself but stayed seated, seemingly delighting in his confusion and mental torture.

"What the fuck?" he snarled his disgust at her "Are you *married* to that thing or something?"

"Oh Seth, listen to yourself" she laughed again, her merriment started to grate on his nerves "Married? That's such a mortal concept"

"Mortal? What the fuck are you then? He asked the question but didn't really know if he wanted the answer.

"I will just say I'm not mortal, I don't think that in your current mental state you could fully comprehend what I actually am. Apart from the fact that I am Astaroths', it amused me to take my Lords' name while in your mortal realm, twisting your conventions you might say. One more thing that I am, I *am* Meridiana."

"B-But, him and you? But we . . . ." Seth stuttered in disbelief at what he was hearing, desperately wanting to wake from what he hoped was another dream.

"Yes Seth, me and him, me and you" she stood and walked around the desk, unbuttoning her jacket, taking it off and throwing it back onto her chair "me and you Seth, again, just say the word."

Seth stood open mouthed as she strutted over to him, unzipping her skirt and letting it fall to the floor, stepping out of it expertly without stopping her motion as she walked.

"I can recreate your dream of me perfectly if you'd like and so much more, any sexual fantasy you might have, I can make it happen no matter what it is. Remember our night at my apartment? You can have that and more, so much more, for eternity if you want. I can fuck you into oblivion every day and night until the end of time if you so desire. Just write the book Seth and I'm yours, wherever, whenever and however you want me, you can have me." She threw her arms around his neck and kissed him passionately.

A deep laughing male voice came sweeping and rumbling from the back of the room. Seth suddenly felt déjà vu from the voice he thought he'd heard at Alexs' apartment but back then he'd dismissed it, he wasn't going to dismiss it this time. He unhooked her arms and pushed her away.

"This isn't real!!" he yelled as he ran to the door and struggled to open it, he heard more laughter behind his back, both male and female and he turned as he fumbled with the door. He saw no man, just the woman he now knew only as Meridiana, standing by her desk in her lingerie, her body convulsing and reacting as if to the intimate touch of a lover, Seth remembered her reacting like that when he touched her, yet she seemingly stood there alone.

"You will write the book Seth" she yelled at him from where she squirmed now as she reclined back over the desk "Of that I can promise you"

As Seth watched, she was 'moved' onto the desk now, as if positioned by an unseen force. Her head tossed from side to side and her silk and lace underwear were visibly and audibly being ripped from her body, scraps of the delicate fabrics were being tossed into the air as her body was stripped clean of all garments and she writhed under an invisible *someone* clearly ravishing her body. Her head then turned to face Seth but kept turning, it turned completely in reverse to her body, more it turned, Seth could hear bones and tendons crunch and crack like dried twigs, still her head rotated to complete a 360 degree revolution before turning again to face Seth. Her tongue, now black and slimy, lolled out of her open mouth as he gawped at the sight and she spoke as if nothing were happening to her, though in an unearthly, guttural voice.

"You will keep your side of the bargain or I cannot help you. You agreed to do what we asked, we kept our side of the pact and you have your wealth and success, now you must do likewise and adhere to the agreement"

"Why me?" he screamed at her as she lay naked and wantonly

"You are perfect for us Seth, you are the one." Hand and bite marks suddenly became clearly visible on her now naked body, her flesh bruising like a peach

"No" he screamed again "let me go"

"As you wish Seth, but on your head be it" as she spoke, her eyes started to bleed yet still she squealed and twisted in horrific ecstasy.

At once the door flung open and the elevator waited patiently to transport him out of this particularly dark and disturbing rabbit hole in the sky. He dived into the elevator and sat on the floor, sweating and crying. As if to taunt him further, the elevator doors waited for a few seconds before closing as did the office door, it felt like an eternity. He looked back into the office, he could see through the huge floor to ceiling windows and he saw the sky turn a sickly shade of green before going black from an impending storm. The thick and durable windows themselves suddenly cracked from a seemingly huge force and the naked Alex/ Meridiana was now bent over her desk and being taken brutally from behind by *someone* or *something* unseen.

"Impale me My Lord" she yelped in both pleasure and pain "Fuck me"

"What's happening to me?" he sobbed as the elevator finally closed on him "What have I done?"

CHAPTER 22

While Seths' mind was being tormented to still further degrees, Lily was back at work in the Hoffman Institute. She spent the morning catching up on paperwork and checking through patient reports from over the weekend as she'd been away. Her mind had been puzzled by Father Duncan during her drive to work but those concerns were pushed away by her worries for Seth. Once at the Hoffman however she'd been able to immerse herself in her job and put other things to the back of her mind.

Lily read the updated files on all her patients to get herself up to speed on any developments which may have taken place in her absence. Happily everything had seemed to run very smoothly without her, although she wasn't entirely sure that that was a good thing! In these days of expenditure reviews and budget cutting, she didn't want to be the highly paid professional who suddenly found herself to be expendable,

As usual, she left her 'priority' patients until last, flicking through the latest entries in Severin Frosts' file she found entries regarding his increasingly aggressive behaviour and a return of his intimidation tactics. Lily desperately hoped that this wasn't going to be a sustained deterioration in his mental state, she had been thrilled by the progress he'd been showing up until the last few months, that was when he had started to become restless and angry again. She decided to go and see Severin, to assess him for herself.

Dr Caine made her way down to the high security wing of the Institute feeling good to be back at work. Some colleagues had referred to her as a workaholic and even obsessive about her job, she preferred terms like 'dedicated' and 'perfectionist' and 'passionate' but still enjoyed other peoples' descriptions as she considered them compliments, no matter how they had been initially intended. As she passed through security gates and identification checks she started to hear voices shouting and gradually they were becoming louder the closer she approached, suddenly she was jolted as an alarm rang out and multiple guards were dispatched at speed to the incident. Lily continued to the final checkpoint through which the rushing guards had also passed, the gates had closed automatically, locking behind them and in front of her.

The security officers were always very professional and hand picked for their positions, Lily had had a hand in appointing a number of them and she trusted them all implicitly to carry out their duties effectively and efficiently. She waited patiently at the gate to be checked through into maximum security, a couple of minutes passed but she understood that some incidents took time to resolve and contain, she had instigated many of the containment protocols herself, she hoped it wasn't anything too serious though.

A guard came out of the office at the checkpoint to confirm Dr Caines' credentials, all the officers knew her but she had insisted on everything being done by the book, safety and security first, she never minded waiting and was always pleasant with the guards, who were just doing their jobs as she wanted it done, properly. He smiled as he checked her identification and she could hear the shouts becoming screams, there seemed to be a lot of anger and hate in the voices as well as the sounds of large objects being thrown across rooms and into walls, Lily winced.

All of a sudden she recognised the distinctive voice of Severin Frost, at his most vicious and hateful. A shiver ran down her spine and a knot appeared in Lilys' stomach, she stood rigid as the guard now seemed to be taking too long to open the gates for her liking, he recognised the voice too and joked

"Are you sure you want to go in there Dr Caine?"

"Open this fucking gate . . . now!!" Lily screamed at him, she didn't know why she had reacted in such a way, it was totally out of character but she somehow knew instinctively that she had to get through that gate immediately. Her response to the guard obviously had the desired effect because he fumbled with the locking mechanism and humbly apologised as he opened up for her and then stood open mouthed as she pushed him aside and ran into the wing to check on her patient.

As Lily arrived at Severins' door, a group of security officers stood in the corridor looking into the room before three guards came out, two limping heavily and the third with blood pouring from a head wound. She pushed past them and saw a fourth guard slumped in the doorway trying to catch his breath and cradling what looked immediately like a broken wrist. Inside the room two more guards were tightening restraints holding an enraged Severin Frost to his bed while a white-coated doctor prepared to inject a sedative-filled syringe, Lily recognised the doctor immediately, Dr Jason Bolton.

"What the hell is going on here?" she shouted as she entered, at the sound of her voice Severin immediately calmed and relaxed, causing the guards and doctor to freeze like statues with surprise. No-one spoke, the guards looked at Dr Bolton, Dr Bolton looked at the guards and all three looked at the now angelic and peaceful Severin Frost.

"I said, what's going on?" as she spoke again Dr Bolton looked up at her from where he crouched over Frost, he stood up straight and gestured for the guards to finish their restraint checks while he put away the sedative and ushered Lily outside the room.

Once out in the corridor, Jason stroked Lilys' arm as if consoling a grieving relative, he smiled and looked into her eyes to gain her trust with his usual mock professional sympathy.

"Don't look at me like that Jason" she snapped

"Lily, there's no need to be like this" his curly hair moved across his forehead as he tilted and inclined his head towards her in a very patronising manner.

"Two things Jason, first, what are you doing here in my Institute? I was told you had been transferred, as you requested. And second, what the hell are you doing to my patient?" straight and to the point

"Okaaaaaay, firstly I was asked to come back and oversee things while you were away."

"I was only away for a few days! Who requested that?" interrupted Lily

"The Director of course, I've done a few weekends over the last few months, just to get a feel for the old place" he smiled seductively which made her flesh crawl, she didn't think he could've made her feel like that "given our history I suggested that he didn't tell you that I was coming in"

"You were brought in to tend to my patients without my authorisation? This is absurd and totally inappropriate, I will be making a formal complaint" she yelled

"Feel free but remember, I know the majority of these patients very well, not quite as well as you, I accept but I do know them. I only left here six months ago and I am still practising, I do know what I'm doing you know"

Jason shouted back at her which only served to inflame her rage and the situation. Lily wanted to scream at him and shout her response, partly for what he was doing to Severin and partly for the way he had treated her. She neither knew nor cared what he was up to now, where he was living or with whom but her feelings were still pretty raw the way he left her for a younger model.

Thankfully her emotions were quickly reined in when the remaining two guards came out of Severins' room, pretending not to have heard the argument, and informed the two doctors that the patient had been secured before they stood side by side at the door, Lily re-entered the room first, in silence.

She surveyed the scene, the table and chair that normally stood in the room were almost unrecognisable, now looking like little more than large splinters. Blood smears and even dents were clearly visible along the walls, Severin now lay wide awake but serene on his bunk as he watched the two psychiatrists.

"What the?" gasped Lily

"Our friend Mr Frost seems to have revisited his past, in terms of his temper I mean." Jason sounded like he was talking about a naughty family dog.

"I'm not your friend" rumbled Severin from his prone position

"Calm Severin, I'm here" replied Lily in a very soothing voice

Jason looked at her curiously and furrowed his brow in consternation, she'd never spoken to a patient like that before in his experience, Lily noticed him watching her.

"That'll be all Dr Bolton" she said as she moved over and showed him the door

"But, don't you want a full report? I should tell you that . . . ."

"Thank you!" Lily cut him off as she ushered him out of the room, she told the guards to wait outside and closed the door behind a very disgruntled Jason Bolton who stormed off, mumbling to himself loudly about a lack of respect and going to see the Director.

Lily looked around the room again and then down at Severin where he lay. She had developed a closer bond than ever with Frost over the last year, a bond that she was both delighted and concerned by, in equal measures, caring for someone in her charge was one thing but they had almost got to the point where they were friends, of sorts at least. Their tone when talking to each other had softened and he had become much more open and receptive to her questions. Some days they had just sat and talked about music or art, politics or sculpture. She saw, or was shown, the cultured man that he had once been before his horrific homicidal urges had taken a grip on his mind. She knew that the other man that she glimpsed, the pleasant and refined character, was in there locked up somewhere, he was only allowed out on occasions to talk to her it seemed, she desperately wanted to help Severin release him from his mental prison cell.

Lily was honoured and flattered that Severins' 'real' self was only for her, if a colleague happened to be accompanying her, Severin immediately clamped his mind shut at he intrusion. Due to this, Lily had whenever possible, declined to let visiting scholars have access to Mr Frost, usually citing a mysterious sickness circulating the maximum security wing.

Prior to her recent conference appearance, Severin had descended into a very dark mood which had become a rarity for him in her presence, he had mumbled on about a huge black storm coming but wouldn't elaborate. Lily had become so concerned at the change in his demeanour that she had decided to cancel her conference date but the Director had refused to send a replacement to the event and insisted that she attend.

Now she wondered if his outburst was the storm that he had mentioned, a storm brewing in his head that had to be freed at some point. With the guards outside and Jason gone to bleat to the Director, Severin seemed more like himself, or at least the self that only she had come to know. Lily sat on the edge of his bed and found herself stroking his brow, she was suddenly very protective of him as he lay there helplessly strapped to his bunk. Their eyes locked and she realised what she was doing, quickly she pulled her hand away, feeling guilty.

"Are you okay?" she spoke in hushed tones

"I am fine my dear doctor, more so than those guards at least. I have missed you greatly." He smiled

"I'm glad" she returned the smile but then checked herself at her lack of professionalism.

"I must speak to you Lily" his familiarity seemed very natural between them now.

"That's what I'm here for" she whispered

"There is a huge storm on the horizon, a very dark storm."

"You mean this wasn't it?" Lily laughed as she looked around the room

"No, far from it, I'm serious Lily, I am greatly concerned for you. You have shown me much kindness and understanding over the years of my incarceration here and especially over the last few months, perhaps you have even given me more than I deserve." He held up his hand to stop her interruption and continued "I do not like thought of you being caught up in the terrible events of the storm that is about to unfold."

There was indeed genuine concern in Frosts' voice and also his eyes where most observers only saw pain, death and a lack of remorse. As close as they had become over recent times, the mood in the room surprised Lily, she was moved by his thoughts for her safety and touched that he could show such emotion to her.

"Severin" she smiled and glowed "thank you, I'm glad you feel comfortable enough to talk to me this way but I'm fine, everything is going well for me"

"No, I fear you won't be fine unless you adhere to my advice" he started to become agitated but not in any violent context and his eyes even more than his words implored her to listen to him.

"Hush Severin, don't excite yourself, we can talk about all this at length tomorrow, I just dropped in to"

"No!" Frost snapped, shocking Lily into silence "Not tomorrow, there may not be many more tomorrows for you"

Lily tensed and edged away from him, as bound and helpless as he was it was easy to forget just what a torrent of rage and fury this man could become just as easy as flicking on a light switch. She, and the guards, had never forgotten that lesson, but just as he sensed how uncomfortable he was making her he calmed again.

"Please don't go, just listen to me" he begged

"Ok, but try to stay calm and lucid, the guards are right outside" not much of a deterrent to Severin Frost but it was all she had.

"I'm sorry my dear Lily, but you have to listen to me, it's your husband"

"Seth? What about him?" Lily was visibly shocked, Frost hadn't mentioned Seth for a very long time, she'd almost forgotten, but not quite, about his references to Seth and Severins' 'dark friends'.

"All I can tell you is that he must, must make the right decision"

"Decision, what decision? Decision about what and why are you bringing Seth up again? I thought we'd got past all this nonsense of you taunting me?" she became frustrated, frustrated at Seth being brought up in such a sinister way and frustrated at the possible backwards step in Severins' progress.

"Please Lily, I am not taunting you. Seths' life has been enriched in many, many ways over the last year and not just with glitz and finance" he smiled at her as he spoke the last "he has got what he always wanted and my dark friends are responsible for it all."

"I don't understand Severin, what have your friends got to do with Seths' career?"

"They gave him the story which is now flaunted in his name, it was a deal, a pact if you will and he is refusing to complete his side of this pact, he is acting without honour, he is refusing to pay the price my dear and I am afraid that you will get caught up in what will follow." He closed his eyes and a tear slipped down his cheek "retribution will be swift and potentially horrendous Lily, you deserve so much better than to be scarred by that."

"Severin, what are these men planning on doing to Seth? Are they going to hurt him? What does he have to do?" urgency now filtered through Lilys' voice as it became shrill with panic.

"He knows what he has to do and he could avoid a lifetime of nightmares, pain, despair and degradation just by doing as he was asked, more to the point, so could you."

"Who are they? Can't we get the police involved?" if only she knew how futile that sounded to Frost.

"Sweet Lily, the police can only help you against bad men, my friends are not mere men, my friends are not ones to be crossed either and there will be consequences, grave consequences. You must persuade him to honour the pact if only for your own self-preservation" sorrowfully he looked at Lily as his words stayed with her.

Lily stood and moved to the door, as she opened it she looked back at him and he nodded as if asking if she agreed, she smiled weakly and nodded her agreement. She didn't understand what the hell was going on or what Seth had done, if anything at all.

"Seth has had chances and enough warnings my dear, he is fast running out of options and even faster running out of time, make him see sense, for both your sakes." Severins' words felt like a veiled threat.

Part of her now hoped that Severin *was* slipping back into delusion, if only to spare her the thought that Seth was somehow in very serious trouble, even danger. However, the thought of Severins' potential downturn also made her leave and head home with a very heavy heart.

After Lily had left, Severin settled back in dark raptures of black delight and closed his eyes, with a satisfied and twisted smile he sighed
"It is done"

Chapter 23

As Lily drove home, confusion and worry reigned supreme in her mind. Professionally she was concerned about the possible deterioration in the mental health of Severin Frost, this was evidenced by the seemingly delusional outburst that she felt she had just witnessed. He had been making such fantastic progress in the last year that it almost made her weep with frustration. It seemed a reasonable assumption to say that Severin had developed feelings for his therapist and his jealousy at her husband, with whom she had reconciled during her time as Frosts' psychiatrist, manifested itself in his wild accusations and threats.

Personally however, she was concerned for Seth, while Lily had been at work he had said he'd be trying to see Dr Roth. Despite her many misgivings about Seths' 'miracle worker' that she had never even heard of, Lily was pleased that he was getting professional help to solve his night terrors. She hoped his day had been fruitful in that respect, their relationship had gone from strength to strength in the last year since they were finally reunited and they were both happier now than either had been in many years previously. Lily didn't want that to end, she had even considered bringing up the idea of having a baby, or if that wasn't possible, maybe adopting.

In between her professional and personal concerns lay the nagging question of whether Severin was telling the truth about his dark friends and Seth, she didn't really believe it was true and didn't *want* to believe it either but the question was there all the same, just festering below the surface. As she arrived home Lily wasn't sure if she wanted to bring the subject up and decided to see how things developed over the evening.

"Hiya" she called as she walked into their home.

There was no reply but she could hear a commotion and a lot of cursing coming from the kitchen and so went to investigate. Lily entered the kitchen to be confronted by a sight that she had rarely seen, Seth actually cooking, well, trying to cook. Seth did not cook in her experience, microwave dinners and ready-made frozen meals were about all he would entertain normally. He loved his food, he loved restaurants, he loved take-away but if she had put him in front of an oven with basic ingredients he would be totally lost. Yet here he was, cook book open as he tried to follow a recipe, pots and pans everywhere, flour and eggs, packets and jars wherever she turned. He looked like a mad scientist from an old fifties movie. Lily lent on the door-frame as she watched him beaver away, completely oblivious to her presence. She smiled to herself at the undoubted effort and concentration that he was putting into his 'experiment'.

"Anything I can do?" she asked, smiling as he jumped at her voice.

"Oh, er, you're home, er, I thought I'd cook for us."

"So I see, did you have a plan going into this or are you just making it up as you go along" she laughed teasingly

"Sorry" he frowned and looked around, realising the mess and chaos he'd created "I just thought you might like . . . ."

His words trailed off as she walked over to him, she threw her arms around his neck and kissed him lovingly. He slid his arms around her waist and squeezed her gently.

"Thank you" she whispered as their lips parted.

"For what?"

"For this of course" she said, gesturing around the room

"Don't thank me, I don't think it's worked out how I planned it" he frowned again.

"Ah, so you did have a plan?" she laughed again playfully "well thank you for the thought anyway, it's very sweet of you to try" she kissed him again.

"Sweet?"

"Sorry, I know you don't like to be called sweet" she lifted a lid and peered into a bubbling pot "Should I try it?"

"Er no," he winced "I wouldn't bother! Take out?"

"I'll get the menus" she laughed again.

They ordered their food and set about cleaning up Seths' mess between them. While they cleaned Lily noticed that he was still as quiet and distant as he had been that morning.

"So how did your day go? Did you go to see Dr Roth?"

At the mention of her name Seth dropped the plate he was holding and it fell to the floor with an almighty crash, shattering everywhere. Lily looked up in surprise while Seth looked decidedly sheepish.

"Oh er yes, I don't think I'm going to see her again though"

"Really? I thought you liked her."

"I did but I'm not comfortable with her, can we change the subject." Seth sounded extremely spikey and defensive but Lily didn't want to push him on what seemed like a delicate subject. She was trained to know when someone had issues to deal with but his demeanour made it obvious to anybody. Personally though she didn't want to start analysing or diagnosing her own husband, she felt she had to tread very carefully.

"Ok" she replied, his sudden change of heart regarding his therapist was baffling but he'd seemed so troubled lately that she didn't want to get into a fight "So, what brought the whole culinary incident on?"

"I just needed to be busy that's all, people say that cooking or gardening and stuff like that can be therapeutic and I've had a lot on my mind so . . . ." He looked at her and saw the concern in her eyes "Plus, I wanted to cook you a great meal, sorry about that again" he laughed

"Gardening next?" she asked

"Not a hope in hell!" he replied and they both laughed together, though each seemed uneasy.

As Seth cleaned up the broken plate the doorbell rang and Lily went to answer it. She brought the freshly delivered Chinese food into the kitchen and unpacked it. They moved to the dining room to eat their banquet and opened a bottle of wine. The couple dined while exchanging pleasantries, loving glances and smiles, Seth innocently asked how Lilys' day had gone and her mood clouded over.

"Not too bad" she replied and hesitated before asking "do you remember me asking if you knew a man called Severin Frost?"

Seth thought for a second or so before shaking his head and continuing to eat.

"A year or so ago? A patient of mine? He said that his Dark Friends knew you?"

The phrase 'dark friends' immediately brought memories back to Seth of a previous time he'd heard it, in Alex/Meridianas' apartment, and all at once everything he'd been trying to suppress came flooding back.

"Like I said, I don't know him" Seth grunted and finished his food then opened another bottle of wine, obviously not wanting to talk "Do you want to watch a DVD?"

"Er sure" replied Lily, puzzled by his eagerness to change the subject again but now sceptical about why.

They moved into the living room and Seth selected his copy of John Boormans' 'Excalibur' and held it up for Lilys' approval.

"Again?" she exclaimed

"Aw come on, it's a classic!" he seemed cheerier now at the thought of a favourite movie and so she agreed.

Seth made the usual preparations, he opened a third bottle of red wine so they would have two bottles ready and he wouldn't have to get up mid-movie. He turned off the lights and lit the large church candles in the fire place. Atmosphere achieved, they both lay entwined on their large suede couch, Seth pulling over the coffee table to within easy reach for their wine and his ashtray and cigarettes. Lily had relented on his smoking in the house as long as he promised to cut down on his habit, something which he hadn't quite managed yet.

The movie started and Lily curled into Seths' chest, they could both put their own privately difficult days behind them now for a couple of hours and enjoy some quality escapism. Three quarters of the way through the movie, Seth noticed that Lily had fallen asleep, he didn't want to disturb her so let her slumber on as he watched the remainder of the film. Just as she always seemed to, Lily woke up as the end credits started to roll.

"I'm sorry" she said as she yawned and stretched while Seth switched off the DVD and poured more wine "none for me, I'm shattered"

Seth stood and ejected the disc then put it away, Lily watched him in silence, the words of Severin coming back to her and she knew she couldn't go to bed with them still gnawing away at the back of her mind. She needed some sort of confirmation in order to treat Frost and also relieve any doubts regarding her husband and his possible involvement with Frost or his 'dark friends'.

"Can I talk to you about something Seth?"

"Course you can" he seemed in a much better mood now

"It's about Severin Frost"

"Lily" he sighed "I've told you, I don't know him. How many more times do I have to say it?"

"I know that but it's just that he brought you and these dark friends of his up a year ago, now, completely out of the blue he's bringing the same thing up again!"

"He's a mental patient darling, forget it" he tried to dismiss the subject as trivial.

"I can't forget it Seth, he's my patient, it's my job"

"For Gods' sake Lily" Seth became exasperated as he genuinely didn't know Frost but also a little intrigued by the 'dark friends' aspect "Right, ok, what's he been saying?" he sighed

"Well for a start he thinks you're in big trouble with his friends!"

"Why? What am I supposed to have done?" Seth took a large gulp of wine; he was feeling guilty suddenly and more than a little uncomfortable.

"Have you made some sort of deal with someone? His friends' maybe?" she asked hopefully and trying not to sound as though she was being judgemental.

Seth stopped drinking immediately and swallowed hard, all colour drained from his face and he sat open mouthed with shock at her words. "Seth? Are you ok?"

"What sort of deal" he whispered

"Your last book, he said his dark friends had given it to you"

Seth sat back down on the couch in silence, staring at the floor. He had no idea what was going on and his whole reality seemed to be crumbling before his very eyes. This Severin Frost suddenly loomed large though he still had no idea who the hell he was, he'd never met him and none of Seths' night time visitors had mentioned him as far as he could remember. However, Frosts' knowledge of the pact that Seth still hoped was all in his mind, gave it substance, a substance that Seth was having difficulty comprehending.

"Seth, what have you done?" Lily was very worried now by the look of ashen terror that had crept over his face "What have you got yourself mixed up in? Who are these 'Dark Friends' Seth? Talk to me, please"

"Lily, you mustn't have anything to do with this man Frost" he sounded frantic

"I can't do that Seth, he's my patient"

"You must keep away from him, he's dangerous" implored Seth

"I can't, now tell me what's going on, first you said that you didn't know him and now you're trying to warn me off!" Lily raised her voice more in frustration than anger.

"I don't know what's going on, that's just the point" he snapped "I really don't know him, honestly but it's the *people* he knows that are dangerous. I don't want you mixed up in . . . whatever's going on".

"Don't yell at me Seth, if you've done something wrong . . . ."

"I think . . . ." he paused

""You think? You think what?" Lily was getting impatient for real answers

"I think that these 'Dark Friends' he tells you about are the same demons that are haunting my dreams" his head dropped further into his chest as he spoke, partly through embarrassment as he knew how crazy he sounded "that's the only explanation I can give you"

There was a deafening silence as they sat there, she stared at him, he stared at the floor before looking up to her for reassurance that he wasn't going completely insane after all.

"But that's just not possible, it's just too bizarre. How?" Lily was flabbergasted at his statement.

"I don't know, I'm not even sure what I'm saying myself. I've heard that phrase 'Dark Friends' before and it all seems connected to my dreams, I wouldn't call the creatures in my nightmare 'friends' but they don't come any darker! And if I'm right, a man who does consider them friends is not someone you should be getting too involved with, whether he's your patient or not"

"But that doesn't mean that they are the same people" Lily was grasping for clarity.

"Well they seem to be under the impression that they gave me the story for 'Suffering Innocence' in my sleep, sort of subliminally I think. They referred to it as a pact, bit of a coincidence that now this Frost is talking about it all to you? How could he know all that if he didn't know them?"

"But they're in your head!" Lily found it difficult to comprehend "Aren't they?"

More silence ensued as they both struggled with the concept of what seemed to be going on. Seth had had a lot more time to rationalise what was happening but he was floundering almost as much as the speechless Lily.

"And to make matters worse" he continued "now they want to collect payment for the pact that I *supposedly* agreed to"

"What do they want from you, money?" it was the obvious thing she could think of but it seemed ridiculous to Seth who suppressed an inappropriate laugh.

"No, not money" he sighed "They want me to write them a book"

"Er, that doesn't sound too bad" Lily was genuinely surprised that that was all he had to do "it seems a small price to pay and not worth getting yourself into such a state over, if they'll leave you alone afterwards. What sort of book?"

"I don't know what sort of book but that's just the point, will they leave me alone afterwards? Am I then just going to be their puppet? Where does it all end? I'm scared Lily, very scared, one of them even came to the book signing the other day! I try to deny that they exist and try to block them out but you see, they aren't just in my head anymore, they're real!" Seths' voice rose in pitch as he became more frantic with the situation

"Seth darling, I'm here for you, you know that. I can get you some professional help if things aren't working out with Dr Roth; I know lots of other respected psychiatrists"

"Lily, it's fucking complicated" he felt as if he was howling inside and no-one would ever truly understand him. "I don't know what's real and what's in my mind. My dreams are coming to life and haunting me, they're manipulating my life. Even this so-called Dr Roth isn't what she said she was and I don't know who I can trust anymore."

"Me Seth, you can trust me, just let me in" she put her hands on his cheeks and lifted his head, looking deep into his eyes as they filled with tears like a frightened little boy, it broke her heart.

"No Lily, you can't get involved in this"

"Let me in Seth" she implored again

"No!" he shouted this time and pulled away out of her reach, he felt awful for doing it but also he felt that it was for her own good. He hated himself for speaking to her so harshly and for locking her out of his problem but he wanted to protect her from whatever was happening to him, this was the only way he knew how.

"Alright! If that's the way you want it" Lily started to cry herself and stood up, Seth reached across and tried to take her hand but she snatched it away "I'm going to bed, I'll leave you with your wine, *sweet dreams*"

Lily went upstairs, leaving Seth wallowing in his turmoil of confusion. He poured himself more wine to block out the pain and sat on the couch in a daze. The way he thought, the less Lily knew, the less involved she was and therefore the safer she would be. He felt he'd told her too much already, he couldn't allow her to be dragged down into the vortex of despair that was gaining a grip on his very existence.

He drank and drank for another hour in order to numb his mind and allow Lily to sleep. When tiredness eventually persuaded him to retire he succumbed and went up to join his beloved. Seth stood in the doorway of their bedroom watching her sleep, he hoped she hadn't cried herself to sleep, she was so beautiful and fragile despite her inner strength, he just wanted to shield her from potential harm. He couldn't even contemplate losing her again.

He wiped another solitary tear from his eye before undressing and gently sliding into bed beside her.

Seth kissed her on the cheek as he wrapped himself around her and whispered
"I love you Lily Munster" as he closed his eyes in the darkness he heard her whisper
"I love you too".

CHAPTER 24

Seths' sleep was broken, not by a noise but by a presence, he sat bolt upright in his bed while Lily lay undisturbed beside him. A man sat in a chair of throne-like proportions, positioned just a few feet from the edge of their bed. The stranger didn't look anything like one of Seths' usual late night callers, no horns, tails, claws or flames, no twisted succubus turning his head, just a man it seemed. Seth was ever vigilant however and refused to let his guard drop, he was all the more concerned purely out of the fact that Lily was still sleeping right there.

The seated man looked very urbane, stylish and elegant; he was dressed in a black three-piece suit and an open-necked dark purple shirt. Though Seth was seeing him by moonlight, there was a clear glow or radiance being given off by the man. Seth got out of bed and retrieved his robe, putting it on before walking around to confront his visitor. The man sat with legs crossed, displaying exquisitely tailored shoes. His forearms lay on the armrests of the huge chair, allowing his hands to droop freely over their ends. His fingers were pale and adorned with silver rings, much like Seths' own, he also had long, sharp yet excellently manicured fingernails.

This was an exceptionally handsome man; cleanly shaven with long, thick black hair swept back and tied. He looked quite muscular and broad across his shoulders, he also seemed deceptively calm and relaxed. The only thing that would set him apart from a modern day movie star or model was his eyes. They burned with a deep, scarlet red as Seth approached; the man smiled causing them to dance like flames.

Seth stopped dead in his tracks as he saw this and he couldn't help but to glance back at his sleeping Lily.

"If I'd have wanted her, I would already have taken her my dear Seth" spoke the man in a very cultured voice with the hint of a European accent that Seth couldn't quite place.

"W-who are you?" he mumbled in reply

"That can't have been the first time you've said that in your sleep recently"

"Please, d-don't hurt her" Seth begged for his wife

"Fear not, I am not here to hurt either of you" the man sat calmly as he studied Seth deeply.

"So, what do you want with me?" instinctively Seth felt more scared of this polite gentleman than the monstrous wretches that had visited him previously; this was a very unnerving presence indeed. His feelings showed themselves in the timbre of his voice, panic was lying just beneath the surface and he knew he had to hold it back.

"Straight to the point Seth, I like that" the man said with a sinister smile "As you wish, you owe me a book."

"B-but I've already told the others that I won't do it, why can't you just leave me alone? I don't even remember this so-called pact anyway; get someone else to write your damn book!"

"Your ignorance is no excuse Caine, you made an agreement and we delivered our part of the bargain, now you must honour your side. You can't run away from us Seth, we WILL get what we want."

"Why should I? What're you going to do if I don't?" Seth surprised himself with his bravado.

"Oh my dear Seth" the man sighed and shook his head "you are looking at this in completely the wrong way"

"Oh really? How should I be looking at it then?"

"You should be asking yourself what *else* I can do for you, as if I haven't done enough for you already with your success and fortune, be under no illusion Caine, you're success and life is all down to me" the man sneered and glared at Seth as he finished his words.

"But I don't even know who the fuck you are!!" replied Seth angrily.

"Yes you do, deep down, in the pit of your stomach and the dark corners of your mind, you know full well who you are talking to, what is more, you also know that you should have a hell of a lot more respect in your voice when you talk to me" he paused and his eyes bored deeply into Seth who stood motionless, the stranger finished "you can be taught respect Caine, you can be taught through fear and pain, should I so wish".

Seth didn't reply, he just slowly sat on the edge of the bed before his legs buckled beneath him from the shock and realisation now dawning on him, a sickly feeling grew in the pit of his stomach and his heart felt heavy in his chest as his knowledge drifted over him like a shroud of misery and darkness,

"Ah, I see the pieces of the puzzle have finally fallen into place" said the now not-so-mysterious stranger "yes, I am the one who sent Mammon and Astaroth and of course Asmodeus. I also conjured the various scenarios of your own torture and death, I have to say that I was especially impressed by your reactions to the succubi that I sent you, I was watching the whole time as I'm sure you've gathered. I noticed your amazement on seeing Angelique in your bathtub and naturally who wouldn't enjoy fucking Richelle? However, it is quite obvious that you were particularly enamoured of the lovely Meridiana, any man would be of course. She is wonderful in her ability to be all things to all men, and women for that matter. She is every fantasy woman you've ever had, all rolled into one delicious specimen, am I right?"

"Satan" replied Seth in a hushed voice.

"Oh come now Caine, you can't be that surprised surely? Yes I am the Fallen One but prefer to think of myself as the Risen One, or better yet the Rising One, for I continue to rise. I am known by many names but if that is the one you choose to know me by, then so be it."

Seth sat in silence as he tried to come to terms with the fact that he was actually sitting in his bedroom conversing with the Devil himself.

"Nothing to say my friend?" Satan asked "then I shall continue, as I was saying, you should be asking yourself what else I can do for you. You should be driving a hard bargain, be greedy, get as much as you can for yourself. That's the mortal way after all, be selfish. You will be providing a great service for me and you deserve great recompense in return." Satan smiled with glee and his eyes lit up further as he watched Seth grapple with his inner turmoil.

"W-what else could you possibly give me? I have all I want" he stammered uneasily.

"That's the spirit, allow me to show you" with that Satan lifted the fingers on his left hand slightly and suddenly they were in a large old stone building.

Satan still sat on his throne, Seth surprisingly, was still sat on his bed and Lily lay asleep in it, yet here they were, transported to another place entirely.

"Where the fuck are we?" Seth gasped as he gazed around the draughty and dusty old cavernous room.

"This is the Franciscan convent of Louviers, this could be a very pleasurable place indeed for a man of your particular tastes." The Devil grinned

Seth stood up and walked cautiously around the old building, he could hear his barefoot falls on the cold stone floor and he stroked the wooden panels on the walls and he touched the furniture gently as if touching furniture for the first time. He could even smell the decay and dust and the old dampness in the air, 'this must be real' he thought to himself. Seth jumped as he was startled at the sound of a bolt being opened, three men in robes entered the room from a creaky and very heavy-looking side door, Seth moved away to the side of the room but they were oblivious to his presence. The robed men moved to the centre of the room and stood in front of a large altar. From the opposite side of the room another door opened and a group of women, also in robes, entered and encircled the men.

"Who are they?" whispered Seth curiously to Satan.

"They are the priests who were the head of this particular convent. Father Pierre David, Father Mathurin Picard in the middle and on the left is Father Thomas Boulle. The women are the nuns of the order" replied Satan with a lecherous smile "in the second quarter of the 17th Century, wonderful things took place here and all in my name." he spoke proudly.

The women disrobed and one of them climbed onto the altar in front of the priests who now also discarded their robes. Self consciously Seth looked back at Lily who lay still in her undisturbed sleep.

"What the hell's going on?" Seth blurted out.

"Ah, Madeline" Satan gazed with delight at the woman now on the altar "That my friend is Madeline Bavent, isn't she beautiful and oh so ripe? The prize of the convent, queen of this particular coven."

"Coven?" queried Seth

"Yes, you see, the good Father David created the coven in my name as I said. He had wonderful and ingenious ways of worship, nuns were encouraged to pray naked in order to satisfy his own voyeuristic tendencies as well as that he also promoted and encouraged lesbianism between the sisters, purely for his own self gratification of course.

Sadly he died in 1628, however his successor was Father Picard who delighted in not only continuing Father Davids' work but building upon it. He introduced ritualistic orgies and under his guidance, the lovely Madeline became the head of the coven, he lasted for fourteen gloriously sin-filled years until dying in 1642. However, this time he had already groomed his successor and that is where Father Boulle comes in. Unfortunately, he only managed to enjoy these beauties until he went on trial on witchcraft charges two years later and was burned alive three years after that."

As he watched the scene unfold before his eyes, Seth couldn't help but become aroused. He felt he couldn't take his eyes from the nun, now known as Madeline, as she writhed in ecstasy on the altar. The rest of the sisters pleasured themselves and each other on the cold stone floor or against the rough walls while the priests gazed around the room with pride at their creation. The scent of sex and sweating flesh filled Seths' nostrils and he turned to see Satan watching him enjoy the show.

"Why the fuck have you brought me here?" he shouted, looking away from the women and trying to block the images from his mind.

"Did you know that Angelique joined the coven for a while to help instruct and encourage the young sisters'? Just think of that my friend!" Satan goaded Seth.

"No! Get us out of here" Seth yelled

The Devil raised his fingers again and the scene immediately vanished. They were back in Seth and Lilys' bedroom. Lily continued to sleep on and Satan studied Seth where he stood at the side of the bed, now next to his wife in a protective stance.

"What was the point of that? Why show me something that happened nearly four hundred years ago?"

"Because, my dear author, that happened as you say, nearly four hundred years ago but it has also happened constantly since 1628 when Father David left your plain and entered mine. That was to be his eternity, his reward for serving me, then as the others died it became theirs too, believe me Seth, they are *more* than satisfied with how their afterlife turned out. Would you like to ask them yourself?"

"No!" snapped Seth "I don't want to talk to any dead priests thank you"

"As you wish" Satan smiled

"That still doesn't explain why you showed it to me"

"Ah yes, well you see, you're a creature of certain *tastes*, as am I, and I feel I can give you pleasure ever after. Unmeasured pleasure, whatever your dark heart requires, that was just a mere sample of my delights."

Seth was speechless, his brow furrowed and his jaw hung open as he shook his head in disbelief at what he was hearing. Absent-mindedly he stroked Lilys' leg through the bed covers as she slept.

"She will grow old Seth, she'll wither and die" The Devil said bluntly.

"So will I" Seth snapped back "But at least we will be together forever"

"You think so? Seth, sooner or later you will have to accept that you are destined to spend your 'forever' with me, not with Lily. That is just the natural order of things, your only choice now is to how you spend that eternity. You can have pleasure so endless that it becomes almost painful or pain so excruciating that you learn to love your tormentors touch. All that will come in time and time is all that you will have to either enjoy or loathe the sensations."

As Satan spoke Seth could almost physically feel the atmosphere in his room change. Suddenly he was aware of a pulsing beat like that of a heart and he moved to the side of the room. The wall seemed to move ever so slightly as if it were breathing, he put his hand on the wall to check for movement and it was damp to the touch. He looked at the Devil who sat impassively on his throne, the throne was clearer now to Seth from where he stood. It was made of bone, human bones, twisted and blackened as if charred then polished but human bones all the same. Across the sides of the throne it seemed to be upholstered in leather, yet the leather seemed to move. The 'leather' was skin, again human skin, a fact made all the clearer when he noticed that there were features in the fleshly covering, a face, a mans' face and as Seth stared in amazement the mouth opened to issue forth a silent scream of intense pain and agony.

When Seth looked back at the wall he saw that it was now streaked with a dark liquid, tentatively he touched the liquid as it oozed thickly. He brought some of it up closer to his eye sight in the dim light, it was blood. As Seth looked around the room in horror, every wall now ran deep with thick red rivers of blood. Not for the first time, Seth stood there with a mixture of bemusement and terror in his eyes.

"Sit down Seth" Satan spoke with calmness and Seth did as he was bid "is there anything that you want to ask me?"

"Why me?" he whispered hoarsely and timidly in his shock

"Why you? A good question. Well, you are undoubtedly good at what you do, or at least you were once upon a time. Your life had fallen apart, you'd lost your money, you'd lost your way, you'd lost your son" he noticed Seth visibly wince at the mention of Jack "I'm sorry about that, it was a tragedy I accept but that was not of our doing I can assure you."

The Devil let all his words seep into Seths' mind before he continued with the rest of Seths' decline and downward spiral to Hell, literally.

"You'd lost your wife and your whole life was crumbling around you, out of control. You had become a drunk and a womaniser; let's just say that you were very susceptible to us. My Legions can be very persuasive, I would go so far as to say that you were the ripest of not-so-forbidden fruits to be picked, the perfect candidate for them, maybe the question should be 'why not you'?'"

"So, why in my dreams? Why not just show yourselves, Angelique did." Seth questioned

"Because mortals are naturally more open during sleep, their guard is down and they feel safe as their body recharges, visitations can be passed off as nightmares. If you were approached as Angelique did, you would not have allowed it to pass into your subconscious where it can play with your mind. However, you were very stubborn in your denial of the pact so Angelique changed things to make you understand that this is all very, *very* real and not just a dream. In you mind you feel as if you are going insane and you just want it to stop, just like you did when we gave you your novel."

Seth sighed, he had no answer, everything seemed to have a strange kind of logic to what Satan was saying and Seth just wanted to wake up, he needed this to be over, even in his dream he knew that he had to wake to clear his mind and think rationally.

"So, what exactly do you want from me?" Seth sighed in surrender.

"Ah, you have come around at last, you will learn in time that resistance to me is a lesson in futility."

"No, I just want to know what you want from me; I haven't said that I'll do what you want yet."

Satan sighed deeply and it sounded like a dark and angry growl, Seth felt the floor rattle beneath his feet and the Devils' nostrils flared at Seths' seeming contempt of him.

"You test my patience at your peril Caine" he snarled "do you still intend to defy me, boy?"

"I want to know what is expected of me, this might be the first of many things you want from me" Seth tried to stay calm and firm and in control.

"Very well, I want you to write another book."

"I gathered that much from your minions" Seths' lack of respect was borne out of his sudden realisation that they actually *needed* him.

"I would be very careful using terms such as that Caine, one day soon enough you will meet those *minions* again. However, the book you will write will be my story"

"Your story?" Seth was puzzled

"That is correct, I feel I have been misrepresented as you would say. All your world sees is good and evil, black and white, your God and me. There is more to the story of the world than anyone knows and you are going to put forth my side of that particular story."

"That's ridiculous" sneered Seth

"Ridiculous? But how do you know what is ridiculous or fact or fiction, how do you separate history from myth and legend, decide between truth and lies? You cannot do any of that until you have all the evidence to make a judgement. Innocent until proven guilty is practically a commandment in your world I believe, is it not? I have been tried and convicted and condemned in the eyes of the majority of mortal minds and all based on what? Dusty old books handed down from generation to generation, stories told and retold. Stories become fragmented and disjointed over time Caine, so that centuries later, very little of the actual truth remains."

"Interesting concept, and if I don't do it?"

Seths' stubbornness was starting to wear thin and Satan leaned forward, suddenly he lurched effortlessly but with amazing speed and reaching out a hand he grabbed Seth by the throat in his vice-like grip. Immediately Seth realised the power and fury of the beast as he stared into those furnace eyes and felt the rancid breath on his face. Seth had been taunting and dismissing something that was way beyond his comprehension, all too late, his situation was starting to dawn on him. He gasped for breath desperately under the awesome yet controlled power threatening to crush his windpipe.

"If you don't, I will take away everything that I have given you" he hissed and snarled through clenched teeth "Everything! I wouldn't kill you straight away of course Caine, I would make you suffer first on this plain before you suffer for eternity in mine. I will start by taking your wealth and bankrupting you, your fame will be tarnished irreparably, your whole life will crumble and you would climb back inside the stinking bottle you crawled out of."

He released his grip on Seth before he lost consciousness, throwing him back onto the bed; Seth rubbed his throat and gasped for air, his eyes wide with fright.

"Moreover Caine, if you cross me, I will take . . . ." Satan didn't finish the sentence, he didn't need to, he just pointed with a long sharpened nail at the sleeping Lily. "We have given you your life back and I can take it all away again, your time is running out Seth, deliver on the pact or your life is mine . . . and everything in it, think on Caine."

With that, he was gone, Seth sat on the edge of his bed sobbing like a child and shivering with fear, trying to decide what he should do next, assuming that is, that he woke up from this nightmare.

CHAPTER 25

Seth rolled over in bed as the morning light poured into his room. He reached out a hand to touch Lily but didn't make contact. Still half asleep he blindly padded around the bed for his wife but she wasn't there. Seth opened his eyes and darted glances around the room, there was no sign of her anywhere. He quickly jumped out of bed and ran into the bathroom, still nothing. His dream quickly came back to him and Seth started to panic, he searched every room upstairs and called her name but still there was no response.

He stood at the top of the staircase and looked down; he could see no-one but could smell burning. Slowly, hesitantly he moved down the stairs not knowing who or what to expect down there. All he wanted was for Lily to be there, alone. Seth crept like a cat through the house and the burning smell intensified, his mind conjured all sorts of horrible images which he tried to force away then he heard Lilys' unmistakable voice emit a yelp, he ran into the kitchen.

"Lily, are you ok?" he yelled, immediately noticing blood on the counter
"I'm fine" she stood at the sink, rigid with surprise at his rapid entrance and cursed to herself.
"You screamed, there's blood!"
"I didn't *scream*, I just cut the tip of my finger off, that's all" she protested
"But you're alright? You're alone?"
"Of course I'm alone, who else did you expect to be here?" she answered as she wrapped a cloth tightly around her finger to stem the blood flow.
"I can smell burning!" he said in desperation, still panicking and frantic.
"Seth, I'm cooking breakfast, I sliced my finger on a knife and that burning is, or was, the toast. What the hell's the matter with you?"

"Oh Lily" he gushed and ran over to where she stood, sweeping her up in a tight and loving embrace.

"Good morning to you too!" she smiled but consternation quickly took over and concern spread across her face.

"Oh darling, I thought he'd taken you." He gasped as he squeezed her more tightly, never wanting to let her go.

"No baby, I'm right here" Lily pulled gently back from the hug to look into his face. His eyes were red and tear-filled and he shivered in his nakedness. She eased him back farther and sat him on a kitchen stool. Quickly she ran upstairs and grabbed his bathrobe before returning and wrapping it around him, rubbing his arms and back in order to warm him up. Her efforts were in vain however, his shivers were from fear not the temperature though her love warmed his heart

"So much blood" Seth uttered in a distant almost child-like voice.

"What?" she frowned before realising he was looking at the counter in some distress and immediately threw a towel over the offending scarlet pool "Don't worry I'll clean it up in a minute, amazing how much a small injury can bleed isn't it?"

He looked at her hand, swathed in the bloody cloth, the bleeding had eventually started to ease so she swapped the stained cloth for a bandage which she applied as quickly as possible in order to attend to her ashen faced husband.

"Now, just who did you think had taken me?" she asked as she poured two cups of strong coffee hoping the caffeine would clear his head a little.

"Er, never mind" he replied, suddenly feeling ridiculous.

"No Seth, don't do that, you need to tell me. If I'm going to help you we need to stick together and that means you telling me everything, so tell me, who was supposed to have taken me?" she passed him a cup as she finished.

"Satan" he said simply as he sighed

"What? Did you just say Satan?" she definitely wasn't expecting that.

"Yes, Satan"

"As in the Devil?" she desperately hoped she had mis-heard him.

"Yes Satan, yes the Devil, Lucifer, Beelzebub or whatever else you want to call him." He felt absolutely stupid and humiliated just saying the words out loud.

"And er, why would er Satan have taken me exactly?"

"Look Lily, I know all this sounds preposterous to you, a woman of science and rationale and logic but this is actually happening to me. Whether it's all in my head or even if turns out to be real, it's still happening and it's driving me insane." Seth clenched his fists in anger at his situation and the adrenalin started to pump through his veins causing him to shake more.

"Aw baby" she moved over and wrapped her arms around him lovingly and kissed his forehead "Then let me help you, tell me what happened, please?"

"Alright" he sighed again, feeling as if the weight of the world was pressing down on him.

"I promise you'll feel better when you've unburdened yourself and got it all out in the open, don't bottle it up darling"

"That's what Dr Roth said" Seth frowned

"Really? Well I won't be charging you" Lily laughed lightly to ease the tension.

"Neither did she" Seth half smiled back

"Oh?"

"It doesn't matter, forget it" he shook his head dismissively.

"Alright, we'll forget her, now tell me what's been happening in your dreams, I know about how you were having all those nightmares about being tortured and then you dreamt of Jack, but since then?" Lily deliberately wanted to avoid bringing Jack up again, she didn't want to get upset and in Seths' current state she felt he wouldn't be able to handle it.

"Well, I started to have dreams of a . . . sexual nature" he paused.

"Go on, sexual dreams are rarely actually about sex, you won't tell me anything that can shock me" she smiled again and stroked his thigh reassuringly.

Seth doubted that but decided straight away that he wasn't going to dwell on the specifics of the sexual side and he certainly wasn't going to mention Meridiana or when he knew her as simply Alex the stunning red-head.

"These sexual dreams were always very dark and they were always interrupted by the sudden manifestation of a demon. The demons knew me and talked to me about my life. The first one, Mammon, told me about how I could one day have everything back the way it used to be."

"That's what Severin told me" Lily said under her breath

"What?"

"Severin Frost, my patient with the 'Dark Friends', he told me I could have it all back. Oh Seth, this is all getting too coincidental." She pulled out a stool and sat beside him, holding his hand tightly "Go on, what else did he say?"

"Nothing really, just that I would be visited again soon. Then I went to see Dr Roth, she told me to open myself up to them and accept and embrace my dreams."

Lily frowned at this and shook her head, they both simultaneously took a drink from their coffee cups and Seth continued his story.

"That night I went home and had another dream, now this is where it gets a little cloudy because I remember the sexual element and the demon Astaroth visiting me but I'm not sure about the conversation. That's when they say that I agreed to the pact but I'm not sure if I did or what I actually agreed to. They would give me my life and success back if I agreed to write a book for them, or so they say.

Anyway, the next morning I woke up with a hellish buzzing and agonising pain in my head. Strangely, the only way to ease it was by writing, I know that sounds stupid but for some reason I was *compelled* to write and it really did work, as if there was a pressure behind a damn and my writing let it all out and released that pressure." He paused and took another drink.

"No darling, that doesn't sound stupid, in your own time just tell me everything you can remember." She looked at the clock on the kitchen wall "I'll be a little late for work but you are my priority." She stroked his face tenderly.

"Anyway" he continued, appreciating the warmth and love from her caress "That became 'Suffering Innocence' and as you know, the success followed as they said it would, I got my fame and fortune back and I'm bigger than I ever was. I even got the dream movie that I never expected" he paused again, shaking his head.

"Are you ok? Do you want to carry on?"

"Yes, you're right, I need to get this out of me." He drained his cup then got up and went to the coffee machine to pour himself some more, he offered Lily a refill but she declined. He stood for the rest of his tale, feeling more relaxed and focused as she had said he would, leaning on the kitchen counter with both hands as he spoke.

"Well all that was a year ago. Then when you were away at the conference I went out for a few drinks with Karl, the funny thing is that I asked him to stay over. I don't know whether that was because I was lonely without you or whether it was because I thought something was going to happen, I can't explain that. As it happens I did get another visitor, this time it was Asmodeus. He was a nasty piece of work and I really don't want to bump into him again, anyway, he told me that I had made this pact and now I had to honour it, I couldn't remember it despite him explaining. In the end I plucked up my courage and basically told him and the whore he was with to fuck off and leave me alone."

Lily sat with raised eyebrows at this revelation, Seths' now clenched fist had started to shake again and she calmed it by placing her hand on top of his.

"That was very brave of you, to stand up to them" she whispered

"Brave or stupid? It seemed a pretty good move at the time because they left, now I'm not so sure it was." His half smile was more a grimace.

"'Anything else?" Lily asked

"Oh yeah, a lot, but do you have time?"

"Plenty, I will always make time for you honey" she smiled again as she looked into his eyes with concern.

"After that" he continued "I felt quite pleased with myself and I went to Simmons & Stanley for the signing session. Everything was going really well, nothing out of the ordinary, when the next the thing I know, I look up and one of the women from the dreams, the sexual part, is standing in front of me, in the shop! I couldn't believe it!"

"Seth" Lily interrupted "I'm not doubting you for a second but did anybody else see her?"

"I know what you're thinking, I thought the same, it must be some sort of hallucination right? But there was people standing in line behind her and after she'd gone, Gus even came over and commented on her!"

"Ok, what did she say?" Lily masked her now mixed feelings, if this woman was real after all, did that mean he'd cheated on her? Was it a dream after all? How much was fact or fiction? Some of it, none of it or all of it?

"She said the same sort of things, that they had kept their part of the pact and now I had to keep mine, basically, or else!" he frowned "Oh and later that day, if you remember, is when that fucking priest came up to me in the alley and told me to stop writing because I'm an abomination and offending the planet, so I punched him a couple of times."

"Is that when Satan comes in?" Lily sighed, wishing she could be more help but also wishing that he'd told her what he'd been dealing with a long time ago when she could've helped intervene in his pain and torment at an earlier stage.

"Yes, I mean no, first I went to see Dr Roth as you suggested"

"And what did she have to say?"

"Well, she had come up in one of those dreams too, with Asmodeus but calling herself Meridiana."

"Why didn't you tell me about her?" Lily felt hurt and a little betrayed and even a touch of jealousy, dream or no dream.

"Because I wasn't sure about anything" he squeezed her hand, now reassuring her "least of all my own sanity. Like I keep saying, I'm still not sure even at this point of what's real and what's in my mind."

"Ok, go on." Lily sighed again.

"She basically let me connect all the dots for myself and then came right out and admitted her part in all of this, she seemed to think of it all like a game, my life and mind is falling apart but she laughed it off. Then she kept saying the same things as Angelique in the bookstore and Asmodeus in the dream" Seth wasn't going to go into the specifics of how Dr Roth/Meridiana tried to tempt and persuade him to keep the pact in her office.

Lily was quiet and contemplating what he had told her so far, a lot of it was difficult to handle, from a strictly professional point of view it all seemed ludicrous, but some of these people were obviously real, at least to Seth, not just in his head. Added to that there was Severin Frost in the back of her own mind, another very real person, with his offer of 'you can have it all back' and his 'Dark Friends', it was clear that he had got a lot to do with this.

"Then last night" Seth brought her up to speed with the latest chapter "I had a visit from Satan himself. You were there with me."

"Oh really?" Lily raised her eyebrows with surprise, she was about to say that she didn't remember or feel anything but knew that it would be even more bizarre and complicated if she had remembered Seths' own dream.

"Yes, he was sat at the foot of the bed on a sort of throne, he didn't look how I imagined he would look. I've never thought he'd be all red with a tail and pitchfork but he just appeared so amazingly handsome and *seductive* I suppose you could say. Anyway he showed me a convent, again while you were sleeping right there, and there was this orgy going on with priests and nuns and things like that. I think he was just trying to get my attention, the upshot of it all was that he could give me anything I ever wanted as long as I write this book for him."

"Did he say what this book was to be of?" asked Lily

"Yes, basically he wants me to be his biographer!"

"His biographer?" Lily was becoming more stunned with each revelation.

"That's right, well pretty much. He wants me to write his side of the story, as he puts it. He wants to let people know there is more to the stories that have been passed down through the ages which have basically given him a bad reputation, now he wants to put his side of the story across."

"Sympathy for the Devil?" Lily half laughed, uneasily

"Hey, that's not a bad title" Seth smiled

"You're not seriously thinking about doing this are you?"

"Do I have much choice? If this all turns out to be real and I continue to refuse, I'm fucked!"

"Seth, listen to me, you really cannot even consider writing this book, have you any idea of the controversy and chaos that this would cause? Have you any idea of the hurt and upset to people and religions all over the world that a book like that would bring?"

"Lily you're sounding like that priest now." He smiled

"And he would be right, you can't do this Seth." Lily wasn't smiling

"Well what would you have me do then?" he threw his hands up in frustration

"Well" Lily thought for a few seconds "Have they caused you any actual physical damage or is it just mental?"

"Apart from the scars on my face from that winged demon, I suppose not."

"Ok then, I need to get you referred to someone" she said.

"Lily, another psychiatrist? To explain it all over again?" Seth was already tired of telling his story.

"Please Seth, I think you need some serious specialised help."

"But darling"

"No buts Seth, please trust me, I have to go to work now but when I'm there I can contact a few colleagues and decide who would be best for you. I've already got a couple in mind but I need to find out who's available at such short notice."

Seth tutted and sighed to himself, rubbing his temples to ease a headache that had started to come over him as he told Lily of the events.

"Please Seth. I know what I'm doing, let me help you." She begged "just give me today to sort it out, just one more day and I'll pull a few strings. Some people owe me favours and I'll explain about the urgency of the situation without going into too much detail over the phone."

"Ok" he sighed again "but I need to get it sorted out as soon as possible, I don't want to be waiting around for ages for an appointment, I don't know when I'm going to get another nasty surprise in my head!"

"No problem" she smiled "I'll get right on it as soon as I get to the institute."

"I'm going to be going out of my mind with all of this today while you're at work."

"I'll tell you what would be a good idea" she said excitedly "research"

"Research of what?" he questioned

"These Demons" Lily replied

"What the fuck?" Seth was less than enamoured by the prospect.

"Listen to me, if we're going to fight this thing, whether it's in your head or not, we'll need all the information we can get. Knowledge is power remember, it could be very useful to be armed."

Lily could be very formidable and tenacious when she got her teeth stuck into something and one of the many reasons why he loved her.

"I suppose so" he admitted with a small grin.

"You've already got piles of books on this sort of thing, you just need to look more deeply into them and study hard, there's the internet too of course." She grinned back at him

"Ok, ok, I get it, thank you for my homework assignment Dr Caine" he lent forward and kissed her and laughed as he did so.

"What're you laughing at?" she smiled

"You're drive, stubbornness, fortitude, all part of the many reasons why I married you."

"And I always thought that it was because of my tight ass and wanton desires" she laughed and kissed him deeply.

"Well that too!"

"Aw baby, now I really have to go darling" she kissed him again "don't worry, we'll beat this together, I love you."

"I love you too" he replied as he watched her leave.

CHAPTER 26

Lily arrived in her office determined and focused, her husbands' mental state was hanging in the balance at the very least, let alone his physical well-being if threats against him were to be believed.

On her arrival her secretary, Linda, had given Lily her messages then brought her a cup of coffee while Lily flicked through her contacts book for colleagues phone numbers. During the drive to work she had mulled over Seths' problems then considered and dismissed her various contemporaries based on her professional opinion of their usefulness and skills in this specific and unique situation, she only wanted the very best. Lily had narrowed down her shortlist to two candidates who were at the top of their profession but also within a reasonable distance to get to as well as being quite accommodating to Lily at such short notice. That shouldn't be a problem if she used a little influence.

Her two choices were both excellent and renowned in their field and she knew that the help of either one of them would be of great benefit to Seth, her chosen ones were Dr George Haslam and Professor Paul Michie. Lily found their phone numbers and called first George Haslam, unfortunately she was told that he'd been involved in a recent car accident and was a few weeks away from returning to full practice. She was assured that it was nothing too serious and she asked for her best wishes to be conveyed to the good doctor, as she hung up she whispered "fuck" under her breath. She was now down to her last shot, otherwise she would have to look at the 'also-rans' in the race.

Lily called Professor Michie and thankfully she was put straight through to him. He was in fine health and delighted to hear from her as it had been some time since they had last spoken regarding a case, they chatted on professional matters for a few minutes out of courtesy. Lily asked after

Professor Michies' family and in turn Paul said how happy he was to hear that Lily and Seth had reconciled. This gave Lily the perfect opportunity to bring up Seth and the real reason for this phone call.

She explained in broad terms about what was going on without giving away too much detail. Lily found herself sitting at her desk with her fingers crossed as she told Paul of the situation and her desperate need for urgency. She was prepared to grovel if necessary but luckily Professor Michie didn't require such things, he said he would be more than happy to help and even told Lily to bring Seth to his home for a private consultation the next day. After thanking the Professor profusely Lily hung up and slumped back in her chair with a sigh. That single phone call and acceptance of help from her colleague seemed to lift a great weight from her shoulders. She drank her coffee and breathed a little more easily before she faced her next challenge.

Lily went to see Severin Frost with determination seeping from every pore of her being. Every guard that she passed on her way to Frost noticed her steely stare, as she arrived at Severins' door more guards awaited her as they had been notified of her visit. The door was unlocked for her and the men made to enter too but she stopped them in their tracks, ordering them to stay outside in no uncertain terms. She went in alone.

Frost was sat in his chair, chained at the wrists to the seat, just as he always was when he was expecting a visitor, the guards always made sure that that protocol was observed.

"Ah my dear Lily" Frost smiled his lecherous lizard smile.

"Dr Caine" she replied coldly

"Oh, I'm sorry, no offence *Dr Caine*, I didn't realise that we were returning to such formalities. To what do I owe the pleasure of you're company on such a glorious morning?"

"Cut the crap Severin, you know exactly why I'm here don't you?"

"My, my, we are forthright today aren't we" Frost mocked with his tone and voice yet his expression seemed to be of stone but with eyes that independently scared her, or rather they would have done on any other day.

"Your *Dark Friends*, who exactly are they and why are they trying to intimidate my husband?"

"Straight to the point, please have a seat doctor" he said

"Ok" she pulled a chair over to sit opposite him "Now tell me what's going on"

"You tell me Lily, what has he told you?"

"He's told me everything" Lily confirmed

"Everything? Hmm brave man, you must be a very forgiving wife." sneered Frost.

"What do you mean by that?" Lily felt he was playing games to weasel his way around her questions as usual.

"We'll get to that later I'm sure" he goaded "if you know everything then there is very little for me to add my dear, he has a pact to fulfil and fulfil it he must, or suffer the consequences, which will be dire."

"Is that a threat? What kind of game are you people playing here?" Lily found herself getting angrier by the second "You're playing with our lives"

"Game? Ha ha ha" he laughed heartily "This is no game Dr Caine, this is very serious, this is real. He must complete his task as agreed, as you are no doubt aware, my friends have delivered as they said they would and now it is his turn. I don't know how many times this must be stated to him, there is no other way out, I do hope he realises that My Lord is not a patient being."

"Your *Lord*? You mean Satan?"

"Who else, my work was all in His name? Did you really think I would have committed the acts with which I was condemned in the name of your God?" Frost sneered again in derision at the very thought.

""I didn't think you committed your crimes in anyones' name, everyone thought that you were simply insane and naturally evil, yet stupidly I tried to help you." Lily shook her head in disappointment.

"More fool you Lily" his tone made a mockery of all the years she had worked with him, trying to understand him, protect him and even defend him in some instances.

"You bastard"

"I say again Lily, he must be all out of chances by now, if Seth doesn't do as he is told he will regret his actions and sadly I think, so will you." His sneer turned to a hardened serious and cold stare.

"I've told you before not to threaten me Severin."

"Why? There is nothing you can do to me my dear doctor, I know that I may well be free of this place one day soon. Maybe I should look you up at home, that would be nice, a more *personal* visit." He said it in a statement of fact rather than an opinion and he finished his words with a lecherous smile that chilled her soul.

"Really?" she steeled herself with composure and smiled back "Severin, you will never be free, even if by some miracle you are freed from this Institute by your reptilian lawyers, you would still be incarcerated somewhere else and for the rest of your life."

"Oh, you think so do you?" his smile gleamed like a smug game show host "We shall see my dear, we shall see."

Lily frowned, did Frost really believe that one day soon or even in the distant future, he would be released back into society to no doubt prey on the weak again? He couldn't possibly have knowledge of that, especially not before Lily, she would have to be consulted anyway and even if she was, she would block any ludicrous plans to free him.

"If anything happens to Seth, I'll . . . ." Lily said quickly to change the subject.

"You'll what?" he taunted "What can you do? Cry?" he had never, even at his darkest, ever spoke to her with such contempt.

She had no answer, at least she couldn't think of one now, her heart raced as she tried to think of a response under his glare but nothing came. Lily stood to leave and Severin spoke again.

"So, he told you everything did he?"

"What are you talking about now?" she asked though she'd had enough of talking to him now, he was starting to repulse her.

"Seth, he told you all? Even about how he met Alex?"

"Alex?" she questioned

"Oh sorry, Dr Roth to you, but Meridiana to me"

"Er, she was his therapist but not anymore" she was confident in her response but feeling very uneasy about anything that was going to come out of his vile mouth.

"Ah, but how did they meet?" he taunted her further now and she knew it.

"Spit it out Severin, what are you getting at" she refused to rise any further to his bait.

"They met in a bar. They went back to her place and they fucked each other til they could fuck no more" he did indeed spit it out at her, he spat it out like cobra venom "is that how you vet your patients Dr Caine? I wish you had, I would've enjoyed that immensely" he leered while he mentally undressed her.

Lily stood still and stared at him, enraged by his accusations but upset, Seth had been evasive about this so-called Dr Roth from the start and this was probably why. How much truth there was in anything that Frost ever said was open to debate but she could feel the tears welling up in her eyes and her fists clenched. She had only one answer to what she'd heard, Lily rushed over and struck him with all her pent up rage and pain and upset, her fist caught him fully in the mouth.

"Shut your filthy mouth!" she screamed as she dealt the blow.

Frost hadn't expected that and spat a dislodged tooth across the room as blood dripped down his chin. He smiled at her, displaying the gap where his tooth had been. Lily stood frozen to the spot, shocked by her own violent actions. On hearing a commotion the guards had entered the room behind her, they asked if everything was alright and Lily said nothing as she stormed out of the room with Severin shouting after her and laughing hysterically to himself

"Last chance Lily, tell Seth that they're coming for him!"

Lily arrived home earlier than Seth had expected, she hadn't wanted to stay at the Hoffman after her altercation with Severin Frost. She had gone back to her office but just sat brooding over the situation that they had become embroiled in. The thought of Seth with another woman cut deep into her heart, despite all his womanising ways during their separation, he had never cheated on her while they were together. He had always said that the idea of another man touching her or her touching someone else made him sick to the stomach, she felt exactly the same, her flesh crawled at the idea of Seth with another woman. She just hoped and prayed that this wasn't true, especially after they had reconciled so perfectly. So she had decided to leave work early, telling herself to deal with one problem at a time, the sanity of Seth and now even her own were the priorities first.

As she entered his office at home she found him at his desk, computer monitor to one side with various occult sites on display as he darted his gaze from them to the various assorted volumes of books laid out in front of him.

"Hi babe" he said cheerfully and looking at his watch "I wasn't expecting you back so soon"

"Rough day" she replied "how's it going?"

"Really well actually, this was a good idea, I've found out quite a bit on these things already."

"You want a coffee?" she sighed and moved to the kitchen without waiting for a reply but Seth was so engrossed in his studies that he didn't reply anyway.

She returned a few minutes later with two cups and kicked her shoes off as she walked over to him. She handed him one and stood behind him, looking over his shoulder at what he was working. She bent forward and kissed him on the top of his head and stroked his shoulders, he reached back with a free hand and stroked the back of her leg without taking his eyes off his subject.

"Are you ok?" he smiled as he looked up

"Fine, tell me what you've found" she didn't want to ask him about Alex Roth or whatever her other name was, they would get all this sorted out first and then they could have a serious discussion at a later date, maybe go away for a weekend first though, she thought.

"Well, first of all, the one calling himself Mammon, I'd heard of him before. He's the ancient Lord of Avarice and Greed, he was said to be like a man-made demon, in ancient texts it was more a term for greed rather than an actual demonic being but he sure as hell looked real to me! He talked about my old life and the monetary benefits and wealth that I could achieve in order to give me a better life."

Seth flicked backwards and forwards through his reference books and alternated also to clicking on differing websites to relay his new found information

"Next we have Astaroth, ruler of forty of hells legions, interestingly enough he may have started out as a female Goddess called Astarte, I wouldn't like to be the one to point that out to him! Ha ha" Seth laughed to himself at the very idea, Astaroth looked every inch the monstrous warrior as opposed to a former Goddess "but he was transformed into a demon and thrown from Heaven for opposing Gods' will, apparently he knows all secrets. Then we have that nasty looking fucker, Asmodeus" Seth pointed out a picture of the creature to which he pulled a face and Lily winced "Head of the Order of the Seraphim, the demon of rage and lust, no shit! I can understand the rage part but lust? The three-headed description I've got here is pretty accurate but it says he's courteous and softly spoken in this book, I suppose it's in the eye of the beholder" Seth smiled up at Lily as he tried to lighten the mood a little.

"Anything else?" she half smiled back

"Er, the convent that *He* showed me at Louvier, that's all factual, I found bits on that. I couldn't find anything on the succubi, oh except for Meridiana, remember her?" Seth didn't know what he was saying by bringing up Alex, so lost in his research was he. Lilly just nodded with gritted teeth as she tried to desperately hold her tongue.

"Well I found a Meridiana in the 10th Century who seduced a young man who later went on to the Papacy just like she said, Pope Sylvester II. It's all very interesting when you delve deeper into it." He smiled again.

"I'll get started on dinner" she said as she stood and went back into the kitchen to take her mind off this Meridiana.

"Hey darling, you have to see this first" he called after her.

She really wasn't in the mood for this but reluctantly she went back into the office to see what else he had dug up.

"Have to see what?" she sighed

"Come here, who does this remind you of?" he said with a grin on his face as he brought up a picture on the computer of an old painting, centuries old, as she drew closer the image hit her like a bolt between the eyes of the unmistakable

"Father Seymour Duncan" she gasped and stood there open-mouthed in shock.

"I know, looks good for his age doesn't he? I wouldn't have hit him so hard if I'd have known he was over four hundred years old" Seth joked and laughed.

"Who is it?" she said in a hushed voice

"It's actually er, Prince Bishop von Dornheim. He ran a witch hunting operation in the 1620s' in Bamberg, is that in Germany or Austria?" he asked "Anyway, he tortured and executed over 600 people in a place called the 'Hexenhaus' or witches house, apparently. Nasty bastard eh?"

"My God" gasped Lily again.

"I know, he's a dead ringer for your priest."

A shiver slipped down Lilys' spine as she looked into those cold and cruel eyes, a man supposedly doing Gods' work, she'd seen and heard enough for one night and left Seth with his new fascination and went back into the kitchen.

Later that evening, after they'd eaten, they sat quietly watching TV, Lily had been relatively quiet since she came home from work and Seth asked her again if she was ok.

"I'm fine" she told him

"No you're not, tell me." He insisted as he turned off the TV.

"Ok, first of all, I've made an appointment for you with Professor Paul Michie, he's a leading psychiatrist and someone who I respect a great deal. He's very kindly offered to help us."

"No problem, how soon can he see me?" Seth seemed very eager and focused all of a sudden which encouraged Lily that they could get through this together after all.

"Tomorrow, at his home. I'm to go round there with you after work, so be ready and I'll pick you up, is that ok?"

"That's great" he said, only then noticing her bruised hand from where she had struck Severin Frost "What did you do to your hand?"

"Oh, I er trapped it in the car door" she lied

Seth felt she wasn't telling the truth but also thought that there was something else on her mind, her sullen mood was a dead giveaway on someone so normally upbeat.

"Please Lily, tell me what's wrong" he asked again

"I went to see Severin Frost again today" she said

"Lily, I thought I told you, you should stay away from him."

"Yes and you also said that you didn't know him!"

"I don't know him! But if he's got anything to do with what's going on then you need to steer clear of him." He protested

They both sighed and stared into space, Seth was curious about this man Frost though. His name had come up too many times and all at bad times.

"Who the hell is he anyway? What's he done, this Frost guy?" Seth asked tentatively.

"He's a priest slayer!" she answered bluntly "He trapped various priests, usually in their own churches, then he tortured, tormented and slaughtered them in cold blood."

"Wow, how many?" asked a clearly shocked Seth.

"Well, seven that he was convicted of, beheading, crucifixion and various other things. He's also thought to have tortured others as well as raping and molesting his way through a convent. He's a pretty sick individual"

"Why isn't he doing multiple life sentences in prison then?"

"Because he had the best legal team that money could buy, simple as that, if you have enough money you can buy your way in or out of pretty much anything I suppose."

Seth was suddenly very quiet after listening to what Lily had said, he seemed to be contemplating or trying to remember something and it seemed to be causing him some distress.

"Seth, what is it?" she asked

"The seven killings, do you remember what they were and in what order they were done?"

"Why?" Lily frowned

"Please Lily, do you remember?" he said sharply

"Ok, ok, just a second, I've got some notes in the filing cabinet"

Lily got up and went to her locked filing cabinet in the office, a few minutes later she returned with a notepad to a very anxious and pensive looking Seth.

"Well, well?" he tried to hurry her

"Just a minute" she complained as she flicked through the pad "Ah, here it is, erm, the first one was skinned alive, second dismembered, third one had their eyes gouged out with Frosts' thumbs, next came disembowelment, five er that was beheading . . . ."

"Followed by another beheading and a crucifixion, correct?" he finished for her

"How could you possibly know that?" Lily sat stunned

"Because in my nightmares of being tortured by his so-called dark friends, that is exactly the same order that I was killed!" all colour had drained from his face as he spoke. "Lily, I beg you, please don't have anything more to do with him."

"It's ok, I have no intention of seeing him again; I'll try to transfer him or put him under another doctor." She was aghast at this new revelation and also at his next request of her.

"Lily, can I ask you to go away for a few days, please"

"What do you mean? I thought we were going to deal with all this together?" Lily was so hurt that he would even ask such a thing.

"We will see it through together, I promise. It's just that with getting that visit from *Him* last night and how terrified I was at just the very thought that I'd lost you, it's making me even crazier than the visions and visitations. I'm going to need all my focus on what I'm going to do and you being here distracts me too much, I'm sorry. You do understand don't you?" his eyes filled with tears and sorrow and she knew how serious he was.

"I'll go and stay with" she began

"No!" he interrupted "don't tell me, if they can get inside my head so easily, they might know where you are, I can't take the chance that they might get to you somehow"

She had already decided that she was going to go and stay with Gus and Natalie, on reflection after listening to Frosts' taunts about Seth and Alex it might prove to be not such a bad idea at the moment she thought.

"Alright, but I can't go until tomorrow night though, I have to take you to see Professor Lipscomb after work remember? Then I'll drop you off back here when we're done and I'll leave you to it, only for a couple of days though and you must promise to keep in touch and let me know how things are going." She stroked his cheek as she spoke "You better phone me every night to say goodnight, or else!"

"I promise" he replied softly and lent forward and kissed her gently.

"Now come on" she smiled "It seems that this is going to be our last night together for a few days so let's make it count and go to bed"

"Whatever you say darling"

CHAPTER 27

They made love that night, tenderly and passionately, as if it were to be their last ever night together. They forgot about everything and everyone else and got lost in each other and the moment. Somehow it seemed like the last conjugal visit for a condemned man awaiting execution and they both felt it. For the most part they slept in each others arms, entwined, not wanting to let go for fear they may never feel each others touch again.

Due to their sexual exertions, sleep came over them both easily and heavily until Seth felt himself being softly rolled over and away from Lily and then gently pushed in the back, slowly he was being inched away from his wife. He was pushed gradually to the edge of the bed, he didn't fight it, in his deep sleep he thought it was just Lily needing more space. She had always been a restless sleeper who took up more than her fair share of the bed and, as always, he obliged without resistance. More and more he felt himself slowly being guided towards the edge until his arm hung out, he lay there still dead to the world until another little nudge pushed him off and towards the floor.

Seth fell to the floor but when he should have made an immediate impact he just kept falling. Falling and falling, over and over, he opened his eyes to nothing but blackness. Head over heels, arms flailing and legs kicking in order to make some kind of contact with something, anything, he had to grab whatever was available to break his seemingly never ending fall, or at least slow himself down. Faster and faster his descent increased, his hair whipped around his face, his cheeks rippled at the force of the air he cut through as he dropped, he opened his mouth and issued forth a shout for help but only silence emerged while his limbs continued to grasp in desperation and more furiously for some sort of self-preservation.

Suddenly and without any kind of warning, Seth landed with a bone-jarring crash on a dusty plain. He clambered to his feet with a groan of pain; from the almost endless fall and the manner of his violent and abrupt halt he felt he should have broken every bone in his body. He was surprised and relieved to find he was still in one very sore piece albeit with a few minor abrasions and bruises. Seth looked around as he brushed the dust from what should be his *sleeping* naked body; this was a place unlike anywhere he had visited before. It reminded him a little of the deserts he had seen on TV or maybe the wild and remote Australian outback, yet it was even more barren than that. He quickly surveyed the scene, no plant life, no birds in the sky; he looked across the ground to notice that there weren't even bugs or insects scuttling around. It summed up the word desolate, the sky itself was red and tinged with purple like an unusual sunset but there was no sun that he could see of any kind yet the place seemed very well illuminated.

He looked this way and that but saw no-one and nothing to break the endless horizon. Seth started to walk, he didn't know where he was walking to or indeed where he was walking away from, he just felt that he should start walking in the direction that his first steps took him in and so off he went. He stumbled naked through the wasteland for what seemed like hours upon hours, his muscles ached, his mouth parched and his lips cracked from the heat of the invisible sun that he thought would have set by now, eventually he stumbled forward and collapsed in a dusty heap of exhaustion in the middle of nowhere. Still he had seen nothing to give him any clue as to his whereabouts, he lay heaving for breath, hot, exhausted and alone, he closed his eyes and felt he was about to die.

An almighty commotion of shouting and cheering caused Seth to open his eyes; he had no idea how long he had been lay face down in the dirt. He now found himself on the edge of a huge gathering, where the hell had all these people suddenly and silently appeared from? Seth was shocked and even more disorientated than before, maybe these people could help him or at least let him know where he was.

He clambered to his feet and stumbled over to the throng. They all stood in a circle with their backs to him and seemed to be watching some sort of event. As he approached it quickly became apparent to him that these weren't people at all, these were beings that were clearly otherworldly. The closer he got to them, the more obvious their otherworldliness became, his head knew that he should be moving in the opposite direction, quickly, but his legs seemed to stagger him straight to *them*.

They were, in the most part, quite tall by mortal standards. The majority of them looked very muscular and either very pale white or very dark of skin. Their most obvious difference to mere humans however was the fact that most of them had wings! Large and leathery, ragged wings growing out of their shoulders in a very natural way as if planned by evolution to be so. Seth immediately recalled his dream of the beast clutching Jack at the bottom of his bed. That image had been terrifying in itself; the difference now though was that there appeared to be at the very least hundreds but more likely thousands of replicas of that monstrous creature.

Seth stopped where he stood as more howls of delight erupted from the hordes. As he tried to peer over them, which was nigh on impossible due to their sheer bulk and height, they suddenly and without warning stepped aside. Not just the ones at the back but as they parted so too did the ones in front of them and the ones in front of them and so on until a clear path had opened up before him, allowing him access to the centre of the ring. Not one had turned to face him or even seemed to acknowledge his presence but they all seemed to notice that he was there. He realised that he had been expected and reluctantly he stepped forward, they didn't move or turn and still didn't face him and Seth took a couple more steps forward. His flesh started to crawl however as he sensed the creatures at the back had now closed ranks and completed the circle again behind him. He stepped forward again and the next lines fell back into place, he knew he wasn't going anywhere but forwards, he had no choice whatsoever. He steeled himself and continued to walk forward as the rest of the legions filtered back into their positions, he now noticed an awful stench in the air, emanating from these 'soldiers', a scent of death and decay, of something dead and left out in the sun for way too long. Seth suddenly felt very small and insignificant surrounded as he was but there was little he could do now, he was here and trapped whether he liked it or not and he definitely did not.

He found himself in a clearing at the centre of a huge ring of demons. He stopped and stared around in awe at the masses, hate and venom oozed from the gathering, as bad as the palpable stench that he could actually physically smell. As he stood directly in front of them, some looked at him with disdain, others with rage and many with a severe bloodlust. He stumbled back from them and further into the centre of the ring, trying to get equidistance from all sides. All at once, as though obeying a silent command, the whole monstrous throng of demons took three steps forward. This caused them to close their ranks still further and tighter and also brought them closer to Seth all around, he stumbled again as he stepped back in fear and fell to the ground, he was unable to go in any direction that was safer, there genuinely was no escape. As he lay on the ground contemplating his own surely inevitable and no doubt gruesome demise at their hands he heard a guttural voice.

"Welcome to *my* world Mr Caine"

Seth looked behind himself from his prone and helpless position in the dust. An enormous throne stood there, he couldn't believe he hadn't seen it when he reluctantly entered the ring but there it stood, it was made of bone and polished black rock, ornately carved befitting a king and lined and upholstered with human flesh, as he had seen before but on a much, much more gigantic scale. Sat on the throne, though barely recognisable from their last meeting, was Satan.

"You weren't expecting to see me again so soon were you Caine?" he smiled

Seth sat on the ground with a horrified look on his face. Satan seemed so much bigger in every respect now than when he appeared previously as the suave and erudite gentleman in Seths' room. He also seemed to glow with power and aggression. He seemed far more animalistic than mortal now, stripped of clothing, his muscular physique rippled with intensity like a wild cat ready to pounce on its' prey. Seth clambered to his feet and gazed at his infernal host.

"Where am I?" Seth asked

"You know exactly where you are" Satan replied somewhat redundantly "This is my realm, I and my kind have visited you and now, I felt it would be prudent for you to visit us"

"W-why?"

"Seth, Seth, Seth" he shook his massive head and sighed "must we go over this yet again?"

"The book?" he cast his eyes down as he spoke with shame

"Congratulations. So are you going to write it? Are you going to fulfil your part of the pact?"

"I can't, it would cause untold damage to the world" Seth sighed at the thought then looked around "I mean *my* world"

"Naturally" said Satan, looking bemused "that is the point Caine, I don't believe for a second that you would be so naïve as to think otherwise or that that wouldn't be the whole purpose of it"

"But how can I do such a thing?" Seth protested

Satan studied Seth for a while, he looked him up and down and pondered this mans morality and somewhat surprising conscience.

"How can you do such a thing? I'll tell you what, while you are my guest here, I'll show you why you *must* do such a thing, how about that?" Satan spoke with an evil grin.

Seth stood frozen to the spot, not sure what to expect or what diabolical treats he was going to have to endure.

"First of all though, do you see the legion to my left?" the Devil said as he lifted his mighty hand to gesture to a group of demons larger in stature still than the ones that Seth had stepped between to get there. "They are the Watchers"

Seth looked at them; he could tell that they were once incredibly handsome beings; they looked like the marble sculptures of heroic figures in ancient Rome or Greece, angelic beauty in alabaster form. Now they looked ravaged by time, battle scarred and broken yet so powerful and ready for war once again. As Seth eyed them they stepped forward to announce their presence fully, there must have been over three hundred of them, snarling, sneering and spitting towards Seth with bared teeth gnashing, ready to strike and devour him in seconds.

"The Watchers, my dear Caine, were so once named because your god created them to watch over, protect and guard humanity. Alas your god obviously didn't fully understand just what he had created with them. The Watchers, quite naturally I think, became fascinated by your mortal women and began teaching mortals the forbidden ways of magick and the arts of war while lusting after and seducing your females. Your god was not pleased with them and in his *wisdom* he decided to banish them from his kingdom, therefore they naturally joined with me in an effort to storm the golden walls and create the holocaust of heaven" Satan sat with a rueful smile as he spoke "*My* Watchers get to enjoy as much female mortal flesh as they can catch" he gloated lecherously and the Watchers howled their approval.

"But you failed" Seth said rather too smugly, causing the grin to drop from the face of Satan and the Watchers to tense their muscular physiques, ready and eager to shred this mortal to pieces.

The Devil sat forward in his seat, looking down at Seth from his throne, glowering at the man. The insolence with which a mere mortal spoke to him made him bristle with fury and he clenched his fists. But then Satan calmed as if realising that a larger picture was to be viewed, he would have his time with Caine and make him pay for his lack of respect when the pact was completed.

"Yes, I suppose you might say my uprising failed" Satan spoke thoughtfully while his hordes looked at each other and then looked at him in uncertainty but he continued "But we will be back, one dark and painfully blessed day. There will be a symphony of black tears shed in Heaven when we destroy the gates and smash the walls as I take my rightful place on my rightful throne with your deposed god grovelling at my feet for mercy. He will not beg for mercy for himself you understand, he will beg for mercy for his children, for you and your kind. You are his weakness and therefore his undoing, you see your kind will have played a huge part in his downfall and you, my dear Caine, will have been the catalyst for it all with your book, or should I say, my book."

Suddenly Seth had a vision placed directly into his mind by Satan of crumbling walls, gates being torn apart, palaces burning and dying angels being thrown from battlements with wings ablaze or hacked to pieces by the Watchers and their cohorts with blood-stained swords, axes and spears. He saw Satan ascend a gold and marble staircase to a bejewelled throne where he sat as surviving angels wept their black tears for their fallen King and his son.

"I cannot be a part of that" Seth whispered hoarsely with emotion as the vile vision ended in smoke, fire, blood and destruction.

"You can and you will Caine" Satan replied firmly.

"Kill me then, because I won't help you to do that, just get it over with" he sighed

"I don't want you dead" laughed the Devil "you are too important to me"

"How can I be that important to you? How can what I write have such a huge impact as to trigger all that as you seem to think?"

"You underestimate yourself, your fame and notoriety coupled with what I have to give you for the book? It will work perfectly. Even if some people don't believe any of my story and think it is a work of fiction, there will inevitably be many mortals, simply starting with your own readers, who *will* believe it. The more that they will believe; the more that they will be able to persuade and convert their weaker minded peers.

Hence, like ripples spreading outwards on a lake of blood, so too, the word will spread. Debate will rage and controversy will ensue, thus the world becomes divided. Your world is already infected and infested by religious intolerance and holy wars, add *my* words to the mix and the potency for this recipe of hate and darkness will increase ten fold. Your world will rip itself to pieces and as your god watches impotently as his creation kills itself, my legions and I will storm his kingdom and take back what should be ours. Hopefully we will do it all with time to spare in order to see the end of his world in flames, then I can force him to watch and he will weep endless tears, then I will recreate life in my dark image."

"You are insane" gasped Seth at the Devils' plan "but I still won't do it"

"Really?" sighed Satan with frustration "I think I can change your mind Seth"

"No, you can't change my mind, now I see what you have in store there is no way I can be a party to that. I'm not a religious man in any way, shape or form, before seeing you in person, I didn't seriously believe that you actually existed but I do know that to aid you in any way would be catastrophic for everyone."

"Ah, but you believe in me now?" Satan smiled

"I'm still not sure, I'm assuming that this is all some lavish nightmare that you've created and eventually I'm going to wake up, hopefully you and these *things*" he gestured at the assembled mass of demons "will be gone again. I may end my days in an asylum somewhere being spoon fed and talking to the walls but I can't help you end the world as I know it, no matter how fucked up it is at times."

"Strong and noble words my friend, I have definitely chosen a man worthy of my company. However, I know, as I said, that I can change your mind."

"No, no you can't, just give it up, I would rather die first." Seth said defiantly.

"Do you remember when you arrived here amongst us?" Satan continued unperturbed by Seths' stubborn refusal

"Yes"

"Do you remember the noise, the cheering and shouting?" Satan teased with a grin.

"Yes, what of it?" Seth was growing weary of his hosts' games.

"You also remember my Watchers?"

"Yes of course, what are you getting at?"

"Now, why were they cast out of Heaven?" Satan asked

"Because they lusted after mortal women and taught man the arts of war and magick" Seth repeated the phrase almost word for word.

"Perfect, you were listening" came the sarcastic reply

"For fucks' sake, just get to the point!" snapped Seth

"The first part of that, they lusted after *mortal* women"

"Er, yeah" all of a sudden Seth started to have a very uneasy feeling in the pit of his stomach.

"Well Seth, put all that together. I need leverage to make you co-operate with my plans, my lust filled Watchers were eager for mortal female flesh, all the cheering and goading, this is my realm remember Seth, I do what I please. Surely there is only one outcome isn't there?"

Seth didn't want to say what had been going through his mind, he didn't even want to consider it himself.

"No response? Alright, I think it would probably be easier to just show you how my legions were entertaining themselves when you arrived."

With that Satan clapped his hands together to an almighty cheer from his army, Seth slowly and reluctantly turned around to see what was happening and the vision before his eyes made him scream.

CHAPTER 28

Two large stone pillars stood erect in the demonic circle, tied between them with arms and legs outstretched was a completely naked woman. Head down with exhaustion she gasped for breath, behind her stood the unmistakable figures of Angelique and Meridiana. They were both dressed as twisted dominatrix', wearing nothing but thigh length boots and thongs all fashioned from human skin. Each held a long black whip with which they were taking it in turns to thrash their unfortunate victim as she struggled to stand, pleading and bleeding. As Seth turned to catch sight of this harrowing scene the woman lifted her head and looked right into his eyes as tears poured down her face and she begged for mercy. "Liiilllllyyyyy!!" he screamed

With each stroke of their lashes, the mass of hellspawn yelled their approval and inched forward for a better view. Seth had crumpled to his knees on seeing his wife being so despicably abused but he gathered his strength and clambered to his feet, dashing to Lilys' aid. Just as he made it to the pillars and her side, two of the Watchers broke rank and caught him, grabbing him by the arms just before he could make contact and touch her. They pulled him back out of reach but close enough that he could still hear her pleas for help, smell her tears, blood and sweat and almost feel the crack of the whip as it flayed her flesh. He hoped that this was some macabre and twisted illusion but the sights, sounds and smells told him otherwise.

Meridiana and Angelique gleefully continued with their sport, urged on by their raucous audiences' screams of delirium. Seth looked at his two captors and while they held him in their vice-like grips they didn't take their eyes off the action in front of them. The Watchers both smiled lecherously as they lived up to their name and Seth stood helpless and closed his own tear-filled eyes. The whipping stopped and Seth opened his eyes hoping that the horror was over, it was not.

The two succubi approached Lily and proceeded to molest her where she hung helplessly. They used their fingers and tongues all over her body, probing every intimate orifice, only pausing their assault to molest each other in the same fashion for their own pleasure, before returning to degrade their victim further to the delight of their demonic on-lookers.

Seth turned his head away from the torture scene and towards the sitting and smiling Satan, who was occasionally glancing to either side and seemingly revelling in the pleasure and joy of his army.

"P-please, stop this." He sobbed as he begged.

The two Watchers picked him up by his arms and carried him back over to their masters' throne where they unceremoniously threw him at Satans' feet. Seth clambered to his knees and grabbed the Devils' foot

"Please, stop it" he begged again,

"I'm sorry Seth; I felt you needed a little more convincing, you did say that there was nothing I could do to persuade you, well, how about this?"

With that the Watchers turned him back around and lifted his head, forcing him to watch as Angelique returned to lashing Lily from behind while Meridiana continued to abuse and molest her from the front. Another brief image came to Seth as he cried, that of Meridianas' head turning completely around on her desk as she was herself molested by the unseen force in her office, he'd hoped that she had been killed during that ordeal yet here she was, in unmarked condition assaulting the love of his life. Seths' tears flowed as his heart raced in anguish and tightened. He slumped forwards but the Watchers held him firm and upright, Seth gasped for air and the pains in his chest grew stronger, shooting now down his arm.

His heart felt like it was in an ever-squeezing vice, crushing the life out of him. He could feel the blood draining from his face and a cold clammy sweat spreading over his whole body. The Watchers raised him up farther and turned him back to their master for analysis. Satan looked down on his victim with disdain.

"Heart problems Mr Caine? How very reminiscent of when you killed your son"

Seth was dropped into the dirt again by the demonic soldiers as they turned their attention back to the 'entertainment'. Seth didn't respond to Satans' jibe, he couldn't.

"I could give you visions of your son watching this if you would prefer? Imagine the look of horror on his face as he watched two of my favourites torturing and raping his mother, that would be delectable. I couldn't actually bring him here of course as alas he is out of even my reach, well for now at least. Once I take my rightful place however, well, things could be different, would you like to see that?" Satan sneered

"N-n-no, I'm begging you to stop this, please." Seth gasped again

"Speaking of your son, do you remember Direth?" Satan ignored his pleas and gestured to his right, a winged-demon stepped forth from the crowd. Through the haze of his tears and pain Seth recognised the leathery beast who had brought an image of his Jack to his bedside nightmare. The creature grimaced and snarled in seeming delight at Seths' demise.

"Direth can visit you every night if you so wish, sometimes with haunting images of your son or maybe even just to ravish and abuse your wife" as the Devil spoke those words a howl of joy erupted from Direth and further screams came from the hordes at Lilys' continued yelps of distress and torment.

Seth couldn't speak though he tried to make his voice heard through the agony and the bedlam now flooding through the demonic throng, he couldn't bring himself to turn and see what was going on behind him; in his head he kept telling himself that it was only a nightmare and that in reality they were both tucked up together in their bed but with each crack of Angeliques' whip and each scream from his wife, that thought became less and less realistic.

"This can be her eternity Seth"

"B-but she has done nothing wrong" Seth found his voice

"That matters not to me, she has done nothing *yet*. You know that I can be extremely persuasive my friend. If I were of a mind to, I could easily manipulate circumstances and turn her to my will." Spoke Satan.

"But, why?"

"To torment you of course, haven't you realised that yet Seth? You are going to spend your eternity here with me, you are going to sit at my side and bask in my reflected glory. Providing that is, that you do as you are told of course and write my book."

"But if I don't, I'm damned anyway, right?"

"Correct, you made a deal with me Mr Caine and the price is your soul, whether you complete your side of the deal is irrelevant as far as your soul being forfeit is concerned. I may have taken it due to how you lived your life anyway but once that you had agreed to the pact" he paused "well it became mine anyway"

Seth knelt in the dirt, broken down, beaten and exhausted, physically and emotionally drained. Tears streaked his cheeks and his mind felt numb at the bleak outlook in front of him, he had no options left, the only thing that really concerned him was Lily. He had to end this living nightmare as soon as possible, for both of them.

"So" he sighed in defeat, though stubborn to the end "If I'm going to spend my forever in your world, where is my incentive?" Seths' physical pain was easing but he stayed down on his knees, crushed and still unable to turn to the horror that he could hear in the background, he had to block it out.

"You're incentive is simply, do you want to spend eternity by my side where you could possibly be enjoying the rewards you have reaped for your services to my crown, remember the priests at Louvier? Well that was a mere trifle compared to the deliciously dark delights that could be afforded to you should you complete our little arrangement. Have you any idea of the power and influence I could allow you to have in my court?" Satan tempted.

Seth looked into the dirt where he knelt, if he was going to spend his days in the womb of damnation, did he have much of a choice? It seemed that, if Satan was to be believed, his dream of one day being reunited with his son was over either way. His only consideration now was Lily.

"What about my wife, what happens to her?" he whispered in grief at the thought of a time without being able to hold her hand.

"Aw Seth, your love for your woman is touching, as I knew it would be" Satan couldn't resist a mocking tone but continued "You would go back to your life together, in time, you can have your happy ever after storybook life as you wish and you will both be unmolested by me or mine. You will be left to live the rest of your lives in peace but when your time comes to an end . . . you will be mine!"

Seth pondered what the Devil had said, it genuinely was the only option, the only way he could have more time of love and peace with Lily. Every moment that he was with her felt like a gift, he thought of the two of them curled up on the couch reading quietly, he thought of walking through the woods together as they often loved to do, he thought of making love to her and the electricity between them. He thought of all those things but his trails of memories were halted when the beast spoke again.

"However, if you fail to comply, my wrath can be just as devastating as my benevolence can be bountiful and endless. As I have told you, you are going to be here with me but have you considered just how long eternity actually is? Either way you will be mine, against me and I will then make it a personal quest to turn Lily to me as well, therefore one day I will have her here with me too, make no mistake. When that day comes I can then make you go through all of this scenario over and over again, each time making it feel fresh and new to your horrified mind. I would have your eyelids removed so that you couldn't even close your eyes to it. Endless pain, endless screams and endless torture. Angelique and Meridiana may eventually grow weary of Lily and require a new victim to persecute, but look around you Seth."

Seth did look around at the salivating hordes no doubt eager for blood and longing to play with Lilys' ripe and luscious mortal flesh, they howled yet more with screams of pleasure.

"Do you think I would ever run out of willing volunteers to take over with what's left of Lily when Angelique and Meridiana have finished with her? No, definitely not, they would be fighting over her. I could have her completely flayed then have one of my many wenches walk around in her skin for the pleasure of my warriors. On the other hand, I could make her a succubus just like Meridiana or Richelle, that way I could send her back into the mortal realm to seduce men and turn them to my will. Just think of that Caine, your wife, your beautiful wife, your Lily prostituted out for endless centuries, over and over again, think of the orgies and how she would be used. Her only payment for her sins is the knowledge that she will be doing my bidding." Satan watched Seth as he knelt in front of him. The rage had been building inside him as the Devil spoke his vile and filthy words, all the time putting lurid images of Lily into his head with each scenario he described.

"One day Seth, this will be your world too. It is just a matter of time and then how you spend it here. One mortal day can feel like an eternity here so just think how long eternity could feel." Satan let that thought hang in Seths' mind for a second before finishing off with the final heart stabbing of "It would feel so much longer too if I forced you to watch your wife doing my bidding, think of that Caine, and imagine if she actually started to enjoy it? You know, I think she might!"

Seth jumped to his feet and dived headlong at Satan, screaming his rage with every fibre of his being as he clawed for the Devils' throat. Satan didn't even flinch as his two Watchers effortlessly caught the man in mid-air. He simply smiled as his guards threw their mortal prey back into the dirt at his feet, where he belonged. Seth knelt in a crumpled, dejected heap, out of questions, out of hope, out of fight.

"Your fate is sealed Caine, all you have to do is accept it and make the best of what time you have left in your world" whispered Satan as he lent forward over Seths' prone body.

"Alright" came the soft reply.

Satan raised his hand in the air, immediately the shouting and screaming from the crowd ceased. So too did the whipping and molestation as every creature gathered there turned to face their master in a deathly silence, all that could be heard was the sobbing of Lily as she hung from the pillars.

"Alright what, Caine?" Satan whispered again.

Seth looked up into the Devils' burning eyes and then he looked out at the vast army of baiting demons hanging on their Kings' every word. Finally he looked over his shoulder at his wife, hanging pitifully broken and bleeding from the pillars as the two succubi stood ready and eager to resume their tortures should the order be given.

"Alright, I'll write your damn book, as you wish." He sobbed in defeat.

Satan raised his hand again, Lily was cut down and the bloodthirsty army cheered again, though this time at their Lords' victory.

"We will leave a glorious trail of destruction together my friend" Satan laughed

"Release her" Seth gasped

"All in good time Caine, you complete our transaction and you will have your lovely woman back warming your bed in no time but not before completion, she is my insurance."

Seth collapsed back to the ground in exhaustion and regret, wondering just what he had exactly agreed to do and what his actions could mean to mankind. Unfortunately, at the moment mankind could wait, all he could really think of was his Lily.

Chapter 29

Seth opened his eyes the following morning with a more than familiar but no less agonising buzzing and ringing in his head. Lily wasn't by his side, despite the agony raging in his skull he knew he just needed to see her face and to know that she was alright. He checked the bathroom but it was empty, he walked along the landing and checked the spare room, nothing. He stood at the top of the stairs and called her name without reply. There was a growing feeling of desperation and loss manifesting itself as a knot in the pit of his stomach and his chest ached as his heart pounded so hard, threatening to burst out through his ribs.

Quietly Seth crept downstairs, his back to the wall as much for support should his legs buckle beneath him, as well as keeping him safe from a surprise attack from behind. The house seemed quiet, too quiet; Lily would be up now and getting ready for work on any normal day. Come to think of it, he had no idea what day it actually was. He kept moving through their home in search of his wife, she wasn't in their office or in the living room. he couldn't smell anything burning or any fresh coffee. He reached the kitchen, the last room in the house that he hadn't checked.

"Please, please, please be in here" he said to himself

He opened the door, nothing. No breakfast, no coffee, no burnt toast, no Lily. He shouted her name at the top of his voice, he noticed for the first time that there was an echo, that only emphasised the emptiness of the house without her and also the emptiness of his life without her.

Seth sat on a kitchen stool and gazed around the room, inside he was panicking even though a part of him also knew that she wasn't going to be there. He tried to think things through, where could she be? She was in his dream, did that mean she could still be in there? Was she trapped in Hell or in his head? Maybe both? Maybe she hadn't really come back to him after all and she was only in his head in the first place, a figment of his imagination? Maybe she was just a part of this whole elaborate twisted game?

Seth felt his mind and life start to unravel as he sat at the kitchen counter, the whole fabric of his life being unpicked at the seams leaving him with nothing but images of what used to be and even those images of better and happier times all of a sudden seemed blurred and bubbled like melting photographs.

Seth found himself softly praying for the safe return of his wife, he hadn't prayed since he was a very little boy but that's just how he felt now, like a frightened little boy.

"Please God let her have gone to work early, please let her come home and say she just didn't want to wake me, please baby just come home, I love you."

He got up and moved back through the house, he saw through the window that Lilys' car was still parked in the driveway. A mixture of joy that she wasn't actually a figment of his imagination and that she had actually come back to him yet the horrible realisation also that she hadn't gone to work early, she should be around the house somewhere, but she wasn't.

Seth moved to the back door and opened it, the house, despite its' size, suddenly seemed to be oppressive and closing in on him. He stepped outside and he noticed a change in the air out there too. It had been one of the hottest and driest Julys' on record yet huge storm clouds loomed above him. The sky was a deep dark grey with a sickly shade of green. Then black storm clouds closed together and not-so-distant thunder growled, as Seth stood and watched the clouds gather, the rain started to fall. It came down quickly and heavily as Seth stood there naked almost hoping for a lightning bolt to strike him and put an end to his torment and misery in one fell swoop, but the bolt didn't come. He stood in the rain until he was soaked through to the bone as the sky seemed to mourn and cry for him and his loss.

He moved back into the house, slick with raindrops which puddled on the floor around him and he shivered, pneumonia would be a blessing now. The demonic presence in his head returned to gnaw away at his mind; he knew what he had to do. Seth went back upstairs and dried himself in the bathroom before getting dressed in the first clothes that came to hand. As he dressed he noticed Lilys' things more and more all around him, her clothes in the linen hamper, her make up on the bathroom shelf, he could smell her scent everywhere, his heart lurched and his tears flowed yet again.

He returned downstairs as he tried to keep his mind together, he poured himself a cup of coffee and then took his seat at the computer. Seth lit a cigarette and drank his coffee, he sat back in his chair and stared at the screen as the cursor blinked at him with familiarity like a dear old friend. He smoked his cigarette and sighed as he waited for the inevitable onslaught and attack on his senses to begin. He didn't have to wait long.

It arrived just as he took another mouthful of coffee, it also arrived with the malevolent and primeval fury of a natural disaster, unsurpassed by anything that he had felt before and it caused him to almost choke on his drink and drop the cup and remainder of the liquid on the desk and tiled floor, the mug smashing on the surface beneath his feet. His body jerked with spasms and his face contorted as if it were undergoing electro-shock therapy. He tried to control his arms and legs but to no avail as they twisted and writhed as if being manipulated by an invisible and sadistic puppet master.

His control over his own body seemed to take an eternity to establish itself, when eventually he did regain some semblance of domination he slumped forward onto his desk panting and gasping for air. His heart raced, which was now becoming a common occurrence to him, his eyes were tightly shut and cold sweat rivered down his spine. He lay with his cheek against the cool wooden desk, his palms resting either side of his head. Seth opened his eyes and all seemed calm, curiously the buzzing in his head seemed to have gone completely. He waited for a few minutes, adopting the same position so as not to disturb the tranquillity that was washing over him. Was that it, was it all over?

Slowly, ever so slowly he raised his head, peace and calm reigned supreme throughout the house. His heart returned to it's normal steady pace as he looked around his office, everything seemed normal and untouched, he eased back into his chair with relief. Seths' hands still resting on the desk as before, he looked like a concert pianist awaiting his cue to begin playing. He moved his bare foot and it came into contact with something sharp and wet causing him to jump, automatically he looked down and noticed the shattered cup and pool of spilt coffee. Seth tutted but before he could even think about getting a cloth to clean up the mess, his left index finger twitched.

He stopped and looked at it, he knew that lots of people had had that happen to them at some point in their lives, but they weren't dealing with the things that he was having to deal with. As Seth watched, the finger did it again, then the thumb and his middle finger followed suit closely joined by the rest of the fingers on his left hand. Seth felt now that the spasms and contortions that he had been subjected to earlier had only just been the prelude, the opening band, now he could feel the headline act warming up and getting ready to take the stage by storm. The fingers on his right hand then mirrored their contemporaries and seemingly took on a life of their own. He tried with both hands to clench his fists but the harder he tried, the more the unseen puppeteer fought back to gain supremacy over his digits.

His possessed hands lurched forward and grabbed Seths' keyboard, drawing it closer to him in order to adopt a more comfortable writing posture, how very considerate!! The fingers sprang into life again at an unbelievable speed, dashing across the keyboard with unerring accuracy, hitting every key as required, no backspacing or deletions and no mistakes to be corrected. Seth stopped watching his hands on the keys and concentrated on the screen, the literature being composed moved up the screen at such a rate that it was difficult to comprehend what it was actually saying. He caught the odd phrase and paragraph, title or chapter number, the hands seemed to know what they were doing and he suddenly felt redundant to the whole process.

For hour upon hour his hands wrote their script, the apocalypse or end of days as most would call it, the catalyst for a new dawn *He* would no doubt term it, the storm outside raged a fitting backdrop to the damnation being created before his eyes. Seths' arms ached as the muscles went into overdrive to feed the fingers with power and energy for the hellish task, all he could do was watch and try to decipher what he could from the demonic text. He tried to stand in order to stretch his limbs but his hands were having none of it and refused to budge from their work.

Unlike the horrific writing process for his previous novel 'Suffering Innocence', allegedly given to him by Satan, this time the evil little gremlin in his skull never returned to chew on his brain. It seemed that they were now just using his body as an instrument for their monstrous plans. The hours stacked up as Seth grew weary and he returned his head to rest on the desktop, bizarrely his hands continued at their frenetic pace undisturbed and Seth slipped into a little sleep.

He woke with a feeling of cramp in his hands, his eyes opened and immediately he noticed the sunlight streaming through the window, the storm had passed over him it seemed, literally and figuratively. He looked up at the screen, it had been finished with the phrase '. . . The End?'

"Cute" he mumbled to himself at the sentiment.

Seth regained his composure and sat upright, he clenched his fists, partly to reassure himself that they were in his control again and partly to get the blood flowing again. He toyed with the idea of simply deleting the whole fucking thing but he knew that that wouldn't be a wise move. It was done at least, his pact had been fulfilled and he just hoped that now he could get on and piece his mind and life back together again. He saved the file and sat back in his chair and yawned, all he wanted now was to hear Lilys' sweet voice and beautiful laugh, he just needed to hear her.

As he stretched and sighed, he could sense someone in the room with him, watching him. He didn't seem phased at all, he had completed everything that had been asked, or demanded, of him and he knew who he expected to be there, standing in the shadows behind him.

"It's done, just as you asked, now give me back my wife and leave me the fuck alone" he said without turning around to see the being.

"Hello Mr Caine" said the intruder

Seth recognised the voice but it wasn't one of his previous demonic visitors, he spun around in his chair to confront the stranger. It was a man standing hidden by the side of the window, the light shining in Seths' eyes making a positive identification difficult.

"Who the fuck are you?" Seth demanded

"Oh, come now Mr Caine, please don't tell me that you've forgotten me" the man said as he stepped out from the shadows and into Seths' clear vision "I'm Father Seymour Duncan, remember?"

"What the . . . how the hell did you get in here and what the fuck do you want?" Seth stood angrily and snarled at the priest.

"Please Mr Caine, we can do without the profanity, I am here to help you"

"I don't need your help and I don't want it now get out of my house."

"But Mr Caine, you are making a very grave mistake" said Seymour

"What are you talking about?" Seth was quickly losing what little patience he had left, he was tired, he had incomparable things going on in his head and the last thing he needed was a priest breaking into his home for a chat "Mistake, what mistake? How long have you been standing there?"

"Long enough Mr Caine, long enough to see what you have been writing and I'm here to help you, more importantly to help the world."

"Very saintly of you but I don't need your help" Seth switched off the computer and moved towards the priest in order to throw him out.

"Caine, you must destroy what you have just written" Seymour said without any pretense.

"Are you fucking insane, first of all, that was just a novel I'm working on and secondly . . . ." Seth stopped, he felt no compulsion to explain himself to anyone, let alone a priest and instead he grabbed Father Duncan by the shoulder to escort him to the door.

"Secondly, your wife is missing and presumably in the gravest of danger?" Seymour finished the thought for him.

Seth stopped dead in his tracks, his mouth gaped open and he felt sick to his stomach.

"How the hell did you know about that?" he gasped

"Also Mr Caine, in the first instance, what you were just writing was anything but *just a novel*. I would've intervened as you were writing it but *they* would've stopped me" He smiled knowingly

"Tell me what you know" Seth shouted at him as he slammed the priest up against the wall of his office.

"I know everything, my friend" said an unshakable and resolute Seymour

"I'm not your friend, priest" snarled Seth to which Father Duncan smiled

"Is something funny?"

"No, you just remind me of somebody; tell me, do you know a Severin Frost?"

Seth released his grip on the holy man and stood in awe at his words, this whole chain of events was getting more bizarre with every twist and turn.

"Severin Frost again?" he whispered

"Don't be too alarmed Mr Caine, I did briefly work with your wife at the Hoffman Institute remember."

"So, what do you want?" asked Seth in a more reasonable tone.

"I have come to reassure you and to help you make the right decision regarding that blasphemous filth that you have just helped to create."

"What do you mean? What decision? There is no decision to make, it's finished"

"Mr Caine, you cannot possibly think of allowing that vile work to be published, surely?"

"It has to be published, there's no other way around it" Seth said with an assured defiance.

"Then if that's the way you feel, I will have to stop you." replied Seymour with an equally determined look in his eye.

"Don't even think about tying to stop me Father, have you any idea of what hangs on that book?"

"I know about your wife my friend, and it grieves me to see anyone in such a horrific predicament, it really does, but you have to look at the bigger picture."

"There is no other picture" Seth gritted his teeth as he spoke with great resolve and a tear in his eye. "My wife is all that matters and the only way I can get her back is to get this book out there."

"But what about the rest of humanity, have you any idea how this will affect them and just how much damage you will cause?" asked Seymour imploringly

"Do you really expect me to leave my wife in the hands of those things just to save the rest of this miserable fucked up planet?"

"Listen to yourself my friend, at how petty and narrow-minded you sound. The needs of the souls of the world could potentially rest in your hands and you would let them all burn just to save a single one."

"How do you know about all of this anyway?" snapped Seth angrily, slightly changing the subject.

"Much like you, I have had visitations but unlike you, mine were of angels not demons which over time have forewarned me of the deeds that you are about to undertake, I was charged with stopping you from carrying out your foul mission, by any means necessary."

"Really, you've had visions of angels? Did they threaten to take away the one and only thing in your life that has any true meaning?" questioned Seth.

"No, of course they didn't, angels do not come to harm or threaten; they asked for my help in this realm, someone was needed to act on their behalf. I was fortunate and honoured enough to be the one chosen for this most glorious of services. It was an honour and a privilege and my duty to comply with their wishes. My dear Mr Caine, you do not fully realise with what you are dealing." Seymour moved away from Seth and towards the computer.

"Neither do you" Seth said firmly as he grabbed the priest by his jacket and pulled him back and around to face him, only then did Seth notice that Father Duncan had withdrawn a knife from his jacket pocket.

Seymour lunged at Seth who quickly moved to the side, narrowly avoiding the blade. The priest slashed left to right and then right to left as Seth backed off out of range. Father Duncan moved back over to the computer and made to pick it up, whether to steal it or to smash it Seth didn't have a clue but either way he wasn't going to let him get away with it.

He ran at the priest and jumped on his back causing Seymour to buckle under the weight and he landed on Seths' desk. They wrestled to the ground for control of the situation and Seymour lunged again with his free right hand still holding the blade, he caught Seth a glancing blow on the shoulder which immediately started to bleed heavily.

Seth cursed the priest and clenched his fist before bringing it down with all his force into Seymours' face, the priests nose collapsed with the strike, blood burst out all over his face and his top lip split through the middle. Stars shone in his eyes with disorientation and Seth picked him up off the floor. He dragged the priest to the front door but just as they arrived there Seymour flayed out almost blindly with his knife now in his left hand, Seth caught him by the wrist and slammed Father Duncans' forearm over his knee, breaking the limb with a sickening crunch and causing him to drop the blade.

Seth opened the front door and dragged the priest outside, Seymour stood bloodied with his left arm dangling uselessly by his side as he gasped for breath from his exertions, Seth held him up by his shirt front.

"I told you the last time you came to see me to fuck off and leave me alone, now I'm telling you that if I see you again or if you get involved in my business I will fucking kill you. None of your angels will save you, now get off my property."

With that Seth swung again with his fist, he hit Seymour on the side of the jaw and felt it crack under the blow, Father Duncan would undoubtedly have been knocked clean across Seths' driveway but for Caine holding onto him.

"This is not over" gasped Seymour, blood spitting out of his mouth as he spoke. Seth had had enough and dragged him down to his high front gates; he unlocked them and dragged the stricken cleric down to street level where he dumped him in the gutter before turning and walking back through the gates and slamming them shut and back to his front door. Over his shoulder he could still hear Father Duncan yelling as best he could with a broken jaw.

"Not over Caine"

Seth didn't even look back; he just slammed the door behind him.

CHAPTER 30

Once back inside his home, Seth took off his blood stained shirt to check the extent of the knife wound in his shoulder. There seemed to be a lot of blood so he went to the bathroom to clean it up, on his way he looked out of the bedroom window to see where Father Duncan was, thankfully the priest seemed to have made his escape, a wise move Seth thought to himself. He continued on to the bathroom, washed away the blood and examined the injury.

"Bastard!" he said in annoyance as he realised that Seymour had actually sliced across one of his tattoos, it didn't seem too deep a gash so he retrieved the first aid box from under the sink, dressed and bandaged it up. He was grateful that he didn't need to go and get stitches after all because he didn't want to leave the house in case he got news of Lily.

Patched up but aching, he went back downstairs, checking all the windows and doors were bolted as he went through the house, just in case the deranged priest decided to pay him another visit. Happy in his security, he poured himself a large single malt scotch and sat in his armchair to let the alcohol numb both the pain in his shoulder and the pain in his heart.

Seth got up for a refill and to get his phone. He felt apprehension which brought the familiar knot back to his stomach as he looked at his phone, 'no news is good news' he thought but really he knew that he *had* to have some information, one way or another, he took another swig from his glass for some liquid courage and dialled Lilys' office number, his mind clutched at straws, her car was still in the drive but maybe she'd walked to work? Too far. Maybe she'd been offered a lift? By who, none of her colleagues lived on this side of town as far as he was aware. Maybe she'd had car trouble? Maybe, maybe, maybe? He hoped and prayed that any one of his unlikely scenarios were true as he waited for Lilys' secretary to answer the fucking phone!!

"Good afternoon, Hoffman Institute, Dr Caines secretary speaking, how may I help you?" the cheery sound of Lindas' voice was like music to Seths' ears, after what he had been dealing with, it was that little touch of normal everyday reality that he craved so desperately.

"Hi Linda, it's Seth" he sighed "could I speak to my wife please, if she's free"

"Oh hello Mr Caine, no I'm sorry Dr Caine isn't available today, er isn't she at home?"

"At home? No, why would you think she was here?"

"Erm, I'm sorry but she didn't come in today, there was a voice mail from her just saying that she wouldn't be in" Linda seemed a little confused and concerned herself.

"So you haven't actually seen her yourself?" Seths' voice became shrill as yet another wave of panic started to wash through his head.

"No, I'm sorry, she left the message around 5am though if that's any help?"

5am? They were both still in bed at that time, although in his dream they were both in a whole other place entirely, a place where time is endless along with the pain and suffering. A chill ran down his spine and he quickly tried to banish the recollections from his nightmare.

"How did she sound?" he asked

"Well, to be honest, not very well, she seemed to have been crying. I don't want to pry but have you two had a fight?" Linda said

Seths' arm lost all power and he slumped back in his chair, the phone in his hand dangling by his side. Oh how he wished they'd had a fight and she'd gone to stay with friends or relatives, that was something mundane and everyday, he could handle that and any amount of ridiculous demands that she would make, he would agree to anything right now to get her back.

"Mr Caine? Mr Caine are you still there? Is everything ok?" Linda still called down the phone line, Seth was numb all over and unable to respond. His thumb moved over the disconnect button as Linda continued to try to get his attention.

"Mr Caine? Mr Cai" he cut her off.

He sat quietly and wondered where she was, he wondered what she was going through, he wondered how or even if he was going to get her back. He decided he had to get himself back together, if there was going to be even the merest hope of rescuing Lily from her hell, literally.

Seth dialled Lilys' mobile, inadvertently, after he had dialled, his fingers crossed and he closed his eyes, like a child not wanting to see what lurked in his darkened bedroom again. The phone rang and rang but he received no answer, suddenly her voice lifted his spirits briefly until he realised it was her voice mail message.

"Lily? Lily? It's Seth darling, if you're there baby please pick up, I love you so much, please just pick up the phone if you can and let me know you're alright, I miss you angel, I need you to come home to me, please just call me and let me know that you're safe." The recorder bleeped to end his message and the tears that had been building up in his eyes as he spoke trickled down his cheeks, he broke down and sobbed like he had never done before, the hurt coursing through his head and heart was leaving him a broken shell of the man that he once was.

Night came down and found him curled up in the foetal position on the floor where he had slipped to at some point during the late afternoon. He still clutched the phone but there had been no calls, no news and no contact of any kind. He tried to ring her again but got no reply, he tried again and again and every time he got her machine and every time he did, a little piece of hope was chipped away from him. Exhausted, he didn't even have the energy to climb the stairs to bed; instead he crawled to the couch and curled back into a ball, hugging his knees close to his chest for comfort.

He woke sometime later at the sound of a car pulling up and he ran to the window only to have his hopes dashed by the neighbours getting out of a taxi and stumbling drunkenly to their house after a night out. Noticing her car again just made any rational explanation for her disappearance seem even more unlikely, which depressed him further.

His eyes were heavy and his wounded shoulder ached and stiffened, he decided that he needed to rest properly and recharge himself in order to think clearly on Lilys' behalf, he would call her again then sleep. He dialled again and waited as it rang, he didn't hold out much hope until it stopped ringing and was answered.

"Lily?" he yelled breathlessly "Lily? Are you there?"

"Hello Seth" came a voice

"Lily?" he questioned, it was a woman but it didn't sound like her.

"Lily's a little, erm, tied up at the moment" mocked the malevolent and child-like voice as it giggled.

"Meridiana!" he gasped

"Ah, you remember me my darling" she said reverting to her normal voice "How are you?"

"Where is she?" he snarled at her through gritted teeth

"She is still here with us my love" she squealed and as if to prove a point he heard a whip crack and Lilys' unmistakable voice scream.

"I have done what was asked of me" he winced at the sound of her scream as he spoke "Now give her back, let her go" he shouted.

"Play nicely Seth, we like her, she's pretty and we don't really want to let her go."

"Give her back!" he screamed down the phone with rage as his blood threatened to boil over. "Or so help me, the book is destroyed"

All he heard was yelps of delight from Meridiana and he assumed Angelique and sobs of pain from Lily, his heart felt as though it had been cleaved in two when the phone went dead but not before he heard Lily scream

"Seeeeeettthhh!!"

He woke up on the couch; he had cried himself to sleep, now he was all cried out. His phone was still in his hand and it bleeped with missed calls, he checked them and they were all from Lilys' phone. He wasn't sure if he wanted to go through all that again. He looked at the times and they were all from the early hours of the morning, clustered together over a two hour period. He played back a couple of them and they were much the same as he had heard the night before. He tried to remain calm as he had listened but quickly cut each one short as he could bear the harrowing content no more, he deleted each one, all but the last one. It had been sent at 9:30am. Seth looked at the clock on the wall; it was now 9:42; that must have been what had woken him up.

Tentatively he brought up the message, again it was from Lilys' phone and again it was another voice mail but this time from a man, he listened intently.

"Good morning, my name is Dr Ross Holland, I'm a consultant at St James Hospital and I'm calling on behalf of Dr Lily Caine. I was hoping Mr Caine, that you would contact me immediately regarding your wife, thank you."

Finally, some hope he thought. She is out of their clutches if he has her phone. Unless, she's lying on a slab in the mortuary, he banished the horrible thought immediately from his mind and called back, he wasn't going to waste time trying to find the hospitals number if just a few minutes ago this doctor was using Lilys' phone. It would be quicker to just ring back, so he pressed recall and it rang, a man answered.

"Hello, Dr Holland? This is Seth Caine, you just called me about my wife, is she ok?" Seths' frantic tone was evidence of him being at his wits end with worry.

"Oh hello Mr Caine, yes this is Dr Holland"

"Yes, yes, my wife, is she alright?"

"Yes Mr Caine, she's here with us, I must say she's in rather a bad way but she's here" he reassured Seth

"Thank God" Seth gasped and another tear slipped down his face though this one was one of joy not sorrow "How is she? Can I see her? What happened?" he knew the answer to the last question more than anyone but he couldn't possibly explain it.

"She will be ok in time but I can't really discuss it over the phone, can you get down here as soon as possible?" asked the doctor.

"I'm on my way" Seth said and hung up, he ordered a taxi and ran upstairs to get changed and put his boots on. He grabbed his phone, cash and smokes and ran to the street to wait for the cab.

Seth arrived at the hospital in record time after bribing the taxi driver with triple the fare, which seemed to do the trick. He burst through the doors and straight to reception where he blurted out his and Lilys' names and that of Dr Holland, he was breathless with panic but luckily a man came over to him and said

"Mr Caine?"

"Yes?"

"I'm Dr Holland, I've been waiting for you, are you alright?" he said as he looked at Seths' pale and ashen face.

"I'm fine, where's my wife?" he gasped

"This way" the doctor led him to a ward and then an empty side room just off the wards' main corridor, in order to prepare him.

"Is she ok Dr Holland?"

"Please, call me Ross, she'll be fine, though she's in quite a bit of pain so we've had to sedate her quite heavily I'm afraid and she should be sleeping now."

"Thank you so much for calling me Doctor, er I mean Ross."

"It's my pleasure, it's unfortunate that we have to meet under such circumstances but you see, I know Dr Caine, or rather, your wife."

"Really, how?" asked Seth

"Well, a couple of months ago, a man came in here in a very bad way, mentally speaking and Dr Caine very kindly came in to assess and review him for us. We got chatting and somehow you came up and I said I'd read some of your books."

"Oh I see, well thank you for that too" said a slightly embarrassed Seth

"The thing is, she was brought in here with no possessions, the staff weren't sure who to contact but I recognised her and checked through her phone for your number."

"She came in here with no possessions at all?"

"Apart from the phone, no, I'm sorry to have to tell you this but . . . ." he paused

"Go on doctor, you aren't going to shock me." Said Seth

"Well, she was actually found wandering around the park next to the hospital, she was completely naked and disorientated, the only thing she had with her was the phone, which seemed very odd in itself, she clutched it so tightly. We couldn't even get her to let go of that because she was so traumatised, we had to sedate her first. We've taken care of her injuries as well, of course. She's hardly said a word apart from the occasional scream or calling out for you."

"Injuries?" Seth sighed with a lump in his throat

"Yes, I'm afraid that she had a significant amount of lacerations across the majority of her body, as well as multiple bruises and abrasions. Luckily we don't think there is any internal bleeding or permanent physical damage. Psychological damage however, that may be more difficult to ascertain, as we are unsure at this point of what she has had to endure, though I'm sure she has been through a terrible ordeal" he sighed and shook his head "it may be sometime before she can tell us exactly what happened to her. I have to tell you also that the police are here and they will want to speak to you at some point too before you leave, I hope you understand?"

"Er, yes, yes, of course" Seth was in a daze

"I'm sure you just want to be alone with her now so I'll take you to her, I'll be in my office just down the corridor if you need me."

He didn't reply, he just allowed himself to be escorted to a private room where Dr Holland silently left him to visit her. Seth gasped as he saw the almost mummified version of his beloved wife, his best friend, his lover, his confidant, his sidekick, his companion, his soulmate, his Lily. He pulled up a chair and sat at her bedside, taking her bandaged hand ever-so-gently in his. Drips of sustaining liquids and analgesia hung beside the bed, pumping valuable fluids back into her system and monitors beeped her pulse rate to him, signifying that her heart still beat, that in itself was a great comfort to him now.

"I'm sorry Lily, I'm so, so sorry" he didn't think he had any tears left to shed but suddenly they came thick and fast, as he buried his head in her blankets and wept uncontrollably.

CHAPTER 31

Seth sat with his silent and heavily wounded wife for over an hour, an hour in which the last of his tears eventually dried up, he tried to talk to her but got no response until eventually she squeezed his finger with hers. He became overjoyed at this which seemed very reminiscent of the first time their baby Jack did the same, how different the circumstances now, how very cruel life can be.

Later on, a nurse came in and very apologetically told him that he had to leave as Lily needed to rest but that he could come back in the evening to visit her, reluctantly he agreed to leave. As he left, a waiting police officer took him into Dr Hollands' office, in order to ask him about the circumstances of her injuries. Another hour passed, this time of questioning, before Seth was relieved to be allowed to go home.

Somehow he had managed to coerce the police down a line of enquiry that Lily must have been abducted as she left for work early the previous morning, they were confused as to why her car hadn't been stolen as well to which he told them that the car had been unreliable recently so he assumed that she had taken a taxi. When they asked why he hadn't reported that she hadn't come home last night, he lied that sometimes she worked very late, he only realised that she hadn't come home when he got the phone call from Dr Holland.

Luckily they hadn't got any other leads to work with and there was no way they would've believed the truth. Seth couldn't believe that they actually fell for his deception but what else could he have said? He was having a hard time coming to terms with the truth as it was. The officer said that they would put out extra patrols and scour the area for clues and evidence as well as canvassing the local residents for sightings of strange men roaming the park or surrounding streets.

"Not to worry sir, we suspect that due to the nature of the attack and your wife's injuries that there were three or four men involved, this will be our top priority, believe me, we will catch these bastards" reassured the officer.

Seth thanked him for his help and asked to be kept informed of the manhunts progress while thinking to himself "Good fucking luck!" He took a taxi home, despite the horrendous state that Lily was in, he was at least delighted that she was alive and satisfied that she would be alright, eventually.

Once at home Seth knew that the nightmare wasn't quite over yet, he still had to get that damned book published. He printed it off his computer and sat with it on his desk in front of him. All the pain, all the heartbreak, all the tears and all the anger that this thing had already caused almost made him want to burn it. Added to that was all the pain and upset that it could eventually cause on its' release, but what was the alternative? He didn't have one. Some may have called him selfish to only think of Lily and himself but who in that position would have done differently? Seth thought, no-one if they were honest.

He had to go and see Gus, the sooner he got the book published, the sooner his debt would be paid in full and Seth hoped *He* would have no further reason to call on him again. In the taxi ride over to Gus' city centre office, Seth sat with the completed manuscript on the seat beside him. He couldn't bring himself to even look at it, he felt as though it pulsed with darkness and hatred. He'd been given a glimpse of the potential for horror and evil that it could unlock and unleash on the world. It threatened to cover mankind with wound upon festering wound, still his conscience tried to twist him up in knots yet as soon as he switched his thoughts to Lily and the unspeakable acts that she had had to endure, his resolve was strengthened again.

The book would be published and when Lily was better they would sell up and flee to the countryside, Lily loved horses, she'd had them as a little girl; that was it! They would buy horses and stables and an isolated farm, no TV, no newspapers, the civilised world at least, would burn but they would live out their days in blessed ignorance of the rest of mankind's problems, simple.

On his arrival at Gus' offices, Seth had already formulated their basic escape plan; retire to the peace and quiet of the countryside. They would at least get to spend their last days alone and undisturbed. He would let the world tear itself to pieces with religion and hate and, he thought, in their idyllic seclusion they wouldn't even know about it until the very end of days.

"Seth, great to see you" called Gus as Seth was shown into his very plush and newly decorated office.

"Hi Gus" Seth half-smiled as his agent finished off a phone call and gestured for him to take a seat, which Seth did.

"Hey, how ya doin buddy?" bellowed Gus as he hung up the telephone "you look like boiled shit by the way"

"Fine thanks, you?" Seth gazed around the room as he spoke, it was very gaudy, very loud and very Gus but it also looked very expensive, again, very Gus! "You're doing very well for yourself I see"

"Absolutely, and a large part of this is down to you my old friend" beamed Gus

"Thanks, but I wouldn't want to take credit for this" Seth raised his eyebrows at Gus' décor.

"You have no taste!" laughed Gus "You want some coffee?"

"No thanks"

"Ok, so to what do I owe the unexpected pleasure of your company?"

"This" Seth threw the manuscript onto Gus' desk.

Gus looked at it as if with awe and wonder, then he looked back at Seth with eyes and mouth open.

"Another book?" he said

"I can tell you're an agent!" Seth sarcastically deadpanned

"No, I mean, you said that you'd had enough and weren't going to do anymore writing"

"Well, let's just call this my last hurrah shall we?"

"I'm stunned, delighted of course, but stunned. What is it?" he asked but before Seth could reply, Gus excitedly asked "is it a follow-up to 'Suffering Innocence'? Oh please say it's a follow-up to 'Suffering Innocence'"

"No"

"Oh, pity, not that you needed a follow-up of course, it's just that with the phenomenal success of that, well, you couldn't fail" he hesitated "I mean, er, I'm sure that this won't fail. But, well, oh you know what I mean"

"Yeah, I know" sighed Seth.

"So, what is it?" asked Gus again

"Just read it, it isn't my usual sort of thing really but I need to get it out as soon as possible, is that ok?"

"Of course, if you wrote a shopping list I'm pretty sure I could get it published right now *and* it'd sell" laughed Gus

"Good to know" Seth looked at the clock on the office wall, he had all afternoon before he could go back to the hospital to see Lily and he had nothing else to do, besides which, he didn't want to go back to their empty house alone either "So, I'll have that cup of coffee now"

"What, you want me to read it now?" Gus was shocked by such urgency

"If you don't mind, you got anything else planned?"

"Well, as it happens, there's nothing that I can't get out of but . . ."

"Black, two sugars please. I've got a few hours to kill so let's get the ball rolling" Seth stood and moved to one of Gus' two large and luxurious new leather couches against the back wall of his office and sprawled out on it.

"Er, ok, I'll get through as much as I can, I suppose I'll get the drift of it at least" he pressed a button on his intercom and asked his assistant for coffee for two.

"I'll be waiting" Seth closed his eyes and relaxed as he left Gus to read.

Four hours later and Seth was nudged awake by Gus who stood over him, he must have drifted off after the coffee, his sleep had understandably been erratic of late and he must have needed it.

"Morning" said Gus

"Hey" Seth stretched and swung his legs round and into a sitting position

"You snore" Gus mumbled

"Big deal"

Gus didn't reply, he just walked back over to his desk and sat down with a half grunt and half sigh. Then he looked over at Seth as he stood and walked back over to join Gus at his desk.

"So, what do you think?" asked Seth

"You really want me to get this published?" Gus looked very concerned

"Definitely"

"In your name"

Seth hesitated, he hadn't thought of that, use a pseudonym, at least he could avoid some of the fall out and inevitable shit storm that would follow, then he thought better of it. Satan wanted this out by Seth Caine, to feed off his infamy and notoriety, anybody could put out a blasphemous book and go unnoticed, also he knew it would be suicide to start playing games now when he was so close to getting his life back together with Lily, finally.

"Of course in my name" he protested

"Hmmm" Gus shook his head with disapproval "I don't know Seth"

"What do you mean?"

"I don't know if I can get this published buddy"

"You mean you can't or you won't?" Seth narrowed his eyes and frowned as he started to get angry.

"Whoa, slow down, it's not really a question of can't or won't, like I said, I can get anything published of yours. It's more a matter of *should* we publish it?"

"I need it published and out there Gus and I need it done yesterday!"

"I haven't read it all yet but it's pretty inflammatory stuff pal" sighed Gus as he shook his head "it's dark, even for you, this could cause a hell of a lot of controversy and not in a good way either"

"Controversy, like sex, always sells, or so you always say" Seth was not going to back down now.

"I know what I always say Seth, but this is gonna cause one hell of a stink, are you ready for that?"

"Of course I'm ready for that" yes Seth would be ready for it because once Lily was up to it, they would be off and lost in the wilderness somewhere.

"Ok, ok, I'll see what I can do, how about a pen name?" Gus clutched at straws again but just to protect his friend and client though he knew that Seth had always hated the idea.

"No! I've just told you, it goes out and it goes out in my name" Seth was determined to see this through to the bitter end now, if only to give Lily and himself freedom, as he saw it "and don't just see what you can do Gus, you *have* to make it happen and as soon as possible"

"Alright, I'll get to it" Gus looked hurt by his friends tone

"I'm sorry Gus" Seth apologised immediately "I just have to get this done, I can't explain why."

"Fair enough, we've made each other very successful over the years, we've been great partners, it's the least I can do."

"Thanks Gus, I won't forget it"

"Actually, with your success recently this should be easy to sell, the movie is still packing them in, then there'll be the DVD sales, this can just ride its' coat tails." Gus smiled

"That's my Gus" Seth returned the smile but with a sickly taste in his mouth, knowing what a big success for this book could mean.

"By the way, how's Lily? Natalie was talking the other day about the four of us going out for a meal soon."

"Well actually Gus" Seth looked again at the clock on the office wall "She isn't good at the moment, I'm on my way back to the hospital to visit her now."

"Hospital!! Jesus Christ, what the fuck happened?" gasped Gus as he rose from his chair

"Erm, well she was attacked outside the house as she was going to work" it seemed that that was what the police were going with so he may as well follow the same line.

"Oh my God Seth, is she alright?" Gus was genuinely shocked and visibly upset.

"She will be but it'll take time, she's in a pretty bad way at the moment" Seth frowned as he thought of her in that hospital bed.

"Fuck, I hope they get the bastards and string them up by their balls, I'm so sorry"

"Thanks" Seth looked down, he hated lying to his friend but much like the police, Gus would think Seth crazy if he had told the truth.

"Natalie'll be devastated, which hospital is she in?"

"St. James" replied Seth

"Would it be ok for us to go and see her?" asked Gus

"Yeah, sure, I know she'd like that but give it a few days will you and let her get her strength back. She's very weak at the moment and she's under sedation."

"Sure buddy, whatever you say, I'll give you a ring in a couple of days and you can let me know when'll be a good time" suddenly Gus felt guilty about giving Seth a hard time over the new book, the guy obviously had more important things on his mind. "and don't you worry about your work, I'll call in some favours again, you've made a lot of people very rich, it's the least that they can do too."

"Oh and on that subject" Seth suddenly decided "I don't want any of the money from it, everyone makes their money but all my royalties go to St. James' Hospital alright?" there was no way Seth could make money from this but at least it could go to a worthy cause and the hospital caring for his wife was the perfect place.

"Well in that case, I'll get on it double quick and I'll do the same with my commission buddy, I'm sure I can get a few donations from elsewhere too" Gus said with genuine heartfelt emotion.

"Thanks Gus, I knew I could count on you" now Seth felt bad for making his old friend feel guilt-ridden in the first place, deep down Gus was a big guy with a big heart "I'll have to go now and see Lily, I'll be in touch"

"Sure thing Seth, please give our love to Lily, we'll be thinking of her"
"Yeah, I know you will, speak to you soon buddy" Seth smiled and held out
his hand for Gus to shake, Gus shook it but grabbed him and added a bear
hug too for good measure, there was almost tears in the big agents eyes as
he released Seth and they bid each other farewell and Seth left to be in the
only place in the world that he ever wanted to be, by his wifes' side.

CHAPTER 32

It was six months before Lily made anything approaching a full recovery from her horrific ordeal. Most of that time was required for hospital treatment to let her wounds heal sufficiently and for her to recuperate her strength in order for her to go home. Seth spent every day and every evening by her side, thankfully no surgery was required, just lots and lots of care, attention and time, and Seth was overflowing with it all.

She needed a further four months off work before she felt fit enough to return, even then it was against Seths' wishes. He hadn't wanted her to go back to work at all but she had persuaded him that she had to keep her mind active and reminded him constantly of her love for her job. Her stubbornness to go back to work frustrated Seth but he knew how much her career meant, therefore a compromise was struck between the two whereas Lily promised to keep her contact with the patients down to a minimum and she concentrated her efforts on paperwork, meetings and administration, for the time being at least. She didn't particularly agree with the arrangement but she knew she could get out of the house and that Seth was only being that way because he loved her so much and wanted to protect her from too much stress and anxiety.

Lily had been back at work for three or four weeks and starting to feel like her old self again, finally. Seths' over-protection had been well-meant and thoughtful but now she was looking forward to getting on with her life again after the 'accident'. Lily had no recollection of what had actually happened to her, a blessing indeed. Seth had concocted a story that she had been involved in a serious car crash and her head injuries were the cause of her memory loss. The other so-called 'true' story of her being attacked by a man or men outside their home was known as fact by the police, Gus and Natalie, Lilys' work colleagues, as well as Karl and various friends and family who were concerned about her prolonged stay in hospital and out of circulation. They had all been asked by Seth to keep up the pretence of a car accident in order to protect Lily from renewed trauma, for the time being at least. He had even gone to the lengths of having her car scraped and buying her a new one while she was in hospital just to keep the story believable, he was only doing it to save her from more anguish. Everyone had respected Seths' wishes although the police had been very reluctant to go along with it. Seth had had to agree that he would contact them if Lilys' memory status changed in any way. He had in turn reasoned with himself that should her memory return, he had just been trying to shield her from the horrible truth.

Various experts had suggested therapy in order to induce her mind to recall the traumatic events that had befallen her, thus allowing her to deal and move past them. Seth had immediately blocked that idea, being the only person that had any real knowledge of what the truth actually was and also what the implications of such revelations could be. The specialists hadn't understood his vehement objections but while she was in hospital they allowed him to oversee her care. Now she was home and recently returned to work, therapy hadn't seemed to be an issue anymore.

Lilys' initial state on her homecoming had been difficult; she had become understandably nervous and jumped at the sound of the phone or a knock at the door, yet she didn't know why. Physically it was tough, Seth changed her dressings daily and inspected for any infection or pain increase, he bathed her, lifting her into and out of the bath. He did everything he could possibly do for her, she hated being dependant on anyone at the best of times but with Seth it was different. Seth had vowed not to leave her side but she gradually craved her independence, hence her desire to get back behind the wheel of her (new) car and into her office.

One particularly difficult day had arrived when the police caught a man who had attacked a woman in the park near to where Lily had been found. Naturally they had wanted to ask her to identify the man in question, in case it had been the same man who had 'attacked' her. Luckily Seth had been there to head them off, telling them that she was still too weak to answer their questions or look at potentially upsetting photos. It was becoming increasingly difficult to keep them away from her and Seth knew that one day soon he might have to tell her the ugly 'truth' that she had been attacked. He knew that he would never tell her the real truth of Angelique and Meridiana, unless she did remember it all, even then he thought of lying and persuading her that it was just a nightmare that she'd had. That was a secret he was hoping to take to the grave with him.

From Seths' professional point of view things were either wonderful or devastating, depending on which side of the situation one stood. His book of Satans' biography entitled 'Sympathy for the Devil: The Truth' had been courting controversy the world over. It had been credited as 'By Seth Caine' but also 'As Told by His Infernal Majesty'. The youth of the day were buying it in their many, many thousands, some just to piss off their parents, some to fit in with their peers while others were using it as part of their alternative lifestyle choice. Seths' long time fans bought it purely because he had written it, some loved the book while others detested it but either way they had all bought a copy leading it to amass huge sales across the globe.

Others who hadn't been aware of its' existence suddenly became curious of the number one best seller, everyone was talking about it, which just led to more publicity and more sales. Seth was even heralded by scholars and teachers due to the fact that people had started to read again rather than playing video-games or texting someone in the next room or chatting to on-line 'friends' about meaningless bullshit to make themselves feel popular. He was being touted for every relevant award in every country where he was published.

The opposite side of that particular coin was that various religious leaders of all faiths were whipping up their flocks of followers against him. Books were being piled up in the street and turned into bonfires, some even with effigies of Seth sitting on top. Gus had simply made the point that even those people had actually bought copies, if the books were being burned, so what, business was business.

What did strike a chord with Seth though was that there had been a spate of church burnings across the world, reminiscent of the ones in Norway during the nineties that he remembered well. Those had been inflamed partly by music, black metal, a style of music close to his heart, as well as nationalistic pride and anti-Christian feelings in the young and deep down he felt that this time he had had more than a part to play himself. Again Gus and Seths' publisher had taken a pragmatic stance and written them all off as coincidence and an act of rebellion by disenfranchised youth.

However, Seth knew that there was a shift in the air, just switching on the news to see more fighting and bloodshed in the name of religion made him wince with guilt and shame. Tension was growing and Seth knew why, lots of people seemed to know why and a growing number of those people were blaming him, at least in part. The problem was that although many learned people talked about unrest and about where the world was heading, only Seth truly knew deep down for sure where that was. He was the only one who knew exactly and fully what he had created and unleashed, and why he had done it, he had seen glimpses of what was to come and he also knew that there was little, if anything that anyone could do to stop it.

Seths' dreams had been untroubled since completing his task, much like the aftermath of 'Suffering Innocence'; then he had been allowed to bask in the wealth and glory that that work had afforded him. That had been until he'd had to pay for the price of his success. Now, nearly two years after the success started, every night he slept he wondered how long it would be before *they* wanted something else from him. Every morning he woke, wracking his brain for a reminder that he had been visited, yet none came. It seemed that now he was to be left to bask again but this time in the pain, tears, misery and sorrow of others the world over.

Occasionally he still had visions of blood-stained and broken angels being tossed dead or dying from battlements. Bleeding wings cleaved from the backs of their celestial hosts lay trampled under foot where they scattered the ground as Satans' hordes hack and bludgeon their way through paradise. The visions made him shiver every time, he regretted writing the book constantly yet now there was nothing he could do. His whole life had become a tissue of lies and deceit. He had been lying to his beloved Lily about her ordeal, lying to the police, lying to their friends and family who were concerned about his wife and holding back his full knowledge of the inferno of holy wars that were threatening to engulf the planet. Only he knew his full involvement and only he had the knowledge of what he had done, only he knew, or so he thought to himself.

Father Seymour Duncan sat in his home, a thick beard had overgrown his chin in the near year since his last encounter with Seth Caine. His arm had set awkwardly and still ached, his nose was crooked from Seth breaking it as was his jaw, despite his thick beard his top lip was still visibly scarred from the poor healing as he hadn't gone to hospital to have his injuries attended to properly, all in the quest to avoid awkward questions. He now sat, like most days in his recent memory, in front of his TV, unmoving and wide-eyed at the images assaulting his senses. He flicked through channels, shocked at the half naked and painted whores (as he saw them) passing themselves off as musical talent, he saw the sickening cult of celebrity which seemed a horror in itself and he saw sports stars sign obscenely lucrative deals to kick or throw balls around a field. He watched all of this in dismay at the world but mostly he watched news footage from around the planet, of terror and bloodshed, war and poverty.

His home smelled of decay from neglect, it smelled of alcohol from the empty and half empty bottles strewn about the place and he himself smelled of the same things too. Seymour wallowed in self-pity; he had let his God down. He knew what had transpired between Seth and the demons, he knew all about the book and he felt he knew what was to follow. Knowing all of his beforehand, he'd had just one task to fulfil, stop the book. He had failed miserably he thought; he felt this every time he opened his eyes in the morning. Every night when he slept, he had nightmares of angels calling his name for help as they were being torn to shreds and slaughtered by ravenous demons intent on overthrowing Heaven and he'd had the chance to stop it but he'd failed.

Every night for nearly a year he had the same terrors and every morning he woke up screaming with anguish at the horror of what he had seen. His nightmares drove Seymour to crawl further inside the multitude of bottles in order to numb his agony and mental torture. The numbing effect never lasted long enough, his TV was there always to remind him of where everything was heading and as soon as he switched it off or when he fell asleep the nightmare would play itself out again in his head, each time seemingly more vivid, bloody and gore-filled than the last.

If pictures and stories of religious unrest throughout the world weren't enough to drive Seymour weeping back to the nearest bottle then reports of Seth Caines' record breaking book certainly were. Every time Caines' face appeared in a news item, which was all too frequent, Seymours' eyes narrowed, his nostrils flared and his fists clenched with rage. Not knowing what time of day, or indeed what day, it was, Seymour prepared to pour his eighth or ninth large Scotch when a voice caused him to jump and drop the bottle to the floor where it spilled onto his filthy carpet.

"Is that really you?" he whispered "Please tell me that you have returned to me."

"I am here Seymour" said he voice

"Oh my light, how I have longed to hear your voice again. I feared you had deserted me just when I needed you most."

"I would never desert you my dear, does that mean you had lost your faith?" she asked

"No, never!" he protested

"That is reassuring, you are troubled and we know this. There are many people troubled in this world by the events which are unfolding and there are so many more people that are in danger."

"I know" his head dropped in shame "and it is my fault"

"No Seymour, it is not your fault and you must not think like this. The problems in this world are far beyond your control" she reassured

Seymour looked around the room, to see her; he had never seen her face or form, just the voice in his mind. There was always a sense that she was physically in the room with him whenever she came to talk and therefore he naturally looked to see her, she had breathed on him to soothe his mind in the past and he had felt her gossamer touch on his face, oh how he wished that he could see her angelic presence.

"But if I had carried out your wishes as you had asked then the world would not be standing on the edge of the abyss waiting to fall in."

"Oh Seymour, there is a long, long way to go before this battle is won or lost. If mankind had more people such as you then maybe they wouldn't be in the turmoil that they find themselves in now, that much is true. This war *can* still end in victory though."

"I feel I am going insane, I see horrendous things when I close my eyes and nightmares even when I open them from all over the globe, it is never ending. I can't escape, I've longed for you to visit me again, it seems such a long time, I admit with shame that I did doubt your existence" he sighed with a heavy heart at his confession.

"I can ease your mind and help you with that at least" she replied

Suddenly a light formed from nothing before his eyes and grew ever brighter and bigger as it formed a shape, Seymour sat in his chair and inched forward with mouth gaping at the sight that he had longed for finally unfolding before him. The light continued to grow as if it were a flame and its' shape morphed and defined itself until it took on a recognisable form, arms, legs, head and body all became clearly visible. Then to Seymour's even greater amazement, another light appeared to the left of the first one. It too gradually transformed and developed until it also took on human scale and shape. Seymour sat back in his chair rigid, not with fear but shock and awe until the first 'light' spoke.

"Is this more tangible evidence of my existence?" she said with a beatific smile.

"M-m-m my angel, I am honoured and humbled" Seymour slithered off his chair and fell to his knees with his head bowed "I am blessed by your presence and unworthy of your revelation to me"

"It is nothing Seymour, we only reveal ourselves when absolutely necessary, you are more than worthy of our presence. You serve as we do, we are all part of the same glorious army in this war and you deserve to know with whom you fight alongside."

"I am blessed a thousand times over; may I be privileged with your names?" Seymour looked in wonder and delirium at the angels but had to keep averting his gaze rather than be overcome by his emotions.

"Of course you may learn our names, your dedication and faith have earned you that right. My name, my dear Seymour, is Meridiana and this is my sister Angelique" her words were like warm honey as they dripped into his mind.

"Meridiana and Angelique, beautiful names worthy of beautiful beings of God, but of course. Thank you for sharing them with me, they are now like songs for my soul." Seymour smiled as tears trickled down his smiling face, the first time that he had smiled in many months.

"You are very welcome my dear Seymour" spoke Angelique for the first time, her voice floated through the air to kiss him on the cheek.

"How may I serve you? I am at your disposal and your humble servant for evermore" he gushed with pride.

"You are aware of what is happening with that blasphemous book?"

"Of course" Seymour said through gritted teeth at the thoughts of Seth Caine "It is a travesty that threatens to soon engulf the world, turning brother against brother, father against son unless its' creator is stopped."

"But I have tried, unsuccessfully, I am not the warrior that you envisaged, clearly" he frowned and bowed his head in shame and disappointment at himself.

Meridiana reached down and put her finger under his chin, tilting his head up to face theirs again. He revelled in her angelic touch and a warm glow emanated out from her fingertip and throughout his whole body as he gazed at their beautiful faces smiling down at him.

"You are more than just a warrior Seymour" Angelique announced

"You are the last of the bloodline of Prince Bishop von Dornheim, a true man of God" said Meridiana with a knowing smile which radiated and seemed to light up the whole room.

"Von Dornheim? I'm sorry, I don't know who that is" Seymour apologised "He lived many centuries ago" replied Angelique "he tried to destroy and rid the world of the cult of the witch; he disposed of hundreds of them in the name of our Lord. You sweetest Seymour, are the last of his descendants." "I had no idea" gasped the priest

"There is no reason why you should have known such a thing my dear." Meridiana spoke again "you see, this is your destiny, your birthright. You have been doing the Lords' work for all of your life, now though, you know the reason why. It is in your blood, you are the heir to a great man of God and your time is now, to stand shoulder to shoulder with him and us in a war to end all wars. You have the chance to play your part; you will go down in history for your detailed role in events. You can strike at the very heart of darkness itself."

Meridianas' battle cry made the hairs stand up on the back of Seymours' neck, he shivered with anticipation, he always felt that he had a purpose in life but never imagined his ancestors held the key to his illustrious future. "I-I-I will do anything to help you" stuttered a shocked and delirious Father Duncan.

"We knew that we could depend on you Seymour, you are thought of in the highest regard"

"I am?" he said, even more breathless and shocked at the thought.

"Yes" smiled Angelique, a smile that felt to Seymour as if she were cradling him in her arms with love and joy.

"Thank you, it is an honour to serve you, as I said, I will do anything you so desire of me."

"That is why we came to you, your task is simple but carries great risk" said Meridiana with sympathy in her eyes.

"Fear not for me, ask me and consider it done" Seymour bowed his head to receive his blessed and holy orders.

Severin Frost lay on his bunk with a satisfied grin of contentment, he clenched his fists and sighed as if in orgasmic rapture and delight.

"Oh my glorious Lord, everything is now in place" he spoke, seemingly to no one "your hour is now finally at hand, soon we will ride over the bodies of the angelic, winged monstrosities that he has created in his palace. We will dine from his table as he whimpers in pain and we will show him no mercy as he begs for his children. For Millennia and a day have you waited and seethed in the shadows to take your rightful throne but your time is soon. Ours will no longer be just the night, for soon we will have the day and everything in it. The world will be yours, to do with as you please, darkness will encompass the Earth and everyone who survives. Oh my Satanic Majesty, hear my words and favour me for the work I have done in your black name. How I long to sit by your side in your new ebony kingdom and witness the annihilation of all his work. To you I pledge forever, my dark allegiance."

CHAPTER 33

"No, I promise you, he'll be there. Alright, I'll see you soon and give my love to Natalie and Alice, bye." Lily hung up the phone and went back upstairs to the just-waking Seth. It was early morning and Lily had been getting ready to go to work when the phone rang. She put a fresh mug of coffee on his bedside table and continued to get dressed.

"Aren't you coming back to bed?" he called playfully from beneath the quilt.

"No, we have to go to work" she replied

"We? You mean you, I'm an author remember, we keep our own hours and play by our own rules" he grinned as he emerged from beneath the covers.

"True" she said "but you still have commitments"

"What're you talking about?" Seth frowned

"Apparently it was agreed two weeks ago that you would appear on TV today, is that right?"

"Er, how did you know about that?" guilt flashed all over his face

"I just got off the phone with Gus" she said "weren't you going to tell me?"

"No, I just er wasn't going to go" Seth sighed

"You have to go Seth, you're committed to promoting you're book"

"But what about you?" he whined

"What about me? I'll be at work"

"Yeah but . . . ." he feebly protested

"Seth, you have to get out and do this. I appreciate all you've done, I really do, but I'm fine now."

"But Lily" he tried to argue in vain

"No" she stopped him "it's for your own good; you've already blown off three signing sessions that I know of. This is your career and you have to take it seriously, you can't just stop showing up because you can't be bothered. You promised Gus that you would do it."

"Only to get him off my back" Seth sulked

"To get him off your back? That's a horrible thing to say, after everything he's done for you. He's one of your best friends not just your agent. He stood by you when things weren't going well in the early days and he always believed in you, sometimes you have to repay that loyalty whether you can be bothered to or not."

"I know, I know" he sighed again. He felt awful letting Gus down, he had been forgiven before because he hadn't wanted to leave Lily alone following her 'accident' but now she was back working again, he didn't really have an excuse. He definitely couldn't give the real reason of him not wanting to promote a heavenly holocaust as a valid defence for his absence.

"So, you're going to go?" she said, it wasn't really meant as a question

"Ermm"

"Seth, if I'd have wanted to marry a recluse or a hermit then I would've done"

"Ok" reluctantly he agreed "I'll go" then he pouted some more.

"Good boy" she smiled and moved to the bed where he still sat. She placed her hand on his cheek, bowed her head to his and kissed him deeply on the mouth. Lily pulled away just as he tried to slip his arms around her waist, knowing full well that he would pull her back into bed.

"I have to go lover, sorry" she stood up and smiled again as she looked down at where his erection had emerged straining from beneath the covers "Hold that thought until tonight" she said as she winked and walked to the bedroom door, purposely wiggling her bottom as she walked.

Seth responded by pouting out his bottom lip and furrowing his brow in his disappointment, Lily looked over her shoulder and laughed lightly in turn before crushing him further by saying.

"Oh and as you're going on TV, wear something nice!"

"Nice!!" Seth shrieked with mock horror at the thought and his head fell into his hands, causing her to laugh more.

"Yes, something nice, you don't need a tie but wear that new purple shirt, I love you in that. Have to go now, see you tonight babe, I love you"

"Love you too angel, bye" Seth replied as Lily left and he fell back into his pillows, frustrated and irritated with the thought of his upcoming television appearance.

Seth stood behind the TV studios smoking a cigarette while he waited for Gus to arrive. During the last six months or so he had cut down considerably on the amount that he smoked, as stressful as the time had been during Lilys' recovery, he'd found himself without the time to smoke. It was forbidden in the hospital of course and he had made up for it in between visits, as soon as he had gotten outside but once his wife had come home he didn't feel it right to smoke anywhere near her and even when she slept he rarely left her side. The last few weeks as she returned to work and a normal life he had simply lost the inclination to smoke and he resolved to quit properly in order to have a longer and healthier life with her, to which she had been delighted. For the time being though, he usually had a pack of cigarettes in his jacket pocket but they were only brought out occasionally, the irritation he felt at having to make a television appearance was one of those occasions.

"Hey buddy, thanks for doing this" Gus called as he approached

"Hi" grunted Seth

"I'm sorry man, I know you hate doing this sort of thing" Gus immediately recognised Seths' reluctance to be there "But you're the talk of the literary world, again, and people want to know about this new book, it's got the world talking and reading and they only seem to be reading your product or at the very least reading about you."

"Hmmm" Seth remained tight lipped and non-committal.

"Seth, business is business, there are the publishers and their share-holders, then there's my share-holders to consider, some of us are taking a lot of heat for you on this, I pushed this book through as a favour to you remember and"

"Ok, ok! I get it" snapped Seth "so, you didn't tell me what puppet show I'll be on"

"Edward Whites' Close Up"

"Oh, really?" said Seth, surprised and at least a little relieved "That's not too bad I suppose."

Edward George White was one of Seths' favourite journalists, he was in his early fifties and had been terrorising public figures and so-called celebrities for over twenty years with his no-nonsense approach and insightful questioning. Seth respected and liked him a great deal, he asked the questions that Seth wanted to ask and he seemed one of the few people in the media with genuine integrity, even amongst the guests that he'd verbally assaulted and interrogated over the years, he was still revered and admired.

"Thought you'd be impressed" smiled Gus

"Alright" Seth finished his cigarette with an air of relief "Let's go then"

"There's one more thing though" Gus hesitated and the smile dropped from his face.

"What?"

"It's a special show . . . so it's going out live" Gus winced as he spoke.

"What? Oh for fucks' sake Gus, live TV?" Seth was less than impressed and even more edgy and nervous than before "Why?"

"Well, because religion is such a hot topic right now they decided to do a special live edition, plus it's being recorded and repeated tonight for prime time, it's even being broadcast live on the internet"

"Oh terrific, any more pressure you want to dump on me?" Seth lit another cigarette and drew heavily on it. "What's the plan then?"

"The plan?" asked Gus

"The plan, the show, what's happening?" snapped Seth

"Well, it's you and a few religious leaders and"

"Oh fucking great! You mean I'm gonna get ambushed?"

"No, no, I wouldn't do that to you. It's a debate about modern attitudes towards religion and the youth of today and faith and stuff like that. Because you're at the centre of a lot of the scandal and all the shit and accusations thanks to the book, they wanted you as a sort of witness for your own defence, not that you're on trial though" Gus pre-empted Seths' next complaint "There's a few others on your side, remember Ian Jones?"

"No!" Seth clenched his fists as he smoked in exasperation.

"Yes you do, the artist that dubbed himself the Messiah and did all those blasphemous photographs"

Seth did actually remember the man, he'd met him at his gallery and even bought a couple of his pictures, though Lily hated them and they had mysteriously vanished from their home. Jones had commented that he was a fan of Seths' work but still wouldn't come down on his exorbitant prices.

"So, what you're telling me is that you've booked me onto some live freakshow?"

"I wouldn't put it that way buddy" Gus tried to smile and half laughed.

"Fucking hell Gus" Seth sighed "Come on, let's get this over with"

Seth ground his cigarette out under his boot and moved to enter the building through the back way but Gus stopped him and eased him around to face the other way.

"We have to go in through the front doors" he said

"Why?" Seth scowled

"Publicity, I'm sorry pal but it's all very high profile and the guests are all asked to enter through the main entrance so that the cameras can get footage of their arrival, think of it like a boxers' big entrance to the ring."

"Ok" Seth gave Gus a withering stare and sighed as they walked around the corner and to the front of the building, on their approach he stopped dead in his tracks and said "Gus, what the fuck?"

A huge mob of people stood amassed around the main entrance to the studios, some with placards thrust in the air while others chanted and waved their fists in anger. A figure was being smuggled through the crowd and as the figure was hit by a protester he reared up and struck back at his assailant, punching the man to the ground, Seth recognised the man as Chris Bamford, a guitarist from a number of his favourite bands from his younger days.

"Nice shot Chris" Seth smiled to himself then his smile faded as he turned to confront Gus "And who the fuck are all they?"

"Er, fans I suppose" offered Gus "though not fans of his" he laughed

"Fans? They're not fans Gus" they could both now hear the anti-Seth Caine chants as the mob caught sight of him approaching "They're fuckin protesters!"

Seth had upset people in the past, sometimes with his books, others were upset by him just being himself when drunk but he'd never seen such bile and vitriol aimed in his direction. Genuine hate and loathing was etched all over the protesters faces as Seth and Gus sheepishly continued their walk up the steps to the main doors.

Security guards and especially drafted-in police officers struggled to hold back the mob as they threatened to break through and lynch Seth. He tried to keep his cool and avoided eye-contact with the crowd, a guard opened the doors and finally they were ushered inside the building.

"What the fuck was that all about?" Seth turned angrily back to Gus

"I'm sorry, I didn't know anything about it, I promise" Gus quickly apologised "It might not be as bad as it looks"

"Just how exactly is all that not as bad as it looks?" Seth was amazed as he pointed at the crowd through the glass doors and they swore and snarled back at him.

"I'm just saying, it's all publicity, you never know, the publishers might have started it all off"

"Why the hell would they do that?" Seth couldn't believe his ears

"Sometimes to get maximum exposure . . . ." Gus started.

"Christ, I don't believe this" Seth asked for directions and left Gus standing in the foyer, explaining the possibilities to himself.

A short time later while sat in the make-up chair, Seth received another little bombshell. Gus came in after catching up and chatting with the shows' producers and he came to reluctantly give Seth the bad news.

"Erm, I'm sorry Seth but . . . ." he hesitated

"But what?"

"Er, it seems that Mr White isn't available to do the show" Gus screwed up his eyes and winced as he said it.

"What, why?"

"It seems he's had some sort of family emergency, they wouldn't say what it was though"

"So, the show's cancelled then?" said Seth with a little smile of relief

"Actually, no, so at least we haven't had a wasted journey" Gus tried to look on the bright side again, annoyingly.

"Who's hosting it Gus?" no smile whatsoever on Seths' face

"Poppy Kyle" Gus tried to say under his breath

"Poppy Kyle? Poppy fuckin Kyle?" Seth shouted "you've got to be fucking kidding me!" Seth was absolutely furious

Ms Kyle was exactly the kind of vapid, vacuous so-called celebrity that Seth hated and loathed with a passion. She was purely a piece of blond eye candy that TV stations rolled out because she managed to get herself in tabloid newspapers due to her latest liaison with a sports, soap opera or pop star, thus guaranteeing ratings. She made all the celebrity magazines and during slow or quiet periods she would 'happen' to be photographed falling out of her dress, and depending on the time of day she would top various 'what's hot and what's not' lists. Poppy had come to prominence through modelling then decided she'd like to have her own chat show, that had resulted in her basically interviewing her friends and, as it turned out most of the time, her future lovers.

"I know Seth, I'm sorry" Gus continued to apologise

"That stupid bitch is totally inappropriate for this" shouted Seth

"I know, I know, don't you think I didn't tell the producers that?"

"So what did they say?"

"That it was short notice; they don't have any choice, on the plus side she just has to stick to a minimal script" Gus tried to placate him.

"Script? It's a fuckin debate isn't it?"

"Yeah but she'll have to ask questions to get the thing going."

"So, she's going to ask scripted questions and we'll respond, then what? She's supposed to follow things up and raise points of view, like Edward White does, isn't she?" Seths' mood wasn't eased no matter how he thought of things.

"Well, yeah but . . . ."

"But nothing Gus, this is gonna be a train wreck, a farce, not exactly an insightful discussion"

"Ok, I'm sorry" Gus inched his way to the door before he delivered the final insult "Oh and the producers also asked me to remind you that this is live television so can you watch your language please."

"Tell them I said to go fuck themselves" Seth screamed over his shoulder.

Chapter 34

T he show started in predictable fashion with Poppy Kyle getting most of the guests' names or credentials wrong then giggling to herself when she was corrected by the producers via her ear piece or by the guests themselves. The frequency of her mistakes was matched only by the amount of eye-rolling from the said guests on both sides who squirmed in embarrassment on her behalf. Various religious figures from differing faiths plus theologians and academics sat in attendance scattered throughout the audience amongst the general public.

The specific holy specialists, ten of them, chosen to hold the debate sat on one side of the studio while on the other sat Seth, alongside him were the artist and self-proclaimed 'messiah' Ian Jones as well as a pagan monk, rock guitarist Chris Bamford and another writer, Paul Miller, who specialised in religious fetishism in sexual practices. This seemed a very one-sided debate, for a start, Seths' 'team' were heavily out numbered, also he seemed to be part of a very disjointed group, he felt as though he was part of an ambush and that they should all have 'scapegoat' written across their foreheads.

Seths' unease grew further when he looked at the audience, there were a few people that were blatantly living an 'alternative' lifestyle and one or two others shouting obscenities or mocking the more overtly religious people sat there. However, those people seemed to be in the minority, in fact, when Seth and his fellow 'outsiders' had made their entrance there seemed to be a mainly hostile reception apart from a few cheers from their own fans and supporters. Seth then noticed that there seemed to be an extremely strong security presence for such a show, some of the officers in attendance were even armed! He couldn't help but wonder what kind of trouble they were expecting from a crowd mainly made up of priests, academics and professors?

Throughout the debate Seth tried to stay as low profile as possible, allowing the 'opposition' to rip into the other guests on his side of the discussion. Normally he would've leapt to their defence in that scenario but something seemed very, very wrong although he couldn't quite put his finger on it. When talk turned to his own work, Seth tried to keep his answers brief and to the point, he wanted to avoid confrontation at all costs and get the hell out of there. It was very out of character for Seth who loved a good argument and debate but he had fulfilled his pact and wanted little to do with any of this now, he still clung to his dream of a countryside escape with Lily.

As regards his latest book, and the powder keg that it had seemingly ignited, he knew that he couldn't defend the content in it and he also knew that that was the main reason that he had been invited on to the show. All he could do was try to steer the conversation back to his previous novels, still controversial in many respects but which he stood by fiercely. Thus he hoped to throw them off talking about 'Sympathy for the Devil', even if he got a lot more heat for his old work, at least he could defend that. For the most part, his ploy worked, when they did round on him he managed to talk his way out of any tight situations.

Seth did notice however that when he deftly avoided answering questions, Poppy seemed to get instructions in her ear piece. This was irritating, as if someone who didn't have the guts to ask probing questions of him to his face was sat in a studio using Poppy as a puppet, it felt more and more like a set-up, a witch-hunt, literally. The audience at times seemed to be getting more restless too, once the show had started, there was very little unrest early on and Seth had hoped his initial fears were unfounded but as the debate unfolded and the subjects became more inflammatory and heated so too did the guests, this transmitted itself to the audience and the tension grew. Heckling, mocking and laughing turned to booing and verbal abuse, it was all clearly audible yet the producers and security guards seemed to do little to quell the problem.

Seth sat there seething, there was something going on which he could sense brewing and almost physically see but he couldn't explain it. The questions were fired at the other guests and they tried valiantly to defend themselves but Seth had had enough, he stood up

"Are you shitting me? This is pathetic" he shouted "it's just a witch hunt"

"Ah, Mr Caine, you've been relatively quiet" said Poppy, not phased by his language as she received more instructions in her ear "it's funny you should mention that, I understand that your previous book, 'Suffering Innocence' dealt with the witchcraft epidemic of the late sixteenth and early seventeenth centuries, would you like to elaborate on a subject which is clearly very close to your heart?"

She portrayed the image of a ventriloquists' dummy or someone badly reading cue cards, what was abundantly clear was that they weren't her words. No matter, Seth had had enough of this circus and he remained standing.

"First of all" he started "Don't refer to it as an epidemic, it wasn't a plague or disease, it was thousands of innocents, men, women and children, all across Europe. They were tortured and murdered by so-called holy fucking men, not by God, but by the fucking church."

The audience gasped at the outburst and more restlessness ensued as people stood to either applaud him or shout with bile at him, the priests on the panel all looked at each other and then at Seth, all with anger on their faces. Poppy Kyle also gasped and turned to the camera.

"I do apologise to our viewers at home for the language Mr Caine just used and I'd like to remind him that this is a live television show" she said

"Don't fuckin apologise on my behalf you half-witted bitch, that book was about the persecution of innocent people, all in the name of your God, people using God for their own ends" he pointed at the priests on the panel and in the audience before continuing "the church was responsible for it all yet it's constantly brushed under the carpet like some dirty little family secret. Before that there were the Crusades to Scandinavia and the Middle East, thousands upon thousands of more innocent people slaughtered because the church wanted to spread their word, peaceful countries with their own Gods and traditions just swept away under the banner of Christianity. Now here you all sit in your fuckin robes pontificating about us and our work, you bastards make me sick to my stomach."

The guests on Seths' side of this supposed debate all stood and applauded him, along with pockets of people in the audience. The majority of them however tried to drown out the cheers with more booing and shouting, threats of violence were clearly heard being aimed at Seth and his contemporaries. The guards immediately became more heightened to the threats and the ugliness of the atmosphere as it suddenly became increasingly darker.

Seth stood watching the chaos unfold, he could see it as a metaphor for the intolerance that was gripping the world outside and he knew he had contributed to it greatly, albeit against his will and to save his wife.

"Stop" he said as he watched the anger develop and the pushing and shoving threatened to turn the show into a riot, no one heard him or at least no one took any notice of him "Stop it" he shouted again to no avail.

Fights broke out throughout the audience, security guards moved in, a little too late, to quell the disturbances yet the cameras kept rolling. Seth noticed that despite the chaos and hatred now sweeping the crowd, one man sat unmoved in the front row. The man just sat calmly staring at Seth with a look of serenity on his face. Seth thought he recognised him but couldn't remember from where. Seth looked away and back to the fighting audience, the 'opposition' had all stood up now and they too were pleading for calm. He watched as the now full scale battle unfolded and shook his head in disbelief, he was struck by the notion that Satan had been right in his prediction of what was to come for this world.

"Please stop" he said and sighed wearily "a war is coming" no one listened and the rioting became more violent and began to spill out of the audience and onto the stage, Seth shook his head and shouted again in desperation and anger "Please, please, can't you see that this is what *He* wants, his war is coming"

Still no one took any notice of him, except for the man sitting in the front row; he was still sitting quietly in his chair despite the fury and anarchy that had erupted around him. Seth couldn't help but look straight at the curious man who now seemed so conspicuous by his demeanour; still Seth couldn't place him though he was sure they had met before, Satan in another guise? Was it Mammon or Astaroth perhaps or maybe another of their minions? Suddenly the man stood up without breaking eye contact with him, the man spoke in a soft and calm voice at odds with the chaos and amazingly, despite the noise and shouting in the studio, it was as if he was whispering directly into Seths' ear.

"You are absolutely right Mr Caine" he said "a war is coming. Unfortunately for you however, you have chosen the wrong side to collaborate with"

The man was thirty feet away in the middle of a riot but his whispered words made Seth shiver with concern, suddenly he recognised the man.

"Father Duncan?" he said

"Yes, I knew that we would meet again, I did tell you that this wasn't over" and with that Seymour reached inside his jacket and pulled out a pistol which he aimed at Seth, the guests now standing closest to Seth immediately scrambled for cover.

"Gun!!" someone yelled from somewhere in the crowd and panic ensued as people scattered away from the stage for their own self-preservation. Security guards separated themselves from out of the crowd immediately and focused their attention on the priest; they drew their weapons and trained them on Father Duncan.

"Put the gun down and lie face down on the floor" they yelled at him

"I did try to warn you Mr Caine, you have gone too far now" said Seymour, ignoring everything and everyone else in the studio.

"Put the fucking gun down, now!!" yelled another guard.

"Wait, calm down, I had to write the book, you don't understand, I had no choice" pleaded Seth.

"No Caine, *you* don't understand, you have spat in the face of God and the church and I cannot allow that."

The studio suddenly seemed very quiet, though there were still people running to the exits, all eyes and guns were focused on the lone priest, all save for Father Duncan whose eyes and gun were focused solely on Seth Caine.

"This is your final warning, put the gun down" the guards' scream shattered the moment.

"Goodbye Mr Caine" Seymour said as he pulled the trigger.

Everything seemed to move in slow motion from that point, the bullet exploded from the barrel of Seymours' pistol and Seth could see in his peripheral vision the security guards reaction as three of them responded with shots of their own. Before they hit Father Duncan however, Seymours' bullet struck Caine in the chest. The shot hit Seth with such force that it knocked him off his feet. He felt his ribs crack as the bullet penetrated him and then he felt something burst inside his torso. Seth fell back onto the floor and lay staring at the ceiling of the studio. The guards' bullets all hit Seymour, one in the shoulder, one in the chest and the third struck him in the temple, killing him instantly before he even slumped back down into his chair.

Seth lay helpless, the bullet had torn through his lung and as he lay there staring at the bright studio lights; he could feel his lungs filling with blood. In the twinkling of the lights above him he could see images of happier times. Chaos and screaming was rife throughout the television set as police and security cleared the remaining guests and audience members out and a medical team rushed onto the stage to attend to Seth.

The lights reminded him of the lights of the emergency services arriving in vain to save Jack and a tear rolled down his cheek at the thought. He still hoped he would get to see his son again though he knew it was doubtful. He cried more at the thought of leaving Lily. She wasn't even here to say goodbye to, if her face could be the last thing that he saw before he died, he knew that he could be at peace. The medical staff ripped open his shirt to assess the damage and he lay staring at the lights, knowing that it was too late. He struggled to breathe as the blood increased in his lungs rapidly, 'this must be what it's like to drown' he thought, he didn't much care for it. An image crystallised in his mind of the single most important day in his life, the day he met Lily.

Then, Seth Caine was gone.

Severin Frost sat alone in his room, conversing with the special visitor in his head. Though he was alone he sat with his head bowed in great reverence, his lips moved as if in silent prayer, guards checked in on him through the window in his door but thought nothing of Severin seemingly talking to himself, how wrong they were.

"My Lord, thank you for honouring me with your dark presence, it has been a great privilege for me to play a part in your plans" he whispered

"My son, you have performed outstandingly well and I thank you for your role and obedience" replied Satan.

"No thanks are warranted, I feel it was, and still is, my duty to serve you however you think fit, just to be your servant is reward enough."

"Nevertheless" spoke the darkness "you will be rewarded, you will not find me an ungrateful master to serve."

"My Lord, I am overwhelmed. I assumed that now you're plan has come full circle that I would not be needed anymore" gasped Frost.

"First of all, my plan has not come to fruition just yet, almost, but not quite and secondly, you are to play a huge part in taking my plan to the next level."

"You Majesty, I am overcome with dark joy at such a prospect, may I inquire as to the nature of your plan and my role in it?" Severins' heart swelled at the idea.

"You may, especially as the time is almost at hand. As you know, everything has worked out very well so far. Mr Caine has performed a sterling job of writing as I expected and his book of my word is selling incredibly well throughout the world. It is already converting and twisting minds" Satan laughed to himself "where there is resistance to the ideas, there will always be at least a little conflict. As the book becomes more prevalent in society it will at least cast doubts over some mortal religious views, then like ripples on a cold dead lake my influence shall spread ever outwards, reaching all corners of the Earth and all mankind."

"Oh what a gloriously black world that would be your Highness, I can almost taste the death and decay" Severin smiled to himself as he spoke in hushed tones.

"Indeed it would, on top of all this I now have the soul of Mr Caine, thanks to him making our little pact. I must commend Angelique and Meridiana for their special roles in condemning not only Seth but also their expertise in sending Father Duncan to his death, not to mention sending his soul to me for the act of murder! I think I will give him extra special attention, a priests soul is always a little more delicious. I would have let you have him Severin for services rendered, but as I mentioned, you still have a major role to play here."

"I understand fully Master and I would indeed have enjoyed inflicting further torment upon him but if you have further plans for me on this plain, then so be it. I am sure he will still be there with you when I finally take my place in the Great Hall" smiled Severin again with glee at the prospect.

"Exactly, which brings me to you and the continuation of my plan, or should that be the sustaining of my plan?"

"Master?" questioned Frost

"You, my dear Severin are to be freed, as I said you would be"

"Free, finally" gasped Frost "that would be wonderful My Lord, I'd always hoped that one day I would be free and I know you have told me of this before but how could even you manipulate such a thing?"

"Do not doubt me now" Satan said with steel in his voice.

"Forgive me My Prince, I do not doubt you, or your word or your will, I was just wondering how you would go about such a task."

"That is not something that you should not concern yourself with, just be content with the knowledge that you will not be in this place for much longer, someone will be coming in to release you, someone that we both know very well."

"That is wonderful news, what will my role be when I am free Majesty?"

"Well, I shall need an Earth bound leader to continue to raise the tension levels, a man whom I can trust to do whatever I ask but also knows and understands my goals, a General on the ground, if you will. I feel that you are eminently qualified for the position. There is much work for us to do in order to drive my word and message forward, do you accept this position?"

"Oh My Lord, I cannot imagine a greater responsibility or honour could be bestowed upon a mere mortal. I will do everything within my power to succeed and drive you on to a great and bloody victory" Severin clenched his fists as the adrenalin coursed through his veins at the prospect.

"You will do well I am sure of that my son, until we speak again, I will now bid you farewell, I will be watching your progress from afar as the world burns and tears itself apart."

Chapter 35

Gus went to see Lily at home a few hours after Seths' death. He had been grief stricken himself, he'd been stood on the opposite side of the stage as the fighting broke out. Everything had seemed like a blur of hostility, anger and rage as security guards had held him back when the guns had been drawn, yet there was an intensely surreal feeling as well, was this actually happening? He had thought to himself. He had also been moved away from the stage when Seth fell and the medical team rushed in, he swore and raged at the officials as he struggled to get past them but was held back, he had been impotent to help his buddy, though in truth there would've been nothing he could've done, except maybe to be there for him, Gus had shouted for his friend but received no reply.

He wanted to contact Lily immediately but knew that she would be at work and in her panic she may have switched on the TV or the internet; that was the last thing Gus wanted. Images of the murder were being played out constantly thanks to the ever-rolling camera crews, he knew that that would only upset her more. She had to hear the awful news from a friend so Gus waited in his car close to their house and waited for Lily to arrive home. She drove past the waiting Gus who allowed her to gather her things and get inside before he pulled up, he didn't want to confront her in the driveway. His gamble that she wouldn't have heard the news paid off in that she greeted him at the door in quite a cheerful mood, all of a sudden he really didn't want to be the one to tell her.

"Hi Gus, how are you?" she chirped with a beaming smile

"Er, hi Lily" he was pale and shaking, his eyes reddened from tears.

"My God Gus, you look awful, Seth did turn up for the show didn't he? I've only just got home myself, I thought he would be back by now"

"Yes he turned up" sighed Gus

"So where is he? I thought you'd be bringing him home" her smile slipped a little as something seemed very wrong.

"Lily, I er . . . . I don't know how to say this" he stammered, his expression caused her heart to race and her stomach to knot and lurch.

"Gus, tell me, it's Seth isn't it" her voice started to tremor with the realisation that all wasn't well at all.

"Yes, he erm . . . ."

"Has he had an accident? Oh my God, he's had an accident, is he okay? Can I see him? Gus, tell me where he is" panic set in as she fired her questions at him.

"Lily" a tear rolled down his cheek as Gus choked on his words

"Please Gus" Lily started to cry and shake "please, what's happened?"

"He's gone Lily, I'm sorry, I'm so sorry" Gus head bowed

Gus' demeanour and words left Lily in no doubt that Seth simply hadn't gone 'somewhere', he was dead; Gus just couldn't bring himself to say *those* words, not regarding his oldest friend.

"No" she whispered "this can't be happening, how? Why?" her tears flowed freely down her face.

"He was shot"

"Shot? But why? Who would kill my Seth?" her knees buckled and she slumped to the floor in her grief.

Gus wasn't quick enough to catch her but he immediately knelt down and embraced her, slowly he lifted her up and eased her into the nearest armchair. He went into the kitchen and poured her a glass of brandy, he returned to see her sobbing with her head in her hands, which broke his heart all over again.

"Who did it Gus?" she sniffed

"That's not important now" he tried to soothe her

"The fuck it's not, who did it?" she snapped "who took my Seth?"

"A priest, a Father Duncan I think" he sighed, shaking his head at the thought

"Seymour Duncan?" Lilys' mouth gaped open with shock as she spoke

"Er, yes, do you know him" said Gus with genuine surprise

"That bastard used to work at the institute a couple of years ago, so what happened Gus?"

"Well" sighed Gus, not really wanting to re-live it but Lily had a right to know "The debate basically got out of hand, there was fighting everywhere and Seth was trying to calm it all down when this guy, this priest, got up in the front row and . . . shot him"

"Was he wearing the purple shirt?" whispered Lily in a very far away voice as she stared into space.

"I'm sorry?" Gus was caught off guard a little.

"Seth, I asked him to wear his purple shirt for TV, I love him in that shirt, it's my favourite" her voice broke again as she tried to fight the tears.

"Aw, Lily" Gus put his arms around her and squeezed her tightly, holding back his own tears "Yes, he was wearing the purple shirt"

"Good boy Seth" she burst into tears

They stayed locked in an embrace of pain and mutual heartbreak for what seemed like hours, rocking backwards and forwards. They parted and they both wiped away their tears and sniffed.

"So, did they catch him then? Seymour Duncan?" she croaked

"Well, he was gunned down too, he's dead" reassured Gus

"Good, the fucker deserves it" anger and grief mixed together in Lilys' voice

"True, the police might have some questions for you, they're trying to figure out what happened and why."

"Seth had a run in with him ages ago, at a bookstore but that's all I know" Lily shrugged her shoulders.

"It's ok, if you need me to come round when the police come over, I will you know?" Gus offered

"Thanks Gus, you're a good friend" she looked into his eyes as the tears returned and asked "did Seth suffer?"

"No, I don't think so; I think it was pretty much instantaneous. Lily, I'm so sorry, I think you should come and stay with us for a few days at least, Natalie wanted to come with me but we couldn't get a sitter at such short notice and didn't think in the circumstances that we should bring Alice."

"You don't have to explain Gus, thanks for telling me in person rather than over the phone."

"It's the least I could do, Natalie's devastated too, we all loved Seth" Gus cleared his throat and took a deep breath as he tried to hold back the tears again.

"Thanks for the offer but I'd rather be left alone for a while if you don't mind."

"Of course, whatever you think is best. Natalie said that she will phone you tomorrow if that's alright and it goes without saying that if you need anything, anything at all, even if you just want to talk, day or night, call us." Gus moved to the door as he spoke.

"Thank you Gus, you've always been a great friend to us both and thank Natalie too, I'll speak to her tomorrow" Lily put her arms around Gus and hugged him tightly.

"Anything, day or night, remember" he said as he left

"I will, thanks again Gus" replied Lily as she closed the door behind him.

Lily sat in Seths' favourite armchair; she drew her knees up into the foetal position and rested her head against the soft leather. The smell immediately brought a smile to her lips and then tears to her eyes as she thought of Seth. As she looked around the house there were a multitude of reminders of her husband, the love of her life. Even when they had been apart during their separation, she knew her heart would always belong to Seth. He was everything she could ever have wanted, he had said the same thing about her on numerous occasions and it always made her heart rise.

When they were younger, they both used to agree that death would be preferable to them breaking up. Their reasoning being that if your partner died you would be devastated but after the grief, you mourn and in time you moved on with your life. Whereas when you break up with someone that you truly love, you grieve but then potentially you would see them again, probably with someone else and you have to grieve and mourn all over again.

Sitting here now she felt that that was just the romantic ideas of youth, nothing could have prepared her for the pain and agony she was going through now, sitting in his chair as the tears rolled endlessly down her face with her heart shattered irreparably into thousands of pieces. She wept and wept throughout the night until eventually she cried herself to sleep.

Seths' funeral had been a quiet affair, Lily had wanted it that way, close friends and family only. The media had wanted to cover it but Lily had refused, thankfully the majority of them had respected her wishes. A handful of photographers waited at the cemetery gates before and after the burial and a few of his fans also stood outside crying and mournful. A large number of wreaths waited at the gates too, along with flowers and candles, some poems, photographs and copies of Seths' books were all laid in tribute like some kind of shrine.

Despite wanting as little fuss as possible, Lily was moved to stop the car she was being driven in, on their way into the cemetery and got out at the gates in order to look at the tributes to her husband. On reading the messages and love from people that hadn't even met him Lily was overcome,

Gus and Karl climbed out of the car behind hers' and got to her just in time to catch her before she collapsed with grief. They eased Lily back into her seat and the small procession continued on its' solemn task.

Despite Gus and Natalie encouraging her to stay with them, Lily insisted that she wanted to go home. As grief-stricken and heartbroken as she was, she knew that she wanted to be alone, she had stayed with them for a couple of days when the loneliness had become too much after Seths' immediate death but now she needed to be by herself. She had seen Seths' execution on television and that had been the catalyst for her to go to Gus and Natalie, on arrival home she made a conscious decision that the TV would remain off for a few days at the very least, there would inevitably be footage of the funeral and that was the last thing she needed to be reminded of now.

She knew that she should eat something; her friends had been reminding her that she should keep her strength up for the last few days but her appetite was completely gone. Everything seemed so pointless and trivial now and even though she knew that they only had her best interests at heart, eating now just seemed without meaning.

Lily took a long relaxing soak in the bath, she felt so tired, physically and emotionally. This was the first time since Seths' death that she could be truly alone and calm, no tears, no screaming inside just numbness, throughout her entire body and mind, she just felt numb.

She lay there allowing the hot water to soothe away her physical aches for over an hour, the priest conducting the funeral service had talked of Seth being reunited with their son Jack, at the time she nearly collapsed but now she smiled at the thought, more so at the thought of one day joining them both for eternity. It was her first smile since she left for work on that fateful morning, the last time that she would ever see her beloved Seth. She imagined him coming into the bathroom as he always did, initially with the premise of talking to her about something, he always admitted later that he loved to just sit and watch her bathe. Other times he would get into the bath behind her and stroke and hold her as they relaxed in blissful silence. Realisation that he would never walk into the bathroom again washed the smile from her face and brought a lump to her throat and another tear to her eye.

After bathing she towelled herself dry and went downstairs to pour herself a large whiskey before switching off the lights and going to bed with scotch in hand. She tried not to think of her husband for fear of breaking down as she climbed between the crisp sheets. Lily finished her drink and hoped that it would aid her sleep then curled up in their king sized bed, it suddenly felt way too big for her alone and she moved over to Seths' side. Immediately she could still faintly smell him and his aftershave on the pillow and despite the tears in her eyes and ache in her heart she snuggled herself more into the pillow as if to absorb every last drop of him. Yet again, she cried herself to sleep.

Lily slept deeply, her body needing to recharge itself following the emotional trauma of the last week, she slept that was, until she was woken by a mans' voice. She felt she must be dreaming as she sat up and saw the shadowy figure of a man sitting in a chair at the foot of the bed.

"Seth?" she whispered in hope

"No my darling Lily, not Seth"

"W-who are you?" she suddenly became very frightened

"I knew your husband very well, don't you recognise me my dear?"

Lily tried to adjust her sight in the darkness and gradually his image came into full view, it was a very well dressed and polite gentleman, Lily recognised him but couldn't place from where.

"How did you get in here?" she asked holding her fear at bay

"I go wherever and whenever I please" he replied

"Please don't hurt me, I don't know what you want but . . . ."

"Hussshhhh" he whispered "I am not here to hurt you my angel, I promise you that" his honeyed words didn't do anything to alleviate Lilys' anxiety and she pulled up the covers to her neck as some sort of protection.

"So, what do you want from me?" she asked again

"I want you to hep me that's all"

"Help you with what?"

"Straight to the point, just like Seth, I like that and I shall be just as forthright in my reply. You see, I have certain friends who find themselves unfortunately 'detained' in your fine institution, to put it bluntly, they must be released" he said with a grin which then quickly faded.

"What do you mean, released? I can't just release people until they are ready to be released and with the correct authorisation. Now for the last time, will you tell me who the hell you are or not?"

"This is regrettable, however, I did anticipate your refusal to be co-operative but we will get to that shortly. As far as my identity is concerned, didn't your husband tell you about me? I believe he did."

"Why are you being so evasive" snapped an increasingly frustrated Lily "just tell me."

"I'm sorry you feel that I'm being evasive, in that case I will show you who I am, let the candour flow."

With those words Lily felt her mind being instantly transported to a hot and dusty plain. Suddenly she seemed to be looking down on a huge circle of beings as they cheered and snarled, her view descended as if zooming in, in order that she could make out the figures as she felt she was floating above the scene. A naked woman was tied between two pillars and she was being tortured, whipped and abused by two scantily clad bitches all, it seemed for the delectation of the twisted demonic throng as it bayed, literally, for blood. A man on his knees in the dirt, screaming for it all to stop as two monsters held him back. Another creature of immense proportions sat laughing with pleasure on a hideous throne. Closer and closer Lilys' mind floated towards the vile pageant, she gasped as she recognised herself being flagellated and violated.

As she sat now on the bed, tears welled in her eyes and her lip trembled in fear and horror as she clasped her hands to her ears to try to block out the sounds of her own screams. This was impossible of course as her screaming was already inside her head. The man in her room sat impassively observing her discomfort with relish. In her mind she seemed forced to survey the traumatic spectacle further, now she looked at the man screaming, she recognised Seth and her heart raced. She called his name but he couldn't hear her, he wept and wailed at his captors in futility and she wept further as she witnessed his helplessness.

The creature on the throne seemed to look up at her floating mind, the only one who acknowledged her presence, he smiled and then with further glee returned his attention to the show, his smile stuck in Lilys' head as she drifted back up and away from the grotesque circle of debauchery and torture. Up, higher and higher until with an almighty jolt she was back in her own body and mind, she sat gasping for breath at the man in her room. He sat there wearing the same malevolent smile she had just witnessed seconds before, her memories came flooding back to her, Seths' nightmares.

"Satan" she whispered hoarsely

"Pleased to make your acquaintance, formally that is" he mocked

"This can't be happening" she whispered again, though more to herself.

"Ah, that is what your husband used to say, eventually though, he came to accept us and believe" grinned Satan

"But . . . h-how did you do that?"

"Do what my dear?"

"That horrible vision" she frowned as she spoke "it was so real"

"Vision? Ha ha" laughed the Devil "That vision as you put it seemed so real because it *was* real my darling."

"No, it can't have been" Lily protested "I was looking at myself, I think I would know if something like that had happened to us"

"Oh my dear sweet innocent Lily, I showed you a different perspective of events but it did happen. What do you think is real and what is imagined? Fact and fiction sometimes blur at the edges, I take it you never did quite manage to recall your memory from your 'accident' did you?"

Lily remained silent; she was still in a daze that she was actually conversing with the Devil himself, or she was dreaming that she was, she wasn't very sure of anything at that moment. She couldn't understand what he was getting at and her mind was still very distorted and fractured regarding her accident. Without waiting for a reply, the fallen one continued.

"If my recollection of events is clear, Seth told you that you'd had a car accident, he told the authorities and your friends that you had been attacked by a random man or men as you left for work. Yet Seth and I know the truth, you were being *pleasured* by my deliciously dark angels, as you just saw for yourself" he grinned callously at her "and I believe that secretly you enjoyed every second of it, as did my legions."

"You lying bastard" Lily said through clenched teeth as she grew enraged at the poisonous words dripping from his mouth.

"Mmmm, anger, that emotion looks very good on you" Satan licked his lips as if savouring a high quality wine, to emphasise his pleasure at her distress.

"What the fuck do you really want?" Lilys' fists now clenched and her brow furrowed, she had never been a violent woman and now, despite her fury, she remained in control enough to realise it would be sheer stupidity to attack someone or *something* like this.

"Severin Frost" he said simply

"Severin Frost? What do you mean?" she seemed puzzled

"It's very simple my sweet, I want my various children released from your *prison*, first of all I want Severin Frost. Therefore I want you, in your capacity as head psychiatrist to acknowledge his sanity and release him first and above all others" he made it all sound so easy

"I can't do that!" she gasped in surprise

"You can my dear and what's more, you will!" he spoke with steel and authority in his voice and darkness flowing from his eyes like a rolling storm.

"I can't, it's not possible and let me be clear, even if I could, I wouldn't" Lilys' defiance in the circumstances shocked even her, or it would've done had she taken a moment to think about it. For now her adrenalin raged.

"Ah Lily, your husband was also very defiant, in the end he did as he was told and got what he deserved."

"You fucking bastard" she spat at him, his words were like acid poured on her emotions.

"You are very wilful Lily and I like it, I shall look forward to breaking your spirit over and over again" he leered "but to get back to the matter in hand, I am ordering you to release Frost."

"Ordering me? You can't order me to do anything. But humour me, why do you want him released anyway?" before he could reply she knew the answer and she slumped back silently on the bed in shock before whispering to herself "his Dark Friends"

"Well done Lily, we are indeed his dark friends" Satan smiled

"And you are his darkest friend of all, he spoke about you" her voice little more than a sigh "he was involved in this thing all along" her voice trailed off as did her thoughts.

"You are correct, he has been playing with you ever since my plan was put into place some time ago, he did an exemplary job too by his reports and the results attained."

"Why? Why Seth? Why Severin, what do you want with him?" she shook her head in disbelief as she tried to take all the information in.

"Seth was merely a pawn, a sizeable pawn but a pawn nonetheless, Severin is required to continue with my plans on your mortal plain, therefore it is imperative that he is free to act on my behalf without restrictions."

"What kind of explanation is that? A pawn? You ripped our lives apart and my husband is now dead because of your stupid plans" Lily screamed at him

"Lily, I owe you no explanation, it is a bigger picture that I gaze upon and Seth has played his part, now it is Severins' turn."

"Is that it? That's all you'll tell me?" she yelled in frustration.

"That's all you need to know, there is another way I can get him released but I thought that I would come to you first, out of respect for a grieving widow" Satan remained calm and relaxed as he merely negotiated his business deal.

It was the first time Lily had even thought of the term 'widow' which crushed her heart but strengthened her spirit.

"You arrogant fuck, I will not release Frost and even if I did diagnose his sanity he would then be transferred to an actual prison so you still wouldn't get him anyway."

"Lily, there are means and ways around little problems such as that, you just need to play your part"

"No way" she snarled at him

"My dear, I can be very persuasive, as I'm sure Seth told you" he sneered back

"No, I don't want to hear anymore of your filthy lies and tricks, now leave me the fuck alone!!" she screamed again as loudly as she could.

"As you wish my dear, think on though, we will talk again" and with that, he was gone.

CHAPTER 36

L ily arrived at work the next day in a state of confusion. She had awoken from a strange dream which she couldn't recollect, with a terrible headache and feeling absolutely exhausted as if she hadn't slept for days. It was her first day back following Seths' death and her secretary seemed extremely surprised to see her back so soon. She had sent Linda to get her some coffee and painkillers in order to relieve the throbbing pains in her skull. Once the caffeine and drugs had arrived and Linda had expressed her sympathies and condolences to Lily, the secretary left her alone having been given the strictest of instructions that Lily was not to be disturbed under any circumstances.

When she had gotten out of bed that morning, Lily had felt numb and overly tired; she had put it down to the emotion of the last week. However, she felt 'strange' as if she were being watched, she hadn't planned to go back to work so soon but with the unusual atmosphere she felt in the house she knew that she had to get out, if only for some fresh air or change of scenery. As soon as she'd started driving she felt drawn towards the Hoffman Institute, she'd pulled up in her parking space without even realising she had driven there.

Lily sat in her office drinking the strong black coffee she'd requested and waiting for the painkillers to kick in. She sat there for over an hour waiting for a feeling of normality that never came, every time she tried to move a limb it felt as though she were sitting in a bath of treacle. Eventually she managed to get up out of her seat and moved over to the large leather sofa in her office, she kicked off her shoes and lay down hoping that a little snooze would shake off the lethargy that seemed to be holding her tightly. She closed her eyes and soon she drifted off to sleep.

Lily found herself standing in front of a huge black door; she didn't know where she was or how she'd gotten there. The door seemed extremely old and thick and was ornately carved with grotesque masks and blasphemous images, as she gazed at the scenes she could make out whimpering and crying coming from the other side of the door. She tried to listen closely by leaning her ear to the large rusty keyhole, it was confirmed to her that someone was in an awful lot of pain and distress inside the room beyond the foreboding door. She tried to halt her breathing to hear more clearly but a blood-curdling scream made her jump and stumble back onto the dusty floor. Her heart raced with fear at what could be happening beyond her vision then someone called out in agony "Lily!"

She gasped with fright but still found the courage deep within her to start clawing and banging at the door, there was no apparent handle and so she groped in the semi-darkness to try to gain access. Her fingers started to bleed as splinters broke away from the ancient wooden door and embedded themselves in her flesh but no matter how hard she struggled, the door just would not budge. Lily yelled in fury and frustration and another scream from inside the room chilled her soul. She collapsed down onto her knees, breathing heavily and crying in her defeat with her head in her blood-stained hands.

As Lily knelt there sobbing, the ancient door creaked, she looked up and saw it open slightly. She quickly clambered to her feet and stepped back, she was very wary in case someone or something was on its' way out of whatever place lay beyond the door. Nothing happened, no being emerged from the room and cautiously she approached. There was now a gap of around an inch or two, not big enough to get through but at least now she could gain some purchase on the door to allow her to get access. Lily took hold of the ancient blockade with both hands and heaved with all her might, it moved, only another couple of inches but she had actually moved it. As it shifted, what seemed like many years of dust fell down from the top of the door and onto her head making her cough and sneeze. This door had obviously not been opened for a long, long time; it even smelled of the centuries.

After dusting herself off she tried again, again it moved a few inches and again dust and a few cobwebs clouded down upon her, she would not be denied. Eventually, with a chorus of tears and screams she managed to open it enough that she could squeeze through and into the darkened room.

The room was dimly lit and enormous as befitting such a monstrous door and it looked just as foreboding; near-darkness surrounded her as she walked through the cavern, just about able to see where she was going. Suddenly she saw something in the centre of the room, a scene lit up as if out of nowhere, solely for her benefit, a crucifixion.

A massive and hideous and abnormal creature stood in front of a large wooden cross with its' back to her. As she slowly, and against her better judgement, walked up to it and she heard it speak.

"Caaaaiiiiiinnnnneeee" it drawled

The voice sounded as if it came from a stinking and steaming sewer, the word it spoke made her stop dead in her tracks. She peered around the demons' bulk to look upon its' victim being nailed to the cross. No matter that she didn't want to see or believe it, she was compelled to know and know she did. Lily screamed in horror and fainted down to the filthy ground as the creature laughed in its' sickly delight.

When Lily came round, the scene in front of her had changed. Now the creature stood holding a large blade as if seemingly waiting for instruction. Seth hung naked by his wrists over a font, he seemed to be unconscious and Lily called his name but got no response.

"Welcome my dear" said another all too familiar voice from behind her.

Lily was still lay in the dirt and dust on the ground, on hearing the voice she clambered to her feet and ran over to Satan who sat on his throne observing the imminent show.

"Please, please stop this" she begged through her tears

"Only you can stop this Lily" he smiled

"How?"

"You know how, release Severin Frost as I asked"

"I can't" she sobbed

"Well my dear, you do seem to have a bit of a quandary on your hands" he said and then to the blade-wielding creature "continue"

The monster grinned and approached the prone and defenceless Seth Caine.

"Wait!" shouted Lily "please wait, what're you going to do to him?"

The beast hesitated and turned to Satan, who held up a hand to at least temporarily halt the torture that was sure to follow, the creature hung its head in disappointment but obeyed its' master.

"Well, you should be familiar with how your husband is to spend eternity. His fate is to be entwined with the past of my associate Mr Frost. You see, my sweet child, do you remember all the things that Severin told you about all his so-called crimes?"

"Y-y-yes" Lily stammered with terror coursing through her veins.

"Of course you do, you should know them better than anyone, anyone that is except Seth. He dreamt about his eternity in the same manner as Severin acted it out. You see, Seth will spend the rest of time as he knows it going through all those events, over and over and over again. Sadly for him however, he will only see and feel them from a victims point of view, he will never be killed by the torture because he is already dead, he will never pass out through the agony, he will just relive the endless pain, continuously, again and again."

"But why? He did as you asked" she wailed

"That he did, however, he did try to warn the public just before he died. I see that quite simply as betrayal, he could have had a wonderful afterlife with dark pleasures at his fingertips but sadly, his morality got in the way and dragged him back down to everyone else's level" Satan sighed in disappointment for added effect "unfortunately that little speech he started has come back to haunt him. There has to be rules you see my darling, my rules, even my world has rules and honour . . . of sorts" he smiled his twisted lecherous smile again.

Lily slumped back down in her helplessness and cried yet more rivers of tears, her back to her husband as she couldn't bear to watch him in pain.

"And you will let him go if I comply?" she whispered through her sobs.

"Seth is mine Lily and cannot be released from here but I can alter his torment, that should be comfort enough for you my child"

"What? You won't release him even if I do release Severin?" anger and despair crept in and flooded her voice.

"I'm sorry Lily but your husband made a pact with me and I now own him, there is no going back on that, he is here to stay"

"Then fuck you!!" she screamed at Satan who seemed genuinely surprised by her will and reaction.

"I am sorry that you still feel that way, to be honest with you, I was hoping that you would also make a pact with me" he leered at her again "I would've enjoyed our time together"

"Forget it you bastard, you can't threaten me because I have nothing left to lose. I realise this is a nightmare because Seth told me all about them and how you got to him. At some point I will wake up and be free of you. My son is gone and he is in a far better place, now I have lost my husband and there is nothing else that can be taken from me" She knew she was right and her defiance had grown as she spoke.

"You are stronger than I gave you credit for and yes you will wake soon from this particular nightmare. My plans will not be disrupted though; I always have an alternative of which you will shortly be aware. As a parting gift to you" he raised and pointed a finger at Seth, the creature was poised and acted swiftly on his command, slicing the blade through the flesh on Seths' thigh.

Lily had spun on her heels as Satan pointed and she watched in horror as her husbands blood came pouring down his legs and dripped off his toes into the font as the beast peeled his leg of flesh like a piece of over-ripe fruit. Seth screamed in agony and jerked on the chains suspending him, Lily screamed in disbelief at the sight and she also jerked upright but upright and onto the floor as she fell from her leather couch in her office.

"Dr Caine, are you okay?" said a voice

"Er, what er yes, I'm fine" replied a very disorientated Lily as she climbed to her feet, self-consciously wiping tears from her eyes and noticed the Institutes' Director standing in her office doorway.

"I'm sorry Sir, I didn't hear you come in, I was just taking a nap. I wouldn't normally but it's been quite a stressful time recently and I haven't been sleeping well and . . . ." Lily felt wracked by guilt at her seeming lack of professionalism. Even with her situation and the immense upheaval in her life, she always tried to remain the utmost professional.

"Don't give it a moments thought Lily, I totally understand what you're going through, I lost my wife a few years ago as you know, that was a terrible time for me and your support was most valued" he said

"Yes, I'm sorry"

"Don't keep apologising either" he smiled "I'm only here to make sure you haven't come back to work too soon as well as to offer my sincerest condolences"

"Thank you Sir" Lily half smiled and she heard her secretary talking to someone through the open door behind the Director, causing her to peer around him.

"Oh, that's the other reason I came" he smiled again "I've finally found you a new consultant"

"Really?" Lily was surprised, especially with recent budget cuts

"Come in" he said as he turned around "Now Dr Caine, I know we've had financial restraints over the last couple of years but with your workload increasing over the same period following Dr Sterlings' sad departure I felt that it was important to bring in a new Senior Consultant as soon as possible. Especially with the one we have found with so many radical new ideas to cut costs and change a few things around here. I spoke with the other board members and they agreed with me. Also with your recent loss I insisted we fill the post immediately in order to take the burden off your shoulders, so, this morning I'm acting as tour guide" he grinned

The new Consultant breezed into the room and Lilys' eyes widened in recognition while her chin nearly hit he floor and the colour drained from her cheeks.

"Are you sure you're alright Dr Caine" asked the Director again

"Er . . . d-don't I know you?" stammered Lily

"Possibly" replied the Consultant "I am so looking forward to working with you Dr Caine, I'm sure we'll get along famously"

"Dr Lily Caine, allow me to introduce you to the new Senior Consultant of the Hoffman Institute, Dr Alexandra Roth"

. . . The End?